CW00506919

Julius Eggeling

The Sacred Books of the East

Vol. XLIII

Julius Eggeling

The Sacred Books of the East

Vol. XLIII

Reprint of the original, first published in 1897.

1st Edition 2023 | ISBN: 978-3-36863-599-2

Verlag (Publisher): Outlook Verlag GmbH, Zeilweg 44, 60439 Frankfurt, Deutschland
Vertretungsberechtigt (Authorized to represent): E. Roepke, Zeilweg 44, 60439 Frankfurt, Deutschland
Druck (Print): Books on Demand GmbH, In de Tarpen 42, 22848 Norderstedt, Deutschland

THE

SACRED BOOKS OF THE EAST

HENRY FROWDE, M.A.

PUBLISHER TO THE UNIVERSITY OF OXFORD

LONDON, EDINBURGH, AND NEW YORK

THE

SACRED BOOKS OF THE EAST

TRANSLATED

BY VARIOUS ORIENTAL SCHOLARS

AND EDITED BY

F. MAX MÜLLER

VOL. XLIII

Oxford

AT THE CLARENDON PRESS

1897

[All rights reserved]

𝔒𝔵𝔣𝔬𝔯𝔡

PRINTED AT THE CLARENDON PRESS
BY HORACE HART, M.A.
PRINTER TO THE UNIVERSITY

THE

SATAPATHA-BRÂHMANA

ACCORDING TO THE TEXT OF THE

MÂDHYANDINA SCHOOL

TRANSLATED BY

JULIUS EGGELING

PART IV

BOOKS VIII, IX, AND X

Oxford

AT THE CLARENDON PRESS

1897

[All rights reserved]

CONTENTS.

EIGHTH KÂNDA.

The Building of the Sacred Fire-altar (continued).

INTRODUCTION.

THE present volume completes the exposition of the
Agnikayana, or construction of the sacred Fire-altar.
Whilst to the general reader the section of the Brâhmana
treating of this ceremony, and extending over no less than
five of its fourteen kândas—or rather more than one-third
of the whole—will probably appear the least inviting part
of the work, a special interest attaches to this ceremony,
and the dogmatic explanation of its details, for the student
of Indian antiquity. The complicated ritual of the Fire-
altar, as has been pointed out before [1], does not seem to
have formed part of the original sacrificial system, but was
probably developed independently of it, and incorporated
with it at a comparatively recent period. There seems,
indeed, some reason to believe that it was elaborated with
a definite object in view, viz. that of making the external
rites and ceremonies of the sacrificial cult the practical
devotional expression of certain dominant speculative
theories of the time. As a matter of fact, the dogmatic
exposition of no other part of the sacrificial ceremonial
reflects so fully and so faithfully as that of the Agnikayana
those cosmogonic and theosophic theories which form
a characteristic feature of the Brâhmana period. In the
present work, that section commences with a cosmogonic
account so elaborate as is hardly to be met with anywhere
else in the Brâhmana literature; and throughout the
course of performance the symbolic import of its details is

---

[1] See part i, introduction, p. xxxi.

explained here, as in other Brâhma*n*as, on the lines of those
cosmogonic speculations.

When, towards the close of the period represented by the
Vedic hymns, inquiring minds began to look beyond the
elemental gods of the traditional belief for some ulterior
source of mundane life and existence, the conception of
a supreme, primordial being, the creator of the universe,
became the favourite topic of speculation. We accordingly
find different poets of that age singing of this uncreate
being under different names,—they call him Visvakarman,
the 'All-worker'; or Hira*n*yagarbha, the 'golden Embryo';
or Purusha, the 'Person'; or Ka, the 'Who?'; or the
heavenly Gandharva Visvávasu, 'All-wealth'; or Pragápati,
the 'Lord of Creatures.' Or they have recourse to a somewhat older figure of the Pantheon, likewise of abstract
conception, and call him Brahma*n*aspati[1], the Lord of
prayer or devotion; a figure which would naturally
commend itself to the priestly mind, and which, indeed, in
a later phase of Hindu religion, came to supply not only
the name of the abstract, impersonal form of the deity, the
world-spirit, but also that of the first of its three personal
forms, the creator of the Hindu triad. Amongst these and
other names by which the supreme deity is thus designated
in the philosophic hymns of the *R*ik and Atharva-veda, the
name of Pragápati, the Lord of Creatures or generation,
plays a very important part in the immediately succeeding
period of literature, viz. that of the Brâhma*n*as.

In the so-called Purusha-hymn (*R*ig-veda X, 90), in which
the supreme spirit is conceived of as *the* Person or Man
(Purusha), born in the beginning, and consisting of 'whatsoever hath been and whatsoever shall be,' the creation of
the visible and invisible universe is represented as originating
from an 'all-offered' sacrifice[2] (yag*ñ*a) in which the Purusha
himself forms the offering-material (havis), or, as one might

---

[1] Cf. *R*ig-veda X, 72, 2.

[2] That is to say, a sacrifice at which not only portions of the sacrificial dish,
or the victim, are offered up to the deities, but where every single part of it is
offered.

say, the victim. In this primeval—or rather timeless,
because ever-proceeding—sacrifice, Time itself, in the shape
of its unit, the Year, is made to take its part, inasmuch as
the three seasons, spring, summer, and autumn, of which it
consists, constitute the ghee, the offering-fuel, and the
oblation respectively. These speculations may be said to
have formed the foundation on which the theory of the
sacrifice, as propounded in the Brâhma*n*as, has been reared.
Pragâpati, who here takes the place of the Purusha, the
world-man, or all-embracing Personality, is offered up anew
in every sacrifice; and inasmuch as the very dismember-
ment of the Lord of Creatures, which took place at that
archetypal sacrifice, was in itself the creation of the universe,
so every sacrifice is also a repetition of that first creative
act. Thus the periodical sacrifice is nothing else than a
microcosmic representation of the ever-proceeding destruc-
tion and renewal of all cosmic life and matter. The theologians of the Brâhma*n*as go, however, an important step
further by identifying the performer, or patron, of the
sacrifice—the Sacrificer—with Pragâpati; and it is this
identification which may perhaps furnish us with a clue to
the reason why the authors of the Brâhma*n*as came to fix
upon 'Pragâpati' as the name of the supreme spirit. The
name 'Lord of Creatures' is, no doubt, in itself a perfectly
appropriate one for the author of all creation and generation;
but seeing that the peculiar doctrine of the Purusha-sûkta
imparted such a decisive direction to subsequent dogmatic
speculation, it might seem rather strange that the name
there chosen to designate the supreme being should have
been discarded, only to be employed occasionally, and then
mostly with a somewhat different application[1]. On the
other hand, the term 'Pragâpati' was manifestly a

---

[1] In its original sense it occurs at the beginning of the Agni*k*ayana-section,
VI, 1, 1, 2 ?, in connection with what might almost be regarded as an exposition of the Purusha-sûkta. The seven original *p*urushas out of which *the*
Purusha comes to be compacted, are apparently intended to account for the
existence of the seven *Ri*shis (explained in the Brâhma*n*as as representing the
vital airs) prior to the creation of the one Purusha. It would seem that they
themselves previously composed the as yet uncorporeal Purusha.

singularly convenient one for the identification of the
Sacrificer with the supreme 'Lord of Creatures'; for,
doubtless, men who could afford to have great and costly
sacrifices. such as those of the Srauta ceremonial, performed
for them—if they were not themselves Brâhmans, in which
case the term might not be inappropriate either—would
almost invariably be 'Lords of Creatures,' i.e. rulers of men
and possessors of cattle, whether they were mighty kings.
or petty rulers, or landed proprietors, or chiefs of clans.   It
may be remarked, in this respect, that there is in the
language of the Brâhmanas a constant play on the word
'pragâ' (progenies), which in one place means 'creature' in
general. whilst in another it has the sense of 'people,
subjects,' and in yet another the even more restricted one
of 'offspring or family.'

How far this identification of the human Sacrificer with
the divine Pragâpati goes back, and whether, when first
adopted, it was applied at once to the whole of the sacrificial
system, or whether it rather originated with a certain
restricted group of ritualists in connection with some
limited portion of the ceremonial such as the Agnikayana.
and became subsequently part and parcel of the sacrificial
theory, it would probably not be easy to determine.   As
regards the symbolic connection of the Sacrificer himself
with the sacrifice, there can at any rate be no doubt that it
was an essential and an intimate one from the very beginning
of the sacrificial practice.   When a man offers to the gods
their favourite food. it is in order to please them and to
gain some special object of his own,---either to make them
strong and inclined for fighting his battles. and to secure
their help for some undertaking of his or against some
danger by which he is threatened ; or to deprecate their
wrath at some offence he knows or fancies he has committed
against them ; or to thank them for past favours, with an
eye, it may be, to new and still greater favours to come.
Gradually, however, the connection becomes a subtler and
more mystic one ; the notion of substitution enters into the
sacrifice : it is in lieu of his own self that man makes the

offering. This notion is a familiar one to the theologians of the Bráhmaṇas, either in the sense that the oblation is sent up to the gods in order to prepare the way for the Sacrificer, and secure a place for him in heaven; or in the sense that along with the burnt-offering the human body of the Sacrificer is mystically consumed, and a new, divine body prepared to serve him in the celestial abodes. Intimately connected with this latter notion we find another, introduced rather vaguely, which makes the sacrifice a mystic union in which the Sacrificer generates from out of the Vedi (f.), or altar-ground, his future, divine self. In this respect Agni, the offering-fire, also appears as the mate of Vedi[1]; but it will be seen that Agni himself is but another form of the divine and the human Praǵápati.

With the introduction of the Praǵápati theory into the sacrificial metaphysics, theological speculation takes a higher flight, developing features not unlike, in some respects, to those of Gnostic philosophy. From a mere act of piety, and of practical, if mystic, significance to the person, or persons, immediately concerned, the sacrifice—in the esoteric view of the metaphysician, at least—becomes an event of cosmic significance. By offering up his own self in sacrifice, Praǵápati becomes dismembered; and all those separated limbs and faculties of his come to form the universe,—all that exists, from the gods and Asuras (the children of Father Praǵápati) down to the worm, the blade of grass, and the smallest particle of inert matter. It requires a new, and ever new, sacrifice to build the dismembered Lord of Creatures up again, and restore him so as to enable him to offer himself up again and again, and renew the universe, and thus keep up the uninterrupted revolution of time and matter. The idea of the dismembered Praǵápati, and of this or that sacrificial act being required to complete and replenish him, occurs throughout the lucubrations of the Bráhmaṇas; but in the exposition of the ordinary forms of sacrifice, this element can hardly be considered as

---

[1] See I, 2, 3, 15 16. From the woman Vedi (otherwise representing the earth) creatures generally are produced; cf. III, 5, 1, 11.

one of vital importance ; whilst in the Agni*k*ayana, on the
contrary, it is of the very essence of the whole performance.
Indeed, it seems to me by no means, unlikely that the
Purusha-Pra*g*âpati dogma was first practically developed
in connection with the ceremony of the Fire-altar[1], and
that, along with the admission of the latter into the regular
sacrificial ceremonial, it was worked into the sacrificial
theory generally. In the Agni*k*ayana section (Kâ*nd*as
VI–X), as has already been stated[2], Sâ*nd*ilya is referred
to as the chief authority in doctrinal matters, whilst in the
remaining portions of the Brâhma*n*a, that place of honour
is assigned to Yâ*gñ*avalkya. Now, it may be worthy of
notice, in connection with this question of the Pra*g*âpati
dogma, that in the list of successive teachers[3] appended to
the Agni*k*ayana section, the transmission of the sacrificial
science—or rather of the science of the Fire-altar, for the
list can only refer to that section—is traced from Sâ*nd*ilya
upwards to Tura Kâvasheya, who is stated to have received
it from Pra*g*âpati ; the Lord of Creatures, on his part,
having received it from the (impersonal) Brahman. Does
not this look almost like a distinct avowal of Sâ*nd*ilya and
his spiritual predecessors being answerable for having
introduced the doctrine of the identity of Pra*g*âpati and the
sacrifice into the sacrificial philosophy ? If such be the
case, the adaptation of this theory to the dogmatic explanation of the other parts of the ceremonial, as far as the
Satapatha-Brâhma*n*a is concerned, might be supposed to
have been carried out about the time of Sa*mg*ivi-putra,
when the union of the two lines of teachers seems to have
taken place[4]. But seeing that the tenth Kâ*nd*a, called the
Mystery, or secret doctrine, of the Fire-altar, was apparently
not at first included in the sacrificial canon of the Vâ*g*a-

---

[1] VI. 2, 2, 21, 'This performance (of the Agni*k*ayana) assuredly belongs to
Pra*g*âpati, for it is Pra*g*âpati he undertakes (to construct) by this performance.'

[2] Part i, introduction, p. xxxi.

[3] For this Va*ms*a, as well as that appended to the last book of the Brâhma*n*a,
see ibid. p. xxxiii, note 1.

[4] Ibid. p. xxxiv ; Max Müller, History of Ancient Sanskrit Literature,
p. 437.

sancyins[1], the mystic speculations in which that section so freely indulges would seem to have been left apart from the regular canon, along with other floating material which was not considered suitable for practical purposes, or indispensable for an intelligent appreciation of the hidden import of the sacrificial rites.

Once granted that the real purport of all sacrificial performances is the restoration of the dismembered Lord of Creatures, and the reconstruction of the All, it cannot be denied that, of all ceremonial observances, the building of the great Fire-altar was the one most admirably adapted for this grand symbolic purpose. The very magnitude of the structure;—nay, its practically illimitable extent[2], coupled with the immense number of single objects— mostly bricks of various kinds—of which it is composed, cannot but offer sufficiently favourable conditions for contriving what might fairly pass for a miniature representation of at least the visible universe. The very name 'Agni,' by which the Fire-altar is invariably designated, indicates from the very outset an identification of cardinal importance— that of Pragâpati with Agni, the god of fire, and the sacrifice. It is a natural enough identification: for, as Pragâpati is the arch-sacrificer, so Agni is the divine sacrificer, the priest of the sacrifice. Hence the constantly occurring triad—Pragâpati, Agni, and (the human) Sacrificer. The identity of the altar and the sacred fire which is ultimately to be placed thereon is throughout insisted upon. Side by side with the forming and baking of the bricks for the altar takes place the process of shaping and baking the fire-pan (ukha). During the year over which the building of the altar is spread, the sacred fire is carried about in the pan by the Sacrificer for a certain time each day. In the same way as the layers of the altar are arranged so as to represent earth, air, and heaven, so the fire-pan is fashioned in such a way as to be a miniature copy of the three worlds[3]. But, while this identity is never lost sight of, it is not an absolute

---

[1] Ibid. p. xxxii.   [2] See X, 2, 3, 17 18; 2, 4, 1 seqq.; 4, 3, 5–8.
[3] VI, 5, 2, 1 seq.; VII, 1, 2, 7–9.

one, but rather one which seems to hold good only for this
special sacrificial performance. Though it may be that we
have to look upon this identification as a serious attempt to
raise Agni, the divine priest, to the position of a supreme
deity, the creator of the universe, such a design seems
nowhere to be expressed in clear and unmistakeable terms.
Nor are the relations between the two deities always
defined consistently. Pragâpati is *the* god above all other
gods ; he is the thirty-fourth god, and includes all the gods
(which Agni does likewise) ; he is the three worlds as well
as the fourth world beyond them [1]. Whilst, thus, he is the
universe, Agni is the child of the universe, the (cosmic)
waters being the womb from which he springs [2]. Whence
a lotus-leaf is placed at the bottom of the fire-altar to
represent the waters and the womb from which Agni-
Pragâpati and the human Sacrificer are to be born. Agni
is both the father and the son of Pragâpati: 'inasmuch as
Pragâpati created Agni, he is Agni's father ; and inasmuch
as Agni restored him, Agni is his father [3].' Yet the two
are separate ; for Pragâpati covets Agni's forms.—forms
(such as Îsâna, the lord : Mahân Devah, the great god ;
Pasupati, the lord of beasts) which are indeed desirable
enough for a supreme Lord of Creatures to possess, and
which might well induce Pragâpati to take up Agni within
his own self. Though, in accordance with an older conception, Agni is still the light or regent of the earth, as
Vâyu, the wind, is that of the air, and the sun that of the
heavens ; it is now explained that really these are but three
forms of the one Agni,—that Agni's splendour in heaven is
Âditya, that in the air Vâyu, and that on earth the (sacrificial) fire [4]. When Pragâpati is dismembered, Agni takes
unto himself the escaping fiery spirit of the god ; and when
he is set up again, Agni becomes the right arm, as Indra
becomes the left one, of the Lord of Creatures. Upon the
whole, however, the peculiar relations between the two
gods may perhaps be defined best in accordance with the

---

[1] IV. 6, 1, 4.   [2] VI. 8, 2, 4-6.
[2] VI, 1, 2, 26.   [4] VI, 7, 4. 4; VII, 1, 1, 22-23.

passage already referred to :—Agni is created by Pragâpati, and he subsequently restores Pragâpati by giving up his own body (the fire-altar) to build up anew the dismembered Lord of Creatures, and by entering into him with his own fiery spirit,—'whence, while being Pragâpati, they yet call him Agni.'

The shape adopted for the altar is that of some large bird—probably an eagle or a falcon—flying towards the east, the gate of heaven. Not that this is the form in which Pragâpati is invariably conceived. On the contrary, he is frequently imagined in the form of a man, and symbolic features are often applied to him which could only fit, or would best fit, a human body. But, being the embodiment of all things, Pragâpati naturally possesses all forms ; whence the shape of a four-footed animal is likewise occasionally applied to the altar [1]. It was, doubtless, both traditional imagery and practical considerations which told in favour of the shape actually chosen. Pragâpati is the sacrifice and the food of the gods [2] ; and Soma, the drink of immortality and at the same time the Moon, is *the* divine food or offering κατ' ἐξοχήν, the uttamam havis [3], or paramâhuti [4], or supreme oblation: hence Pragâpati is Soma [5]. But Soma was brought down from heaven by the bird-shaped Gâyatri ; and the sacrifice itself is fashioned like a bird [6]. In one passage [7], certain authorities are referred to as making the altar (Agni) take the form of a bird in order to carry the Sacrificer to heaven ; but the author himself there insists dogmatically on the traditional connection of the altar with Pragâpati: that it was by assuming that form that the vital airs became Pragâpati [8] ; and that in that

---

[1] See, for instance, VIII, 1, 4. 3.   [2] V, 1, 1, 2.
[3] Rig-veda IX, 107, 1.   [4] Sat. Br. VI, 6, 3, 7.
[5] See, for instance, VI, 2, 2. 16; X. 4, 2, 1.
[6] IV, 1, 2, 25.   [7] VI, 1, 2, 36 ; cf. XI, 4, 1, 16.
[8] This can only refer to the cosmological statement at the beginning of the same Kânda, where the seven Rishis, or vital airs, are said to have combined to form the bird-shaped Purusha or Pragâpati. Though nothing is said there of their having themselves been shaped like birds, this might perhaps be inferred from the use of the term 'purusha' with reference to them. In the Purusha-sûkta nothing whatever is said of a birdlike form, either in regard to the Rishis,

form he created the gods who, on their part, became
immortal by assuming the birdlike form—and apparently
flying up to heaven, which would seem to imply that the
Sacrificer himself is to fly up to heaven in form of the
bird-shaped altar, there to become immortal. It is not,
however, only with the Moon, amongst heavenly luminaries,
that Pragâpati is identified, but also with the Sun; for the
latter, as we have seen, is but one of the three forms of Agni,
and the fire on the great altar is itself the Sun [1]; whilst the
notion of the sun being fashioned like a bird flying through
space is not an unfamiliar one to the poets of the Vedic
age. More familiar, however, to the authors of the Brâhmanas, as it is more in keeping with the mystic origin of
Pragâpati, is the identification of the latter, not with the
solar orb itself, but with the man (purusha) in the sun, the
real shedder of light and life. This gold man plays an
important part in the speculations of the Agnirahasya[2],
where he is represented as identical with the man (purusha)
in the (right) eye—the individualised Purusha, as it were;
whilst his counterpart in the Fire-altar is the solid gold man
(purusha) laid down, below the centre of the first layer, on
a gold plate, representing the sun, lying itself on the lotus-
leaf already referred to as the womb whence Agni springs.
And this gold man in the altar, then, is no other than
Agni-Pragâpati and the Sacrificer: above him—in the first,
third, and fifth layers—lie the three naturally-perforated
bricks, representing the three worlds through which he
will have to pass on his way to the fourth, invisible, world,
the realm of immortal life. We thus meet here again with the
hallowed, old name of the Lord of Being, only to be made
use of for new mystic combinations.

As the personified totality of all being, Pragâpati, however, not only represents the phenomena and aspects of
space, but also those of time,—he is Father Time. But
just as, in the material process of building up the Fire-altar,
the infinite dimensions of space require to be reduced to

or the Purusha; the latter being, on the contrary, imagined in the form of
a gigantic man.

[1] VI, 1, 2, 20; 3, 1, 13.   [2] X, 5, 2, 1 seq.

finite proportions, so, in regard to time, the year, as the lowest complete revolution of time, is taken to represent the Lord of Creation :—he is Father Year ; and accordingly Agni, the Fire-altar, takes a full year to complete. And, in the same way, Agni, the sacrificial fire, from the time of his being generated in the fire-pan, as the womb, requires to be carried about by the Sacrificer for a whole year, to be matured by him before the child Agni can be born and placed on the Fire-altar. The reason why the Sacrificer must do so is, of course, that Agni, being the child of the universe—that is of Pragâpati and the Sacrificer,—the latter, at the time when the fire is kindled in the fire-pan, has, as it were, to take Agni within his own self [1], and has afterwards to produce him from out of his own self when mature.

But whilst, in regard to Agni-Pragâpati, the year during which the altar is erected represents the infinitude of time, to the mortal Sacrificer it will not be so until he shall have departed this life ; and, as a rule, he would probably not be anxious there and then to end his earthly career. Nor is such an effort of renunciation demanded of him, but, on the contrary, the sacrificial theory holds out to the pious performer of this holy ceremony the prospect of his living up to the full extent of the perfect man's life, a hundred years ; this term of years being thus recognised as another unit of time, so to speak, viz. that of a complete lifetime. Yet, be it sooner or be it later, the life of every creature comes to an end ; and since time works its havoc on all material existence, and carries off generation after genera-tion, the Supreme Lord of generation, Father Time, as he is the giver of all life, so he is likewise that ender of all things—Death. And so the Sacrificer, as the human counterpart of the Lord of Creatures, with the end of his present life, becomes himself Death,—Death ceases to have power over him, and he is for ever removed from the life of material existence, trouble, and illusion, to the realms of light and everlasting bliss.

[1] VII, 4, 1, 1.

And here we get the Supreme Lord in his last aspect : nay, his one true and real aspect, in which the Sacrificer will himself come to share,—that of pure intellectuality, pure spirituality,—he is Mind : such is the ultimate source of being, the one Self, the Purusha, the Brahman. The author of the Mystery of Agni attempts to reveal the process of evolution by which this one true Self, through sacrifice carried on by means of the Arka-fires of his own innate fervour and devotion, comes to manifest himself in the material universe ; and—as the sum total of the wisdom of Sândilya—he urges upon the searcher after truth to meditate on that Self, made up of intelligence, and endowed with a body of spirit, a form of light, and an etherial nature, . . . holding sway over all the regions and pervading this All, being itself speechless and devoid of mental affects ;—and bids him believe that ' even as a grain of rice, or the smallest granule of millet, so is the golden Purusha in the heart ; even as a smokeless light, it is greater than the sky, greater than the ether, greater than the earth, greater than all existing things ; that Self of the spirit is my Self : on passing away from hence I shall obtain that Self. And, verily, whosoever has this trust, for him there is no uncertainty.'

As the practical application of the Agni-Pragâpati mystery to the sacrificial ritual consists mainly in the erection of the Fire-altar and the ceremonies connected with the fire-pan, which fell almost entirely within the province of the Adhvaryu priest, it is naturally in his text-books, in the Yagur-veda, that the mystic theory has become fully elaborated. Yet, though the two other classes of priests, the Hotris and Udgâtris[1], take, upon the whole, a comparatively subsidiary part in the year's performance symbolising the reconstruction of the Lord of Creatures, they have found another solemn opportunity, subsequently to the completion of the Fire-altar, for making up for any

---

[1] They take part, however, in such ceremonies as the doing homage to the completed Fire-altar by means of the Parimâds ; cf. p. 288, note 2 of this volume.

shortcomings in this respect, viz. the Mahâvrata, or Great Rite.

The brick altar, when complete, might apparently be used at once for any kind of Soma-sacrifice[1]; but whether, if this were to be merely a one-day performance, it might be made a Mahâvrata day (in which case it must be an Agnish/oma), seems somewhat doubtful[2]. As a rule, however, at any rate, the Mahâvrata was performed in connection, not with an ekâha or ahina, but with a sacrificial session (sattra): and since sacrificial sessions, it would seem, could only be undertaken by Brâhmans who would at the same time be the Sacrificers—or rather Grihapatis (masters of the house or householders) as the Sattrins are called—and their own officiating priests, the Mahâvrata would thus generally, if not invariably, be reserved for Brâhmans[3]. Indeed, in our Brâhmana (IX. 5, 2, 12-13) the rule is laid down that no one may officiate for another person at the Agnikayana, the Mahâvrata (sâman), and the Mahad Uktham; and dire consequences are predicted in the case of any one who does so: —'for, indeed, these (rites) are his divine, immortal body; and he who performs them for another person, makes over to another his divine body, and a withered trunk is all that remains.' And, though other authorities are then referred to who merely prescribe, as a penance for those who have officiated at these ceremonies for others, that they should either perform them for themselves or cause others to perform them again, the author

---

[1] Our Brâhmana, X, 2, 5, 16, says that, if a man cannot press Soma for a year, he should perform the Visvajit Atirâtra with all the Prishthas, and at that performance he should give away all his property. These, however, were doubtless by no means the only alternatives.

[2] See, however, Sâyana on Ait. Âr. V, 1, 1, 1, where it is distinctly stated that the Mahâvrata may either be performed as an Ekâha, or as part of either an Ahina, or a Sattra.—Kâtyâyana, XVI, 1, 2, lays down the rule that though the building of an altar is not a necessary condition for the performance of a Soma-sacrifice, it is indispensable in the case of a Soma-sacrifice performed with the Mahâvrata.

[3] That is to say, as Sacrificers. Persons of other castes of course took part in the proceedings of this day. In the various accounts of these proceedings, no alternative ceremonies seem anywhere referred to in case the Sacrificers themselves belong to different castes.

adheres to his opinion that there is no atonement for such
an offence. There can be no doubt, however, that the
Agni*k*ayana, at any rate, was not restricted to the Brâhma*n*ical order[1] ; and this passage, if it does not merely
record a former sacrificial practice, has probably to be
understood in the sense that one must not officiate for
another at an Agni*k*ayana which is to be followed by a
Soma-sacrifice with the Mahâvrata. If the Sattra performed
was one of the shortest kind, viz. a Dvâda*s*âha, or twelve
days' performance—consisting of a Da*s*arâtra, preceded
and followed by an Atirâtra—the Mahâvrata was inserted,
it would seem, between the Da*s*arâtra and the final Atirâtra.
Usually, however, the Sattra, like the Agni*k*ayana, lasted
a full year ; the favourite form being the ' Gavâm ayanam,'
arranged, in accordance with the progress of the sun, in two
halves, an ascending and a descending one, divided by
a central day, the Vishuvat. The Mahâvrata was performed on the last day but one of the year, the day before
the final Atirâtra, being itself preceded (as it was in the
case of the Dvâda*s*âha) by a Da*s*arâtra, or ten days' performance. Now, the chief feature of the Mahâvrata day
is the chanting,—in connection with a special cup of Soma-
juice, the Mahâvratiya-graha—of the Mahâvrata-sâman[2],
as the Hot*ri*'s P*ri*sh*th*a-stotra at the midday service ; this
chant being followed by the recitation of the Mahad Uktham[3], or Great Litany, by the Hot*ri*. The special feature,
however, of these two ceremonies, which recalls the mystic
Agni-Pra*g*âpati doctrine, is the supposed birdlike form of
both the chant and the litany. The Lord of Creatures, as
the embodiment of all things, also represents the ' trayî
vidyâ,' or sacred threefold science, the Veda. Accordingly,
the Stomas (hymn-forms) of the single Sâmans (chanted

---

[1] See, for instance, *S*at. Br. VI, 6, 3, 12-15, where directions are given as to
certain alternatives of performance at the initiation ceremony in case the Sacrificer is either a Kshatriya, or a Purohita, or any other person. The ceremonies
connected with the consecration of the Sacrificer (IX, 3, 4, 1 seqq.) point
chiefly to a king.

[2] See p. 282, note 5 of the present volume.

[3] See notes to pp. 110-113 of this volume.

verses) composing the Stotra or hymn of praise (the Mahâvrata-sâman), on the one hand, and the verses and metres of the recited litany, on the other, are so arranged and explained as to make up the different parts of a bird's body. It need scarcely be remarked that, whilst in the case of the altar the task of bringing out at least a rough resemblance to a flying bird offered no great difficulties, it is altogether beyond the capabilities of vocal performances such as the chant and the recitation of hymns and detached verses. But the very fact that this symbolism is only a matter of definition and make-believe, makes it all the more characteristic of the great hold which the Praɡâpati theory had gained upon the sacerdotal mind.

The question as to whether these compositions themselves might seem to show any signs of comparatively recent introduction of this symbolism requires further investigation before it can be answered. Of the Mahâvrata-sâman we have virtually a single version, with only indications of certain substitutions which may be made in the choice of texts and tunes: the parts of the bird's body represented by the single Sâmans being in the order—head, right wing, left wing, tail, and trunk. Of the Mahad Uktham, on the other hand, we possess two different versions, those of the Aitareya and the Sânkhâyana schools of Ri̯g-veda theologians. Both of them start with the hymns representing the trunk of the bird; but otherwise there is so marked a difference between them, both as to arrangement and the choice of verses and hymns, that it seems pretty clear that, whilst there must have existed already a certain traditional form of the litany when these two schools separated, it was not yet of a sufficiently settled character to prevent such serious discrepancies to arise as those exhibited by the two rituals. This point being, however, of too technical a nature to be entered upon in this place, its further investigation must be reserved for some other opportunity.

SATAPATHA-BRÂHMANA.

EIGHTH KÂNDA.

THE BUILDING OF THE SACRED FIRE-ALTAR
(continued).

THE CONSTRUCTION OF THE FIRST LAYER
(continued).

FIRST ADHYÂYA. FIRST BRÂHMANA.

1. He lays down the Prânabhritah (breath-holders)[1] : now, the Prânabhritah being the vital

---

[1] The construction of the first of the five layers of the altar which, as far as the special bricks are concerned, is now nearing its completion, may be briefly recapitulated here. The altar (agni) is constructed in the form of a bird, the body (âtman) of which consists of a square, usually measuring four man's lengths, or forty feet (Indian = c. 30 ft. Engl.) on each side. The ground of the 'body' having been ploughed, watered, and sown with seeds of all kinds of herbs, a square mound, the so-called uttaravedi, measuring a yuga (yoke = 7 ft. Ind.) on each side, is thrown up in the middle of the 'body,' and the whole of the latter then made level with it. In the centre of the 'body' thus raised, where the two 'spines'—connecting the middle of each of the four sides of the square with that of the opposite side—meet, the priest puts down a lotus-leaf, and thereon the gold plate (a symbol of the sun) which the Sacrificer wore round his neck during the time of initiation. On this plate he then lays a small gold figure of a man (representing Agni-Pragâpati, as well as the Sacrificer himself), so as to lie on his back with the head towards the east; and beside him he places two offering-spoons, one on each side, filled with ghee and sour curds

airs, it is the vital airs he thereby bestows upon
(Agni). He lays them down in the first layer;—
that which is the first layer is the forepart (ground-
part) of Agni : it is thus in front that he puts (into
Agni) the vital airs, whence there are (in creatures)
these (orifices of the) vital airs in front.

respectively. Upon the man he then places a brick with naturally-
formed holes in it (or a porous stone), a so-called Svayam-âtrinnâ
(self-perforated one), of which there are three in the altar, viz. in
the centre of the first, third, and fifth layers, supposed to represent
the earth, air, and sky respectively, and by their holes to allow the
Sacrificer (in effigy) to breathe, and ultimately to pass through on
his way to the eternal abodes. On this stone he lays down a plant
of dûrvâ grass—with the root lying on the brick, and the twigs
hanging down—meant to represent vegetation on earth, and food
for the Sacrificer. Thereupon he puts down in front (east) of the
central stone, on the 'spine,' a Dviyagus brick ; in front of that, on
both sides of the spine, two Retahsik; then in front of them, one
Visvagyotis; then again two Ritavyâh; and finally the Ashâdhâ, representing the Sacrificer's consecrated consort. These
bricks, each of which is a pada (foot, Ind.) square, occupy nearly
one-third of the line from the centre to the middle of the front side
of the 'body' of the altar. South and north of the Ashâdhâ,
leaving the space of two bricks, he places a live tortoise, facing the
gold man, and a wooden mortar and pestle respectively. On the
mortar he places the ukhâ, or fire-pan, filled with sand and milk ;
and thereon the heads of the five victims, after chips of gold have
been thrust into their mouths, nostrils, eyes, and ears. At each of
the four ends of the two 'spines' he then puts down five Apasyâh
bricks, the middle one lying on the spine itself, with two on each
side of it. The last set of five bricks, those laid down at the north
(or left) end of the 'cross-spine,' are also called Khandasyâh by the
Brâhmana. He now proceeds to lay down the Prânabhritah,
meant to represent the orifices of the vital airs, in five sets of ten
bricks each. The first four sets are placed on the four diagonals
connecting the centre with the four corners of the body of the altar,
beginning from the corner (? or, according to some, optionally from
the centre), in the order S.E., N.W., S.W., N.E. ; the fifth set being
then laid down round the central stone at the distance (or, on the
range) of the retahsik bricks. See the diagram at p. 17.

2. He lays them down by ten and ten, for there are ten vital airs; and even though 'ten-ten' may mean many times, here they mean only ten. Five times he puts on ten (bricks) each time: for it is those five (kinds of sacrificial) animals he bestows, and there are ten vital airs in each animal: upon all of them he thus bestows the vital airs. He lays down (the bricks) so as not to be separated from the animals: he thus bestows vital airs not separated from the animals. He lays them down on every side: on every side he thus bestows on them (orifices of) the vital airs.

3. And again why he lays down the Prânabhritah. From Pragâpati, when relaxed (by producing creatures), the vital airs departed. To them, having become deities, he spake, 'Come ye to me, return ye unto me that wherewith ye have gone out of me!'—'Well then, create thou that food which we will await here looking on!'—'Well then, let us both create!'—'So be it!'—So both the final airs and Pragâpati created that food, these Prânabhrit (bricks).

4. In front (of the altar) he lays down (ten bricks [1],— the first) with (Vâg. S. XIII, 54), 'This one in front, the Existent,'—in front, doubtless, is Agni; and as to why he speaks of him (as being) 'in front,' it is because they take out the fire (from the Gârhapatya) towards the front, and attend on Agni towards the front [2]. And as to why he says 'the

---

[1] Whilst standing in front (east) of the altar, he puts down the first set of ten bricks on the line from the south-west corner (or right shoulder) of the altar towards the centre. The formulas with which each set of ten bricks are deposited are spread over three paragraphs, the first of which gives that of the first brick, the second those for two to eight, the third for the last two.

[2] Viz. in taking out the fire from the Gârhapatya and transferring

existent (bhuva),' Agni is indeed the existent, for it
is through Agni that everything exists (bhû) here.
Agni, indeed, having become the breath, remained
in front [1] : it is that very form [2] he now bestows
(on Agni).

5. [The others with], 'His, the Existent's son,
the Breath,'—from out of that form, fire, he (Pragâpati) fashioned the breath ;—'Spring, the son of
the breath,'—from out of the breath he fashioned
the spring-season [3];—'The Gâyatrî, the daughter
of the Spring,'—from out of the spring-season he
fashioned the Gâyatrî metre ;—'From the Gâyatrî
the Gâyatra,'—from out of the Gâyatrî metre he
fashioned the Gâyatra [4] hymn-tune ;—'From the
Gâyatra the Upâmsu,'—from out of the Gâyatra
hymn - tune he fashioned the Upâmsu-graha [5] ;—

---

it to the Âhavanîya, as well as in approaching the sacrificial fire for
offerings. It should also be borne in mind that the altar (agni) is
built in form of an eagle flying towards the east, or front.

[1] See VII, 5, 1, 7, 'The breath is taken in from the front backwards.'—In the text 'prâno hâgnir bhûtvâ purastât tasthau,' I take
'prânah' to be the predicate.

[2] At VII, 4, 1, 16, the vital air is called Pragâpati's (Agni's)
pleasing form (or part).

[3] For a similar connection of the East with the Gâyatrî, the
Rathantara, the Trivrit, the Spring, and the Brahman (priesthood)
see V, 4, 1, 3. (part iii, p. 91).

[4] The Gâyatra-sâman is the simplest, and by far the most
common of all hymn-tunes. It is especially used in connection
with the trivrit-stoma, or nine-versed hymn, and is invariably employed for the Bahishpavamâna-stotra. It is also the tune of the
first triplet both of the Mâdhyandina and Ârbhava-pavamâna ; as
well as for all the four Âgya-stotras.

[5] See part ii, pp. 238 seqq., where this soma-cup is repeatedly
connected with the Gâyatrî. Though its pressing is performed by
three turns of eight, eleven, and twelve beatings respectively,
representing the three chief metres, it is expressly stated (IV, 1, 1, 14)

'From the Upâmsu the Trivrit,'—from out of the Upâmsu-graha he fashioned the nine-versed hymn-form;—'From the Trivrit the Rathantara,'—from out of the Trivrit-stoma he fashioned the Rathantara-prishtha [1].

6. 'The Rishi Vasishtha [2],'—the Rishi Vasishtha, doubtless, is the breath : inasmuch as it is the chief (thing) therefore it is Vasishtha (the most excellent) ; or inasmuch as it abides (with living beings) as the best abider (vastri), therefore also it is Vasishtha.—'By thee, taken by Pragâpati,'—that is, 'by thee, created by Pragâpati,'—'I take breath for my descendants (and people)!'—therewith he introduced the breath from the front. Separately he lays down (these ten bricks): what separate desires there are in the breath, those he thereby lays into it. Only once he settles them [3]: he thereby makes it one breath; but were he to settle them each separately, he assuredly would cut the breath asunder. This brick is trivrit (three-fold): the formula, the settling, and the sûdadohas [4], that is threefold, and threefold is Agni.—as great as

---

that he who is desirous of obtaining holiness, should press eight times at each turn.

[1] For this and the other Prishtha-sâmans see part iii, introd. pp. xvi, xx seqq.

[2] In Taitt. S. IV, 3, 2, 1, this formula is connected with the preceding one.—'from the Rathantara (was produced) the Rishi Vasishtha.' Similarly in the corresponding passages of the subsequent sets of bricks.

[3] The sâdana, or settling, consists in the formula, 'By that deity, Angiras-like, lie thou steady!' being pronounced over the bricks. See VI, 1, 2, 28.

[4] For the sûdadohas verse, the pronunciation of which, together with the 'settling,' constitutes the two necessary (nitya) ceremonies, see part iii, p. 307.

Agni is, as great as is his measure, so much he lays down (on the altar) by so doing.

7. And on the right (south) side [1], with (Vâg. S. XIII, 55), 'This one on the right, the all-worker,'—the all-worker (visvakarman), doubtless, is this Vâyu (the wind) who blows here, for it is he that makes everything here ; and because he speaks of him as (being) 'on the right,' therefore it is in the south that he blows most. Vâyu, indeed, having become the mind, remained in the right side (of the body): it is that form (part) he now bestows (on Agni).

8. 'His, the all-worker's child, the Mind,'—from out of that (all-working) form, the wind, he fashioned the mind ; —'the summer, the son of the mind,'—from out of the mind he fashioned the summer season [2] ;—'the Trish/ubh, the daughter of Summer,'—from out of the summer season he fashioned the Trish/ubh metre ;—'from the Trish-/ubh the Svâra tune,'—from out of the Trish/ubh metre he created the Svâra hymn-tune [3] ;—'from

---

[1] Whilst standing on the right (south) side of the altar he lays down the third set of ten Prânabhritah, viz. those on the diagonal from the south-west corner (or right thigh) towards the centre. Whilst, in the actual performance, these bricks are only laid down after those referred to in paragraphs 1–3 of the next Brâhmana, the author, in his explanation of the formulas, follows the course of the sun from left to right.

[2] For a similar combination of the south with the Trish/ubh metre, the Brihat-sâman, the Pankadasa-stoma, the summer season, and the Kshatra, see V, 4, 1, 4 (part iii, p. 91).

[3] Svâra-sâman is called a chanted verse which has no special concluding nidhana, or finale, but in which the svarita (circumflex), or first rising then falling pitch (e.g., f–g–f) of the final vowel, takes the place of the finale ; whence 'svâra' is often explained by 'svaranidhana,' i.e. having the svara (svarita) for its nidhana.   See

the Svâra the Antaryâma,'—from out of the
Svâra-sâman he fashioned the Antaryâma graha;—
'from the Antaryâma the Pañkadasa,'—from
out of the Antaryâma-cup he fashioned the fifteen-
versed hymn-form;—'from the Pañkadasa the
Brihat,'—from out of the Pañkadasa-stoma he
fashioned the Brihat-prishtha.

9. 'The Rishi Bharadvâga,'—the Rishi Bharadvâga, doubtless, is the mind;—'vâga' means 'food,'
and he who possesses a mind, possesses (bharati)
food, 'vâga;' therefore the Rishi Bharadvâga is the
mind.—'By thee, taken by Pragâpati,'—that is,
'by thee, created by Pragâpati;'—'I take the mind
for my descendants!'—therewith he introduced
the mind from the right side. Separately he lays
down (these ten bricks): what separate desires there
are in the mind, those he thereby lays into it. Only
once he settles them: he thereby makes it one
mind; but were he to settle them each separately,

Pañk. Br. IX, 3, 11, where a svâra-sâman is prescribed in case the
Udgâtris have previously committed an excess in their chanting.
The last tristich of the Mâdhyandina-pavamânastotra of the Agnishtoma, the Ausana-sâman (to Sâma-v., vol. ii, pp. 27-29), is chanted
in this way, probably in order to make good the excess committed
in the preceding triplet, the Yaudhâgaya (ii, pp. 25, 26), in which each
verse is chanted with three nidhanas, one at the end, and two inserted
inside the sâman. Lâty. Srautas. VI, 9, 6, the svâra-sâmans thus
treated are called 'padânusvârâni;' whilst those with which the
musical syllables 'hâ-i' are used with a similar effect, are called
'hâikârasvârâni.' As an instance of the former, the Ausana (Sâma-v.,
vol. iii, p. 81) is adduced, and of the latter the Vâmadevya (iii, p. 89).
It is not only the final syllable of a sâman, however, that may be
modulated in this way, but also that of a musical section of the
sâman; cf. Pañk. Br. X, 12, 2, where the Udgîtha is to be so treated
to make up for the preceding Prastâva, chanted without a Stobha.
Sacrificial calls such as the 'Svâhâ' and 'Vashat' are also modulated
in this way,' ib. VII, 3, 26; XI, 5, 26.

he assuredly would cut asunder the mind. This
brick is threefold: the meaning of this has been
explained.

SECOND BRÂHMANA.

1. And at the back (western part of the altar),
with (Vâg. S. XIII, 56), 'This one behind, the
all-embracer;'—the all-embracer, doubtless, is
yonder sun, for as soon as[1] he rises, all this embracing space comes into existence. And because
he speaks of him as (being) 'behind,' therefore one
sees him only when he goes towards the back
(west). The Sun, indeed, having become the eye,
remained behind: it is that form he now bestows
(on Agni).

2. 'His, the all-embracer's child, the Eye,'—
from out of that (all-embracing) form, the Sun, he
fashioned the eye;—'the rains, the offspring
of the eye,'—from out of the eye he fashioned the
rainy season;—'the Gagatî, the daughter of the
rains,'—from out of the rainy season he fashioned
the Gagatî metre;—'from the Gagatî the Rik-
sama,'—from out of the Gagatî metre he fashioned
the Riksama hymn-tune[2];—'from the Riksama

---

[1] Or, perhaps, 'only when' (yadi-eva).

[2] No explanation of this sâman has been found anywhere.
Sâyana, on the corresponding formula, Taitt. S. IV, 3, 4, 2 (where
the term is spelt rik-sama), merely remarks that it is 'a kind of
sâman.' The meaning of the term 'similar to a rik' would seem
to indicate a hymn-tune involving little, or no, modification of the
text chanted to it. At V, 4, 1, 5 it is the Vairûpa-sâman which
(together with the Gagatî, the Saptadasa-stoma, the rainy season,
and the Vis) is in this way connected with the West. Now the
textual parts of the Pañkanidhanam Vairûpam (Sâma-v., vol. v,
pp. 387, 575-6), ordinarily used as a prishtha-sâman, show

the Sukra,' from out of the *R*iksama-sâman he
fashioned the Sukra-graha ;—' from the Sukra the
Saptada*s*a,'—from out of the Sukra cup he
fashioned the seventeen-versed hymn-form ;—' from
the Saptada*s*a the Vairûpa,'—from out of the
Saptada*s*a-stoma he fashioned the Vairûpa-*pr*ish*th*a.

3. ' The *R*ishi *G*amadagni,'—the *R*ishi *G*amadagni, doubtless, is the eye : inasmuch as thereby
the world of the living (*g*a*g*at) sees and thinks,
therefore the *R*ishi *G*amadagni is the eye.—' By
thee, taken by Pra*g*âpati,'—that is, ' by thee,
created by Pra*g*âpati,'—' I take the eye for my
descendants,' therewith he introduced the eye
from behind. Separately he lays down (these ten
bricks) : what separate desires there are in the eye
those he thereby lays into it. Only once he settles
them : he thereby makes this eye one ; but were he
to settle them each separately, he assuredly would
cut the eye asunder. This is a threefold brick : the
meaning of this has been explained.

4. And on the left (upper, north) side, with (Vâ*g*.
S. XIII, 57), ' This, on the upper side, heaven,'
—in the upper sphere, doubtless, are the regions
(quarters) ; and as to why he speaks of them as
being ' on the upper (left) side,' the regions, indeed,

hardly any modifications on the original verses (Sâma-v., vol. ii,
p. 278), even less so indeed than the simple Vairûpa-sâman (Sâma-v.,
vol. i, p. 572), and possibly '*r*iksama' (if it does not apply to
a whole class of sâmans) may be another name for the Vairûpa (of
which there are two other forms, Sâma-v., vol. i, pp. 425, 438) in its
simplest form. The Vairûpa, in its *pr*ish*th*a form, would in that
case, indeed, have originated from the *R*iksama-sâman. It is true,
however, that there is no special connection between the other
Pr*ish*th*a-sâmans and the respective hymn-tune with which they
are symbolically connected in the foregoing formulas.

are above everything here. And as to why he
says, 'heaven (or, the light),' the regions, indeed, are
the heavenly world (or world of light). The regions,
having become the ear, remained above: it is that
form he now bestows (on Agni).

5. 'Its, heaven's, child, the Ear,'—from out of
that form, the regions, he fashioned the ear;—'the
autumn, the daughter of the ear,'—from out of
the ear he fashioned the autumn season;—'Anushtubh, the daughter of the autumn,'—from out of
the autumn season he fashioned the Anushtubh
metre;—'from the Anushtubh the Aida,'—from
out of the Anushtubh metre he fashioned the Aida-
sâman[1];—'from the Aida the Manthin,'— from
out of the Aida-sâman he fashioned the Manthin
cup;—'from the Manthin the Ekavimsa,'—from
out of the Manthi-graha he fashioned the twenty-
one-versed hymn-form;—'from the Ekavimsa
the Vairâga,'—from out of the Ekavimsa-stoma
he fashioned the Vairâga-prishtha.

6. 'The Rishi Visvâmitra,'—the Rishi Visvâmitra ('all-friend'), doubtless, is the ear: because
therewith one hears in every direction, and because
there is a friend (mitra) to it on every side, therefore
the ear is the Rishi Visvâmitra.—'By thee, taken
by Pragâpati,'—that is, 'by thee, erected by Pragâpati;'—'I take the ear for my descendants,'

---

[1] Aida-sâmans are those sâmans which have the word 'idâ' for
their nidhana, or chorus. Such sâmans are, e.g. the Vairûpa (Sâma-v.,
vol. v, p. 387) and the Raurava (iii, 83), the latter of which forms
the central sâman of the Mâdhyandina-pavamâna-stotra. What
connection there can be between the Aida and the Vairâga-prishtha
(Sâma-v., vol. v. p. 391 ; cf. vol. i, pp. 814-5) it is not easy to see.
In Sat. Br. V, 4, 1, 6 the North is connected with the Anu-shtubh,
the Vairâga-sâman, the Ekavimsa and the autumn.

—therewith he introduced the ear from the left (or upper) side. Separately he lays down (these bricks): what separate desires there are in the ear, those he thereby lays into it. Only once he settles them: he thereby makes the ear one; but were he to settle them each separately, he assuredly would cut the ear asunder. This is a threefold brick: the meaning of this has been explained.

7. Then in the centre, with (Vâg. S. XIII, 58), 'This one, above, the mind,'—above, doubtless, is the moon; and as to why he speaks of him as (being) 'above,' the moon is indeed above; and as to why he says, ' the mind,' the mind (mati), doubtless, is speech, for by means of speech everything thinks (man) here[1]. The moon, having become speech, remained above: it is that form he now bestows (on Agni).

8. 'Its, the mind's, daughter, Speech,'—from out of that form, the moon, he fashioned speech;— 'Winter, the son of Speech,'—from out of speech he fashioned the winter season;—' Pankti, the daughter of Winter,'—from out of the winter season he fashioned the Pankti metre;—'from the Pankti the Nidhanavat,'—from out of the Pankti metre he fashioned the Nidhanavat-sâman[2];— 'from the Nidhanavat the Âgrayana,'—from out of the Nidhanavat-sâman he fashioned the Âgrayana cup;—'from the Âgrayana the Trinava and Trayastrimsa,'—from out of the Âgrayana-graha he fashioned the thrice-nine-versed and the three-and-thirty-versed hymn-forms;—

---

[1] Or, perhaps, one thinks everything here.

[2] That is a sâman which has a special nidhana, or chorus, added at the end (or inserted in the middle) of it.

'from the Trinava and Trayastrimsa the Sâkvara and Raivata,'—from out of the Trinava and Trayastrimsa-stomas he fashioned the Sâkvara and Raivata-prishthas[1].

9. 'The Rishi Visvakarman,'—the Rishi Visvakarman ('the all-worker'), doubtless, is Speech, for by speech everything here is done; hence the Rishi Visvakarman is speech :—'By thee, taken by Pragâpati,'—that is, 'by thee, created by Pragâpati;'—'I take speech for my descendants,'—therewith he introduced speech from above. Separately he lays down (these bricks): what separate desires there are in speech, those he now lays into it. Only once he settles them: he thereby makes speech one; but were he to settle them each separately, he assuredly would cut speech asunder. This is a threefold brick : the meaning of this has been explained.

10. This, then, is that same food which both the vital airs and Pragâpati created: just so great indeed is the whole sacrifice, and the sacrifice is the food of the gods.

11. He lays them down by ten and ten,—of ten syllables consists the Virâg (metre), and the Virâg is all food: he thus bestows on him (Agni) the whole food. He puts them down on every side: on every side he thus bestows the whole food on him. And verily these same Virâg (verses) sustain those vital airs, and inasmuch as they sustain (bhri) the vital airs (prâna) they are called Prânabhritah.

---

[1] For these Prishtha-sâmans see part iii, introd. pp. xx–xxi. In V, 4, 1, 7 the upper region is symbolically connected with the Pankti metre, the Sâkvara and Raivata-sâmans, the Trinava and Trayastrimsa-stomas, and the winter and dewy seasons.

THIRD BRÂHMANA.

1. As to this they say, 'What are the vital airs (prâna), and what the Prânabhritah?'—The vital airs are just the vital airs, and the Prânabhritah (holders of the vital airs) are the limbs, for the limbs do hold the vital airs. But, indeed, the vital airs are the vital airs, and the Prânabhrit is food, for food does uphold the vital airs.

2. As to this they say, 'How do all these (Prâna-bhrit-bricks) of him (Agni and the Sacrificer) come to be of Pragâpati's nature?'—Doubtless in that with all of them he says, 'By thee, taken by Pragâpati:' it is in this way, indeed, that they all come to be for him of Pragâpati's nature [1].

3. As to this they say, 'As they chant and recite for the cup when drawn, wherefore, then, does he put in verses and hymn-tunes [2] before (the drawing of) the cups?'—Doubtless, the completion of the sacrificial work has to be kept in view;—now with the opening hymn-verse the cup is drawn; and on the verse (rik) the tune (sâman) is sung: this means that he thereby puts in for him (Agni) both the verses and hymn-tunes before (the drawing of) the cups. And when after (the drawing of) the cups there are the chanting (of the Stotra) and the recita-tion (of the Sastra): this means that thereby he puts in for him both the stomas (hymn-forms) and the prishtha (sâmans) after (the drawing of) the cups [3].

---

[1] Or, come to be (Agni-) Pragâpati's (prâgâpatyâ bhavanti).

[2] In laying down the different sets of Prânabhrit-bricks the priest is said (in VIII, 1, 1, 5; 8; 2, 2; 5; 8) symbolically to put into the sacrificial work (or into the altar, Agni) both verses or metres (as Gâyatrî, Trishtubh, &c.) and hymn-tunes (as Gâyatra, Svâra, &c.).

[3] It is not quite clear whether this is the correct construction of

4. As to this they say, 'If these three are done together—the soma-cup, the chant, and the recitation,—and he puts in only the soma-cup and the chant, how comes the recitation also in this case to be put (into the sacrificial work) for him[1]?' But, surely, what the chant is that is the recitation[2]: for on whatsoever (verses) they chant a tune, those same (verses) he (the Hotri) recites thereafter[3]; and in this way, indeed, the Sastra also comes in this case to be put in for him.

5. As to this they say, 'When he speaks first of three in the same way as of a father's son[4], how, then, does this correspond as regards the rik and sâman?' The sâman, doubtless, is the husband of the

the text, especially as, in the paragraph referred to in the last note, it is not only the metres and tunes that are supposed to be put in along with the Prânabhritah, but also the stomas and prishtha-sâmans.

[1] Only soma-cups (graha) and hymn-tunes (sâman) and hymn-forms (stoma) are specially named in connection with these bricks, but no sastras.

[2] Every stotra, chanted by the Udgâtris, is followed by a sastra recited by the Hotri or one of his assistants.

[3] Most chants (stotra) consisting of a single triplet (e.g. the Prishtha-stotras at the midday service) have their text (stotriya-rika) included in the corresponding sastra recited by the Hotri, or one of the Hotrakas; it being followed, on its part, by the recitation of an analogous triplet (anurûpa, 'similar or corresponding,' i.e. antistrophe) usually commencing with the very same word, or words, as the stotriya.

[4] As in the case of the first (south-west) set of bricks, VIII, 1, 1, 4–6, he puts down the first four with 'This one, in front, the existent,' 'His, the existent's son, the breath,' 'Spring, the son of the breath,' and 'The Gâyatrî, the daughter of spring,'—implying three generations from father to son (or daughter). In the formulas of the remaining bricks of each set referring to the metres (or verses, rik) and hymn-tunes (sâman) the statement of descent is expressed more vaguely by, 'From the Gâyatrî (is derived) the Gâyatra,' &c.

Rik; and hence were he also in their case to speak as of a father's son, it would be as if he spoke of him who is the husband, as of the son: therefore it corresponds as regards the rik and sâman. 'And why does he thrice carry on (the generation from father to son)?'—father, son, and grandson: it is these he thereby carries on; and therefore one and the same (man) offers (food) to them [1].

6. Those (bricks) which he lays down in front are the holders of the upward air (the breath, prâna); those behind are the eye-holders, the holders of the downward air (apâna) [2]; those on the right side are the mind-holders, the holders of the circulating air (vyâna); those on the left side are the ear-holders, the holders of the outward air (udâna); and those in the middle are the speech-holders, the holders of the pervading air (samâna).

7. Now the Karakâdhvaryus, indeed, lay down different (bricks) as holders of the downward air, of the circulating air, of the outward air, of the pervading air, as eye-holders, mind-holders, ear-holders, and speech-holders; but let him not do this, for they do what is excessive, and in this (our) way, indeed, all those forms are laid (into Agni).

8. Now, when he has laid down (the bricks) in

---

[1] At the offerings to the Fathers, or deceased ancestors, oblations are made to the father, grandfather, and great-grandfather; see II, 4. 2. 2, 3.

[2] Sâyana, on Taitt. S. IV, 3. 3, explains 'prâna' by 'bahihsamkârarûpa,' and 'apâna' by 'punarantahsamkârarûpa;' see also part i, p. 120. note 2; but cp. Maitry-up. II, 6; H. Walter, Hathayoga-pradîpikâ, p. xviii. Beside the fifty bricks called 'Prânabhritah,' the Taittirîyas also place fifty Apânabhritah in the first layer of the altar.

front, he lays down those at the back (of the altar) ; for the upward air, becoming the downward air, passes along thus from the tips of the fingers ; and the downward air, becoming the upward air, passes along thus from the tips of the toes : hence when, after laying down (the bricks) in front, he lays down those at the back, he thereby makes these two breathings continuous and connects them ; whence these two breathings are continuous and connected.

9. And when he has laid down those on the right side, he lays down those on the left side ; for the outward air, becoming the circulating air, passes along thus from the tips of the fingers[1] ; and the circulating air, becoming the outward air, passes along thus from the tips of the fingers[1] : hence when, after laying down (the bricks) on the right side, he lays down those on the left side, he thereby makes these two breathings continuous and connects them; whence these two breathings are continuous and connected.

10. And those (bricks) which he lays down in the centre are the vital air ; he lays them down on the range of the two Reta*h*si*k* (bricks), for the reta*h*si*k* are the ribs, and the ribs are the middle : he thus lays the vital air into him (Agni and the Sacrificer) in the very middle (of the body). On every side he lays down (the central bricks)[2] : in every part he thus

---

[1] ? Or, perhaps, the fingers and toes. The same word (aṅguli), having both meanings, makes it difficult exactly to understand these processes. The available MSS. of Harisvâmin's commentary unfortunately afford no help.

[2] That is to say, he lays down the fifth set round the (central) Svayamâtri*nn*â, on the range of the two Reta*h*si*k* bricks. It is,

lays vital air into him; and in the same way indeed
that intestinal breath (channel) is turned all round

however, not quite clear in what particular manner this fifth set of
ten bricks is to be arranged round the centre so as to touch one
another. The two Reta*h*sik bricks, occupying each a space of
a square foot north and south of the spine, are separated from the
central (Svayamâtr*inn*â) brick by the Dviyagus brick a foot square.
The inner side of the reta*h*sik-space would thus be a foot and
a half, and their outer side two feet and a half, distant from the
central point of the altar. The reta*h*sik range, properly speaking,
would thus consist of a circular rim, obtained by drawing two

THE CENTRAL PART OF THE FIRST LAYER.

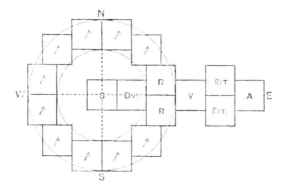

concentric circles round the centre, with diameters of one and a half
and two and a half feet respectively. On this rim (allowing for the
corners of the bricks jutting out) room would have to be found for
twelve bricks of a foot square, viz. the two reta*h*sik, already lying
on the eastern side, south and north of the spine, and ten prâna-
bh*r*is. The way in which these latter were arranged would
probably be this: on each of the three other sides two bricks were
laid down so as to join each other in a line with the respective
'spine,' similarly to the two reta*h*sik bricks on the east side; and
the four remaining bricks would then be placed in the four
corners—the twelve bricks thus forming, as nearly as could be,
a circular rim. In the construction of the altar, this reta*h*sik range
is determined by a cord being stretched from the centre to the
east end of the altar, after the special bricks of the first layer have

the navel. He lays them down both lengthwise
and crosswise [1], whence there are here in the body
(channels of) the vital airs both lengthwise and crosswise. He lays them down touching each other: he
thereby makes these vital airs continuous and connects them; whence these (channels of the) vital
airs are continuous and connected.

FOURTH BRÂHMANA.

1. Now some lay down (these bricks) so as to be
in contact with the (gold) man, for he is the vital
air, and him these (bricks) sustain; and because
they sustain (bh*ri*) the vital air (prâ*na*), therefore
they are called 'Prâ*na*bh*rita*h.' Let him not do so:
the vital air is indeed the same as that gold man,
but this body of his extends to as far here as this
fire (altar) has been marked out. Hence to what-

---

been laid down, knots being then made in the cord over the middle
of each of the special bricks. The reta*h*si*k* range is consequently
ascertained, in subsequent layers, by a circle drawn round the
centre, with that part of the cord marked by the central and the
reta*h*si*k* knot for the diameter. The foregoing diagram shows that
portion of the first layer which contains the continuous row of
special bricks laid down first, viz. Svayamâtr*rinn*â, Dviyagus, two
Reta*h*si*k*, Vi*s*vag*y*otis, two *R*itavyâ, and Ashâ*dh*â; and further the
central (or fifth) set of ten prâ*na*bh*rita*h, placed round the central
brick on the range of the reta*h*si*k*.

[1] Each special brick is marked on its upper surface with (usually
three) parallel lines. Now the bricks are always laid down in such
a way that their lines run parallel to the adjoining spine, whence
those on the east and west sides have their lines running lengthwise
(west to east), and those on the north and south sides crosswise
(north to south). As to the four corner bricks there is some
uncertainty on this point, but if we may judge from the analogy
of the second layer in this respect, the bricks of the south-east and
north-west corners would be eastward-lined, and those of the north-
east and south-west corners northward-lined.

ever limb of his these (breath-holders) were not to reach, that limb of his the vital air would not reach; and, to be sure, to whatever limb the vital air does not reach, that either dries up or withers away: let him therefore lay down these (bricks) so as to be in contact with the enclosing stones; and by those which he lays down in the middle this body of his is filled up, and they at least are not separated from him.

2. Here now they say, 'Whereas in (the formulas) "This one, in front, the existent—this one, on the right, the all-worker—this one, behind, the all-embracer—this, on the left, heaven—this one, above, the mind"—they (these bricks) are defined as exactly opposite the quarters, why, then, does he lay down these (bricks) in sidelong places¹?' Well, the Prânabhritah are the vital airs; and if he were to place them exactly opposite the quarters, then this breath would only pass forward and backward; but inasmuch as he now lays down these (bricks) thus defined in sidelong places, therefore this breath, whilst being a backward and forward one, passes sideways along all the limbs and the whole body.

3. Now that Agni (the altar) is an animal, and (as such) he is even now made up whole and entire,—those (bricks) which he lays down in front are his fore-feet, and those behind are his thighs; and those

---

¹ That is to say, why does he not place them at the ends of the spines, but at the corners of the (square) body, i.e. in places intermediate between the lines running in the direction of the points of the compass? When speaking of the regions, or quarters, it should be borne in mind that they also include a fifth direction, viz. the perpendicular or vertical line (both upward and downward) at any given point of the plane.

which he places in the middle are that body of his.
He places these in the region of the two reta*h*si*k*
(bricks), for the reta*h*si*k* are the ribs, and the ribs
are the middle, and that body is in the middle (of
the limbs). He places them all round, for that
body extends all round.

4. Here now they say, 'Whereas in the first (four)
sets he lays down a single stoma and a single
p*r*ish*th*a each time, why, then, does he lay down
here (in the centre) two stomas and two p*r*ish*th*as?'
Well, this (central set) is his (Agni's) body: he thus
makes the body (trunk) the best, the largest, the
most vigorous of limbs[1]; whence that body is the
best, the largest, and most vigorous of limbs.

5. Here now they say, 'How does that Agni of
his become made up whole and entire in brick after
brick?'—Well, the formula is the marrow, the brick
the bone, the settling the flesh, the sûdadohas the
skins, the formula of the purisha (fillings of earth)
the hair, and the purisha the food: and thus indeed
that Agni of his becomes made up whole and entire
in brick after brick.

6. That Agni is possessed of all vital power:
verily, whosoever knows that Agni to be possessed
of all vital power (âyus), attains his full measure of
life (âyus).

7. Now, then, as to the contraction and expansion
(of the body). Now some cause the built (altar) in
this way[2] to be possessed of (the power of) contraction and expansion: that Agni indeed is an animal;

---

[1] Or,—better, larger, and more vigorous than the limbs.
[2] Viz. by touching, or stroking along, the layer of the altar, and
muttering the subsequent formulas.

and when an animal contracts and expands its limbs, it develops strength by them.

8. [Vâg. S. XXVII, 45] 'Thou art Samvatsara,—thou art Parivatsara,—thou art Idâvatsara,—thou art Idvatsara,—thou art Vatsara. —May thy dawns prosper[1]!—may thy days and nights prosper!—may thy half-months prosper!—may thy months prosper!—may thy seasons prosper!—may thy year prosper!— For going and coming contract and expand thyself!—Of Eagle-build thou art: by that deity, Angiras-like, lie thou steady[2]!'

9. Sâ*ya*yani also once said, 'Some one heard (the sound)[3] of the cracking wings of the (altar) when touched with this (formula): let him therefore by all means touch it therewith!'

10. And Svargit Nâgnagita or Nagnagit, the Gândhâra, once said, 'Contraction and expansion surely are the breath, for in whatever part of the body there is breath that it both contracts and expands: let him breathe upon it from outside when completely built: he thereby lays breath, the (power of) contraction and expansion, into it, and so it contracts and expands.' But indeed what he there said as to that contraction and expansion, it was only one of the princely order who said it; and assuredly were they to breathe upon it from outside a hundred

---

[1] Or, perhaps, 'may the dawns chime in (fit in) with thee!'

[2] For this last part of the formula ('by that deity,' &c.), the so-called settling-formula, see part iii, p. 307, note 1.

[3] Harisvâmin (Ind. Off. MS. 657) seems to supply 'sabdam:' the sound of the cracking being taken as a sign of the powerful effect of the formula. Unfortunately, however, the MS. of the commentary is hopelessly incorrect.

times, or a thousand times, they could not lay breath
into it. Whatever breath there is in the (main) body
that alone is the breath : hence when he lays down
the Prâ*na*bh*ri*ta*h* (breath-holders), he thereby lays
breath, the (power of) contraction and expansion,
into it ; and so it contracts and expands. He then
lays down two Lokam*pri*nâ (bricks) in that corner[1]:
the meaning of them (will be explained) further on[2].
He throws loose earth (on the layer) : the meaning
of this (will be explained) further on[3].

THE SECOND LAYER.

SECOND ADHYÂYA.   FIRST BRÂHMANA.

1. He lays down the second layer. For now the
gods, having laid down the first layer, mounted it.

---

[1] Viz. in the south-east corner, or on the right shoulder, of the
altar. From these two lokam*pri*nâs (or space-fillers) he starts
filling up, in two turns, the still available spaces of the 'body' of
the altar, as also the whole of the two wings and the tail. For
other particulars as to the way in which these are laid down, see
VIII, 7, 2, 1 seqq. The 'body' of an ordinary altar requires in this
layer 1028 lokam*pri*nâs of three different kinds, viz. a foot (Ind.), half
a foot, and a quarter of a foot square, occupying together a space
of 321 square feet, whilst the 98 special (yagushmati) bricks fill up
a space of 79 square feet. Each wing requires 309 lokam*pri*nâs
of together 120 square feet ; whilst the tail takes 283 such bricks,
of together 110 square feet. The total number of lokam*pri*nâs in
the layer thus amounts to 1929 of all sizes, equal to 671 square
feet. If (as is done in Kâty. Srautas. XVII, 7, 21) the 21 bricks
of the Gârhapatya (part iii, p. 304) are added to this number, the
total number of lokam*pri*nâs is 1,950. Similarly, in the second,
third, and fourth layers ; whilst the last layer requires about a
thousand lokam*pri*nâs more than any of the others, viz. 2,922, or,
including the special hearths, 3,000. The total number of such
bricks required—including the 21 of the Gârhapatya—amounts to
10,800. Cp. Weber, Ind. Stud. XIII, p. 255.

[2] See VIII, 7, 2, 1 seq.   [3] See VIII, 7, 3, 1 seq.

But, indeed, the first layer is this (terrestrial) world : it is this same world which, when completed, they mounted.

2. They spake, 'Meditate ye!'—whereby, doubtless, they meant to say, 'Seek ye a layer! Seek ye (to build) from hence upwards!' Whilst meditating, they saw this second layer : what there is above the earth, and on this side of the atmosphere, that world was to their mind, as it were, unfirm and unsettled.

3. They said to the Asvins, 'Ye two are Brahmans and physicians : lay ye down for us this second layer!'—'What will therefrom accrue unto us?'—'Ye two shall be the Adhvaryus at this our Agni-kityâ.'—'So be it!'—The Asvins laid down for them that second layer : whence they say, 'The Asvins are the Adhvaryus of the gods.'

4. He lays down (the first Âsvinî[1] brick, with

---

[1] The main portion of the special bricks of the second layer consists of five, or (if, for the nonce, we take the two southern sets of half-bricks as one) of four sets of four bricks each, or of together sixteen bricks, each measuring a foot square, placed on the range of the reta/sik bricks so as to form the outer rim of a square measuring five feet on each side, and having in the middle a blank square of nine square feet. Each of the four sides of the reta/sik rim contains a complete set of four bricks ; but as there are five bricks on each side, the one in the left-hand corner (looking at them from the centre of the square) is counted along with the adjoining set. Each set, proceeding from left to right (that is, in sunwise fashion), consists of the following bricks,—âsvinî, vaisvadevi, prâna/bhrit, and apasyâ, the last of these occupying the corner spaces. The southern bricks consist, however, of two sets of half-bricks (running with their long sides from west to east), counted as the second and fifth set respectively. The eastern and western bricks are laid down so that their line-marks (which, in the case of the bricks of the second and fourth layers, are of an indefinite number) run from west to east ; whilst those of the southern

Vâg. S. XIV, 1), 'Thou art firmly-founded,
firmly-seated, firm!' for what is steady and settled, that is firm. Now that world was to their
minds, as it were, unfirm and unsettled: having
thereby made it firm, steady, they (the Asvins) went
on laying down (bricks).—'Seat thee fitly in thy
firm seat!'—that is, 'Seat thee fitly in thy steady
seat;'—'enjoying the first appearance of the
Ukhya,'—the Ukhya, doubtless, is this Agni; and
that first layer is indeed his first appearance: thus,
'enjoying that.'—'May the Asvins, the Adhvaryus, settle you here!' for the Asvins, as
Adhvaryus, did lay down (this brick).

and northern ones run from south to north. All the five bricks of
each class, beginning with the âsvinîs, are laid down at the same
time, proceeding again in sunwise fashion (east, south, &c.); the

THE CENTRAL PART OF THE SECOND LAYER.

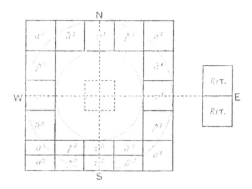

order of the procedure being only interrupted by the two *Rîtavyâ*
bricks being laid down, immediately after the placing of the five
âsvinî, exactly over the two *rîtavyâs* of the first layer, that is to say
in the fifth (easterly) space from the centre, north and south of the
spine. The only other special bricks of the second layer are
nineteen vayasyâs placed at the four ends of the two spines, viz.
four in the east, and five in each of the other quarters.

5. [The second Asvini he lays down, with Vâg. S. XIV, 2], 'Nest-like, fat, wise,'—a nest, as it were, is indeed the second layer[1];—'seat thee in the soft seat of the earth!'—the second layer, no doubt, is the earth: thus, 'Sit on her pleasant seat!'—'May the Rudras, the Vasus sing thy praises!'—that is, 'May those deities sing thy praises!'—'Replenish them, O Brahman, for happiness!'—that is, 'Favour them, O Brahman, with a view to happiness.'—'May the Asvins, the Adhvaryus, settle thee here!' for the Asvins, as Adhvaryus, did lay down (this brick).

6. [The third Asvini brick he lays down, with Vâg. S. XIV, 3], 'By thine own powers seat thee here, a holder of powers,'—that is, 'By thy own energy seat thee here;'—'in the gods' favour for high joy!' that is, 'for the favour of the gods, for great joy[2];'—'be thou kind, as a father to his son!'—that is, 'As a father is gentle, kind, to his son, so be thou kind!'—'rest thou readily accessible with thy form!'—the form, doubtless, is the body: thus, 'rest thou with readily accessible body!' —'May the Asvins, the Adhvaryus, settle thee here!' for the Asvins, as Adhvaryus, did lay down (this brick).

---

[1] This comparison doubtless refers to the way in which the central portion of the special bricks of this layer are arranged so as completely to enclose an empty space in the middle. In the first layer there was, no doubt, a similar enclosure of bricks as the retahsik range, but the central space was not left quite empty. In the end, however, the empty spaces are in both cases filled up by 'space-fillers.'

[2] The author seems to take 'rama' as an adjective (= ramaniya), as does Mahîdhara, who interprets the formula as meaning 'for the gods' great, cheerful happiness.'

7. [The fourth Âsvinî he lays down, with Vâg. S. XIV, 4], 'Thou art the earth's soil-cover,'—the first layer, doubtless, is the earth, and this, the second (layer) is, as it were, its soil-cover (purîsha)—'her sap[1], in truth,'—that is, 'her essence, in truth,'—'May the All-gods sing thy praises!'—that is, 'May all the gods sing thy praises!'—'Seat thee here, laden with stomas, and rich in fat!'—whatever hymn-forms he will be spreading (constructing) thereon by them this (brick) is laden with stomas[2]; —'Gain for us by sacrifice wealth (dravinâ, pl.) with offspring (adj. sing.)!'—that is, 'Gain for us, by sacrifice, wealth (dravinam, sing.) with offspring!' —'May the Asvins, the Adhvaryus, settle thee here!' for the Asvins, as Adhvaryus, did lay down (this brick).

8. These (bricks) are those regions (quarters); he places them on the range of the two retahsik (bricks), for the retahsik are these two (worlds): he thereby places the regions within these two (worlds), whence there are regions within these two (worlds). He lays down (these bricks) in every direction: he thus places the regions in all (the four) directions, whence the regions are in all directions. [He places them] on all sides so as to face each other[3]: he thereby

---

[1] The word 'apsas,' which western philologists usually take to mean 'cheek,' is here apparently connected with 'ap,' water.

[2] Literally, 'having stomas on her back.' Mahîdhara interprets 'stoma-prishthâ' by 'possessed of stomas and Prishthâs.' Sâyana, on Taitt. S. III, 7, 2, 7, by '(Prishtha-)stotras performed with stomas.'

[3] 'Samyañk' may either mean 'tending to one and the same point,' or 'running in the same direction, parallel to each other.' It is probably in the former sense that we have to take it here, though not quite literally, but in so far as the line-marks of these

makes the regions on all sides face each other, and
hence the regions on all sides face each other.   He
lays (the bricks) down separately, settles them
separately, and pronounces the sûdadohas over them
separately, for separate are the regions.

9. He then lays down the fifth regional (or Âsvinî
brick).   Now that region is the one above [1]; and
that same region above, doubtless, is yonder sun : it
is yonder sun he thus places thereon.   He places
this (brick) within the southern regional one [2] : he
thus places yonder sun within the southern region,
and therefore he moves within the southern region.

10. [He lays it down, with Vâg. S. XIV, 5]. 'I
settle thee upon the back of Aditi,'—Aditi
doubtless is this (earth) : it is upon her, as a foundation, that he thus founds him (Agni) ;—' the holder

---

bricks, if continued towards the centre of the altar, intersect one
another.   As applied to the quarters this meaning would then
modify itself to that of 'facing each other.'   On the other hand, it
is quite possible that the meaning of 'tending in the same direction'
is the one intended; and it would in that case probably apply to
the fact that the sets opposite to each other have their line-marks
running in the same direction, or are parallel to each other; and
this meaning would seem to be implied to the quarters where the
author supports his argument by the fact that the wind blows, and
the rain falls, in the same direction in all the four quarters (VIII,
2, 3, 2 ; 5).   It is curious that the expression is used by the author
in connection with the âsvinî, prânabhrit, and apasyâ, but not
with the vaisvadevî, the line-marks of which all meet in one central
point, which is not the case with the others.   At VIII, 3, 1, 11, on
the other hand, it is used again in connection with the Dîsyâ bricks,
which, in the third layer, occupy exactly the same spaces as the
Vaisvadevîs do here.

[1] Or, that direction is the one upward (from here).

[2] That is to say, he places it immediately north of the southern
âsvinî, so as to fill up the unoccupied, inner half of the space (of
a foot square).

of the air, the supporter of the regions, the ruler of beings,'—for he (the sun) is indeed the holder of the air, the supporter of the regions, and the ruler of beings;—'thou art the wave, the drop, of water,'—the wave, doubtless, means the essence;—'Viśvakarman is thy *Ri*shi!'—Viśvakarman (the all-shaper), doubtless, is Pra*g*âpati: thus, 'Thou art fashioned by Pra*g*âpati.'—'May the Aśvins, the Adhvaryus, settle thee here!' for the Aśvins, as Adhvaryus, did lay down (this brick).

11. Now as to why he lays down these Âśvini (bricks). When Pra*g*âpati had become relaxed (disjointed), the deities took him and went away in different directions. Now what part of him there was above the feet and below the waist, that part of him the two Aśvins took and kept going away from him.

12. He said to them, 'Come to me and restore unto me that wherewith ye have gone away from me!'—'What will accrue to us therefrom?'—'That part of my body shall be sacred unto you!'—'So be it!' so the Aśvins restored that (part) unto him.

13. Now these five Âśvini (bricks) are that same (part) of his (Agni's) body; and when he now puts them into this (layer of the altar), he thereby restores to him what (part) of his body these (bricks) are: that is why he puts them into this (layer).

14. 'Thou art firmly founded, firmly seated, firm,' he says, for whatsoever is steady and established that is firm. Now that part of his (Pra*g*âpati-Agni's) body was, as it were, unsteady, unfirm; and having made it steady and firm they (the Aśvins) restored it to him.

15. 'Nestlike, fat, wise,' he says, for this indeed

is as a nest for his body.—'By thine own powers
seat thee here, a holder of powers,' he says, for they
did make that (part) of him powerful.—'Thou art
the Earth's soil-cover,' he says, for that (lower part)
of his body is, as it were, in connection with the
soil-cover. At the range of the Reta*h*si*k* (he places
the bricks),—the Reta*h*si*k* are the ribs, for level
with the ribs, as it were, is that (part) of his body.
He places them on every side, for on every side the
Asvins restored that (part) of his (Pragâpati's) body.

16. He then lays down two *R*îtavyâ[1] (seasonal
bricks) ;—these two, the *R*îtavyâ, are the seasons
(*r*îtu) : it is the seasons he thus bestows thereon.
[He lays them down, with Vâg. S. XIV, 6], 'Sukra
and *Su*/*i*, the two summer-seasons ;'—these are
the names of these two : it is with their names that
he thus lays them down. There are two bricks, for
a season consists of two months. He settles them
once only : he thereby makes (the two months) one
season.

17. And as to why he lays down these two in this
(layer) :—this Agni (fire-altar) is the year, and the
year is these worlds. Now that part of him which
is above the earth and below the atmosphere, is this
second layer : and that same part of him (Agni, the
year,) is the summer season. And when he lays
down those two in this (layer), he thereby restores
to him (Agni) that part of his body which these two
are : this is why he lays down these two (bricks) in
this (layer).

---

[1] These two bricks are placed exactly upon the two *R*îtavyâs of
the first layer, that is, in the fifth space from the centre ; see p. 1,
note 1.

18. And, again, as to why he lays down these two in this (layer). This fire-altar is Pragâpati, and Pragâpati is the year. Now that (part) of him which is above the feet and below the waist is this second layer; and that same part of him is the summer season. Thus when he lays down those two in this (layer), he thereby restores to him that (part) of his body which these two are: this is why he lays down these two (bricks) in this (layer).

SECOND BRÂHMANA.

1. He then lays down the Vaisvadevi (All-gods' bricks). For this second layer is that one which the Asvins at that time laid down for them (the gods); and by laying it down they became everything here whatsoever there is here.

2. The gods spake, 'The Asvins have become everything here: think ye upon this as to how we also may share in it!' They said, 'Meditate ye (kit)!' whereby, no doubt, they meant to say, 'Seek ye a layer (kiti)! seek ye in what way we also may share in it!' whilst meditating, they saw these Vaisvadevi (All-gods') bricks.

3. They said, 'The Asvins have become everything here: with the help of the Asvins let us lay down (bricks) along with the Asvins' layer!' With the help of the Asvins they accordingly laid down (bricks) along with the Asvins' layer, whence they call this the Asvins' layer. Hence the end of these (bricks) is the same as that of the former ones; for they laid them down with the help of the Asvins along with the Asvins' layer.

4. And, again, as to why he lays down the All-

gods' (bricks). These indeed are those same All-gods
who saw this second layer, and who came nigh with
that life-sap: it is them he thereby bestows, that is,
all these creatures. He lays them down in the range of
the Retahsik; for the Retahsik are these two (heaven
and earth): within these two (worlds) he thus places
creatures; whence there are creatures within these
two (worlds). He places (bricks) on every side: he
thus places creatures everywhere, whence there are
creatures everywhere. He places them alongside of
the regional ones [1]: he thus places creatures in the
regions (quarters); whence there are creatures in all
the (four) quarters.

5. And, again, as to why he lays down the All-
gods' (bricks). When Pragâpati had become relaxed,
all creatures went forth from the midst of him, from
that birth-place of theirs. When that (central part)
of his body had been restored, they entered him.

6. Now the Pragâpati who become relaxed is this
very Agni (fire-altar) that is now being built up; and
the creatures who went forth from the midst of him
are these same All-gods' bricks; and when he lays
these down, he causes those creatures, which went
forth from the midst of him, to enter him. In the
range of the Retahsik (he places the Vaisvadevî
bricks), for the Retahsik are the ribs, and the ribs

[1] The Asvinî (or Divyâ) bricks were placed in a circle round
the centre, at the distance of a foot from where the central brick
(Svayamâtrinnâ) was placed in the first layer,—that is to say, in the
third place from the centre. They were, moreover, placed in the
second space (or at the distance of half a foot) from the two spines,
see p. 23, note 1. The five Vaisvadevîs are then placed alongside of the Asvinîs, so as to fill up the 'first spaces,' that is to say,
to lie on the spines themselves; each of the two half-foot bricks
laid down in the south being, as it were, halved by the spine.

are the middle: he thus causes the creatures to enter him in the very middle. He places them on all sides: on all sides he thus causes the creatures to enter him.

7. And, again, as to why he lays down the Vaisvadevi (bricks). At that time, when that (part) of his body had been restored, Pragâpati desired, 'May I create creatures, may I be reproduced!' Having entered into union with the seasons, the waters, the vital airs, the year, and the Asvins, he produced these creatures; and in like manner does this Sacrificer, by entering into union with those deities, now produce these creatures. Hence with all (of these bricks, the word) sagush ('in union with') recurs.

8. [He lays down the Vaisvadevi bricks, with Vâg. S. XIV, 7], 'In union with the seasons,'—he thereby produced the seasons, and having entered into union with the seasons he produced (creatures);—'in union with the ranges,'—the ranges, doubtless, are the waters, for by water everything is ranged (distributed or produced) here: having entered into union with the waters he produced (creatures);—'in union with the gods,'— he thereby produced the gods,—those who are called 'gods[1];'—'in union with the life-sustaining gods,'—the life-sustaining gods, doubtless, are the vital airs, for by the vital airs everything living here is sustained: or, the life-sustaining gods are the metres, for by the metres (sacred writ) everything living is sustained here; having entered into union with the vital airs he produced creatures;—

---

[1] Lit. what they (viz. the Vedic hymns, according to the commentator) call gods:—Yat kimkid ity eva vedavâdâ âkakshate.

'for Agni Vaisvânara,'—Agni Vaisvânara ('belonging to all men '), doubtless, is the year: having entered into union with the year he produced creatures;—'May the Asvins, the Adhvaryus, settle thee here!'—having entered into union with the Asvins he produced creatures.

9. 'In union with the Vasus,' he says on the right side: he thereby produced the Vasus;—'in union with the Rudras,' he says at the back: he thereby produced the Rudras;—'in union with the Âdityas,' he says on the left side: he thereby produced the Âdityas;—'in union with the All-gods,' he says upwards: he thereby produced the All-gods. These (bricks) have the same beginning and end, but are different in the middle: as to their having the same beginning and end, it is because having become united with the deities in front and behind, he produced creatures: and as to their being different in the middle, it is that each time he produced different creatures from within him.

THIRD BRÂHMANA.

1. He then lays down the Prânabhrit (bricks). For at that time the gods said, 'Meditate ye!' whereby, doubtless, they meant to say, 'Seek ye a layer!' Whilst meditating, they saw even that layer, the wind: they put it into that (fire-altar), and in like manner does he (the priest) now put it therein.

2. He lays down the Prânabhrits,—wind, doubtless, is breath: it is wind (air) he thus bestows upon him (Agni). On the range of the Retahsik (they are placed); for the Retahsik are these two (worlds): it is within these two (worlds) that he thus places the wind; whence there is wind within these two (worlds).

He places them on every side : he thus places wind
on all sides, whence the wind is everywhere. [He
places them so as] on every side to run in the same
direction¹: he thus makes the wind everywhere (to
blow) in the same direction, whence, having become
united, it blows from all quarters in the same direction. He lays them down alongside of the regional
(bricks)²: he thereby places the wind in the regions,
whence there is wind in all the regions.

3. And, again, as to why he lays down the Prâṇabhṛïts;—it is that he thereby bestows vital airs
on these creatures. He places them so as not to
be separated from the Vaiśvadevis : he thereby
bestows vital airs not separated from the creatures.
[He lays them down with, Vâg̠. S. XIV, 8], 'Preserve   mine   up-breathing!   Preserve   my
down - breathing!   Preserve   my   through-
breathing! Make mine eye shine far and wide!
Make mine ear resound!' He thereby bestows
on them properly constituted vital airs.

4. He then lays down the Apasyâ (bricks). For
the gods, at that time, spake, 'Meditate ye!' whereby,
doubtless, they meant to say, 'Seek ye a layer!'
Whilst meditating, they saw even that layer, rain :

¹ That is, the bricks placed in opposite quarters, run in the same
direction : see p. 26, note 3.

² The Prâṇabhṛïts are placed beside the Vaiśvadevis so as to
be separated from them by the respective section of the anûkas or
'spines' (dividing the square 'body' of the altar into four quarters).
Each Vaiśvadevî would thus be enclosed between an Âśvinî and
a Prâṇabhṛït; but whilst the Âśvinî and Vaiśvadevî are placed in the
same section (or quarter) of the altar, the Prâṇabhṛït comes to lie
in the adjoining section, moving in the sunwise direction from left
to right.

they put it into that (fire-altar) and in like manner does he now put it therein.

5. He put on the Apasyâs; for rain is water (ap); it is rain he thereby puts into it (the altar; or into him, Agni). On the range of the Retahsik (he places them), for, the Retahsik being these two (worlds), it is on these two (worlds) that he thereby bestows rain, whence it rains therein. He places them on every side: he thus puts rain everywhere, whence it rains everywhere. [He places them] so as everywhere to run in the same direction[1]: he thereby bestows rain (falling) everywhere in the same direction, whence the rain falls everywhere, and from all quarters, in the same direction. He places them alongside of those referring to the wind[2]: he thereby puts rain into the wind, whence rain follows to whatever quarter the wind goes.

6. And, again, as to why he lays down Apasyâs,—he thereby puts water into the vital airs. He places them so as not to be separated from the Prânabhrits: he thus places the water so as not to be separate from the vital airs. Moreover, water is food: he thus introduces food not separated from (the channels of) the vital airs. [He lays them down with, Vâg. S. XIV, 8], 'Make the waters swell! Quicken the plants! Bless thou the two-footed! Protect the four-footed! Draw thou rain from the sky!' He thereby puts water that is made fit, into those (vital airs).

---

[1] See p. 26, note 3.

[2] The five Apasyâ bricks are placed immediately to the right of the Prânabhrits (looking towards the latter from the centre of the altar), so as to fill up the four remaining spaces between the four sets of bricks on the range of the Retahsik.

7. He then lays down the *Khandasyâ*[1] (bricks);—for the gods, at that time, spake, 'Meditate ye!' whereby, doubtless, they meant to say, 'Seek ye a layer!' Whilst meditating, they saw even that layer, cattle (or beasts): they put it therein, and, in like manner, does he now put it therein.

8. He lays down the *Khandasyâs*; for the metres (*khandas*) are cattle: it is cattle he thus puts into it (or, bestows on him, Agni). On every side (he places them): he thereby places cattle (or beasts) everywhere, whence there are cattle everywhere. He places them alongside of the Apasyâs: he thus establishes the cattle on (or, near) water, whence cattle thrive when it rains.

9. And, again, as to why he lays down *Khandasyâs*. When Pragâpati was relaxed, the cattle, having become metres, went from him. Gâyatrî, having become a metre, overtook them by dint of her vigour; and as to how Gâyatri overtook them, it is that this is the quickest (shortest) metre. And so Pragâpati, in the form of that (Gâyatri), by dint of his vigour, overtook those cattle.

10. [He lays down four in front, with, Vâg. S. XIV, 9], 'The head is vigour,'— Pragâpati, doubtless, is the head: it is he that became vigour;—'Pragâpati the metre,'— Pragâpati indeed became a metre.

11. 'The Kshatra is vigour,'—the Kshatra, doubtless, is Pragâpati, it is he that became vigour; —'the pleasure-giving metre,'—what is unde-

---

[1] These are otherwise called Vayasyâ (conferring vigour, or vitality), each formula containing the word vayas, 'vitality, force.' There are nineteen such bricks which are placed on the four ends of the two 'spines,' viz. four on the front, or east end of the spine proper, and five on the hind end of it as well as on each end of the 'cross-spine.'

fined that is pleasure-giving; and Pragâpati is undefined, and Pragâpati indeed became a metre.

12. 'Support is vigour,'—the support, doubtless, is Pragâpati : it is he that became vigour ;—'the over-lord the metre,'—the over-lord, doubtless, is Pragâpati, and Pragâpati indeed became a metre.

13. 'The All-worker is vigour,'—the All-worker, doubtless, is Pragâpati : it is he that became vigour ;—'the highest lord the metre,'—Pragâpati, the highest lord, doubtless, is the waters, for they (the waters of heaven) are in the highest place : Pragâpati, the highest lord, indeed became a metre.

14. These then are four kinds of vigour, and four metres ; this (makes) eight,—the Gâyatrî consists of eight syllables : this, assuredly, is that same Gâyatrî in the form of which Pragâpati then, by his vigour, overtook those cattle ; whence they say of worn-out cattle that they are overtaken by vigour (or, age), and hence (the word) 'vigour' recurs with all (these bricks). And those cattle which went away from him (Pragâpati) are these fifteen other (formulas) : the cattle are a thunderbolt, and the thunderbolt is fifteenfold : whence he who possesses cattle, drives off the evildoer, for the thunderbolt drives off the evildoer for him. And in whatever direction, therefore, the possessor of cattle goes, that he finds torn up by the thunderbolt.

FOURTH BRÂHMANA.

1. 'The he-goat is vigour[1],'—the he-goat he overtook by his vigour ;—'gapless the metre,'—

---

[1] Mahîdhara, in accordance with the explanation added by the Brâhmana to this and the corresponding formulas in the succeeding paragraphs. takes 'vayas' as a defective instrumental (vayasâ). It is, however, very doubtful whether such an interpretation of the formula was intended by the author of the Brâhmana.

the gapless metre, doubtless, is the Ekapadâ: in the form of Ekapadâ (metre) the goats indeed went forth (from Pragâpati).

2. 'The ram is vigour,'—the ram he overtook by his vigour;—'ample the metre,'—the ample metre, doubtless, is the Dvipadâ: in the form of the Dvipadâ the sheep indeed went forth.

3. 'Man is vigour,'—the man he overtook by his vigour;—'slow the metre,'—the slow metre, doubtless, is the Pankti: in the form of the Pankti the men indeed went forth.

4. 'The tiger is vigour,'—the tiger he overtook by his vigour;—'unassailable the metre,'—the unassailable metre, doubtless, is the Virâg, for the Virâg is food, and food is unassailable; in the form of the Virâg the tigers indeed went forth.

5. 'The lion is vigour,'—the lion he overtook by his vigour;—'the covering the metre,'—the covering metre, doubtless, is the Ati*kkh*andas, for that covers (includes) all metres: in the form of the Ati*kkh*andas the lions indeed went forth. And so he places undefined metres along with defined beasts.

6. 'The ox is vigour,'—the ox he overtook by his vigour;—'the Br*ih*atî the metre,'—in the form of the Br*ih*atî the oxen indeed went forth.

7. 'The bull is vigour,'—the bull he overtook by his vigour;—'the Kakubh the metre,'—in the form of the Kakubh the bulls indeed went forth.

8. 'The steer is vigour,'—the steer he overtook by his vigour;—'the Satobr*ih*atî the metre,'—in the form of the Satobr*ih*atî the steers indeed went forth.

9. 'The bullock is vigour,'—the bullock he overtook by his vigour;—'the Pankti the metre,' —in the form of the Pankti the bullocks indeed went forth.

10. 'The milch cow is vigour,'—the milch cow he overtook by his vigour;—'the Gagati the metre,'—in the form of the Gagati the milch cows indeed went forth.

11. 'The calf of eighteen months is vigour,' —the calf of eighteen months he overtook by his vigour;—'the Trish/ubh the metre,'—in the form of the Trish/ubh the calves of eighteen months indeed went forth.

12. 'The two-year-old bull is vigour,'—the two-year-old bull he overtook by his vigour;—'the Virâg the metre,'—in the form of the Virâg the two-year-old kine indeed went forth.

13. 'The bull of two years and a half is vigour,'—the bull of two years and a half he overtook by his vigour;—'the Gâyatrî the metre,'— in the form of the Gâyatrî the kine of two years and a half indeed went forth.

14. 'The three-year-old bull is vigour,'— the three-year-old bull he overtook by his vigour; —'the Ush/ih the metre,'—in the form of the Ush/ih the three-year-old kine indeed went forth.

15. 'The four-year-old bull is vigour,'—the four-year-old bull he overtook by his vigour;—'the Anush/ubh the metre,'—in the form of the Anush/ubh the four-year-old kine indeed went forth.

16. These then are those very beasts which Pragâpati overtook by his vigour. The animal he (the priest) mentions first, then vigour, then the

metre, for having hemmed them in with vigour and
the metre, he put them into himself, and made them
his own; and in like manner does he (the sacrificer)
now hem them in with vigour and the metre, and
put them into himself, and make them his own.

17. Now that animal is the same as Agni : (as
such) he is even now made up whole and entire.
Those (bricks) which he places in front are his head;
those on the right and left sides are his body, and
those behind his tail.

18. He first lays down those in front, for of an
animal that is born the head is born first.   Having
then laid down those on the right (south) side, he
lays down those on the left (north) side, thinking,
'Together with its sides this body shall be born.'
Then those behind, for of (the animal) that is born
the tail is born last.

19. The metres which are longest, and the animals
which are biggest, he puts in the middle : he thus
makes the animal biggest towards the middle;
whence the animal is biggest towards the middle.
And the animals which are the strongest he puts on
the right side : he thus makes the right side of an
animal the stronger ; whence the right side of an
animal is the stronger.

20. The fore and hind parts he makes smallest ;
for inasmuch as those (bricks in front) are only four
in number [1], thereby they are the smallest ; and
inasmuch as here (at the back) he puts the smallest
animals, thereby these are the smallest : he thus
makes the fore and hind parts of an animal the
smallest, whence the fore and hind parts of an animal

---

[1] See p. 35, note 3.

are the smallest; and hence the animal rises and
sits down by its fore and hind parts.   He then lays
down two Lokamprinâ (bricks) in that corner [1]:
the significance of them (will be explained) further
on [2].   He throws loose earth on the layer: the significance of this (will be explained) further on [3].

THE THIRD LAYER.

THIRD ADHYÂYA.   FIRST BRÂHMANA.

1. He lays down the third layer.   For the gods,
having laid down the second layer, now ascended it:
but, indeed, they thereby completed and ascended
to what is above the earth and below the atmosphere.

2. They spake, 'Meditate ye!' whereby, indeed,
they meant to say, 'Seek ye a layer! Seek ye (to
build) upwards from hence!'   Whilst meditating,
they saw the great third layer, even the air: that
world pleased them.

3. They said to Indra and Agni, 'Lay ye down
for us this third layer!'—'What will accrue unto
us therefrom?'—'Ye two shall be the best of us!'
—'So be it!'   Accordingly Indra and Agni laid
down for them that third layer; and hence people
say, 'Indra and Agni are the best of gods.'

4. He accordingly lays it down by means of Indra
and Agni, and settles it by means of Visvakarman [4],

---

[1] Whilst, in laying down the Lokamprinâs of the first layer, he
started from the right shoulder (or south-east corner) of the altar
(see p. 22, note 1), in this layer he begins from the right hip (or
south-west corner), filling up the available spaces, in two turns, in
sunwise fashion.

[2] See VII, 7, 2, 4 seq.   [3] See VIII, 7, 3, 1 seq.

[4] For the connection of these deities with the third layer, and the

for indeed Indra and Agni, as well as Visvakarman, saw this third layer: this is why he lays it down by means of Indra and Agni, and settles it by means of Visvakarman.

5. And, again, as to why he lays it down by means of Indra and Agni, and settles it by means of Visvakarman. When Pragâpati had become relaxed (disjointed), the deities took him and went off in different directions. Indra and Agni, and Visvakarman took his middle part, and kept going away from him.

6. He said to them, 'Come ye to me and restore ye to me wherewith ye are going from me!'—'What will accrue unto us therefrom?'—'That (part) of my body shall be sacred unto you!'—'So be it!' So Indra and Agni, and Visvakarman restored that (part) unto him.

7. Now that central Svayam-â*trinnâ* (naturally-perforated brick) [1] is that very (part) of his body ;—when he now lays down that (brick), he thereby restores to him that (part) of his (Pragâpati's) body which this (brick represents) : this is why he now lays down that (brick).

8. [Vâg. S. XIV, 11], 'O Indra and Agni, make ye fast the brick so as not to shake!' as the text so the sense ;—'with thy back thou forcest asunder the earth, and the sky, and the air;' for with its back this (brick) indeed forces asunder the earth, and the sky, and the air.

9. [Vâg. S. XIV, 12], 'May Visvakarman settle

---

air, see also VI, 2, 3, 3. Visvakarman is likewise the deity by which the Visvagyotis-brick, representing Vâyu (the wind), the regent of the air-world, is settled; see VIII, 3, 2, 3.

[1] See part iii, p. 155, note 8.

thee,' for Visvakarman saw this third layer:—'on
the back of the air, thee the wide, the broad
one!' for this (brick) indeed is the wide and broad
back of the air:—'support thou the air, make
fast the air, injure not the air!' that is, 'support
thou thine own self (body), make fast thine own self,
injure not thine own self!'

10. 'For all up-breathing, and down-breathing, and through-breathing, and out-breathing!'
for the naturally-perforated (brick) is the vital air, and
the vital air serves for everything here;—'for a
resting-place and moving-place!' for the naturally-perforated (brick) is these worlds, and these
worlds are indeed a resting-place and a moving-
place;—'May Vâyu shelter thee!' that is, 'May
Vâyu protect thee!'—'with grand prosperity!'
that is, 'with great prosperity;'—'with most
auspicious protection!'—that is, 'with what protection is most auspicious.' Having settled it[1], he
pronounces the Sûdadohas[2] over it; the meaning of
this has been explained. He then sings a sâman:
the meaning of this (will be explained) further on[3].

11. He then lays down (five) Disyâ (regional
bricks)[4]. Now the regional ones, doubtless, are

---

[1] Viz. by the concluding formula, 'With the help of that deity,
Angiras-like, lie thou steady!' see part iii. p. 301, note 3.

[2] Viz. Vâg. S. XII, 55 (Rig-veda S. VIII, 69, 3), 'At his birth
the well-like milking, speckled ones mix the Soma, the clans of
the gods in the three spheres of the heavens.' See part iii, p. 307,
note 2.

[3] VIII, 7, 4, 1 seq.

[4] The five Disyâs are placed on the spines in the four directions
at the retahsik range, just over where the five Vaisvadevî bricks
were placed in the second layer (see the sketch, p. 24). Between
them and the central (naturally-perforated) brick there is thus an

the regions: it is the regions he thus bestows (on the air-world). And these are those same regions not separated (from the air) wherewith Vâyu on that occasion[1] stepped nigh: it is them he thereby bestows. But prior to these same (bricks) he lays down[2] both the bunch of Darbha grass and the clod-bricks; and these (diśyâs) being yonder sun[3], he thus places yonder sun over the regions, and builds him up upon (or, in) the regions. But were these (laid down) at the same time (as the bunch of grass and the clod-bricks), they would be outside (of the altar); and outside of the womb (foundation), indeed, is that sacrificial work regarding the fire-altar which is done prior to the lotus-leaf[4]. When he

---

empty space a foot square, and the two southern Diśyâs are half-bricks lying north and south of each other.

[1] See VI, 2, 3, 4. The second naturally-perforated brick represents the air-world with which Vâyu, the wind, is most closely associated.

[2] That is to say, he laid them down on the site of the altar, before the first layer was commenced, viz. the darbha-bunch in the centre of the 'body' of the altar, where the two spines (anûka) intersect each other (VII, 2, 3, 1 seqq.); and the clod-bricks (logeshŧakâ) on the four ends of the two spines (VII, 3, 1, 13 seqq.), that is, in the middle of each of the four sides of the square of which the 'body' consists.

[3] The symbolic interpretation here seems somewhat confused, inasmuch as the Diśyâs, which are now apparently identified with the sun, have just been stated to represent the regions. At VI, 7, 1, 17 the sun was represented as the central point of the universe to which these three worlds are linked by means of the quarters (as by the strings of a scale). The clod-bricks, on the other hand, were indeed, in VII, 3, 1, 13, identified with the regions (quarters); and the bunch of grass, being laid down in the centre, might be regarded as marking the fifth region, that upwards from here. Cf. IX, 5, 1, 36.

[4] The lotus-leaf is placed in the centre of the altar when the first layer is about to be laid down. See VII, 4, 1, 7 seqq., where

now brings and lays down these (bricks), he thereby
establishes them in the womb, on the lotus-leaf, and
thus these (bricks) are not outside (the fire-altar).
He lays them down so as not to be separated [1] from
the naturally-perforated one; for the middle [2] naturally-perforated one is the air: he thus places the
regions so as not to be separate from the air.
Subsequently [3] (to the central brick he lays them
down): subsequently to the air he thus sets up the
regions. In all (four) directions he places them: he
thus places the regions (quarters) in all directions,
whence the regions are in all (four) directions. [He
places them] on all sides so as to face each other: he
thereby makes the regions on all sides face each other,
and hence the regions on all sides face each other [4].

12. And, again, as to why he lays down the re-
gionals. The regions, doubtless, are the metres—the
eastern region being the Gâyatri, the southern the
Trishtubh, the western the Gagati, the northern
the Anushtubh, and the upper region the Pankti;—
and the metres are animals [5], and the middlemost
layer is the air: he thus places animals in the air,

---

it is explained as representing the foundation of the fire-altar, or
rather, the womb whence Agni is born.

[1] That is, not separated therefrom by other special bricks;
though the full space of one brick is left between the Disyâs and
the central brick. Perhaps, however, 'anantarhita' here means
'immediately after.'

[2] That is, the second of the three svayam-âtrinnâs, the one in
the third layer.

[3] Uttara seems here and elsewhere to have a double meaning,
viz. that of subsequent, and upper, or left, inasmuch as looking
towards these bricks from the centre of the altar, they are placed
to the left of the particular section of the anûkas.

[4] See p. 26, note 3.

[5] The metres are commonly represented as cattle.

and hence there are animals that have their abode
in the air[1].

13. And, again, as to why he lays down the re-
gionals. The regions, doubtless, are the metres, and
the metres are animals, and animals are food, and
the middlemost layer is the middle: he thus puts
food in the middle (of the body). He places them
so as not to be separated (by special bricks) from
the naturally-perforated one; for the naturally-perforated one is the vital air: he thus places the food
so as not to be separated from the vital air. Subsequently (to the central brick he lays them down):
subsequently to (or upon) the vital air he thus places
food. On the range of the Reta*h*si*k* (he places them):
the Reta*h*si*k* being the ribs, and the ribs being the
middle (of the body), he thus places the food in the
middle of this (Agni's body). On every side he
places them: from everywhere he thus supplies him
with food.

14. [He lays them down, with. Vâg. S. XIV, 13],
'Thou art the queen, the Eastern region!
Thou art the far-ruler, the Southern region!
Thou art the all-ruler, the Western region!
Thou art the self-ruler, the Northern region!
Thou art the supreme ruler, the Great region!'
these are their names: he thus lays them down
whilst naming them. Separately he lays them down,
separately he settles them, and separately he pronounces the Sûdadohas over them, for separate are
the regions.

---

[1] That is all (four-footed) animals that dwell on, not in, the
earth. The Gâyatrî metre, at any rate, is also represented as a bird
which fetches the Soma from heaven, but it is not the air as such
that is intended here, but the face of the earth.

SECOND BRÂHMANA.

1. He then lays down a Visvagyotis (all-light brick). Now the middle Visvagyotis is Vâyu [1], for Vâyu (the wind) is all the light in the air-world: it is Vâyu he thus places therein. He places it so as not to be separated from the regional (bricks): he thus places Vâyu in the regions, and hence there is wind in all the regions.

2. And, again, as to why he lays down the Visvagyotis,—the Visvagyotis, doubtless, is offspring (or creatures), for offspring indeed is all the light: he thus lays generative power (into that world). He places it so as not to be separated from the regional ones [2]: he thus places creatures in the regions, and hence there are creatures in all the regions.

3. [He lays it down, with, Vâg. S. XIV, 14], 'May Visvakarman settle thee!' for Visvakarman saw this third layer [3];—'on the back of the air, thee the brilliant one!' for on the back of the air that brilliant Vâyu indeed is.

4. 'For all up-breathing, down-breathing, through-breathing,'—for the Visvagyotis is breath,

---

[1] The three Visvagyotis bricks, placed in (the fourth easterly place from the centre of) the first, third and fifth layer respectively, are supposed to represent the regents of the three worlds—earth, air and sky—which these three layers represent, viz. Agni, Vâyu and Âditya (Sûrya). See VI, 3, 3, 16.

[2] Though, properly speaking, the Visvagyotis lies close to only one of the Disyâs, viz. the eastern one, it may at any rate be said to lie close to the range of the Disyâs. Here, too, the sense 'immediately after, not separated from them in respect of time,' would suit even better.

[3] See VIII, 3, 1, 4 with note.

and breath indeed is (necessary) for this entire
universe;—'give all the light!'—that is, 'give the
whole light;'—'Vâyu is thine over-lord,'—it is
Vâyu he thus makes the over-lord of that (layer and
the air-world). Having settled it, he pronounces
the Sûdadohas over it : the significance of this has
been explained.

5. He then lays down two *Ri*tavyâ (seasonal [1]
bricks) ;—the two seasonal ones being the same as
the seasons, it is the seasons he thus places therein.—
[Vâg. S. XIV, 15], 'Nabha and Nabhasya, the
two rainy seasons,' these are the names of those
two (bricks) : it is by their names he thus lays them
down. There are two (such) bricks, for a season
consists of two months. He settles them once only :
he thereby makes (the two months) one season.
He places them on avakâ-plants and covers them

THE CENTRAL PART OF THE THIRD LAYER.

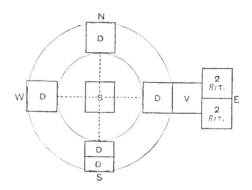

---

[1] These two *Ri*tavyâs are placed beside (east of) the Visvagyotis, one north of the other, just over those of the first and
second layers, that is to say, in the fifth space from the centre. In
the present case, however, these bricks are only of half the usual
thickness; two others, of similar size, being placed upon them.

with avakâ-plants [1]; for avakâ-plants mean water: he thus bestows water on that season, whence it rains most abundantly in that season.

6. Then the two upper ones, with (Vâg. S. XIV, 16), 'Isha and Ûrga, the two autumnal seasons,' —these are the names of those two (bricks): it is by their names he thus lays them down. There are two (such) bricks, for a season consists of two months. He settles them only once : he thereby makes (the two months) one season. He places them on avakâ-plants, for the avakâ-plants mean water : he thus bestows water before that season, whence it rains before that season. He does not cover them afterwards, whence it does not likewise rain after (that season).

7. And as to why he places these (four bricks) in this (layer),—this fire-altar is the year, and the year is the same as these worlds, and the middlemost layer is the air (-world) thereof; and the rainy season and autumn are the air (-world) thereof: hence when he places them in this (layer), he thereby restores to him (Agni) what (part) of his body these (formed),— this is why he places them in this (layer).

8. And, again, as to why he places them in this (layer),—this Agni (the fire-altar) is Pragâpati, and Pragâpati is the year. Now the middlemost layer is the middle of this (altar), and the rainy season and the autumn are the middle of that (year) : hence when he places them in this (layer), he thereby restores to him (Agni-Pragâpati) what part of his

---

[1] As in the case of the live tortoise, in the first layer ; see VII, 5, 1, 11 with note—' Blyxa octandra, a grassy plant growing in marshy land ("lotus-flower." Weber, Ind. Stud. XIII, p. 250).'

body these (formed),—this is why he places them in this (layer).

9. There are here four seasonal (bricks) he lays down in the middlemost layer; and two in each of the other layers,—animals (cattle) are four-footed, and the middlemost layer is the air: he thus places animals in the air, and hence there are animals that have their abode in the air.

10. And, again, why there are four,—animals are four-footed, and animals are food; and the middle-most layer is the middle (of Agni's body): he thus puts food in the middle.

11. And, again, why there are four,—'antariksha' (air) consists of four syllables, and the other layers (*k*iti) consist of two syllables; hence as much as the air consists of, so much he makes it in laying it down.

12. And, again, why there are four,—this Agni (altar), doubtless, is an animal: he thus makes the animal biggest towards the middle; whence an animal is biggest towards the middle.

13. There are here four *K*itavyâs, the Visva*g*yotis being the fifth, and five Di*s*yâs,—this makes ten: the Virâ*g* consists of ten syllables, and the Virâ*g* is food, and the middlemost layer is the middle;—he thus puts food in the middle (of the body). He lays them down so as not to be separated from the naturally-perforated one [1], for the naturally-perforated one is the vital air: he thus places the food so as not to be separated from the vital air. Subsequently (to the central brick) he lays them down: sub-

---

[1] That is to say, the three sets of bricks are not separated by any others from the Svayamâtr*inn*â.

sequently to (or upon) the vital air he thus places food.

14. He then lays down the Prâ*n*abh*ri*t[1] (bricks);—the Prâ*n*abh*ri*ts (breath-holders), doubtless, are the vital airs : it is the vital airs he thus lays into (Agni's body). There are ten of them, for there are ten vital airs. He places them in the forepart (of the altar),—for there are these vital airs in front,—with (Vâg. S. XIV, 17), ' Protect my vital strength! protect mine up-breathing! protect my down-breathing! protect my through-breathing! protect mine eye! protect mine ear! increase my speech! animate my mind! protect my soul (or body)! give me light!'—He lays them down so as not to be separated from the seasonal ones, for the vital air is wind: he thus establishes the wind in the seasons.

THIRD BRÂHMANA.

1. He then lays down the *Kh*andasyâ[2] (metres' bricks). Now the metres are cattle, and the middle-most layer is the air: he thus places cattle in the air, whence cattle have their abode in the air.

---

[1] The ten Prâ*n*abh*ri*ts are placed—five on each side of the spine—either along the edge of the altar, or so as to leave the space of one foot between them and the edge, to afford room for another set of bricks, the Vâlakhilyâs.

[2] The thirty-six *Kh*andasyâ bricks are laid down, in three sets of twelve each, along the edge of the body of the altar where the two wings and the tail join it; six bricks being placed on each side of the respective spine. At the back the bricks are not, however, placed close to the edge separating the body from the tail, but sufficient space is left (a foot wide) for another set of bricks to be laid down behind the *Kh*andasyâs.

2. And, again, as to why he lays down *Kh*andasyâs,—the metres are cattle, and cattle are food,
and the middlemost layer is the middle (of Agni, the
altar): he thus places food in the middle (of Agni's
body).

3. He lays them down by twelves,—for the *G*agatî
consists of twelve syllables, and the *G*agatî is cattle,
and the middlemost layer is the air: he thus places
cattle in the air, whence cattle have their abode in
the air.

4. And, again, why (he lays them down) by
twelves,—the *G*agatî consists of twelve syllables,
and the *G*agatî is cattle, and cattle is food, and the
middlemost layer is the middle: he thus places food
in the middle. He places them so as not to be
separated from the Prâ*n*abh*ri*ts: he thus places the
food so as not to be separated from the vital airs;
subsequently (to them he places them): he thus
bestows food after (bestowing) the vital airs.

5. [He lays down the right set, with, Vâ*g*. S. XIV,
18], 'The metre Measure;'—the measure (mâ),
doubtless, is this (terrestrial) world, for this world
is, as it were, measured (mita);—'the metre Fore-
measure!'—the fore-measure (pramâ), doubtless, is
the air-world, for the air-world is, as it were, measured
forward from this world;—'The metre Counter-
measure,'—the counter-measure (pratimâ), doubtless,
is yonder (heavenly) world, for yonder world is, as it
were, counter-measured [1] in the air;—'The metre
Asrîvayas,'—'asrîvayas,' doubtless, is food: whatever food there is in these worlds that is 'asrîvayas.'
Or, whatever food (anna) flows (sravati) from these

---

[1] That is, made a counterfeit, or copy, of the earth.

worlds that is 'asrivayas.'   Hereafter, now, he puts
down only defined metres

6. 'The Pankti metre! the Ushnih metre!
the Brihati metre! the Anushtubh metre! the
Virâg metre! the Gâyatri metre! the Trishtubh metre! the Gagati metre!' these eight
defined metres, including the Virâg, he puts down.
—[The back set, with, Vâg. S. XIV, 19], 'The
metre Earth! the metre Air! the metre
Heaven! the metre Years! the metre Stars!
the metre Speech! the metre Mind! the metre
Husbandry! the metre Gold! the metre Cow!
the metre Goat! the metre Horse!' he thus
puts down those metres which are sacred to those
particular deities.—[The left set, with, Vâg. S. XIV,
20], 'The deity Fire! the deity Wind! the
deity Sun! the deity Moon! the deity Vasa-
vah! the deity Rudrâh! the deity Âdityâh!
the deity Marutah! the deity Visve Devâh!
the deity Brihaspati! the deity Indra! the
deity Varuna!'—these deities, doubtless, are
metres : it is these he thus lays down.

7. He lays down both defined and undefined
(metres). Were he to lay down such as are all
defined, then the food would have an end, it would
fail ; and (were he to lay down) such as are all
undefined, then the food would be invisible, and
one would not see it at all.   He lays down both
defined and undefined ones : hence the defined
(certain) food which is eaten does not fail.

8. These then are those (sets of) twelve he lays
down,—that makes thirty-six, and the Brihati
consists of thirty-six syllables : this is that same
Brihati, the air, which the gods then saw as a third

layer. In that (br*i*hati set of bricks) the gods come last (or, are highest).

9. And, again, as to why he lays down these bricks. When Pragâpati became relaxed, all living beings went from him in all directions.

10. Now that same Pragâpati who became relaxed is this very Agni (fire-altar) that is now being built up; and those living beings which went from him are these bricks: hence when he lays down these (bricks), he thereby puts back into him (Pragâpati-Agni) those same living beings which went from him.

11. Now when he first lays down ten (Prâ*n*abhr*i*ts), they are the moon. There are ten of these,—the Virâg consists of ten syllables, and the Virâg is food, and the moon is food. And when subsequently he lays down thirty-six (*Kh*andasyâs), they are the half-months and months—twenty-four half-months and twelve months: the moon, doubtless, is the year, and all living beings.

12. And when the gods restored him (Pragâpati-Agni), they put all those living beings inside him, and in like manner does this one now put them therein. He lays them down so as not to be separated from the seasonal (bricks): he thus establishes all living beings in the seasons.

Fourth Brâhmana.

1. He then lays down the Vâlakhilyâs;—the Vâlakhilyâs, doubtless, are the vital airs: it is the vital airs he thus lays (into Agni). And as to why they are called Vâlakhilyâs,— what (unploughed piece of ground lies) between two cultivated fields is called

'khila;' and these (channels of the) vital airs[1] are
separated from each other by the width of a horse-
hair (vâla), and because they are separated from
each other by the width of a horse-hair, they (the
bricks) are called Vâlakhilyâs.

2. He places seven in front, and seven at the back.
When he places seven in front, he thereby restores
to him those seven (organs of the) vital airs here in
front.

3. And those seven which (he places) behind he
thereby makes the counter-breathings to those (first
breathings); and hence by means of (the channels of)
these breathings he passes over the food which he
eats with those (other) breathings.

4. And, again, as to why he places seven in front,—
there are seven (channels of the) vital airs here in
the front part (of the animal)[2]—the four upper and
lower parts of the fore-feet, the head, the neck, and
what is above the navel that is the sixth, for in each
limb there is a vital air: this makes seven vital airs
here in front; it is them he thus lays into him
(Agni-Pragâpati).

5. And as to what seven (bricks) he places behind,—there are seven vital airs here in the back
part—the four thighs and knee-bones, the two feet,
and what is below the navel that is the seventh, for
in each limb there is a vital air: this makes seven
vital airs here at the back; it is them he thus lays
into him.

6. [He lays them down, with, Vâg. S. XIV, 21, 22],
'The head thou art, the ruler! steady thou

---

[1] Or, these bricks representing the vital airs.
[2] Or, in the upper part of man.

art, steadfast! a holder thou art, a hold!'—
'A guider, a ruler! a guider thou art, a guide!
steady thou art, a steadier!' he truly bestows
steady vital airs unto him.

7. And, again, as to why he lays down the
Vâlakhilyâs,—it was by means of the Vâlakhilyâs
that the gods then ranged over these worlds, both
from hence upwards and from yonder downwards;
and in like manner does the sacrifice now, by means
of the Vâlakhilyâs, range over these worlds, both
from hence upwards and from yonder downwards.

8. By 'The head thou art, the ruler!' they
stepped on this (terrestrial) world; by 'Steady
thou art, steadfast!' on the air-world; by 'A holder
thou art, a hold!' on that (heavenly) world.—
'For life-strength (I bestow) thee! for vigour
thee! for husbandry thee! for prosperity thee!'
There are four (kinds of) four-footed (domestic)
animals, and (domestic) animals are food : by means
of this food, these four four-footed animals, they
(the gods) established themselves in yonder world;
and in like manner does the Sacrificer now by means
of this food, these four four-footed animals, establish
himself in yonder world.

9. That was, as it were, an ascent away from
hence; but this (earth) is a foothold : the gods came
back to this foothold; and in like manner does the
Sacrificer now come back to this foothold.

10. By 'A guider, a ruler!' they stepped on that
(heavenly) world; by 'A guider thou art, a guide!'
on the air-world; by 'Steady thou art, a steadier!'
on this (terrestial) world.—'For sap (I bestow) thee!
for strength thee! for wealth thee! for thrift
thee!'—There are four four-footed (domestic) animals,

and (domestic) animals are food: by means of this
food, these four four-footed animals, they (the gods)
established themselves in this world; and in like
manner does the Sacrificer, by means of this food,
these four four-footed animals, establish himself in
this world.

11. Now as to the restoration (of Pragâpati-Agni).
Those eleven bricks he lays down [1], which (constitute) that first anuvâka [2], are the air and this body
(of Agni, the altar). And as to why there are eleven
of these, it is because the Trish/ubh consists of
eleven syllables, and the air is of the trish/ubh
nature. And the sixty subsequent (bricks) are Vâyu,
Pragâpati, Agni, the Sacrificer.

12. Those which he places in front are his head:
there are ten [3] of them, because there are ten vital
airs, and the head is (the focus of) the vital airs.
He places them in front, because the head (of an
animal) is here in front.

13. And those which he places on the right (south)
side are that (part) of him which is above the waist
and below the head. And those at the back are
that (part) of him which is above the feet and below
the waist. Those on the left (north) side are the
feet themselves.

14. And the seven (Vâlakhilyâs) which he places
in front are these seven vital airs here in the forepart (of an animal): it is these he thus puts into

---

[1] That is to say, the first eleven bricks of the third layer, viz.
one svayamâtri*nnâ*, four disyâs, one vi*s*vagyotis, and four *ri*tavyâs.

[2] The formulas used with these bricks, Vâg. S. XIV, 11–16, constitute the first anuvâka of the texts relating to the third layer
(XIV, 11–22).

[3] Viz. ten Prâ*n*abh*ri*s. see VIII, 3. 2, 14.

him (Agni). He places them so as not to be separated from those ten (Prâ*n*abh*r*its) : he thereby puts in vital airs that are not separate from the head.

15. And the seven he places at the back (of the altar) are those seven vital airs behind : it is these he thereby puts into him. He places them so as not to be separated from those twelve (*Kh*andasyâs): he thereby puts into him vital airs that are not separate from the body. That same Vâyu-Pragâpati is turned round in all directions in this trish*t*ubh-like air; and when he lays down the third layer, having made up both Vâyu (the wind) and the air, he thereby adds them to himself. He then puts down two Lokamp*ri*nâ (space-filling bricks) in that corner [1] : the significance of them (will be explained) further on [2]. He throws loose earth (on the layer): the significance of this (will be explained) further on [3].

THE FOURTH LAYER.

Fourth Adhyâya. First Brâhmana.

1. He lays down the fourth layer. For the gods having laid down the third layer, now ascended; but, the third layer being the air; it was the air which, having completed it, they ascended.

2. They spake, 'Meditate ye!' whereby, indeed,

---

[1] Whilst, in laying down the Lokamp*ri*nâs of the first and second layers, he started from the south-east and south-west corners respectively, in the third layer he starts from the left hip (or north-west corner) of the altar; filling up the available spaces in two turns, in sunwise fashion. Cf. p. 22, note 1 ; and p. 41, note 1.

[2] See VIII, 7, 2, 4 seq.

[3] See VIII, 7, 3, 1 seq.

they meant to say, 'Seek ye a layer! Seek ye (to build) from hence upwards!' Whilst meditating, they saw that fourth layer, (to wit) what is above the air and below the heavens; that world was to their minds, as it were, unstable and unsettled.

3. They said to the Brahman, 'We will lay thee down (or, set thee up) here!'—'What will therefrom accrue to me?'—'Thou shalt be the highest of us!'—'So be it!' They accordingly laid the Brahman down here, whence people say that the Brahman is the highest of gods. Now, by this fourth layer these two, heaven and earth, are upheld, and the fourth layer is the Brahman, whence people say that heaven and earth are upheld by the Brahman. He lays down the Stomas (hymn-forms)[1]: the stomas being the vital airs, and the Brahman also being the vital airs, it is the Brahman he thereby lays down.

4. And, again, as to why he lays down the Stomas. The gods, at that time, said to Pragâpati, 'We will lay thee down here!'—'So be it!' He did not say, 'What will therefrom accrue unto me?' but whenever Pragâpati wished to obtain anything from the gods, they said, 'What will therefrom accrue to us?' And hence even now if a father wishes to obtain anything from his sons, they say, 'What will there-

---

[1] This refers to the first eighteen bricks of the fourth layer; but as the names of the bricks (ish/akâ, f.) are invariably of the feminine gender, it is doubtful whether stoma (m.), in this case, is meant as the designation of these bricks, or merely as their symbolical analogon. In the former case, one would rather, from the analogy of other bricks, expect some such term as 'stomyâ.' To the first four of them Mahîdhara, on Vâg. S. XIV, 23, applies the epithet mrityumohini, or 'confounders of death.'

from accrue unto us?' and when the sons (wish to obtain anything) from the father, he says, 'So be it!' for in this way Pragâpati and the gods used of old to converse together. He lays down the Stomas: the stomas being the vital airs, and Pragâpati also being the vital airs, it is Pragâpati he thus lays down.

5. And, again, as to why he lays down the Stomas. Those vital airs, the *Ri*shis[1], that saw this fourth layer[2], and who stepped nigh with that essential element (of the altar), are these (vital airs): it is them he now lays down. He lays down the Stomas :—the stomas being the vital airs, and the *Ri*shis also being the vital airs, it is the *Ri*shis he thus lays down.

6. And, again, as to why he lays down the Stomas. When Pragâpati had become relaxed (disjointed), the gods took him and went away. Vâyu, taking that (part) of him which was above the waist and below the head, kept going away from him, having become the deities and the forms of the year.

7. He spake to him, 'Come to me and restore to me that wherewith thou hast gone from me!'— 'What will therefrom accrue unto me?'—'That part of my self shall be sacred unto thee!'—'So be it!' thus Vâyu restored that unto him.

8. Those eighteen (bricks[3]) which there are at

---

[1] See VI, 1, 1, 1; VII, 2, 3, 5.

[2] See VI, 2, 3, 7, 8.

[3] These eighteen bricks, representing the Stomas, or hymn-forms, are laid down in the following order. At each end of the spine (running from west to east) one brick, of the size of the shank (from knee to ankle), is placed, with its line-marks running from west to east; the eastern one being placed north, and the western one south, of the spine. Thereupon an ordinary brick, a foot square, is placed

first, are that very (part) of his (Pragâpati's) body; and when he places them in this (layer), he thereby restores to him that (part) of his body which these (form): therefore he places them in this (layer). He lays down the Stomas: the stomas being the vital airs, and Vâyu (the wind) also being the vital airs, it is Vâyu he thus lays down.

9. In front he lays down one, with (Vâg. S. XIV, 23), 'The swift one, the Trivrit!' he therewith lays down that hymn-form which is trivrit (threefold, or thrice-three-versed). And as to why he calls it 'the swift one,' it is because this, indeed, is the swiftest of stomas. But the swift threefold one, doubtless, is Vâyu: he exists in these three worlds. And as to why he calls him 'the swift one,' it is because he is the swiftest of all beings: being (or, in the form of) Vâyu it remained in front,— it is that form he now lays down.

10. [The back one [1], with], 'The bright one [2], the Pañkadasa!' he therewith lays down that

at the southern end of the 'cross-spine,' so as to lie on the spine (though not apparently exactly in the middle, but so that only one-fourth of the brick lies on one side of the spine) with its line-marks running from south to north; and a second brick of the same size is placed on the north, but so as to leave the full space of another such brick between it and the northern edge of the altar. Behind (west of) the front brick, fourteen half-foot bricks are then laid down, in a row from north to south, seven on each side of the spine.

[1] The formulas of the first four of these (stoma) bricks are not given here (in paragraphs 9–12) in the order in which the bricks are actually laid down, viz. E. W. S. N., but in the order E. S. N. W.; cp. Kâtyây. Srautas. XVII, 10, 6–9. For a symbolic explanation of this change of order see VIII, 4, 4, 1 seq.

[2] Or, perhaps, 'the angry one.' The author of the Brâhmana, however, evidently connects 'bhânta' with the root 'bhâ,' to shine.

hymn-form which is fifteenfold (fifteen-versed).
And when he calls it 'the bright one,' it is that
the bright one is the thunderbolt, and the thunderbolt is fifteenfold. But the bright, fifteenfold one,
doubtless, also is the Moon : he waxes during fifteen
days, and wanes during fifteen days. And as to his
calling him 'the bright one,' the Moon indeed shines:
being the Moon it remained on the right side,—it is
that form he now lays down.

11. [The left (north) one, with], 'The (aerial)
space, the Saptadasa!' he therewith lays down
that hymn-form which is seventeenfold. And as
to his calling it 'the space,'—the (aerial) space is
Pragâpati, and the seventeenfold one is Pragâpati.
But indeed the seventeenfold space also is the year :
in it there are twelve months and five seasons.
And as to his calling it space, the year indeed is
space : being space, it remained on the left side,—
it is that form he now lays down.

12. [The right (south) one, with], 'The upholder,
the Ekavimsa!' he therewith lays down that hymn-
form which is twenty-one-fold. And as to his calling
it 'the upholder,'—the upholder means a foothold,
and the Ekavimsa is a foothold. But indeed the
twenty-one-fold upholder also is yonder sun: to
him belong the twelve months, the five seasons,
these three worlds, and yonder sun himself is the
upholder, the twenty-one-fold. And as to his calling
him 'the upholder,'—when he sets everything here
holds its peace: being the sun, it remained at the
back,—it is that form he now lays down; and the
forms of the year he lays down.

13. 'Speed, the Ashtâdasa!' he therewith lays
down that hymn-form which is eighteenfold. Now,

speed, the eighteenfold one, doubtless, is the year: in it there are twelve months, five seasons, and the year itself is speed, the eighteenfold. And as to his calling it 'speed,' the year indeed speeds all beings: it is that form he now lays down.

14. 'Heat, the Navadasa!' he therewith lays down that hymn-form which is nineteenfold. But heat, the nineteenfold one, doubtless, is the year: in it there are twelve months, six seasons, and the year itself is heat, the nineteenfold. And as to his calling it 'heat,' the year indeed burns all beings: it is that form he now lays down.

15. 'Victorious assault, the Savimsa!' he therewith lays down that hymn-form which is twenty-fold. But victorious assault, the twentyfold one, doubtless, is the year: in it there are twelve months, seven seasons, and the year itself is victorious assault, the twentyfold. And as to why he calls it 'victorious assault,' the year indeed assails all beings: it is that form he now lays down.

16. 'Vigour, the Dvâvimsa!' he therewith lays down that hymn-form which is twenty-two-fold. But vigour, the twenty-two-fold one, doubtless is the year: in it there are twelve months, seven seasons, the two, day and night, and the year itself is vigour, the twenty-two-fold. And as to why he calls it 'vigour,' the year is indeed the most vigorous of all existing things: it is that form he now lays down.

17. 'The array, the Trayovimsa!' he therewith lays down that hymn-form which is twenty-three-fold. But array, the twenty-three-fold one, doubtless, means the year: in it there are thirteen months, seven seasons, the two, day and night, and the year itself is the array, the twenty-three-fold.

And as to his calling it 'array,' the year is indeed arrayed over all beings : it is that form he now lays down.

18. 'The womb, the *K*aturvi*m*sa!' he therewith lays down that hymn-form which is twenty-four-fold. But the womb, the twenty-four-fold one, doubtless, is the year : in it there are twenty-four half-months. And as to his calling it 'the womb,' the year is indeed the womb of all beings : it is that form he now lays down.

19. 'The embryos, the Pa*ñk*avi*m*sa!' he therewith lays down that hymn-form which is twenty-five-fold. But the embryos, the twenty-five-fold one, doubtless, is the year : in it there are twenty-four half-months, and the year itself is the embryos, the twenty-five-fold. And as to his calling it 'the embryos,'—the year, as an embryo, in the shape of the thirteenth month, enters the seasons : it is that form he now lays down.

20. 'Strength, the Tri*n*ava!' he therewith lays down that hymn-form which is thrice ninefold. And as to his calling it 'strength,'—strength (o*g*as) means the thunderbolt (va*g*ra), and the Tri*n*ava is a thunderbolt. But strength also means the year : in it there are twenty-four half-months, the two, day and night, and the year itself is strength, the thrice-ninefold. And as to his calling it 'strength,' the year indeed is the strength of all beings : it is that form he now lays down.

21. 'Design, the Ekatri*m*sa!' he therewith lays down that hymn-form which is thirty-one-fold. But design, the thirty-one-fold, doubtless, means the year : in it there are twenty-four half-months, six seasons, and the year itself is design, the thirty-one-fold. And

as to his calling it 'design,' the year indeed designs (makes, forms) all beings : it is that form he now lays down.

22. 'The foundation, the Trayastrimsa!' he therewith lays down that hymn-form which is thirty-three-fold. And as to why he calls it 'the foundation,' the thirty-three-fold is indeed a foundation. But indeed the foundation, the thirty-three-fold, also is the year : in it there are twenty-four half-months, six seasons, the two, day and night, and the year itself is the foundation, the thirty-three-fold. And as to his calling it 'the foundation,' the year is indeed the foundation of all beings : it is that form he now lays down.

23. 'The range of the ruddy one, the Katu-strimsa!' he therewith lays down that hymn-form which is thirty-four-fold. But the range of the ruddy one (the sun), the thirty-four-fold one, doubtless, is the year : in it there are twenty-four half-months, seven seasons, the two, day and night, and the year itself is the range of the ruddy one, the thirty-four-fold. And as to his calling it 'the range of the ruddy one,' the range of the ruddy one, doubtless, means supreme sway, and the thirty-four-fold one means supreme sway : it is that form he now lays down.

24. 'The firmament, the Shattrimsa!' he therewith lays down that hymn-form which is thirty-six-fold. But the firmament, the thirty-six-fold one, doubtless, is the year : in it there are twenty-four half-moons, and twelve months. And as to why he calls it 'the firmament' (nâkam), it is because there is no pain (na akam) for whosoever goes there. And the firmament indeed is the year, the heavenly world is the year : it is that form he now lays down.

25. 'The revolving sphere, the Ash/â/atvâ-rimsa!' he therewith lays down that hymn-form which is forty-eight-fold. But the revolving sphere, the forty-eight-fold, doubtless, is the year: in it there are twenty-six half-months, thirteen months, seven seasons, and the two, day and night. And as to his calling it 'the revolving sphere,' from the year all creatures indeed are evolved: it is that form he now lays down.

26. 'The stay, the Katush/oma!' he therewith lays down the chant of praise consisting of four stomas [1]. And as to his calling it 'the stay,'—stay means support, and the Katush/oma is a support. But the stay, the Katush/oma, doubtless, is Vâyu (the wind), for he sings from all those four quarters. And as to his calling him 'the stay,'—stay means support; and the wind indeed is the support of all beings: it is that form he now lays down. The wind he places first and last: by the wind he thus encloses all these beings on both sides.

27. These, then, are eighteen bricks he lays down; this makes two Trivr/ts,—the Trivr/t being breath, and breath being wind, this layer is Vâyu.

28. And as to why there are eighteen,—the year is eighteenfold: twelve months and six seasons. And Pragâpati indeed is the year, Pragâpati is eighteenfold: as great as Agni is, as great as is his measure, so great he makes it when he lays it down.

Second Brâhmana.

1. He then lays down the Spr/ta/ [2] (freeing

---

[1] For particulars on the Katush/oma, see note on XIII, 1, 3, 4.

[2] The ten Spr/ta/ are placed in close connection with the preceding set;—viz. at the front and back ends of the spine, two

bricks). For when that (part) of his body had been restored, Pragâpati became pregnant with all beings: whilst they were in his womb, evil, death, seized them.

2. He spake to the gods, 'With you I will free all these beings from evil, from death [1]!'—'What will accrue unto us therefrom?'—'Choose ye!' said he. —'Let there be a share for us!' said some to him. 'Let lordship be unto us!' said others. Having bestowed a share on some, and lordship on others, he freed all beings from evil, from death: and inasmuch as he freed (spri) them, therefore (those bricks are called) 'Sprítah.' And in like manner does this Sacrificer, by bestowing a share on some, and lordship on others, now free all beings from evil, from death; and hence (the word) 'sprítam (freed)' recurs with all of them.

3. [He lays them down [2], with, Vâg. S. XIV, 24–26], 'Agni's share thou art, Dikshâ's lordship!' —Dikshâ, doubtless, is Speech: having bestowed a share on Agni, he bestows lordship on Speech;— 'the Brahman is freed; the Trivrit-stoma!'— by means of the thrice-threefold hymn-form he freed

---

bricks, exactly corresponding in size to those already lying there, are placed south and north of these respectively. Similarly two bricks, a foot square, are placed on the 'cross-spine' immediately north of the two stoma-bricks lying there. The remaining six bricks are then placed behind the row of fourteen 'stomas' in the front part of the altar, three on each side of the spine.

[1] Or, from that evil, death.

[2] In the case of the first four Sprítah, as in that of the corresponding Stomas (see p. 61, note 1), while the bricks themselves are laid down in the order E.W.N.S., the order in which the formulas are given in paragraphs 3–6, is that of E.N.S.W.—Cp. Kâty. Srautas. XVII, 10, 11–14. For a symbolical explanation of this change of order, see VIII, 4, 4, 1 seq.

the Brahman (priesthood) for living beings from evil,
from death.

4. 'Indra's share thou art, Vish*n*u's lordship!'—Having bestowed a share on Indra, he
bestowed lordship on Vish*n*u;—'the Kshatra is
freed; the Pañ*k*ada*s*a-stoma!'—by means of the
fifteenfold hymn-form he freed the Kshatra (nobility)
for living beings from evil, from death.

5. 'The man-viewers' share thou art, the
creator's lordship!'—the man-viewers, doubtless,
are the gods : having bestowed a share on the gods,
he bestowed lordship on the creator ;—'the birth-
place is freed, the Saptada*s*a-stoma!'—the birth-
place, doubtless, is the peasantry : by means of the
seventeenfold hymn-form he frees the peasantry for
living beings from evil, from death.

6. 'Mitra's share thou art, Varu*n*a's lordship!'—Mitra, doubtless, is the out-breathing, and
Varu*n*a the down-breathing : having bestowed a
share on the out-breathing, he bestowed lordship on
the down-breathing ;—'heaven's rain, the wind is
freed; the Ekavi*m*sa-stoma!'—by means of the
twenty-one-fold hymn-form he frees both rain and
wind for living beings from evil, from death.

7. 'The Vasus' share thou art, the Rudras'
lordship!'—having bestowed a share on the Vasus,
he bestowed lordship on the Rudras ;—'the four-
footed is freed, the *K*aturvi*m*sa-stoma!'—by
means of the twenty-five-fold hymn-form he freed
the four-footed for living beings from evil, from
death.

8. 'The Âdityas' share thou art, the Maruts'
lordship!'—having bestowed a share on the Âdityas, he bestowed lordship on the Maruts ;—'the

embryos are freed, the Pañkavimsa-stoma!'—
by means of the twenty-five-fold hymn-form he freed
the embryos for living beings from evil, from death.

9. 'Aditi's share thou art, Pûshan's lordship!'—Aditi, doubtless, is this (earth): having
bestowed a share on her, he bestowed lordship on
Pûshan,—'vigour is freed; the Trinava-stoma!'
by means of the thrice-ninefold hymn-form he freed
vigour for living beings from evil, from death.

10. 'God Savitrî's share thou art, Brihaspati's lordship!'—having bestowed a share on the
god Savitrî, he bestows lordship on Brihaspati;—
'the facing quarters are freed, the Katush-
toma!'—by means of the chant of praise consisting
of four stomas he freed all the (four) quarters for
living beings from evil, from death.

11. 'The Yavas' share thou art, the Ayavas'
lordship!'—the Yavas, doubtless, are the first (light)
fortnights, and the Ayavas the latter (dark) fortnights, for these gain (yu) and obtain (â-yu) everything here[1]: having bestowed a share on the first
fortnights, he bestowed lordship on the latter fortnights;—'the creatures are freed, the Katus-
katvârimsa-stoma!'—by means of the forty-four-
fold hymn-form he freed all creatures from evil, from
death.

12. 'The Ribhus' share thou art, the All-
gods' lordship!'—having bestowed a share on the
Ribhus, he bestowed lordship on the Visve-Devâh;—

---

[1] This is clearly a fanciful etymology. If 'yava' and 'ayava,' in
the sense of the bright and dark fortnights, are really genuine terms,
it is more likely that they are derived from y u, 'to keep off,'—the
bright half of the moon being looked upon as capable of averting
evil spirits, and the dark half as the reverse of this.

'the living being is freed, the Trayastri*m*sa-
stoma!'—by means of the thirty-three-fold hymn-
form he freed all living beings from evil, from death ;
and in like manner does the Sacrificer, by means of
the thirty-three-fold hymn-form, now free all living
beings from evil, from death.

13. These, then, are ten bricks he lays down,—the
Virâg consists of ten syllables, and Agni is Virâg
(wide-shining) ; there are ten regions, and Agni is
the regions ; there are ten vital airs, and Agni is the
vital airs : as great as Agni is, as great as is his
measure, by so much he thus frees all these creatures
from evil, from death.

14. He then lays down two *R*itavyâs[1] (seasonal
bricks) ;—the seasonal ones being the same as the
seasons, it is the seasons he thus lays down ;—with
(Vâg. S. XIV, 27), 'Saha and Sahasya, the two
winter-seasons!' These are the names of those
two, it is with their names he thus lays them down.
There are two such bricks, for a season consists of
two months. Only once he settles them : he thus
makes (the two months) one season.

15. And as to why he places these two (bricks) in
this (layer),—this Agni (fire-altar) is the year, and
the year is these worlds : what part thereof is above
the air, and below the sky, that is this fourth layer,
and that is the winter-season thereof ; and when he
places these two in this (layer), he thereby restores
to him (Pragâpati-Agni, the year and fire-altar)
what part of his body these two (constitute). This
is why he places these two in this (layer).

---

[1] These are placed over the *R*itavyâs of the preceding layers.
viz. in the fifth place to the east of the centre, south and north of
the spine.

16. And, again, as to why he places these two in this (layer),—this Agni is Pragâpati, and Pragâpati is the year: what (part) of him there is above the waist, and below the head, that is this fourth layer, and that is the winter-season of him (or, of it, the year). And when he places these two in this (layer), he thereby restores to him what part of his body these two (constitute). This is why he places these two in this (layer).

Third Brâhmana.

1. He then lays down the S*rish*/is[1] (creations). For Pragâpati, having freed all beings from evil,

---

[1] The seventeen S*rish*/is are to be placed round the centre, along the reta*hsik* range, in such a way that nine bricks lie south

THE CENTRAL PART OF THE FOURTH LAYER.

(Seventeen s*rish*/i and two *rtavyâ*.)

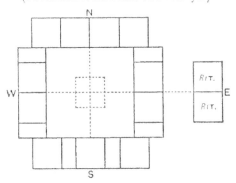

and eight bricks north, of the spine; and that five bricks form the southern side, and four bricks each of the three other sides. Whilst the bricks of the south side are further specified as consisting of a brick, a foot square, lying on the cross-spine, being flanked on both sides by half-foot bricks, and these again by square bricks; no particulars are given regarding the other sides. Most likely, however, as indicated in the accompanying sketch, four square bricks, two on each side of the cross-spine, are to form the left (north) side, whilst the front and hind sides are to consist of two

from death, he now desired, 'May I produce creatures, may I procreate!'

2. He spake unto the vital airs[1], 'Together with you, I will here bring forth creatures!'—'Wherewith shall we sing praises[2]?'—'With me and with your-

---

square bricks lying north and south of the spine, and flanked by half-foot bricks.

[1] That is, to the deities representing the vital airs, viz. the regions, &c. Mahîdh.

[2] Professor Delbrück, in his Altindische Syntax, pp. 136, 257, 265, takes 'stoshyâmahe' in this passage in a passive sense—'by whom shall we be praised?' I think, however, that this is a mistake, and Harisvâmin's commentary certainly takes it in the same sense as I have done; and, indeed, the paragraphs which follow seem to me to make it quite clear that no other interpretation is possible. Pragâpati is about to perform the 'sr/sh/is,' i.e. the creation of living beings by means of sacrifice (his own self). He requires the assistance of the Prânas (vital airs) in order to produce creatures endowed with breath, and he also appeals to (the three most prominent of) them in their capacity as R/shis (VI, 1, 1, 1 seq.) to officiate as his (Udgâtr/) priests. They ask, 'Wherewith shall we sing praises?' and he answers, 'With me and with your own selves.' The 'wherewith,' according to Harisvâmin, refers both to the 'stotriyâ' verses to be used, and to the deities of the sr/sh/i-stotras. That the former, at all events, is indeed the case, a glance at the subsequent paragraphs shows, where the stotriyâs are identified with the vital airs, and, when their number (ten) becomes exhausted, with parts of the year (Pragâpati), and of his (the Sacrificer's, or Pragâpati's) body. As regards the deities whom Harisvâmin considers to be likewise implied, this also is by no means improbable, though I must confess that it did not occur to me, before I looked at the commentary. In the Udgâtr/'s text-books, the chanting of stotras is usually interpreted as symbolising the production of 'food' (cf., for instance, Tândya-Br. I, 3, 6, 'annam karishyâmy annam pravishyâmy annam ganayishyâmi'), whilst here it seems identified with the production of life, or breath itself (cf. ib. 5, 'br/haspatis tvâ yunaktu devebhyah prânâya &c.'); and, accordingly, in Sat. Br. X, 3, 1, 1, 7, the principal vital air, the breath proper, is called 'praganana-prâna.'

selves!'—'So be it!' So they sang praises both
with the vital airs and with Pragâpati; and whatsoever the gods do, that they do with praise, that—
praise being sacrifice—they do with sacrifice. Hence
(the words) 'they sang praises' recur with all (these
bricks).

3. [They lay them down, with, Vâg. S. XIV, 28–
31], 'With one they sang praises,'—the one,
doubtless, is speech: it is with speech they then
sang praises;—'creatures were conceived,'—
creatures indeed were now conceived;—'Pragâpati was the lord!'—Pragâpati indeed was now
the lord.

4. 'With three they sang praises,'—there are
three vital airs: the out-breathing, the up-breathing,
and the through-breathing: it is with them they
then sang praises;—'the Brahman was created,'—
the priesthood indeed was now created;—'Brahmanaspati was the lord!' Brahmanaspati indeed
was now the lord.

5. 'With five they sang praises,'—what (four)
vital airs there are here, with mind as a fifth: it is
with them they then sang praises;—'the living
beings were created,'—the living beings indeed
were now created;—'the lord of beings was the
lord!'—the lord of beings indeed was now the lord.

6. 'With seven they sang praises,'—what seven
vital airs there are here in the head: it is with them
they then sang praises;—'the seven Rishis were
created,'—the seven Rishis indeed were now
created;—'the creator was the lord!'—the creator
indeed was now the lord.

7. 'With nine they sang praises,'—there are
nine vital airs, seven in the head, and two downward

ones : it is with them they then sang praises ;—'the Fathers were created,'—the Fathers indeed were now created ;—'Aditi was the ruler!'—Aditi indeed was now the ruler.

8. 'With eleven they sang praises,'—there are ten vital airs, and the trunk is the eleventh : it is therewith they then sang praises ;—'the seasons were created,'—the seasons indeed were now created ;—'the seasonal periods were the lords!'—the seasonal periods indeed were now the lords.

9. 'With thirteen they sang praises,'—there are ten vital airs, and two feet, and the trunk is the thirteenth : it is therewith they then sang praises ;—'the months were created,'—the months indeed were now created ;—'the year was the lord!'—the year indeed was now the lord.

10. 'With fifteen they sang praises,'—there are ten fingers, four fore-arms and upper arms, and what is above the navel is the fifteenth : it is therewith they then sang praises ;—'the Kshatra was created,'—the nobility indeed was now created ;—'Indra was the lord!'—Indra indeed was now the lord.

11. 'With seventeen they sang praises,'—there are ten toes, four thighs and shanks, two feet, and what is below the navel is the seventeenth : it is therewith they then sang praises ;—'the tame animals were created,'—the tame animals indeed were now created ;—'Brihaspati was the lord!'—Brihaspati indeed was now the lord.

12. 'With nineteen they sang praises,'—there are ten fingers, and nine vital airs : it is with these they then sang praises ;—'the Sûdra and Ârya were created,'—the Sûdra and Ârya indeed

were now created;—'the day and night were the rulers!'—the day and night indeed were now the rulers.

13. 'With twenty-one they sang praises,'— there are ten fingers, ten toes, and the trunk is the twenty-first: it is therewith that they then sang praises;—'the one-hoofed animals were created,'—the one-hoofed animals indeed were now created;—'Varuna was the lord!'—Varuna indeed was now the lord.

14. 'With twenty-three they sang praises,'— there are ten fingers, ten toes, two feet, and the trunk is the twenty-third: it is therewith they then sang praises;—'the small animals were created,'— the small animals indeed were now created;— 'Pûshan was the lord!'—Pûshan indeed was now the lord.

15. 'With twenty-five they sang praises,'— there are ten fingers, ten toes, four limbs, and the trunk is the twenty-fifth: it is therewith they then sang praises;—'the wild animals were created,' —the wild animals indeed were now created;— 'Vâyu was the lord!'—Vâyu indeed was now the lord.

16. 'With twenty-seven they sang praises,'— there are ten fingers, ten toes, four limbs, two feet, and the trunk is the twenty-seventh: it is therewith they then sang praises;—'Heaven and Earth went asunder,'—heaven and earth indeed now went asunder;—'the Vasus, Rudras and Âdityas separated along with them: they indeed were the lords!' and they indeed were now the lords.

17. 'With twenty-nine they sang praises,'—

there are ten fingers, ten toes, and nine vital airs:
it is with these they then sang praises ;—'the trees
were created,'—the trees indeed were now created ;
—'Soma was the lord,'—Soma indeed was now
the lord.

18. 'With thirty-one they sang praises,'—
there are ten fingers, ten toes, ten vital airs, and
the trunk is the thirty-first: it is therewith they then
sang praises ;—'the creatures were created,'—
the creatures indeed were now created ;—'the
Yavas and Ayavas were the lords,'—the bright
and dark fortnights indeed were now the lords.

19. 'With thirty-three they sang praises,'—
there are ten fingers, ten toes, ten vital airs, two
feet, and the trunk is the thirty-third: it is therewith
they then sang praises ;—'the living beings lay
quiet,'—all living beings now indeed lay quiet;—
'Pragâpati, the supreme, was the lord!'—
Pragâpati, the supreme, indeed was now the lord.

20. These, then, are seventeen bricks he lays
down,—the year, Pragâpati, is seventeenfold, he is
the progenitor: it is thus by this seventeenfold year,
by Pragâpati, the progenitor, that he caused these
creatures to be generated. And what he generated,
he created; and inasmuch as he created (srig),
therefore they are called creations (srishti). Having
created them, he made them enter his own self: and
in like manner does the Sacrificer now cause these
creatures to be generated by that seventeenfold year,
by Pragâpati, the progenitor; and having created
them, he makes them enter his own self[1]. On the

---

[1] That is, he makes them pass into his own power, makes them
his own.

range of the Reta/si/ (he lays down these bricks):
the Reta/si/ being the ribs, and the ribs the middle
(of the body), it is in the very middle that he causes
these creatures to enter him. He lays them on all
sides: from all sides he thus makes these creatures
to enter him.

Fourth Brâhmana.

1. Now, then, as to the order of proceeding.
That (brick) which contains the Trivrit (thrice-
threefold stoma) he places in front, that containing the
twenty-one-fold (stoma) at the back, that containing
the fifteenfold (stoma) on the right (south) side, that
containing the seventeenfold (stoma) on the left
(north) side.

2. Now when the one containing the Trivrit had
been laid down, Death lay in wait for Pragâpati in
the one (on the south side) containing the fifteenfold
(stoma), thinking, 'After that he will lay down this
one: I will here seize upon him!' He (Pragâpati)
was aware of him, and having seen him, he walked
round and laid down (at the back) the (brick) containing the twenty-one-fold (stoma). Death came
thither, and he (Pragâpati) laid down the one (on the
south side) containing the fifteenfold (stoma). Death
came to the fifteenfold one, and he (Pragâpati) laid
down the one (on the north side) containing the
seventeenfold (stoma). It was here [1] that he put
down and confounded Death; and in like manner
does the Sacrificer now put down and confound all
evils.

---

[1] That is, in the laying down of these bricks. For the order
followed in laying down the bricks, see also p. 67, note 2.

3. Then as to the subsequent (bricks). Alongside of the one (in front) containing the Trivṛit he lays down one containing the Trivṛit; alongside of that (at the back) containing the Ekaviṃsa (he lays down) one containing the Ekaviṃsa; alongside of that (on the south, or right, side) containing the Pañkadasa (he lays down) one containing the Saptadasa; alongside of that (on the north, or left, side) containing the Saptadasa (he lays down) one containing the Pañkadasa. And because he thus changes in laying them down [1], therefore they (the bricks) are of diverse stomas; and because these stomas are then otherwise with regard to the former ones [2], therefore also they (the bricks) are of diverse stomas. And in this way the gods laid them down, and otherwise the Asuras; whereupon the gods succeeded, and the Asuras came to naught: he who knows this, succeeds of himself, and his hateful enemy comes to naught.

4. Now, this Agni (fire-altar) is an animal, and he is made up (restored) here whole and entire. His head is the two (bricks) containing the Trivṛit; and as to why these two are such as contain the Trivṛit, —the head is threefold (trivṛit). There are two of them, because the head consists of two bones (kapâla). He lays them down in front, for this head is in the front (of the animal).

5. The two (behind) containing the Ekaviṃsa are the foundation (the feet). And as to why these are such as contain the Ekaviṃsa,—the Ekaviṃsa is

---

[1] The Sanskrit text, as usual, makes our gerundial clause the principal clause: 'because he lays them down in changing them.'

[2] On the south side a Spṛit representing the Saptadasa is placed immediately north of a stoma (brick) representing the Pañkadasa; and vice versâ on the north (left) side.

a foundation. There are two of them, because the
foundation is a pair (of feet). He places them
behind, because this foundation (the hind-feet) is
behind.

6. The two containing the Pańkadasa[1] are the
arms (or fore-feet). And as to why these are such
as contain the Pańkadasa,—the arms are fifteenfold.
There are two of them, because these arms are two.
He places them on the sides, because these two
arms are at the sides.

7. The two containing the Saptadasa are food.
And as to why they are such as contain the Saptadasa,—food is seventeenfold. There are two of them,
because 'anna' (food) has two syllables. He lays
them down close to those containing the Pańkadasa :
he thus puts the food close to the arms. Those
containing the Pańkadasa are on the outside, and
those containing the Saptadasa on the inside : he
thus encloses the food on both sides by the arms.

8. And those he places in the middle are the
body (trunk). He places them on the range of the
Retahsik (bricks), for—the Retahsik being the ribs,
and the ribs being the middle (of the body)—this
body is in the middle (of the limbs)[2]. He places them
in every direction, for this body (extends) in every
direction. And as to what other (space) there is
besides this, that is left over ;—and what is left over
for the gods, that is these metres ;—and as to these

---

[1] Viz. the southern one of the two on the south (right) side, and
the northern one of the two on the north (left) side.

[2] Atha yâ madhya upadadhâti sa âtmâ, tâ retahsikor vclayo-
padadhâti—prishtayo vai retahsikau, madhyam u prishtayo—
madhyato hy ayam âtmâ.—Here the two clauses with 'vai' are
inserted to substantiate the reason introduced by 'hi.'

metres, they are cattle;—and as to cattle, they are (objects of) good fortune;—and as to these (objects of) good fortune, they are yonder sun : he is that one to the south of them.

9. Now some lay down these (rows of bricks [1]) immediately after the two containing the Trivr̪it, saying, 'They are the tongue and the jaws : those fourteen are the jaws, and those six are the tongue.' Let him not do so : they cause a redundancy,—it would be just as if one were to put two other jaws to the already existing jaws, as if one were to put another tongue to the already existing tongue. That (brick) wherein the head is indeed (includes) the jaws and the tongue.

10. Now some lay down (these bricks) in the intermediate (south-eastern) space of it (the altar) [2], saying, 'This is the sun : we thus place yonder sun in that direction.' Let him not do so : surely there are those other rites [3] by which he places him in that (direction).

11. Some, again, lay them down on the right

---

[1] Viz. the row of fourteen bricks lying behind the two front bricks, and the row of six bricks again placed behind these. It will be remembered that only the northern one of the two front bricks was laid down at first, and that then three others were placed in the different directions, after which the row of fourteen was laid down behind the front one ; and similarly the laying down of the second front brick was separated from that of the second row by the laying down of three other bricks in the different quarters.

[2] In that case, the two shank-sized bricks are laid down in the south-east corner, and the rows of smaller bricks are placed to the north of them. See Kâty. Srautas. XIV, 10, 4.

[3] See, for instance, VI, 7, 3, 9 where the Ukhya Agni, representing the sun, is held up by the Agnikit (sacrificer) in the south-easterly direction. The south-east corner is sacred to Agni.

(south [1]) side, saying, 'We thus place these signs of good fortune (punyâ lakshmî) on the right side :' whence he who has a mark [2] (lakshman) on his right side is said to have good luck (punya-lakshmika), and on the left side in the case of a woman [3]; for the woman has her position on the left side (of the man): therefore it is done thus. But let him place them in front; for where the head is there are also the jaws and the tongue: and thus he places the signs of good fortune at the head (or, in the mouth, mukhatah), whence they say that he who has a (peculiar) mark in his mouth [4] has good luck.

12. This, indeed, is Brahman's layer: inasmuch as they (the gods) laid down the Brahman [5], therefore it is Brahman's layer. It is Pragâpati's layer: inasmuch as they laid down Pragâpati [6], it is Pragâpati's layer. It is the Rishis' layer: inasmuch as they laid down the Rishis [7], it is the Rishis' layer. It is Vâyu's layer: inasmuch as they laid down Vâyu [8], it is Vâyu's layer. It is the Stomas' layer: inasmuch as they laid down the hymn-forms [9], it is the Stomas'

---

[1] In that case, they are laid down north of the two bricks lying on the southern end of the cross-spine, first the row of fourteen, and then, north of these, the row of six.

[2] Yasya dakshinapârsve lakshanam kiyasya vâ varne vâ kimtarâtmakam (?) bhavati; comm.

[3] This clause is rather abrupt, and is, moreover, hardly logical. It is not clear whether it is the two southern bricks that are compared with the woman, or the bricks to be placed alongside of them on the north (left) side.

[4] Viz. such as an excess of sharp teeth (incisors)—yasya mukhalakshanam dakshinadamshtrâtirekâdi bhavati; comm.

[5] See VIII, 4, 1, 3.   [6] See VIII, 4, 1, 4.
[7] See VIII, 4, 1, 5.   [8] See VIII, 4, 1, 8.
[9] See VIII, 4, 1, 4 seq.

layer. It is the layer of the vital airs: inasmuch as they laid down the vital airs [1], it is the layer of the vital airs. Hence, whatsoever one may know, that comes to be included in the ancestry, in the kinship [2] of this layer.—He then lays down two Lokampr*in*âs (space-filling bricks) in that corner [3]: the significance of these (will be explained) farther on [4]. He throws loose soil thereon: the significance of this (will be explained) farther on [5].

THE FIFTH LAYER.

FIFTH ADHYÂYA. FIRST BRÂHMANA.

1. He lays down the fifth layer. For now, having laid down the fourth layer, the gods mounted it,— having completed what is above the air, and below the sky, they mounted it.

2. They spake, 'Meditate ye (*k*etay)!' whereby, doubtless, they meant to say, 'Seek ye a layer (*k*iti)! Seek ye from hence upwards!' Whilst meditating, they saw that fifth layer, the far-shining heaven: that world pleased them.

3. They desired, 'Would that we could make that world foeless, undisturbed!' They spake, 'Think ye upon this, how we shall make this world

---

[1] See VIII, 4, 1, 5.

[2] Or, in the (symbolic) meaning. The literal reading of the clause is,—'Thereby this layer of his becomes possessed of an ancestry and kinship (or mystic sense).'

[3] Viz. in the north-east corner, or on the left shoulder, whence, in two turns, the available spaces of the altar are filled up. In laying down the Lokampr*in*âs of the first three layers he started from the south-east, the south-west, and the north-west corners respectively. Cf. p. 22, note 1; p. 41, note 1; p. 58, note 1.

[4] See VIII, 7, 2, 4 seq.   [5] See VIII, 7, 3, 1 seq.

foeless, undisturbed!' They spake, 'Meditate ye!'
whereby, indeed, they meant to say, 'Seek ye a
layer! Seek ye how we shall make this world
foeless, undisturbed!'

4. Whilst meditating, they saw these Asapatnâ
('foeless') bricks; they laid them down, and by
means of them they made that world foeless, undisturbed; and because by means of them they
made that world foeless, undisturbed, these (are
called) Asapatnâs. And in like manner does the
Sacrificer, by laying them down, now make that
world foeless, undisturbed. On all (four) sides he
lays them down: on all sides he thus makes that
world foeless, undisturbed. He places them on the
other side: he thereby makes that whole world foeless, undisturbed.

5. He then lays down the Virâgs [1] (far-shining
bricks): this Virâg, indeed, is that far-shining (virâg)
fifth layer which the gods saw. He lays them down
by tens: the Virâg (metre) consists of ten syllables,
and this layer is 'virâg.' He places them on every
side; for he who shines (rules) in one direction only,
does not shine far and wide, but whosoever shines in
all directions, he alone shines far and wide.

6. And as to why he lays down those Asapatnâs.
Now at that time, when that (part) of his body had
been restored, evil beset Pragâpati on every side.
He saw those foeless bricks, and laid them down,
and by means of them he drove off evil, for foe means
evil; and because, by means of them he drove off the
foe, evil, therefore they are (called) 'foeless' (bricks).

---

[1] For particulars respecting these, also called Khandasyâh, see
VIII, 5, 2, 1, seq.

7. And what the gods did, the same is done now. Evil, indeed, does not now beset this (Sacrificer), but when he now does this, it is that he wants to do what the gods did; and he thereby drives off whatever evil, whatever foe besets him; and because, by means of them, he drives off the foe, evil, therefore they are (called) the 'foeless' (bricks). He places them on every side: he thereby drives off the foe, evil, on every side. He places them on the other side: from his whole self he thereby drives off the foe, evil.

8. He lays down (one) in front [1], with (Vâg. S. XV, 1), 'O Agni, drive away the foes of ours that are born, drive back those unborn, O knower of beings! cheer us, kindly and unfrowning! may we be in thy threefold-sheltering, steadfast protection!' as the text so the sense. Then behind, with (Vâg. S. XV, 2), 'With might drive away the foes of ours that are born,

---

[1] The first four of the five Asapatnâs are laid down near the four ends of the spines (in the order east, west, south, north); their exact place being the second space on the left side of the spine (in looking towards them from the centre), that is to say, the space of one (? or half a) foot being left between them and the respective spine. Their position thus is the same as those of the Asvinîs in the second layer (see p. 31, note 1) except that these were placed on the Retahsik range instead of at the ends of the spines. The line-marks of these four bricks run parallel to the respective spines. The fifth Asapatnâ is thus laid down north of the southern one, so as to leave the space of a cubit (about a foot and a half) between them. These latter two Asapatnâs are full-sized bricks (one foot square), and not half-sized, as were the two southern Asvinîs. Moreover, whilst the southern Asapatnâ has its line-marks running parallel to the adjoining cross-spine (south to north), the fifth Asapatnâ has them running from west to east (? as well as from south to north).

drive back, O knower of beings, those unborn!
cheer us with kindly feeling! may we prevail!
drive off our foes!' as the text so the sense.

9. That which is (placed) in front is Agni, and
that behind is Agni: with Agni he (Pragâpati) then
drove away evil both in front and in the rear; and
in like manner now does the Sacrificer with Agni
drive away evil both in front and in the rear.

10. Then on the right (south) side, with (Vâg. S.
XV, 3), 'The sixteenfold Stoma, vigour, wealth!'
The Trish/ubh consists of eleven syllables, and—the
air being of Trish/ubh nature—there are (in the air)
four quarters. The thunderbolt is fifteenfold, and
yonder sun is the sixteenfold wielder of that thunderbolt: with that thunderbolt, with that Trish/ubh,
he (Pragâpati) drove away evil in the south; and in
like manner does the Sacrificer, with that thunderbolt, with that Trish/ubh, now drive away evil in
the south.

11. Then on the left (north) side, with, 'The
forty-four-fold Stoma, lustre, wealth!' The
Trish/ubh consists of forty-four syllables, and the
thunderbolt is of Trish/ubh nature: with that forty-
four-fold thunderbolt, with that Trish/ubh, he (Pragâpati) drove away evil in the north; and in like
manner does the Sacrificer, with that thunderbolt,
with that Trish/ubh, now drive away evil in the north.

12. Then in the middle (the fifth), with, 'Agni's
soil-cover thou art!'—the fourth layer indeed
is the Brahman, and the Brahman is Agni, and this,
the fifth layer is, as it were, the (soil-)cover of that
(fourth layer);—'his sap, in truth: may the All-
gods sing thy praises! Seat thee here, laden
with Stomas, and rich in fat! Gain for us, by

sacrifice, wealth with offspring!' as the text so
the sense.

13. This one he lays down with its line-marks
running eastward and crosswise[1]; for by that one
Pragâpati then cut out the root of evil, and in like
manner does this (Sacrificer) now thereby cut out the
root of evil. On the right (south) side (from the
centre he places it), for the thunderbolt has a string[2]
on the right side :—inside the one in the southern
quarter, for it is for the sake of extension that he
leaves that space.

14. The one which (lies) in front is the out-
breathing, the one at the back the off-breathing :
by the out-breathing he (Pragâpati) then drove away
evil in front, and by the off-breathing in the rear ;
and in like manner does the Sacrificer now by the
out-breathing drive away evil in front, and by the
off-breathing in the rear.

15. And the two on both sides (of the spine) are
the two arms : whatever evil there was sideways of
him, that he drove away with his arms ; and in like
manner does this Sacrificer now drive away with his
arms whatever evil there is sideways of him.

---

[1] That is to say, crosswise, or marked in the opposite direction
to the Asapatnâ brick near it, viz. to the one placed east of the
southern end of the cross-spine which (like all bricks placed between shoulder and thigh) has its line-marks running from south to
north. The fifth Asapatnâ, lying immediately north of that southern
one, thus has its line-marks parallel, not (as one would expect) to
the cross-spine, but to the further removed spine.

[2] This is a doubtful rendering of 'udyâma,' which is accepted by
the St. Petersb. Dict. for 'shad-udyâma,'·at VI, 7, 1, 16, 18 ; whilst
in the present case ' dakshi*n*ata-udyâma' seems to be taken by it to
mean 'southward erected, southward drawn (aufgespannt).' Udyâma, in the sense ' extension,' might mean a protruding part,
serving as a handle.

16. The soil-bedded one[1] means food: whatever evil there was above him, that he (Pragâpati) drove away by means of food: and in like manner does the Sacrificer now, by means of food, drive away whatever evil there is above him.

17. And, verily, whenever he, knowing this, breathes out, he thereby drives away the evil which is in front of him; and when he breathes backward, he thereby (drives away) that which is in the rear; and when he does work with his arms, he thereby (drives away) that which is sideways of him; and when he eats food, he thereby (drives away) that (evil) which is above him: at all times, indeed, even while sleeping, does he who knows this drive away evil. Hence, one must not speak ill of him who knows this, lest one should be his evil (enemy).

SECOND BRÂHMANA.

1. He then lays down those *Kh*andasyâs[2] (relating to the metres). For Pragâpati, having freed himself from evil, death, asked for food; hence, to this day, a sick man, when he gets better, asks for food; and people have hope for him, thinking, 'He asks for food, he will live.' The gods gave him that food, these (bricks) relating to the metres; for the metres are cattle, and cattle are food. They (the metres) pleased him, and inasmuch as they pleased (*kh*and) him they are (called) metres (*kh*andas).

2. He lays them down by tens,—the Virâg consists of ten syllables, and all food is 'virâg'

---

[1] That is, the fifth Asapatnâ, which has a bed or layer of loose soil (purîsha) spread under it.

[2] The *Kh*andasyâ or Virâg bricks are laid down at the end of the spines, ten in each quarter.

(shining, or ruling) : he thus bestows all food on him.
On all (four) sides he places them : from all sides he
thus bestows food on him.

3. [He lays them down, with, Vâg. S. XV, 4. 5],
'The Course metre,'—the 'course' metre, doubtless, is this (terrestrial) world ; — 'the Expanse
metre,'—the 'expanse' metre, doubtless, is the air ;
'the Blissful metre,'—the 'blissful' metre, doubtless, is the sky ;—'the Encircler metre,'—the
'encircler' metre, doubtless, is the regions ;—'the
Vestment metre,'—the 'vestment' metre, doubtless, is food ;—'the Mind metre,'—the 'mind'
metre, doubtless, is Pragâpati ; 'the Extent metre,'
—the 'extent' metre, doubtless, is yonder sun.

4. 'The Stream metre,'—the 'stream' metre,
doubtless, is the breath ;—'the Sea metre,'—the
'sea' metre, doubtless, is the mind ;—'the Flood
metre,'—the 'flood' metre, doubtless, is speech ;—
'the Kakubh (peak) metre,'—the 'Kakubh' metre,
doubtless, is the out (and in)-breathing;—'the Three-
peaked metre,'—the 'three-peaked' metre, doubtless, is the up-breathing ;—'the Wisdom metre,'—
the 'wisdom' metre, doubtless, is the threefold
science ;—'the Arikupa metre,'—the 'Arikupa[1]'
metre, doubtless, is the water;—'the Aksharapankti metre,'—the Aksharapankti (row of syllables) metre, doubtless, is yonder (heavenly) world ;—
'the Padapankti metre,'—the Padapankti (row of
words or steps) metre, doubtless, is this (terrestrial)
world ;—'the Vish/ârapankti metre,'—the Vish-
/ârapankti (row of expansion) metre, doubtless, is the
regions;—'the Bright Razor metre,'—the 'bright

---

[1] A word of doubtful meaning (? drinking its own windings).

razor' metre, doubtless, is yonder sun;—'the Vestment metre, the Investment metre,'—the 'vestment' metre, doubtless, is food, and the 'investment' metre is food.

5. 'The Uniting metre,'—the 'uniting' metre, doubtless, is the night;—'the Separating metre,' —the 'separating' metre, doubtless, is the day;— 'the Brihat metre,'—the 'brihat' (great) metre, doubtless, is yonder world;—'the Rathantara metre,'—the 'rathantara' metre, doubtless, is this world;—'the Troop metre,'—the 'troop' metre, doubtless, is the wind;—'the Yoke metre,'—the 'yoke' metre, doubtless, is the air;—'the Devourer metre,'—the 'devourer' metre, doubtless, is food;— 'the Bright metre,'—the 'bright' metre, doubtless, is the fire;—'the Samstubh metre, the Anush-tubh metre,'—the 'samstubh' metre, doubtless, is speech, and the 'anushtubh' metre is speech;— 'the Course metre, the Expanse metre,'—the meaning of this has been explained.

6. 'The Strength metre,'—the 'strength' metre, doubtless, is food;—'the Strength-maker metre,' the 'strength-maker' metre, doubtless, is Agni (the fire);—'the Striver metre,'—the 'striver' metre, doubtless, is yonder world;—'the Ample metre,'— the 'ample' metre, doubtless, is this world;—'the Cover metre,'—the 'cover' metre, doubtless, is the air;—'the Unclimbable metre,'—the 'unclimbable' metre, doubtless, is yonder sun;—'the Slow metre,' —the 'slow' metre, doubtless, is the Pankti;—'the Ankânka metre,'—the 'ankânka'[1] metre, doubtless, is water.

---

[1] Another word of doubtful meaning (? winding-winding).

7. Now of those which he lays down in front, the first is the out (and in)-breathing, the second the through-breathing, the third the up-breathing, the fourth the up-breathing, the fifth the through-breathing, the sixth the out-breathing, the seventh the out-breathing, the eighth the through-breathing, the ninth the up-breathing, and the tenth, in this case, is the Sacrificer himself: this same Sacrificer, being raised and firmly established on this Virâg (brick), made up of breath, lays down (bricks) extending both backward and forward, for the breathings move both backward and forward.

8. And of those on the right (south) side, the first is Agni (fire), the second Vâyu (the wind), the third Âditya (the sun), the fourth Âditya, the fifth Vâyu, the sixth Agni, the seventh Agni, the eighth Vâyu, the ninth Âditya, and the tenth, in this case, is the Sacrificer himself: this same Sacrificer, being raised and firmly established on this Virâg, made up of deities, puts on (bricks) extending both hitherwards and thitherwards, for those gods move both hitherwards and thitherwards.

9. And of those behind, the first is this (terrestrial) world, the second the air, the third the sky, the fourth the sky, the fifth the air, the sixth this world, the seventh this world, the eighth the air, the ninth the sky, and the tenth, in this case, is the Sacrificer himself: this same Sacrificer, being raised and firmly established on that Virâg, made up of the worlds, lays down (bricks) extending both hitherwards and thitherwards ;—whence these worlds extend both hitherwards and thitherwards.

10. And of those on the left (north) side, the first is the summer, the second the rainy season, the

third the winter, the fourth the winter, the fifth the rainy season, the sixth the summer, the seventh the summer, the eighth the rainy season, the ninth the winter, and the tenth, in this case, is the Sacrificer himself: this same Sacrificer, being raised and firmly established on that Virâg, made up of the seasons, lays down (bricks) extending both hither-wards and thitherwards;—whence those seasons move both hitherwards and thitherwards [1].

11. And, again, those which he lays down in front are the vital airs. There are ten of them, for there are ten vital airs. He places them in the front part, for these vital airs are in the front part.

12. And those on the right (south) side are the deities,—Agni, the Earth, Vâyu, the Air, Âditya, the Sky, Kandra (the moon), the Stars, Food, and Water.

13. And those behind are the regions (quarters),— four regions, four intermediate regions, the upper region, and this (earth).

14. And those on the left (north) side are the months,—two spring-months, two summer-months, two months of the rainy season, two autumn-months, and two winter-months.

15. And, again, the first ten are this (terrestrial) world, the second the air, the third the sky. By the first set of ten they (the gods) ascended this (earth), by the second the air, by the third the sky; and in like manner does the Sacrificer now, by the first set of ten, ascend this (earth), by the second the air, and by the third the sky.

16. This, then, is, as it were, an ascent away from

---

[1] That is to say, they come and go.

here; but this (earth) is the foundation: the gods
came back to this (earth), the foundation; and in like
manner does the Sacrificer now come back to this
(earth), the foundation.   And that last set of ten is
this world: hence, even as (takes place) that start
from the first set of ten, so from the last; for this is
the same,—those two sets of ten (the first and last)
are this (terrestrial) world.

17. Now these are forty bricks and forty formulas,—that makes eighty, and eighty (asîti) means
food[1]: thus whatever he now says that he makes
to be food, asîti, and gives it him, and thereby
gratifies him (Agni).

Third Brâhmana.

1. He then lays down the Stomabhâgâ (praise-
sharing bricks).   For at that time Indra set his
mind upon that food of Pragâpati, and tried to go
from him.   He spake, 'Why dost thou go from me?
why dost thou leave me?'—'Give me the essence
of that food: enter me therewith!'—'So be it!' so
he gave him the essence of that food, and entered
him therewith.

2. Now he who was that Pragâpati is this very
Agni (the fire-altar) that is now being built up; and
that food is these Khandasyâ (bricks); and that
essence of food is these Stomabhâgâs; and he who
was Indra is yonder Âditya (the sun): he indeed is
the Stoma (hymn of praise), for whatsoever praises
they sing, it is him they praise thereby,—it is to
that same Stoma he gave a share; and inasmuch as

---

[1] The author apparently connects 'asîti' with the root 'as,' to eat.

he gave a share (bhâga) to that Stoma, these are
(called) Stomabhâgâs.

3. [He lays them down, with, Vâg. S. XV, 6. 7].
'By the ray quicken thou the truth for truth!'
—the ray, doubtless, is that (sun), and ray is food:
having put together that (sun) and the essence
thereof, he makes it enter his own self;—'by the
starting, by the law, quicken the law!'—the
starting, doubtless, is that (sun), and the starting also
means food: having put together that (sun) and
the essence thereof, he makes it enter his own self;
—'by the going after, by the sky, quicken the
sky!'—the going after, doubtless, is that (sun), and
the going after also means food; having put together
that (sun) and the essence thereof, he makes it enter
his own self. Thus whatever he mentions here,
that and the essence thereof he puts together and
makes it enter his own self: 'By such and such
quicken thou such and such!'—'Such and such
thou art: for such and such (I deposit) thee!'—
'By the lord, by strength, quicken strength!'
thus they (the bricks) are divided into three kinds,
for food is of three kinds.

4. And as to why he lays down the Stomabhâgâs.
Now the gods, having laid down the far-shining
layer, mounted it. They spake, 'Meditate ye!'
whereby, doubtless, they meant to say, 'Seek ye
a layer!' Whilst meditating, they saw even the
firmament, the heavenly world, and laid it down.
Now that same firmament, the heavenly world, indeed is the same as these Stomabhâgâs, and thus
in laying down these, he lays down the firmament,
the heavenly world.

5. The first three (bricks) are this (terrestrial)

world, the second (three) the air, and the third
(three) the sky, the fourth the eastern, the fifth the
southern, the sixth the western, and the seventh the
northern regions.

6. These twenty-one bricks, then, are these
worlds and the regions, and these worlds and the
regions are a foundation, and these worlds and
the regions are twenty-one : whence they say, 'the
Ekaviṃsa (twenty-one-fold) is a foundation.'

7. And the eight bricks which remain over are
the Gâyatrî consisting of eight syllables ; but the
Gâyatrî is the Brahman, and as to that Brahman,
it is yonder burning disk : it burns, while firmly-
established on that twenty-one-fold one, as on
a foundation, whence it does not fall down.

8. Now some lay down a thirtieth (Stomabhâgâ),
with, 'Beautifully arrayed, quicken thou the
kshatra for the kshatra!' saying, 'Of thirty
syllables is the Virâg (metre) and this layer is
virâg (far-shining).' But let him not do so : they
(who do so) exceed (this layer so as not to
be) amounting to the twenty-one-fold, and to the
Gâyatrî ; and that undiminished Virâg, doubtless, is
the world of Indra: in the world of Indra they raise
a spiteful enemy of equal power (to Indra), and
thrust Indra out of the world of Indra. And at his
own sacrifice the Sacrificer assuredly is Indra: in
the Sacrificer's realm they raise for the Sacrificer
a spiteful enemy of equal power, and thrust the
Sacrificer out of the Sacrificer's own realm. But,
surely, that fire which they bring hither is no other
than this Sacrificer: by means of his foundation it
is he who is the thirtieth (brick) in this (layer).

FOURTH BRÂHMANA.

1. He lays them down on the range of the Ashâdhâ; for the Ashâdhâ is speech, and this (set of bricks [1]) is the essence (of food): he thus lays into speech the essence of food; whence it is through (the channel of) speech that one distinguishes the essence of food for all the limbs.

2. And, again, as to why (on the range) of the Ashâdhâ;—the Ashâdhâ, doubtless, is this (earth), and the Stomabhâgâs are yonder sun: he thus establishes yonder sun upon this earth as a firm foundation.

3. And, again, why (on that) of the Ashâdhâ;— the Ashâdhâ, doubtless, is this (earth), and the Stomabhâgâs are the heart: he thus lays into this (earth) the heart, the mind: whence on this (earth) one thinks with the heart, with the mind. He lays them down on every side: he thus places the heart, the mind everywhere; whence everywhere on this (earth) one thinks with the heart, with the mind. And, moreover, these (bricks) are lucky signs: he places them on all sides; whence they say of him who has a (lucky) sign (lakshman) on every (or any) side that he has good luck (punyalakshmika).

4. He then covers them with loose soil: for loose soil (purisha) means food, and this (set of bricks) is the essence (of food): he thus makes it invisible, for invisible, as it were, is the essence of food.

5. And, again, as to why (he covers it) with loose

---

[1] Or, this fire-altar.

soil;—loose soil, doubtless, means food, and this (set of bricks) is the essence: he thus joins and unites the food and its essence.

6. And, again, as to why with loose soil;—the Stomabhâgâs are the heart, and the loose soil is the pericardium: he thus encloses the heart in the pericardium.

7. And, again, as to why with loose soil;—this fire-altar is the year, and by means of the soil-coverings of the layers he divides it: those first four layers are four seasons. And having laid down the Stomabhâgâs, he throws loose soil thereon: that is the fifth layer, that is the fifth season.

8. Here now they say, 'Since the other layers conclude with Lokamprinâs (space-filling bricks), and no space-filler is laid down in this (layer): what, then, is the space-filler therein?' The space-filler, surely, is yonder sun, and this layer is he; and this is of itself[1] a space-filling layer. And what there is above this (layer) up to the covering of soil that is the sixth layer, that is the sixth season.

9. He then throws down the loose soil. Thereon he lays down the Vikarni and the naturally-perforated (brick); he bestrews them with chips of gold, and places the fire thereon: that is the seventh layer, that is the seventh season.

10. But, indeed, there are only six of them; for as to the Vikarni and the Svayam-âtrinnâ, they belong to the sixth layer.

11. And, indeed, there are only five of them,—on the other (layers) he throws down the loose soil with a prayer, and here (he does so) silently: in that

---

[1] Or, and he (the sun) himself.

respect this is not a layer. And the other layers
end with space-fillers, but here he lays down no
space-filler: in that respect also this is not a layer.

12. And, indeed, there are only three of them,—
the first layer is this very (terrestrial) world; and
the uppermost (layer) is the sky; and those three
(intermediate layers) are the air, for there is, as it
were, only one air here: thus (there are) three, or
five, or six, or seven of them.

SIXTH ADHYÂYA. FIRST BRÂHMANA.

1. He lays down the Nâka sads (firmament-seated
bricks): the firmament-seated ones, assuredly, are the
gods. In this (layer) that whole fire-altar becomes
completed, and therein these (bricks are) the firmament (nâka), the world of heaven: it is therein that
the gods seated themselves; and inasmuch as the
gods seated themselves on that firmament, in the
world of heaven, the gods are the firmament-seated.
And in like manner does the Sacrificer, when he lays
down these (bricks), now seat himself on that firmament, in the world of heaven.

2. And, again, why he lays down the Nâkasads.
Now at that time the gods saw that firmament, the
world of heaven, these Stomabhâgâs [1]. They spake,

---

[1] The central portion of the fifth layer is here characterised as
symbolically representing the firmament, the blue canopy of heaven,
and the region of bliss beyond it. The outer rim of this central
structure is formed by a continuous ring of twenty-nine Stomabhâgâ (st) bricks representing, it would seem, the horizon on
which the vault of heaven rests. There is some doubt as to the exact
manner in which this ring of bricks is to be arranged. According
to Kâty. Srautas. XVII, 11, 10, fifteen bricks are to be placed south
(and fourteen north) of the anûka, or spine (running through the

'Think ye upon this, how we may seat ourselves on that firmament, in the world of heaven!' They spake,

centre from west to east). As regards the southern semicircle, the fifteen bricks are to be distributed in such a way that eight fall within the south-easterly, and seven into the south-westerly, quadrant. Some such arrangement as that adopted in the diagram below would seem to be what is intended. It will be seen that this arrangement includes two half-size bricks in the south-easterly

THE CENTRAL PART OF THE FIFTH LAYER.

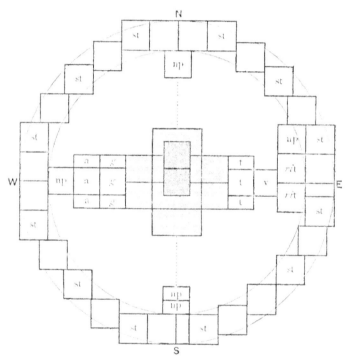

quadrant, the one lying immediately south of the 'spine,' and the other immediately east of the 'cross-spine.' It is an awkward fact, however, that one of the commentators on the Sûtra referred to, states that there are to be two half-foot bricks, (one) on each side of the spine—that is, as would seem, the 'cross-spine.' I cannot but think, however, that this must be a mistake, as otherwise it would seem to make the construction of a continuous ring impossible. Inside this ring, on the adjoining range (viz. the *Rñavyâ*

'Meditate ye! seek ye a layer!' whereby, indeed,
they said, 'Seek ye this, how we may seat ourselves
on this firmament, in the world of heaven!'

3. Whilst meditating, they saw these bricks, the
Nâkasads, and placed them on (the altar): by means
of them they seated themselves on that firmament,
in the world of heaven; and inasmuch as through
them they seated themselves (sad) on that firmament
(nâka), in the world of heaven, these are the Nâka-
sad (bricks): and in like manner does the Sacrificer,
when he lays down these (bricks), now seat himself
on that firmament, in the world of heaven.

range, being the fifth range from the centre, see the diagram of the
first layer, p. 17), five Nâkasads (n) are placed on the spines,
with the exception of the eastern one, which is to be placed in the
second space north of the spine, that is to say, a foot from it (so
as to leave space between it and the spine for the left Ritavyâ;
cf. VIII, 7, 1, 11, with note). In the south two half-sized bricks are
laid down instead of one full-sized one. All these five bricks are of
half the usual thickness so as to allow five others, the Pankakûḍâs
(p), being placed upon them. Of the khandasyâs, or bricks
representing the metres, only three sets (of three bricks each, viz.
a full-sized one flanked on either side by a half-sized one) fall within
the circle formed by the stomabhâgâ-ring, viz. the trishṭubhs (t),
gagatis (g), and anushṭubhs (a). The remaining space in the
centre is now filled up by the Gârhapatya hearth, consisting of
eight bricks. Thereon is placed a second layer of eight bricks
exactly corresponding to the first, and called Punaskiti. This
pile (marked by hatching in the sketch) thus rises above the fifth
layer by the full depth of a brick. He then lays down the two
Ritavyâs (rit) just within the ring on the east side; and the
Visvagyotis (v), representing the sun, immediately west of them.
Having now filled up the available spaces of the layer with
Lokamprinâs, and scattered loose soil on it, he finally lays down
two perforated bricks (marked in the sketch by cross-hatching), the
Vikarnî and the Svayamâtrinnâ, so that the latter lies exactly
in the centre, and the former immediately north of it, over the
'cross-spine.'

4. He places them in the (four) quarters; for that firmament, the world of heaven, is the quarters: he thus establishes them in the world of heaven. On the range of the *Ri*tavyâs (he places them); for the *Ri*tavyâs (seasonal bricks) are the year, and the world of heaven is the year: it is in the world of heaven he thus establishes them. Within the Stomabhâgâs (he places them); for this is the firmament, the world of heaven: it is therein he thus establishes them.

5. In front he lays down one, with (Vâg. S. XV, 10), 'Queen thou art, the Eastern region,' for a queen indeed the eastern region is;—'The divine Vasus are thine overlords [1],' for the divine Vasus are indeed the overlords of that region;—'Agni is the repeller of shafts,' for Agni, indeed, is here the repeller of shafts;—'The Triv*ri*t-Stoma may uphold thee on earth!' for by the threefold hymn(-form) this one is indeed upheld on earth;—'The Âgya-*s*astra may support thee for steadiness' sake [2]!' for by the Âgya-*s*astra it is indeed supported on earth for steadiness' sake;—'the Rathantara-sâman for stability in the air!' for by the Rathantara-sâman it is indeed established in the air;—'May the *Ri*shis, the first-born, magnify [3] thee among the gods!'—the *Ri*shis, the first-born, doubtless, are the vital airs [4], for they are the first-born Brahman [5];—'with the measure, the width of the sky!'—that is, 'as great as the sky is, so much in width may they broaden thee!'—

---

[1] Or, perhaps, 'the Vasus are thy divine overlords;' but see paragraph 9.

[2] Lit. for unwaveringness (so as not to totter).

[3] Lit. broaden, widen.

[4] See VI, 1, 1, 1; VII, 2, 3, 5.   [5] See VI, 1, 1, 8.

'And he, the upholder, and the overlord.'—
these two are speech and mind, for these two uphold
everything here;—'may they all, of one mind,
settle thee, and the Sacrificer, on the back of
the firmament, in the world of heaven!' as the
text, so its import.

6. Then on the right (south) side (he lays down
one [1]), with (Vâg. S. XV, 11), 'Wide-ruling thou
art, the southern region,' for wide-ruling indeed
is that southern region;—'The divine Rudras are
thine overlords,' for the divine Rudras are indeed
the overlords of that region;—'Indra is the repeller
of shafts,' for Indra, indeed, is here the repeller of
shafts;—'The Pañkadasa-stoma may uphold
thee on earth!' for by the fifteenfold hymn it is
indeed upheld on earth;—'The Praüga-sastra
may support thee for steadiness' sake!' for by
the Praüga-sastra it is indeed supported on earth for
steadiness' sake;—'the Brihat-sâman for stability
in the air!' for by the Brihat-sâman it is indeed
established in the air;—'May the Rishis, the
first-born, magnify thee among gods . . .!' the
import of this (and the rest) has been explained.

7. Then behind (he lays down one), with (Vâg. S.
XV, 12), 'All-ruling thou art, the western
region,' for all-ruling indeed is that western region;
—'The divine Âdityas are thine overlords,' for
the divine Âdityas are indeed the overlords of that
region;—'Varuna is the repeller of shafts,' for
Varuna, indeed, is here the repeller of shafts;—
'The Saptadasa-stoma may uphold thee on

---

[1] That is, the southern of the two half-sized ones to be placed in
this quarter.

earth!' for by the seventeenfold hymn it is indeed
upheld on earth;—'The Marutvatîya-sastra may
support thee for steadiness' sake!' for by the
Marutvatîya-sastra it is indeed supported on earth
for steadiness' sake :—'the Vairûpa-sâman for
stability in the air!' for by the Vairûpa-sâman it
is indeed established in the air;—'May the *R*ishis,
the first-born, magnify thee among the gods
...!' the import of this has been explained.

8. Then on the left (north) side (he lays down
one), with (Vâg. S. XV, 13), 'Self-ruling thou art,
the northern region,' for self-ruling that northern
region indeed is;—'The divine Maruts are thine
overlords,' for the divine Maruts are indeed the
overlords of that region;—'Soma is the repeller
of shafts,' for Soma, indeed, is here the repeller of
shafts;—'The Ekavimsa-stoma may uphold
thee on earth!' for by the twenty-one-fold hymn
this one is indeed upheld on earth;—'The Nishkevalya-sastra may support thee for steadiness' sake!' for by the Nishkevalya-sastra it is
indeed supported on earth for steadiness' sake;—
'the Vairâga-sâman for stability in the air!'
for by the Vairâga-sâman it is indeed established in
the air;—'May the *R*ishis, the first-born,
magnify thee among the gods...!' the import
of this has been explained.

9. Then in the middle (he lays down one [1]), with
(Vâg. S. XV, 14), 'The sovereign mistress thou
art, the Great region!' for the sovereign mistress
that great region indeed is;—'the All-gods are

---

[1] That is, he lays down a half-sized brick immediately north of
the southern one, and thus in the direction of the centre from that
brick.

thine overlords,' for the All-gods are indeed the
overlords of that region ;—' Brihaspati is the repeller of shafts,' for Brihaspati, indeed, is here the
repeller of shafts ;—' The Trinava- and Trayastrimsa-stomas may uphold thee on earth ;'—
for by the twenty-nine-fold and thirty-three-fold
hymns this one is indeed upheld on earth ;—' The
Vaisvadeva- and Âgnimâruta-sastras may support thee for steadiness' sake!' for by the Vais-
vadeva- and Âgnimâruta-sastras it is indeed supported
on earth for steadiness' sake ;—' May the Rishis,
the first-born, magnify thee among the gods
. . .!' the import of this has been explained.

10. Thus much, indeed, is the whole sacrifice, and
the sacrifice is the self of the gods : it was after
making the sacrifice their own self that the gods
seated themselves on that firmament, in the world
of heaven ; and in like manner does the Sacrificer
now, after making the sacrifice his own self, seat
himself on that firmament, in the world of heaven.

11. He then lays down the Pañkakûdâ ('five-
knobbed') bricks ; for the Nâkasads are (parts of)
the sacrifice, and so indeed are the Pañkakûdâs the
sacrifice : the Nâkasads are these four sacrificial
priests together with the Sacrificer as the fifth ; and
the Pañkakûdâs are the Hotrâs[1]. Now the Hotrâs
are additional (to the officiating staff, or to the
Hotri) and whatever is additional is an excrescence
(kûda) ; and hence, as they are five additional (bricks),
they are (called) Pañkakûdâs[2].

---

[1] That is, the offices of Hotrakas, or assistants to the Hotri.

[2] These bricks would seem to have had some kind of protuber-
ances or bulgings (kûda), or perhaps tufts, resembling a man's
crest-lock or top-knot (kûdâ). Possibly, however, these five bricks,

12. And, again, as to why he lays down the Nâkasad-Pañkakûdâs;—it is for the sake of completeness; for the Nâkasads are the self, and the Pañkakûdâs the mate, and this, the mate, doubtless, is one half of the self; for when one is with his mate[1], then he is whole and complete.

13. And, again, as to why he lays down the Nâkasad-Pañkakûdâs;—the Nâkasads are the self, and the Pañkakûdâs are offspring (or subjects)[2]. Now progeny is something additional to the self, and whatever is additional is an excrescence; and hence, as they are five additional ones, they are (called) Pañkakûdâs.

14. And, again, as to why he lays down the Nâkasad-Pañkakûdâs;—the Nâkasads are the regions, and the Pañkakûdâs, too, are the regions: what five regions there are on this side of yonder sun, they are the Nâkasads, and those which are on the other side are the Pañkakûdâs. Now those regions which are on the other side of yonder sun are additional, and what is additional is an excrescence (kûda): and hence, as they are five additional ones, they are called Pañkakûdâs.

15. And, again, as to why he lays down the Pañkakûdâs. Now, at that time the gods were afraid lest the fiends, the Rakshas, should destroy

---

being placed on the top of the Nâkasads, are themselves here represented as something additional. Such, at any rate, seems to be the definition of the term given in the text above and in parag. 13. The MS. of the commentary reads, 'kâyasya vai tat pâvargita*m* (!) sa kûdah kesapuñgah.'

[1] This, doubtless, is here the meaning of mithunam; and similarly in I, 7, 2, 11, we ought to translate, 'The vashatkâra is the mate of those two (anuvâkyâ and yâgyâ).'

[2] See paragraph 21.

these worlds of theirs from above.   They put those protectors over these worlds, to wit, those shafts and missiles; and in like manner does the Sacrificer now put those protectors over these worlds, to wit, those shafts and missiles.

16. He places one in front, with (Vâg. S. XV, 15), 'This one in front, the yellow-haired one,'—Agni, no doubt, is in front; and as to his saying of him as (being) 'in front,' it is because they take him out (of the Gârhapatya hearth) towards the front, and attend upon him towards the front[1]; and as to why he calls him yellow-haired, it is because Agni is, as it were, yellow;—'the sun-rayed one,' for Agni's rays are like those of the sun;—'and Rathagritsa and Rathaugas[2], his commander and his chieftain,' the two spring-months are these two;—'and the nymphs Puñgikasthalâ and Kratusthalâ[3],'—'quarter and intermediate quarter,' said Mâhitthi; but army and battle these two are;—'mordacious beasts the shaft, manslaughter the missile,'—inasmuch as they fight in army and battle, those mordacious beasts are the shaft; 'manslaughter the missile,'—inasmuch as they slay one another, manslaughter is the missile;—'to them be homage!' it is to them he pays homage;—'be they gracious unto us!' they are indeed gracious to him;—'he whom we hate, and he who hates us,

---

[1] See p. 3, note 2.

[2] That is, 'skilled in chariot (-fight),' and 'mighty in chariot (-fight).'

[3] The meaning of these names is rather obscure: the symbolical explanations 'army and battle' might seem to point to some such meanings as 'grounded on heaps' and 'grounded on intelligence (or plan).'

him we put into their jaws!' whomsoever he hates, and whoever hates him, him he puts into their jaws. 'N. N. I put into their jaws,' thus he may name him whom he hates, and thereafter he will not be there any more. Let him disregard this also, for indeed marked out of himself is he whom he who knows this hates.

17. Then on the right (south) side (he places one), with (Vâg. S. XV, 16), 'This one on the right, the all-worker,' the all-worker is this Vâyu (the wind) who blows here, for he makes everything here ; and because he speaks of him as (being) 'on the right,' therefore it is in the south that he blows most ; — 'and Rathasvana (chariot-noise) and Rathekitra (glorious on the chariot), his commander and chieftain;' these are the two summer-months ;—'and the two nymphs, Menakâ and Sahaganyâ,'—'quarter and intermediate quarter,' said Mâhitthi ; but these two are heaven and earth;—'Goblins the shaft, demons the missile;' for goblins indeed are here the shaft (weapon), and demons the missile ;—'to them be homage ...!' the import of this has been explained.

18. Then behind (in the west, he lays down a brick), with (Vâg. S. XV, 17), 'This one behind, the all-embracer,'—the all-embracer, doubtless, is yonder sun ; for as soon as he rises all this embracing space comes into existence ; and because he speaks of him as (being) 'behind,' therefore one sees him only when he goes towards the back (west);—'and Rathaprota (fixed on the chariot) and Asama-ratha (of matchless chariot), his commander and chieftain;' these are the two rainy months ;—'and the nymphs Pramlokanti (the setting one) and

Anumlokanti (the rising one),'—'quarter and intermediate quarter,' said Mâhitthi, but they are day and night, for these two set and rise; 'tigers the shaft, snakes the missile,' for indeed tigers are here the shaft, and snakes the missile;—'to them be homage . . .!' the import of this has been explained.

19. Then on the left (north) side (he places one), with (Vâg. S. XV, 17), 'This one on the left, of everflowing blessings;' on the left is the sacrifice; and as to why he speaks of it as 'on the left,' it is because the sacrifice is performed from the left (north) side; and as to why he speaks of it as 'of ever-flowing blessings (samyadvasu),' they do indeed flow together (samyanti) to the sacrifice, thinking, 'this is a blessing;'—'and Târkshya and Arishtanemi, his commander and chieftain,' these are the two autumn-months; 'and the nymphs Visvâki (the all-inclined) and Ghritâki (the ghee-inclined),'—'quarter and intermediate quarter,' said Mâhitthi, but they are the vedi (altar) and the offering-spoon, for the altar is all-inclined [1], and the offering-spoon is ghee-inclined;—'water the shaft, wind the missile,'—water indeed is here the shaft, and wind the missile, for from this side it blows hot, and from that side cold;—'to them be homage . . .!' the import of this has been explained.

20. Then in the middle (he lays down one), with (Vâg. S. XV, 19), 'This one above, the boon-bestower [2],' the one above, doubtless, is Parganya (the rain-god); and when he speaks of him as (being)

---

[1] That is, extending in every direction, or open (common) to all.

[2] Lit. 'he whose boons are (bestowed) hitherwards.'

'above,' it is because Parganya is indeed above; and
when he calls him the boon-bestower, it is because
from there the boon, rain, food for creatures, is
bestowed hitherwards;—'and Senagit (the con-
queror of armies) and Sushena (leader of a fine
army), his commander and chieftain,' these are
the two winter-months;—'and the nymphs,
Urvasî and Pûrvaskitti,'—'quarter and intermediate quarter,' said Mâhitthi, but they are oblation
and dakshinâ (priest's sacrificial fee);—'thunder
the shaft, lightning the missile,' for indeed
thunder is here the shaft, and lightning the
missile;—'to them be homage . . .!' the import
of this has been explained.

21. These, then, are the shafts and missiles which
the gods then put as protectors over these worlds,
and as to offspring (or subjects [1]), they are the commander and chieftain; and as to the mates, they are
those nymphs,—having thus become complete with
offspring and with mates, the gods seated themselves
on that firmament, in the world of heaven; and in
like manner does the Sacrificer, having become complete with offspring and a mate, now seat himself on
that firmament, in the world of heaven.

22. Now, these are ten (Nâkasad-Pañkakûdâ)
bricks he lays down;—of ten syllables the Virâg
consists, and this layer is virâg (far-shining). There
are, however, only five of them, for he lays them
down by two and two. And, verily, they are
prayers for prosperity to Agni (the fire-altar). He
places them in the last layer, for this, the last, layer
is the end of Agni: it is thus at the end that he

---

[1] See paragraph 13.

pronounces the prayers for prosperity to Agni.
There are five of them, for at the sacrifice there are
five prayers for prosperity [1].   Between (each) two he
throws loose soil, for these two bricks being fires, he
does so fearing lest these two fires should blaze up
together.   And, moreover, loose soil means food : it
is thus by means of food that he brings about
concord between them.

23. Now, then, as to the order of proceeding.
Having laid down (a brick) in front, he lays down
those on the right, behind, on the left, and in the
middle.   Then the upper ones: having first laid
down one in front, he lays down those on the right,
on the left, in the middle, and behind.   And, indeed,
the world of heaven is entered from below, for the
gods, having at that time, closed up these worlds
on all sides, entered the world of heaven from below ;
and in like manner does the Sacrificer now, having
closed up these worlds on all sides, enter the world
of heaven from below.

SECOND BRÂHMANA.

1. He lays down *Khandasyâs* [2] (bricks pertaining
to the metres).   Completed now was the entire

---

[1] Viz. for long life, offspring, cattle, social distinction, and a seat
in heaven ;—see the Sûktavâka I. 9, 1, 12 seqq.

[2] The *Khandasyâs* represent the principal metres, the formulas
used in laying down the bricks being composed in the respective
metres.   They consist of ten sets of three bricks each, representing
the ten metres, and an additional (thirty-first) brick representing
the Atikhandas, or redundant metre.   Each of the ten sets consists
of a central brick of full size (a foot square) placed on one of the
two spines, and flanked on the two sides not in contact with the
spines by two half-size bricks, viz. :—1. gâyatrî at the east end of
the 'spine'; 2. trishtubh on the Retahsik range (joining the

Agni (fire-altar). He now wished for distinction[1];
for, indeed, heretofore he was not equal thereto, that
he should sustain distinction; whence people here
say even to this day, 'This one is not equal to
sustain distinction, either in regard to kingship or
to headmanship.' The gods bestowed on him this
distinction, these *Khandasyás*; for the metres
(*Khandas*) are cattle, and cattle are food, and (a
position of) distinction is food.

2. He lays down triplets, for the beast is threefold—father, mother, son; and, embryo, amnion,
chorion; and food also is threefold—ploughing, rain,
seed. One of them is an Ati*khandas*[2] (excessive
metre); for even whilst being one, that one is beyond
all the metres. And as to that distinction, it is this
great hymn of praise[3]; and as to this great hymn of
praise, it is these *Khandasyás*.

Gârhapatya on the front, or east, side); 3. *gagatî*, on the Reta*hsik*
range (joining the Gârhapatya on the west side); 4. anush/ubh,
immediately behind (west) of the preceding set; 5. b*rî*hatî, immediately in front (east) of the Ashâ*dhâ* range (on which the ring of
Stomabhâgâs lies); 6. ush*ni*h, immediately behind (west of) the
Gâyatrîs; 7. kakubh, immediately in front of the b*rî*hatî bricks;
8. pankti, at the right (south) end of the 'cross-spine'; 9. padapankti, at the left (north) end of the 'cross-spine'; 10. the single
ati*khandas*, immediately in front (east) of the fifth Asapatnâ (see
p. 84, note 1); 11. (three) dvipadâ at the back, or west, end of
the 'spine.'

[1] That is, a position of honour, or dignity (*srî*).

[2] By the metres, here and in the sequel, we have to understand
bricks laid down with verses of the respective metres (Vâg. S. XV,
20 seq.).

[3] That is, the so-called Great Litany (mahad uktham) recited,
by the Hot*ri*, in response to the Mahâvrata-sâman, or Chant of the
Great Rite, at the midday service of the last but one day—the
so-called Mahâvrata day—of the sacrificial session called 'Gavâm
ayanam,' or 'cows' walk.' The Great Litany consists of numerous

3. Gâyatrî verses are the head thereof, Trishtubh verses the body, Gagatî verses the spine, and Pankti verses the wings; and of each of those Kakubh verses he takes four syllables[1], and adds them to

hymns, and some detached verses and prose formulas; the whole matter recited being stated to amount to as many syllables as would make up a thousand Brihatî verses (of thirty-six syllables each)—or 36,000 syllables in all.   From an analysis I have made of the Mahad uktham (or Brihad uktham, as it is also called) as contained in MS. Ind. Off. 1729 D, I find it very difficult to check the accuracy of this statement; my own calculation yielding somewhere about 37,200 syllables.   By leaving out of account the prose formulas, as well as certain repetitions, this gross amount might, however, be reduced to something approximating the stated number of syllables; and, indeed, the calculation was probably not meant to be a strictly accurate one.   Cf. II, 3, 3, 19, 20 (where read Litany, instead of Chant), part ii, p. 430.   See also IX, 1, 1, 44; 3, 3, 19; 5, 2, 12.

[1] The three Kakubh verses (Vâg. S. XV, 38–40) consist each of three pâdas, of eight, twelve, and eight syllables respectively, making together twenty-eight syllables.   In muttering these verses, whilst laying down the Kakubh bricks, he is to omit four syllables from the middle pâda of each verse (so as to make it equal to the other two pâdas), and mutter the words thus omitted at the beginning of the verse (XV, 47) used in laying down the Atikhandas brick.   The syllables omitted make up complete words in each case, viz. 'bhadrâ râtih' at the beginning of the middle pâda of the first verse, 'vritra-tûrye' at the end of the middle pâda of the second verse, and 'ava sthirâ' at the beginning of the second pâda of the third verse. The remaining portions of the Kakubh verses consist each of twenty-four syllables, or a Gâyatrî verse.   The references here made to the different parts of the Mahad uktham are not quite clear, and seem to point to a somewhat different arrangement of that sastra from that known from the Aitareyâranyaka and the Sânkhâyana-sûtra.   The head, indeed, consists of Gâyatrî verses, viz. Rig-veda I, 7, either the whole, or, according to some, only certain verses of it; the first three, or nine, verses also forming the opening triplet, or triplets, of the Mahâvrata-sâman, the chanting of which precedes the recitation of the Great Litany.— For the trunk (âtman) consisting of trishtubh verses, see p. 113, note 1. The Pankti verses, on the other hand, said to form the wings, would seem to be Rig-veda VIII, 40 (consisting of mahâpanktis),

the Ati*kh*andas: that is just (what makes) that
Ati*kh*andas (excessive metre). The others result in
Gâyatrîs: this is just that fourscore of Gâyatrîs[1],
the B*ri*hatîs (make up) the Bârhata one, and the
Ush*n*ihs the Aush*n*iha one. And as to the Va*s*a
hymn[2], the two half-verses, the Aindrâgna (hymn),
and the insertion, they are Ati*kh*andas; and as to

---

which in the Aitareya arrangement forms the thighs, whilst *S*ânkhâ-
yana makes it part of the tail; and the *G*agatîs here referred to as
constituting the spine would seem to be X, 50, which immediately
follows the hymn just referred to, and is not otherwise identified
with any special part of the body. The MSS. of Harisvâmin's
commentary are unfortunately hopelessly corrupt in this place.

[1] The Great Litany begins with seven sets of hymns and verses,
meant symbolically to represent certain parts of Agni-Pra*g*âpati's
bird-shaped body which the ceremony is intended to reconstruct,
viz. the trunk, neck, head, the roots (sinews) of the wings, the right
and left wings, and the tail, between each two of which the so-called
Sûdadohas verse (*R*ig-veda VIII, 69, 3), meant to represent the vital
air pervading the body, is inserted, as it also is between (and before)
the succeeding parts. In the first place there follow three eighties
of triplets (or, 3 sets of 240 verses each) in the Gâyatrî, B*ri*hatî
and Ush*n*ih metres respectively. Then comes the Va*s*a hymn
representing the belly, and finally a course of recitations (beginning
with hymn VIII, 40) forming the thighs. For the part which the
number eighty plays in the Agni*k*ayana ceremony, see Weber, Ind.
Stud. XIII, p. 167. The term for 'eighty,' viz. 'a*s*îti,' gives rise to
a constant etymological play. Sâya*n*a, on Aitareyâra*n*yaka I, 4, 3, 1,
takes it in the sense of 'food' (cf. above, VIII, 5, 2, 17); whilst the
Âra*n*yaka itself takes it in that of 'obtainment':—yad evâsmin
loke ya*s*o, yan maho, yan mithuna*m*, yad annâdya*m*, yâ 'pa*k*tis tad
a*s*navai, tad âpnavâni, tad avaru*n*adhai, tan me 'sad iti.

[2] This is the hymn *R*ig-veda VIII, 46, ascribed to Va*s*a A*s*vya,
and remarkable for the variety of metres in which the different
verses are composed. In the Aitareya recension of the Maha*d*
uktham (which is followed in the MS. of this *s*astra referred to in
the preceding notes) only the first twenty verses are recited, but
verse 15 being divided into two verses, a dvipadâ and an ekapadâ,
they are thus made to consist of twenty-one verses.

the Nada-verse[1], the Sûdadohas, the pâda-appen-
dages, and whatever Anush/ubh matter there is,
they make up the Anush/ubhs.

4. Dvipadâ verses are the feet. Thus much is
the great hymn of praise, and the great hymn of
praise means distinction : the gods bestowed upon
him (Agni) all that distinction, and so does this
(Sacrificer) bestow upon him all that distinction.

5. And, again, as to why he lays down the Khandasyâs. The gods at that time saw that firmament,
the world of heaven, to wit, those Stomabhâgâs, and
entered it. Of those entering, Pragâpati entered

---

[1] The Nada-verse, Rig-veda VIII, 69, 2 (in the ushnih metre)
deriving its name from its first word 'nadam,' plays a peculiar
part in the recitation of the Great Litany. The opening set of
recitations, representing the trunk, consists of twenty-two trish/ubh
verses : these are recited in such a way that after each pâda (or
quarter of a verse) one of the four pâdas of the Nada-verse is
inserted. The chief object of this insertion seems to be a metrical
one, viz. that of making each two pâdas (trish/ubh = eleven, and
ushnih = seven syllables) to form half a brihati verse (eighteen
syllables), the whole Litany being computed by brihati verses.
Moreover, of v. 3 of the first Trish/ubh hymn of this set (Rig-veda
X, 120) only the first two pâdas are recited at this stage (whilst the
remaining two are recited in different places later on), and this
half-verse is followed by a brihati and a satobrihati pâda (VII, 32,
23 c, and VI, 46, 2 c), after which the recitation proceeds with
verse 4 of the first hymn. This seems to account for one of the two
half-verses here referred to, whilst the other would seem to be
VII, 20, 1 a, b, recited later on in the sastra. Cf. Prof. F. Max
Müller's translation of Aitareyâr., Sacred Books of the East, vol. i,
p. 181 seqq.—The Aindrâgna hymn is VIII, 40, 1–9 ; 11 ; 12, being
the first hymn of the portion representing the thighs. It consists of
ten mahâpankti verses (6 × 8 syllables)— each of which is split up
into two Gâyatri verses (3 × 8 syllables)— and one trish/ubh verse.—
The chief anush/ubh verses are those of Rig-veda I, 11, 1–8, which
are recited in a peculiar way (towards the end of the sastra), the last
pâda of each verse interchanging with the first pâda of the next verse.

last; and thus Pragâpati is the same as these *Khandasyâs*.

6. Gâyatrîs are his head; and as to its being Gâyatrîs, it is because the head is of Gâyatri nature[1]. There are three, for the head is threefold. He places them on the forepart (of the altar), for the head (of the animal or bird) is in front.

7. Trish/ubhs are the chest: he places them on the range of the two Reta/sik; for the Reta/sik are the ribs, and the ribs lie against the chest.

8. *Gagatis* are the hips; at whatever distance from the naturally-perforated (central) brick he places the Trish/ubhs in front, at the same distance from it he places the *Gagatis* behind; for that naturally-perforated brick is this vital air in the middle (of the body), and as far from that vital air as the chest is in front, so far are the hips behind.

9. Anush/ubhs are the thighs: he places them close to the *Gagatis*, and thereby places the thighs close to the hips.

10. B*ri*hatis are the ribs, Kakubhs the breast-bone. The B*ri*hatis he places between the Trish/ubhs and Kakubhs, whence these ribs are fastened on both sides, on the breast-bone and the costal cartilages[2].

11. Ush/ihs are the neck: he places them close to the Gâyatris, and thereby places the neck close to the head.

12. Pańktis are the wings: and as to their being

---

[1] Either because the Gâyatri is the foremost and noblest of metres (whence its symbolical connection with the priestly office and caste), and the one used for the first stoma at the Soma-sacrifice; or on account of its being best adapted for singing. For the threefold nature of the head, as consisting of skin, bone, and brain, see XII, 2, 4, 9.

[2] That is, on both sides of the chest; see XII, 2, 4, 11, with note.

Panktis, it is because the wings are of Pankti (five-fold) nature. He places them sideways, for these wings are sideways. Whatever metre is larger that he places on the right side: he thus makes the right half of the animal the stronger, and hence the right side of an animal is the stronger.

13. An Atikhandas is the belly; for the metres are cattle, and cattle are food, and food is (what fills) the belly, because it is the belly that eats the food: hence when the belly gets the food, it becomes eaten and used up. And inasmuch as this (brick) eats (atti) the metres (khandas), the cattle, it is called Attikhandas, for Attikhandas is really what is mystically called Atikhandas; for the gods love the mystic.

14. A (brick) covered with loose soil is the womb. These two he lays close to each other, for the belly and the womb are close to each other. They are connected with loose soil, for loose soil means flesh, and both the belly and the womb are connected with flesh. The former is an Atikhandas, the latter a soil-bedded one (purishavati), for the belly is higher, and the womb lower.

15. He places them so as to extend eastwards, for in an easterly direction [1] this Agni (fire-altar) is built; and, moreover, in one moving forward, both the belly and the womb are moving forward. Out-side the Stomabhâgâs (he places them), for the Stomabhâgâs are the heart, and the heart is highest, then (comes) the belly, then the womb.

16. He places them south of the naturally-per-forated (brick). Now, in the first layer, he places

---

[1] Or, as one tending (flying) eastwards.

both the belly and the womb north of the naturally-perforated one [1]; for that naturally-perforated one, indeed, is what this vital air in the middle (of the body) is: he thus places the belly and the womb on both sides of that (central) vital air, and hence the belly and the womb are on both sides of that central vital air.

17. The Dvipadâs are the feet (the stand);—and as to its being Dvipadâs (verses of two feet), it is because the feet are a pair. There are three (such verses), for a stand [2] (tripod) is threefold. He lays them down at the back, for the feet are at the back (of the body).

18. That body of his (Agni) is well-made;—and, indeed, for whomsoever they thus make that body of his so as to be well-made, he becomes possessed of that body of his as a well-made one; but for whomsoever they make it otherwise than that, for him they make that body of his so as to be ill-made, and he becomes possessed of an ill-made body.

19. It is with reference to this that these two sâma-nidhanas (finales of sâman-hymns) are uttered, —'The light (is) in the highest heaven of the gods,' and, 'The gods (are) in the highest heaven of the

---

[1] According to VII. 5, 1, 38, the fire-pan is supposed to represent the belly, and the mortar the yoni; and these two were, in the first layer, placed north of the svayam-âtriṇnâ, or naturally-perforated brick, so as to leave the space of a full brick between them and that central brick of the layer; cf. VII, 5, 1, 13. In the sketch of the central part of the first layer (p. 17), the two northernmost bricks, marked p, represent the fire-pan and mortar.

[2] That is, the feet and back part of the body, or the tail, the latter, in a sitting bird, forming, as it were, a third foot or support to the body.

light;'—for when on that occasion the gods were
entering (heaven), Pragâpati was the last to enter:
that is why he says, 'The light (is) in the highest
heaven of the gods.' And as to why he says, 'The
gods (are) in the highest heaven of light,'—the light,
doubtless, is this Agni (the fire-altar), and it is on
his highest layer that all the gods have thus entered:
this is why he says, 'The gods are in the highest
heaven of light.'

THIRD BRÂHMANA.

1. He lays down the Gârhapatya. For the
gods, having obtained this much, thought they had
succeeded. They spake, 'Whereby have we succeeded in this?'—'By means of the Gârhapatya,'
they said; 'for, after building the Gârhapatya [1] and
mounting thereon, we saw the first layer, from the
first (we saw) the second, from the second the third,
from the third the fourth, from the fourth the fifth,
and from the fifth this one.'

2. They spake, 'Think ye upon this, how there
may be success here for us!' They spake, 'Meditate ye (kit)!' whereby, indeed, they meant to say,
'Seek ye a layer (kiti)! seek ye whereby there may
be success here for us!'

3. Whilst meditating, they said this: 'Let us
bring this one here and put it on (the fire-altar)!'
Having brought this (Gârhapatya) here, they put it

---

[1] For the building of the separate Gârhapatya hearth, on which
the sacred fire was transferred from the Ukhâ (fire-pan), see part iii.
p. 298 seq.; its sketch, p. 302. A similar hearth is now built on
the fifth layer of the Âhavanîya fire-altar.

on. They disputed about it:—in the front part (of the fifth layer) the Vasus, on the right side the Rudras, on the hind part the Âdityas, on the left side the Maruts, and above it the Visve Devâs said, 'Here let us lay it down! here let us lay it down!'

4. They spake, 'Let us lay it down in the middle: when laid down in our midst, it will belong to all of us.' They laid it down in the middle (of the fifth layer), and thus they laid that success into the self (or the body of the altar);—in the middle (they laid it): they thus laid that success into the very middle of (Agni's and their own) self. And in like manner does the Sacrificer, when he lays down the Gârhapatya, lay that success into (his own) self; and (by laying it down) in the middle, he lays that success into the very middle of the self.

5. And, again, as to why he lays down the Gârhapatya. The Gârhapatya, doubtless, is food, and this built Agni is an eater: it is to the eater he thus offers that food;—in the centre (he lays down the Gârhapatya): in the very middle (of the body) he thus lays food into him.

6. And, again, as to why he lays down the Gârhapatya. The world of the gods, doubtless, is the Vedi (altar-ground); but that (original Gârhapatya) is built up outside the Vedi: thus, when he brings it here and lays it down (on the fire-altar), he then establishes it (or him, Agni) on the Vedi, in the world of the gods.

7. And, again, as to why he lays down the Gârhapatya. The lotus-leaf[1], doubtless, is a womb, but

---

[1] For the lotus-leaf, which is the first thing laid down in the centre

that (Gârhapatya) is built up outside the womb, and outside of the womb indeed takes place that performance regarding the fire-altar which takes place prior to the (laying down of the) lotus-leaf: thus, when they bring it (the Gârhapatya) here and lay it down, he then establishes it in the womb, on the lotus-leaf; and thus indeed it is not outside. Eight bricks he lays down : the significance of this has been explained[1]. He builds it up with the same formulas and in the same order, for this one is the same as that (former Gârhapatya Agni) : he thus brings it (or him) here and lays it down.

8. He then lays down the Punaskiti[2]. Now at that time the gods, having built the Gârhapatya, did not find success therein ; for the Gârhapatya pile is a womb, and success in a womb consists in seed, in generative power ; and in this womb they saw no seed, no generative power.

9. They spake, ' Think ye upon this, how we may lay seed and generative power into this womb!' They spake, 'Meditate ye!' whereby, indeed, they meant to say, 'Seek ye a layer! seek ye that we may lay seed and generative power into this womb!'

10. Whilst meditating, they saw this Punaskiti, and put it on (the Gârhapatya), and thereby laid seed and generative power into this womb ;—in the centre (they placed it) : they thus laid seed and

of the altar-site on which the (Âhavaniya) altar is to be raised, see VII, 4, 1, 7 seqq. The Gârhapatya had been built previous to that (VII, 1, 1, 1 seqq.).

[1] See VII, 1, 1, 19 seqq.

[2] The Punaskiti (re-piling) is a second pile or layer of eight bricks corresponding exactly to the first, and placed thereon.

generative power into the very middle of this womb.
And in like manner does the Sacrificer now, when
he lays down the Punaskiti, lay seed and generative
power into this womb;—in the centre (he lays it
down): he thus lays seed and generative power into
the very middle of this womb.

11. Now some lay it down on the hind part (of
the bird-like altar), because it is from the hind part
that seed is introduced,—(to wit) on the juncture of
the tail (and the body), for it is from (the part near)
the tail that seed is introduced. Let him not do
this, for they who do this lay seed and generative
power outside the womb; but let him rather place
it in the centre: he thus lays seed and generative
power right into the womb.

12. He lays down eight bricks,— the Gâyatri
(metre) consists of eight syllables, and Agni (the
fire-altar) is of Gâyatri nature: as great as Agni is,
as great as is his measure, so great he thus introduces him in the form of seed. Five times he 'settles'
it,— of five layers consists the fire-altar, five seasons
make a year, and Agni is the year: as great as Agni
is, as great as is his measure, by so much he thus
introduces him in the form of seed. Eight bricks he
'settles' five times, that makes thirteen,—thirteen
months make a year, and there are thirteen 'layer-
fillings' of the altar: as great as Agni is, as great
as is his measure, so great he thus becomes.

13. And as to why he lays down the Punaskiti.
Now, in laying down the Gârhapatya (hearth) upon
the Âhavanîya, he surely does what is improper;
but when he lays down the Punaskiti he thereby
brings this Agni (or altar) that has been built, and
builds it up again thereon; and because he again

(punas) builds up (*ki*) that (Agni) already built, therefore (this is called) Puna*ski*ti.

14. Now some lay down the Gârhapatya on the hind part, and the Puna*ski*ti on the front part (of the built altar), for these two are the Âhavanîya and the Gârhapatya, and these two fires are (placed) in this way[1]. Let him not do this, for the Gârhapatya is this (terrestrial) world, and the Âhavanîya is the sky; and above this (earth) surely is yonder (sky); let him therefore place it (the Puna*ski*ti) on the top of that (Gârhapatya).

15. And as to why he lays down both the Gârhapatya and the Puna*ski*ti. These two, doubtless, are the Vedi and the Uttaravedi (high-altar) of Agni. Now those two former (altars of this kind) which he throws up[2] belong to the Soma-sacrifice, but these belong to the fire-altar; and when, after laying down these two, he deposits Agni (the fire) thereon, then he establishes him both on the Vedi and the Uttaravedi.

16. And, again, as to why he lays down the Puna*ski*ti. This, doubtless, is a repeated sacrifice (punaryag*ñ*a), and higher (than the ordinary sacrifice) is this worship of the gods: he thus sets up a repeated sacrifice, and the higher worship of the gods; and the repeated sacrifice inclines (accrues) to him.

17. And, again, as to why he lays down the

---

[1] In the ordinary sacrifices the Gârhapatya hearth is placed behind (west of), and the Âhavanîya on the front (or east) end of, the Vedi.

[2] That is, at the performance of an ordinary Soma-sacrifice. For the vedi and uttaravedi on that occasion, see III, 5, 1, 1 seqq.; 12 seqq. (part ii. p. 111 seqq.)

Punaskiti. This (altar), doubtless, is that same Agni whom in the beginning the vital airs, the Rishis, made up[1]. He now builds him up again; and inasmuch as he again (punas) builds up (ki) that (Agni) already built, therefore also it is (called) Punaskiti.

18. [He lays down the first brick, with, Vâg. S. XV, 49], 'With what fervour the Rishis entered upon the sacrificial session,'—he thereby means those Rishis (the vital airs);—'kindling the fire and gaining the light,'—that is, 'kindling the fire, and gaining the heavenly world;'—'upon that firmament I place the Fire,'—the firmament, doubtless, is the heavenly world;—'whom thinkers call the straw-spreader,'—the thinkers (or men) are they who are wise; and 'straw-spreader' he says, because he (Agni) has ever the (sacrificial) straw spread for him.

19. [The second brick, with, Vâg. S. XV, 50], 'With our wives let us follow him, O gods! with our sons and brothers, or our golden treasures;'—that is, 'let us follow him with our all;'—'gaining the firmament in the world of righteousness;'—the firmament, doubtless, is the heavenly world: thus, 'gaining the heavenly world in the world of righteousness;'—'above the third luminous back of the sky,'—for this, indeed, is the third luminous back of the sky where this (Agni) now burns[2].

---

[1] See part iii, p. 143.

[2] That is, on this altar where the fire will soon be burning. It seems also to refer to the sun burning over the third heaven—as the counterpart of the Agni of the fire-altar.

20. [The third brick, with, Vâg. S. XV, 51], 'Unto the centre of speech did he mount, the nimble,'—for this, indeed, is the centre of speech where he now is built up; and 'the nimble (bhuranyu),' that is, 'the sustainer [1] (bhartar);'—'this Agni, the good lord, the heedful,'—that is, 'this Agni, the lord of the good, the heeding one;'—'established upon the back of the earth, he the brilliant,'——that is, 'established on the back of the earth, the shining one;'—'let him tread under foot any hostile!'—that is, 'let him tread under foot all evildoers.'

21. [The fourth brick, with, Vâg. S. XV, 52], 'This Agni, the most mettlesome bestower of strength,'—that is, 'the most vigorous bestower of strength;'—'may he glow a thousandfold, unremitting,'—that is, 'may he shine a thousand-fold, not unheedful;'—'blazing in the middle of the sea,'—the sea, doubtless, means these worlds: thus, 'shining in these worlds;'—'go forth to the divine abodes!'—that is, 'go forth to the heavenly world!'

22. [The fifth brick, with, Vâg. S. XV, 53], 'Gather ye together! draw ye nigh together!'—he thereby says to those Rishis, 'Gather ye him together! draw ye nigh to him together!'—'Make ye Agni's [2] paths to lead to the gods!'—as the text so the meaning;—'making the parents

---

[1] That is, the sustainer of the world (gagad-bhartar), according to Mahîdhara; an etymological play on the word 'bhuranyu.'

[2] The texts have 'agne,' O Agni! the verbal form 'krinu-dhvam' being explained by Mahîdhara as an irregular singular form for 'krinu,' (make thou). The verse seems, however, corrupt.

young again,'—the young parents, doubtless, are
speech and mind, and these two fires also are
speech and mind ;—'in thee hath he spun
out this thread,'—he thereby means that thread
(of the sacrifice) which has been spun out by the
*R*ishis.

23. [The sixth brick, with, Vâg. S. XV, 54],
'Awake, O Agni, and be watchful!'—he thereby
says to this Agni, ' Wake thou over this one[1], and
watch thou over him!'—'Wish and fulfilment,
meet ye and he together[2]!'—as the text, so
the meaning ;—'Upon this, the higher seat,'—
the higher seat, doubtless, is the sky ;—'sit ye
down, O All-gods, and the Sacrificer!'—he
thereby makes the Sacrificer sit down together with
the Vi*s*ve Devâs.

24. [The seventh brick, with, Vâg. S. XV, 55],
'Whereby thou carriest a thousand, whereby,
O Agni, all wealth,'—for that, indeed, is his most
acceptable power whereby he carries a thousand,
and all wealth ;—'thereby lead thou this sacrifice of ours unto the light to go to the gods!'
—that is, 'thereby lead thou this our sacrifice to
the heavenly world to go to the gods.'—[The eighth
brick, with, Vâg. S. XV, 56], ' This is thy natural
womb . . .;'—the meaning of this has been ex-

---

[1] The author (not Mahîdhara) seems rather to take ' udbu-
dhyasva' in a transitive sense ('wake thou him'), as Mahîdhara
certainly does the second imperative ' pratigâg*ri*hi,' 'make him
(the Sacrificer) careful!'

[2] The text has the 2nd person dual, which Mahîdhara explains
by the 3rd dual (yagamânena saha sa*m*sr*ish*/e bhavatâm—' May
the two become united with the Sacrificer '), because of the nomi-
native ' ish/âpûrve,' instead of the vocative.

plained[1]. Eight bricks he lays down : the meaning
of this also has been explained[2].

SEVENTH ADHYÂYA. FIRST BRÂHMANA.

1. He lays down two *Ri*tavyâ (seasonal bricks).
The seasonal (bricks) are the same as these seasons :
it is the seasons he thereby lays down. And, indeed, the seasonal ones are everything here, for the
seasonal ones are the year, and the year is everything here : he thus lays down everything here.
And generative power they also are,—for the
seasonal ones are the year, and the year means
generative power : it is generative power he thus
lays down (or bestows on Agni and the Sacrificer).

2. And, again, as to why he lays down seasonal
(bricks),—the seasonal (ones) are the nobility and
these other bricks are the peasantry : he thus
places the nobility as the eater among the peasantry.
He lays down (some of) them in all the layers : he
thus places the nobility as the eater among the
whole people[3].

3. And, again, as to why he lays down seasonal
(bricks),—this fire-altar is the year, and it is joined
together by means of the seasonal (bricks) : he thus
makes the year continuous, and joins it together, by
means of the seasons. These (formulas of the
seasonal bricks) begin in a different way, but end
in the same way ; for the seasons were created, and,
when created, they were different.

4. They spake, ' While being thus, we shall not be

---

[1] Viz. VII, 1, 1, 28. [2] Viz. VII, 1, 1, 32.
[3] Or, he places the chieftaincy in every clan.

able to procreate : let us unite with our forms!'
They united in each single season with their forms,
whence there is in each single season the form of all
the seasons.   As to their (formulas) beginning in
a different way, it is because they were created
different (or separately) ; and as to their ending in
the same way, it is because they united with their
forms.

5. He lays them down, with (Vâg. S. XV, 57),
'Tapa and Tapasya, the two dewy seasons,'—
these are the names of these two : it is thus by their
names that he lays them down.   Tapa (the burner),
doubtless, is yonder sun : from him these two
seasons are not separated ; and inasmuch as these
two seasons are not separated from him, they are
called Tapa and Tapasya.

6. 'Agni's coupling-link thou art,'—this fire-
altar is the year, and it is joined together by means
of the seasonal (bricks) : he thus makes the year
continuous, and joins it together by means of the
seasons ;—' May Heaven and earth fit into one
another! may the waters and plants fit into
each other!'—he thereby makes everything here [1]
to fit in by means of the seasons :—' May the fires
fit into one another, each singly, working
harmoniously together for my supremacy!'—
for these single bricks are the same as those fires :
he thus says this so that they may fit in with each
other for the supremacy of those two seasons ;—
'whatever fires there are, at one with each
other, within these two, Heaven and Earth;'—
as the text is, so is its meaning ;—' let them draw

---

[1] Or, all this universe.

together, fitting in with the two dewy seasons,
even as the gods draw together unto Indra;'—
that is, 'even as the gods are drawing together
round Indra, so may they draw together for
supremacy round these two seasons.' Two bricks
there are, because the season consists of two
months. Only once he 'settles' them: he thereby
makes the season to be one.

7. And as to why he now lays down these two;—
this fire-altar is the year, and the year is these
worlds: the fifth layer of this (altar) is the sky,
and the dewy season of this (year) is the sky; and
when he now lays down these two (bricks), he
thereby restores to his (Agni's) body what these two
are thereto: this is why he now lays down these
two (bricks).

8. And, again, as to why he now lays down these
two;—this Agni (the fire-altar) is Pragâpati (the
lord of generation), and Pragâpati is the year: the
fifth layer is his (Agni's) head, and the dewy season
is its (the year's) head; and when he now lays down
these two (bricks), he thereby restores to his (or its)
body what these two are thereto: this is why he
now lays down these two (bricks).

9. He lays down the two seasonal ones prior
to the naturally-perforated one and to the Visvagyotis; for the last naturally-perforated one is the
sky[1], and the last Visvagyotis[2] (all-light brick) is

---

[1] For the symbolic meaning of the three svayam-âtrinnâs, as
the central bricks of the first and third layers, and the one lying on
the centre of the fifth layer, see part iii, p. 155, note 8.

[2] On the three Visvagyotis bricks, placed in the same layers, as
representing the gods Agni, Vâyu and Âditya respectively, see
VI, 3, 3, 16; 5, 3, 3.

the sun: he thus places the seasons on this side
of the sky and the sun; whence the seasons are
on this side thereof. But generative power there
also is (in these seasonal bricks)[1]: he thus places
generative power on this side of the sky and the
sun; whence procreation takes place only on this
side of them, but stationary, indeed, is procreation
beyond them, for just as many gods as there were
of old, so many there are now.

10. Now, the (first) two seasonal (bricks) he lays
down subsequently to the first naturally-perforated
one, and to the first Visvagyotis; for the first
naturally-perforated one is this (earth), and the first
Visvagyotis is Agni: thereupon he places the
seasons, whence the seasons are upwards from this
(earth). But generative power there also is therein:
he thus places generative power above this (earth);
whence procreation only takes place above (upon,
not under) this (earth).

11. Let him not derange these (seasonal bricks)[2]
lest he should derange the seasons, for deranged are

---

[1] Or, But these (bricks) also are (or mean) generative power,
cf. paragraph 1.

[2] That is, he is not to shift them from their proper place, but
place each subsequent pair exactly on those laid down before.
As a matter of fact, however, these two bricks (if we determine their
site by mere calculation) would seem, in the fifth layer, to lie
by half a foot further away from the central point, than the Ritavyâs
of the other layers do. This is owing to the fact that whilst, in
the layers in which a Svayamâtrinnâ lies in the middle, only one
half of these central bricks lie on the east side of the central point,
in the present layer the eastern portion of the Gârhapatya (occupying the central part of the layer) consists of full-sized bricks.
This discrepancy of half a foot was probably made good by some
space being left, which was afterwards filled up with earth; unless,
indeed, the Svayamâtrinnâs, as apparently natural stones, were
allowed to somewhat exceed the ordinary size of bricks.

the seasons for him who dies: hence, in whatever place he lays down the first two, there let him lay down all.

12. But the seasonal (bricks), indeed, are also these (three) worlds: by the (different) layers he thus builds up these worlds one above the other. And the seasonal (bricks), indeed, are also the nobility: by the (different) layers he thus builds up the nobility above (the peasantry). And the seasonal ones, indeed, are also the year: by the (different) layers he thus builds up the year. Let him not thereafter place over them any other brick with a sacrificial formula, lest he should place the peasantry above the nobility.

13. Now these same (bricks) are indeed stepping-stones, for by means of the seasonal (bricks) the gods then stepped over these worlds, both from hence upwards and from above downwards: and in like manner does the Sacrificer now, by means of the seasonal (bricks), step over these worlds, both from hence upwards and from above downwards.

14. Now, the Karakâdhvaryus lay down here yet other 'stepping-stones'; but let him not do so, for they do what is redundant, and these are indeed (all) the stepping-stones.

15. He then lays down a Visvagyotis (all-light brick):—the last Visvagyotis, doubtless, is the sun, for in yonder (celestial) world the sun, indeed, is 'all the light': it is the sun he thereby sets up.

16. And, again, as to why he lays down a Visvagyotis:—the Visvagyotis, doubtless, means progeny, for progeny indeed is all the light:—he thus lays generative power into it (or into him, Agni and the Sacrificer).

17. He lays down the Visvagyotis prior to the naturally-perforated one;—for the last naturally-perforated one is the sky, and the last Visvagyotis is the sun: he thus places the sun on this side (below) the sky, whence he burns only on this side thereof. But there also is generative power therein : he thus places generative power on this side of the sky, whence procreation takes place only on this side thereof.

18. Now the (first) Visvagyotis he lays down subsequent to the first naturally-perforated one ; for the first naturally-perforated one is this (earth), and the first Visvagyotis is Agni: he thus sets up Agni upwards from this (earth), whence the fire blazes upwards from here. But there also is generative power therein: he thus places generative power above this (earth), whence procreation only takes place above this (earth).

19. And the (second) Visvagyotis he lays down subsequent to the second naturally-perforated one (in the third, or central) layer; for the second naturally-perforated one is the air, and the second Visvagyotis is Vâyu (the wind) : he thus places the wind in the air, whence that wind (has his abode) in the air.

20. These (three) then are the lights ;—and when he lays down these (three Visvagyotis bricks) in this way, he thereby sets up those same lights so as to face each other; and hence the fire blazes upwards from this (earth), and yonder sun shines downwards, and that wind blows sideways in the air.

21. [He 'settles' the Visvagyotis, with, Vâg. S. XV, 58], 'May Paramesh*th*in settle thee'—for Paramesh*th*in saw this fifth layer ;—'on the back

of the sky, thee, the luminous one!'—for on the back of the sky is yonder luminous sun.

22. 'For all out-breathing, and off-breathing, and through-breathing,'—for the Visvagyotis is the breath, and breath, indeed, is (necessary) for everything here;—'bestow thou all the light!'—that is, 'bestow thou the whole (or every) light:' —'Sûrya is thine overlord,'—he thereby makes Sûrya (the sun) its overlord. Having 'settled' it, he pronounces the Sûdadohas on it: its (symbolical) meaning has been told[1].

23. Now, these (bricks) are indeed stepping-stones, for by means of the Visvagyotis (bricks) the gods then stepped over these worlds, both from hence upwards, and from above downwards: and in like manner does the Sacrificer now, by means of the Visvagyotis, step over these worlds, both from hence upwards, and from above downwards.

24. Now, the Karakâdhvaryus lay down here yet other 'stepping-stones'; but let him not do so, for they do what is redundant, and these are indeed the stepping-stones.

SECOND BRÂHMANA.

1. He then lays down a Lokamprinâ[2] (space-filling brick); the Lokamprinâ, doubtless, is yonder

---

[1] For this verse see part iii, p. 307, note 2; for its symbolic meaning (as the breath, or vital air) VII, 1, 1, 15; 26. See also VIII, 7, 3, 21, where the verse itself is explained.

[2] In laying down the Lokamprinâs of the fifth layer, he begins, as in the first layer, from the right shoulder, or the south-east corner, of the altar, but so that in this case the first 'space-filler' is laid down, not at the corner, but a cubit to the west of it. Starting from that spot, he fills up the available spaces, in two turns, moving in the sunwise fashion.

sun, for he fills these worlds : it is thus yonder sun
he thereby sets up. He lays down this (Lokamprinâ) in all the (five) layers, for those layers are
these (three) worlds[1]: he thus places the sun in (all)
these worlds, whence he shines for all these worlds.

2. And, again, as to why he lays down a Lokamprinâ,—the Lokamprinâ, doubtless, is the nobility
(or chieftaincy)[2], and these other bricks are the
peasants (or clansmen): he thus places the nobility
(or chieftain), as the eater, among the peasantry.
He lays it down in all the layers: he thus places
the nobility, as the eater, among the whole peasantry
(or in every clan).

3. Now this is only a single (brick): he thus
makes the nobility (or the chieftaincy) and (social)
distinction to attach to a single (person). And
what second (such brick there is) that is its mate,
—a mate, doubtless, is one half of one's own self,
for when one is with a mate then he is whole and
complete : (thus it is laid down) for the sake of
completeness. With a single formula he lays down
many bricks[3]: he thereby endows the nobility pre-

---

[1] Rather, the first, second, and third layers are the three worlds.

[2] At VI. 1, 2, 25 Tândya was made to maintain that the Yagushmatis, or bricks laid down with special formulas, were the nobility,
and that the Lokamprinâs, laid down with one and the same formula,
were the peasants, and as the noble (or chieftain) required a
numerous clan for his subsistence, there should be fewer of the
former kind of bricks, than the established practice was. This
view was however rejected by the author of the Brâhmana, and here,
in opposition to that view, the Lokamprinâ is identified with the
nobility, and the Yagushmatis with the clan.

[3] The common formula used with these bricks, and from which
they derive their name—beginning as it does 'Lokam prina,' 'Fill
the space !' see parag. 6—is pronounced once only after every ten
such bricks, and after any odd ones at the end.

eminently with power[1], and makes the nobility more powerful than the peasantry. And the other (bricks) he lays down singly, with separate formulas: he thereby makes the peasantry less powerful than the nobility, differing in speech, and of different thoughts (from one another).

4. The first two (Lokamprinâs) he lays down in that (south-east) corner: he thereby places yonder sun in that quarter: from this (earth) he follows him (the sun) from that (place) there[2]; from this (earth) he follows him from that (place) there; from this (earth) he follows him from that (place) there; from this (earth) he follows him from that (place) there.

5. And in whatever place he lays down the first two (bricks), let him there lay down alongside of

---

[1] In the translation of VII. 5. 2. 14 (part iii, p. 404), the passage 'having taken possession of the man by strength,' which was based on a wrong reading (see Weber, Berl. Cat. II, p. 69), should read thus: 'having pre-eminently endowed man with power' (or, perhaps, 'having placed him above (others) in respect of power,' St. Petersb. Dict.)

[2] I do not know whether 'atas' might be taken here in the sense of 'thither,' or whether it goes along with 'tasmât,' merely strengthening it. The meaning in either case would seem to be this. In the first turn of filling up the empty spaces he first moves along from the south-east corner (the point where the sun rises) to the back or west end of the spine (the place where the sun sets) and the central brick; and having thus, as it were, touched the earth again, he proceeds from there in the same sunwise fashion, filling up the north part of the altar until he reaches the east end of the spine, and there, as it were, touches the earth once more. In the second turn he again begins (with the second brick) in the south-east, and repeats the same process, in filling up the south part of the altar, and completing at the south-east corner. The laying down of the Lokamprinâs would thus be supposed to occupy the full space of two days and two nights.

them the last two (bricks) : for (otherwise) having
once revolved round these worlds, that sun would
not pass by them. Let him lay down the two last
alongside the two first by reaching over them : he
thus causes that sun to pass by these worlds ; and
hence that sun revolves incessantly round these
worlds again and again (from left) to right.

6. [He lays them down, with, Vâg. S. XV, 59].
'Fill the space! fill the gap!'—that is, 'fill up
the space! fill up the gap;'—'and lie thou steady!'
— that is, 'and lie thou firm, settled!'—'Indra and
Agni, and Br*i*haspati, have settled thee in this
womb;' that is, 'Indra and Agni, and Br*i*haspati,
have established thee in this womb.' Thus (he
establishes them) by an anush*t*ubh verse ; for the
Anush*t*ubh is speech, and Indra is speech, and the
'space-filler' is Indra. He does not settle them, for
that (sun) is unsettled. He pronounces the Sûdadohas on them, for the Sûdadohas is vital air : he
thus makes him (Agni) continuous and joins him
together by means of the vital air.

7. Here now they say, 'How does that Lokam-
p*r*inâ become of unimpaired strength ?' Well, the
Lokamp*r*inâ is yonder sun, and he assuredly is of
unimpaired strength. And the Lokamp*r*inâ also
is speech, and of unimpaired strength assuredly is
speech.

8. Having laid down those (bricks) possessed of
(special) sacrificial formulas, he covers (the altar)
with the Lokamp*r*inâ ; for the bricks possessed of
formulas mean food, and the Lokamp*r*inâ means
the body : he thus encloses the food in the body,
whence food enclosed in the body is the body
itself.

9. Those (bricks) possessed of formulas he places on the body (of the altar) itself, not on the wings and tail : he thus puts food into the body ; and whatever food is put into the body that benefits both the body and the wings and tail; but that which he puts on the wings and tail benefits neither the body, nor the wings and tail.

10. On the body (of the altar) he places both (bricks) possessed of formulas and Lokamprinâs ; whence that body (of a bird) is, as it were, twice as thick. On the wings and tail (he places) only Lokamprinâs, whence the wings and tail are, as it were, thinner. On the body (of the altar) he places them both lengthwise and crosswise, for the bricks are bones : hence these bones in the body run both lengthwise and crosswise. On the wings and tail (he places them so as to be) turned away (from the body), for in the wings and tail there is not a single transverse bone. And this, indeed, is the difference between a built and an unbuilt (altar) : suchlike is the built one, different therefrom the unbuilt one [1].

11. The Svayamâtrinnâ (naturally - perforated brick) he encloses with Lokamprinâ (bricks) ; for the naturally-perforated one is the breath, and the 'space-filler' is the sun : he thus kindles the breath by means of the sun, whence this breath (of ours) is warm. With that (kind of brick) he fills up the whole body : he thereby kindles the whole body by means of the sun, whence this whole body (of ours) is warm. And this, indeed, is the difference between one that will live and one that will die :

---

[1] That is, one not properly built.

he that will live is warm, and he that will die is cold.

12. From the corner in which he lays down the first two (Lokamp*rinâ*s) he goes on filling up (the altar) by tens up to the Svayamât*rinnâ*. In the same way he goes on filling it up from left to right behind the naturally-perforated one up to (the brick on) the cross-spine [1]. He then fills it up whilst returning to that limit [2].

13. The body (of the altar) he fills up first, for of (a bird) that is produced, the body is produced first, then the right wing, then the tail, then the left (wing) : that is in the rightward (sunwise) way, for this is (the way) with the gods, and thus, indeed, yonder sun moves along these worlds from left to right.

14. The Lokamp*rinâ*, doubtless, is the same as the vital air ; he therewith fills up the whole body (of the altar) : he thus puts vital air into the whole body. If he were not to reach any member thereof, then the vital air would not reach that member of him (Agni); and whatever member the vital air does not reach, that, assuredly, either dries up or withers away : let him therefore fill up therewith the whole of it.

15. The wings and tail he builds on to the body, for the wings and tail grow on to the body ; but were he first to lay down those (bricks) turned away (from the body), it would be as if he were to take a limb from elsewhere and put it on again.

---

[1] This would seem to be the Vikar*ni* (see VIII, 7, 3, 9 seqq.) which, however, like the central Svayamât*rinnâ*, is only to be laid down after the layer has been levelled up.

[2] Viz. to the east end of the 'spine.'

16. Let him not lay down either a broken (brick) or a black one; for one that is broken causes failure, and sickly is that form which is black : 'Lest I should make up a sickly body,' he thinks[1]. Let him not throw aside an unbroken (brick), lest he should put what is not sickly outside the body. Whatever (bricks), in counting from the dhishnya hearths, should exceed a Virâg[2], and not make up another, such (bricks) indeed cause failure : let him break them and throw them[3] (ut-kir) on the heap of rubbish (utkara), for the heap of rubbish is the seat of what is redundant: thus he thereby settles them where there is the seat of that which is redundant.

17. Now, then, of the measures of the bricks. In the first and last layers let him lay down (bricks) of a foot (square), for the foot is a support; and the hand is the same as the foot. The largest (bricks) should be of the measure of the thigh-bone, for there is no bone larger than the thigh-bone. Three layers should have (their bricks) marked with three lines, for threefold are these worlds : and two (layers

[1] Here, as so often before, the effect to be avoided is expressed by a clause in *oratio directa* with ' ned '; the inserted clause with ' vai ' indicating the reason why that effect is to be dreaded. To adapt the passage to our own mode of diction, we should have to translate :—Let him not lay down either a broken brick or a black one, lest he should form a sickly body ; for a brick which is broken comes to grief, and what is black is of sickly appearance.—In the next sentence of the translation, the direct form of speech has been discarded.

[2] The pâda of the Virâg consists of ten, and a whole Virâg stanza of thirty (or forty), syllables. Hence the number of the bricks is to be divisible by ten.

[3] Or, perhaps, dig them in.

may consist) of (bricks) marked with an indefinite number of lines, for these two layers are the flavour, and the flavour is indefinite ; but all (the layers) should rather have (bricks) marked with three lines, for threefold are all these worlds.

18. Now, then, of the location[1] of (special) bricks. Any (special) brick he knows, provided with a formula, let him place in the middle (third) layer ; for the middle layer is the air, and the air, doubtless, is the location of all beings. Moreover, bricks with (special) formulas are food, and the middle layer is the belly : he thus puts food into the belly.

19. Here, now, they say, 'Let him not lay down (such special bricks) lest he should do what is excessive.' But he may, nevertheless, lay them down ; for such bricks are laid down for (the fulfilment of special) wishes, and in wishes there is nothing excessive. But let him rather not lay them down, for just that much the gods then did.

Third Brâhmana.

1. He now throws loose soil (on the layer) ; for the loose soil means flesh : he thus covers him (Agni) with flesh. [He does so] after having laid down the bricks ;—the bricks are the bone : he thus covers the bone with flesh.

2. He also strews it on (the place where lies) the naturally-perforated (brick), for the naturally-perforated one means vital air, and the loose soil

---

[1] Âvapana has also the meaning of 'throwing in, insertion,' which is likewise understood here, whilst further on in this paragraph ('the air is the âvapanam of all beings') it can scarcely have this meaning (? something injected). Cf. IX, 4, 2, 27.

means food : he thus puts food into (the channels of)
the vital air. In that manner[1] he covers the whole
body (of the altar) ; whence the food which is put
into (the channels of) the vital air benefits the whole
body, extends over the whole body.

3. 'Let him not strew it on (the place of) the
naturally-perforated one,' say some, 'lest he
should stop up (the channels of) the vital airs, for
the naturally-perforated one is the vital air.' Let
him, nevertheless, strew it, for the vital airs are
sustained by food, and whoever eats no food his
(channels of the) vital airs grow up (and close):
hence he for whom they act thus, comes to exist in
yonder world even like a dry, hollow tube. Let him,
therefore, by all means strew (loose soil) on (the
place of) the naturally-perforated one.

4. Having strewed it on the svayamâtr*innâ*
(place) he goes on covering (the altar) from the
(brick) on the cross-spine up to the enclosing-stones.
In the same way he goes on covering it from left to
right behind the naturally-perforated one up to the
one on the cross-spine again.

5. The body (of the altar) he covers first, for of
(a bird) that is produced, the body is the first to be
produced ; then the right wing, then the tail, then
the left wing : that is in the rightward (sunwise)
way, for this is (the way) with the gods.

6. Now this loose soil, indeed, is the vital air ;
he therewith covers the whole body : he thus puts
vital air into the whole body. And, assuredly,
whatsoever member thereof he should not reach,
that member of him (Agni) the vital air would not

---

[1] Or, therewith (with loose soil).

reach ; and whatever member the vital air does not reach that either dries up or withers away : let him, therefore, cover it entirely therewith.

7. [He scatters the loose soil[1], with, Vâg. S. XV, 56; *Rig*-veda I, 11, 1], 'They all have magnified Indra,'—for all beings, indeed, magnify Indra ;— 'the voices, him, of ocean-wide extent,'—he thereby alludes to his greatness :—'the foremost of charioteers,'—for of charioteers he is the greatest charioteer ;—'the lordly lord of viands,' —viands mean food : thus, ' the lordly lord of food.' With this anush/ubh verse addressed to Indra he scatters it ; for the loose soil belongs to Indra : that (layer of) loose soil is one half of Agni (the fire-altar), the (other) half is the collection of bricks.

8. Here, now, they say, ' Whilst he lays down the bricks with all kinds of metres, and with (verses addressed to) all deities, he now scatters (the soil) with a single (verse) addressed to a single deity,— how is this one half of Agni ?' Indra, surely, is equal to all the gods ; hence in that he scatters it with a (verse) addressed to Indra, this (soil) is one half of Agni. And as to its being (done) with an anush/ubh verse,—the Anush/ubh is speech, and all metres are speech : thereby also it is one half.

9. He then lays down the Vikar*n*i and Svayam-át*rinn*à (bricks),—the Vikar*n*i is Vâyu (the wind), and the last naturally-perforated one is the sky : he thus sets up both the wind and the sky. He lays them down as the last (highest), for wind and sky are the highest ; and close together, for wind and

---

[1] Taking it from the edge of the *K*ât*v*âla or pit, cf. VII, 1, 1, 36.

sky are close together. The Vikar*ni* he lays down
first : he thereby places the wind on this side of the
sky; whence that wind blows only on this side
(thereof).

10. And, again, as to why he lays down the
Vikar*ni*. When, on that (former) occasion, they
make the horse smell (the pile of bricks of) the
(first) layer[1], then yonder sun strings these worlds
to himself on a thread. Now that thread is the
same as the wind; and that wind is the same as
this Vikar*ni* : thus when he lays down the latter,
then yonder sun strings to himself these worlds on
a thread.

11. And, again, as to why he lays down the
Vikar*ni* and the Svayamâtr*inn*â; the Vikar*ni*,
doubtless, is vital power, and the naturally-perforated
one is vital air: he thus bestows both vital power
and vital air. He lays them down as the two last
(highest bricks), because vital power and vital air
are the two highest (endowments); and close together, because vital power and vital air are closely
(bound) together. The upper (northern) Vikar*ni*
he lays down first[2]: he thereby encloses the vital
air on both sides in vital power.

12. [He lays it down, with, Vâg. S. XV, 62 : *Rig-
veda* VII, 3, 2], 'When, like a snorting steed,
that longeth for the pasture, he started forth
from the great enclosure, then the wind
fanned his flame, and black then was thy
path;'—for when the wind fans his (Agni's) flame,

---

[1] See VII. 3, 2, 13.

[2] As 'uttarâm' means both 'northern' and 'higher,' so 'pûrvâm'
means both 'first' and 'eastern,' hence, by a whimsical play on
these double meanings, 'on both (or two) sides.'

then his path does become black. With a trish/ubh
verse he lays it down, because Vâyu (the wind) is of
trish/ubh nature; with one relating to Agni, because
it is Agni's performance; with an undefined one,
because Vâyu is undefined. And as to his saying
'the wind,' Vâyu indeed is the wind.

13. He then lays down the Svayamâtr*iṇṇ*â, with
(Vâg. S. XV, 63), 'I seat thee in the seat of the
vital power,'—the vital power, doubtless, is yonder
(sun), and his seat this is;—'the animating,'—for
he (the sun) animates all this universe;—'in the
shadow,'—for in his shadow all this universe is;—
'in the heart of the sea,'—for this, indeed, is the
heart of the (aerial) sea¹;—'the radiant, the luminous,'—for radiant and luminous is the sky;—
'thou that illumines the sky, the earth and
the wide air;'—for thus, indeed, does he (the sun)
illumine these worlds.

14. 'May Paramesh/*/*in settle thee,'—for
Paramesh/*/*in saw this fifth layer².

15. And, again, as to why he lays it down by
means of Paramesh/*/*in. When Pragâpati had
become disjointed, the deities took him and went
off in different directions. Paramesh/*/*in took his
head, and kept going away from him.

16. He spake to him, 'Come to me and restore
unto me that wherewith thou hast gone from me!'
—'What will therefrom accrue to me?'—'That part
of my body shall be sacred to thee!'—'So be it!'
So Paramesh/*/*in restored that to him.

17. Now that last self-perforated (brick) is just

---

¹ The topmost naturally-perforated brick represents the heavens.
² See VI, 2, 3, 5; 10.

that part of him (Pragâpati-Agni); and when he now lays it down in this place, he thereby restores to him what part of his body this is: that is why he lays it down in this place.

18. 'On the back of the sky, thee, the wide and broad one!'—for this (top of the altar) is indeed the back of the sky, and it is both wide and broad[1];—'Sustain thou the sky! make firm the sky! injure not the sky!'—that is, 'Sustain thy self, make firm thy self, injure not thy self (body)!'

19. 'For all out-breathing, off-breathing, through-breathing, up-breathing!'—the naturally-perforated (brick) is the vital air, and the vital air truly serves for everything here;—'for a resting-place, for a moving-place!'—the naturally-perforated (bricks) are these worlds, and these worlds are the resting-place and the moving-place;—'May Sûrya guard thee,'—that is, 'May Sûrya protect thee,'—'with mighty well-being.'—that is, 'with great well-being;'—'with the safest roof!'—that is, 'with whatever roof (abode) is the safest.'

20. Separately he lays them down, for separate are wind and sky; and once only he 'settles' them: he thereby makes them the same, for vital power and vital air are the same. They are both of them stones and both of them naturally-perforated; for vital power and vital air are the same. He then pronounces the Sûdadohas over them,—the Sûdadohas means vital air; he thus makes them

---

[1] Though, in the text of the formula, the adjectives are feminine, and evidently refer to the brick, the author here makes them neuter, referring them to 'prishṭham,' the back (of the sky).

continuous, joins them together by means of the vital air.

21. 'Those his well-like milking ones[1],'— a well (sûda) means water, and milking means food;—'the speckled ones mix the Soma,'—the speckled (cow) means food;—'at the birth of the gods,'—the birth of the gods is the year;—'the tribes,'—the tribes (vis), doubtless, are the sacrifice, for all beings are ranged (vish/a)[2] under the sacrifice;—'in the three spheres of the heavens,'— the three spheres of the heavens, doubtless, are the (three) pressings (of Soma): he thus means the pressings. With an anush/ubh verse (he performs this rite), for the Anush/ubh is speech, and speech (includes) all vital airs; and by means of speech, that is vital air, he thus makes these two (bricks) continuous, and joins them together. This same Sûdadohas, whilst being a single (verse), extends over all the bricks, whence—the Sûdadohas being the vital air—this vital air, whilst being one only, extends over all the limbs, over the whole body.

FOURTH BRÂHMANA.

1. On the (three) naturally-perforated (bricks) he (the Sacrificer) sings sâmans; for the naturally-perforated ones are these (three) worlds; and they

---

[1] Part iii, p. 307, note 2, the following translation of this difficult and obscure verse was proposed: —'At his birth the well-like milking, speckled ones mix the Soma (draught), the clans of the gods in the three spheres of the heavens.'

[2] Literally, have entered, or settled. At XIV, 8, 13, 3, the same etymological word-play occurs, only 'food (anne)' being substituted for 'sacrifice (yagñe)'; where the St. Petersb. Dict. takes 'vish/a' in the sense of 'entered, i.e. contained.'

are just these (ordinary) stones. The gods, having laid them down, saw them as such: that they were dry stones.

2. They spake, 'Think ye upon this, how we may lay sap, the means of subsistence, into these worlds!' They spake, 'Meditate ye!' whereby, doubtless, they meant to say, 'Seek ye a layer! seek ye how we may lay sap, the means of subsistence, into these worlds!'

3. Whilst meditating, they saw these sâmans (hymn-tunes), and sang them; and by means of them they laid sap, the means of subsistence, into these worlds; and in like manner does the Sacrificer now, when he sings these sâmans, lay sap, the means of subsistence, into these worlds.

4. Over the naturally-perforated ones he sings them: the naturally-perforated ones being these worlds, it is into these worlds that he thereby lays sap, the means of subsistence.

5. He sings (the tunes) on the (mystic) words 'Bhûs, Bhuvas, Svar';—bhûs (earth), doubtless, is this world, bhuvas is the air-world, and svar (light) is yonder world: into these worlds he thereby lays sap, the means of subsistence.

6. They have different preludes, and the same finale [1]; and as to their having different preludes, it

---

[1] These hymn-tunes are given, Sâm. Ved. V, p. 487, in the way in which they are here to be chanted. They consist entirely of the respective words, separated four times by musical interjections (stobhas) inserted between them, ending with the common finale: thus, (1) bhû*h*–bhû*h*–hoyi–bhû*h*–hoyi–bhû*h*–hâ–ûvâ–e–suvargyotí–*h*; (2) bhuva*h*–bhuva*h*–hoyi–bhuva*h*–hâ–ûvâ–e–suvargyotí–*h*; (3) suvá*h* suva*h*–hoyi–suva*h*–hoyi–suva*h*–hâ–ûvâ–e–suvargyotí–*h*. Along with these, as to be chanted on the same model, are given, (4) the 'satya*m* sâman,' beginning 'satyâm–satyam–hoyi' &c., and

is because they (the gods) saw them separately;
and as to their having the same finale (nidhana), it
is because there is only one foundation, only one
finale to the sacrifice—even heaven: therefore they
have 'svar-gyotis (heaven-light)' for their finale.

7. He then bestrews him (Agni, the fire-altar and
Agni's body) with chips of gold. Now that whole
Agni had been completed, and the gods bestowed
on him immortality, that highest form; and in like
manner does this one now bestow upon him that
highest, immortal form [1].

8. And, again, as to why he bestrews him with
chips of gold. Now on that former occasion he
first lays into him that pleasing form, the gold
plate and the (gold) man [2]; and he now decks him
all over with a pleasing form.

9. With two hundred (chips he bestrews him)
each time,—two-footed is the Sacrificer, and Agni

---

(5) the 'purusha-sâman,' beginning 'purushâh-purusha-hoyi' &c.:
which are similarly chanted by the Sacrificer at the beginning of
the first layer, when laying down the lotus leaf (part iii, p. 363,
where note 1 should be corrected in accordance with the present
note), and the gold man (ib. p. 369, where the note requires
likewise to be corrected), as the '*K*itre gâyati,' 'he sings on the
bright one,' of the text cannot refer to the '*K*itra-sâman' there
referred to. Cf. Lâ*t*y. S. I, 5, 8.—In regard to these sâmans (hymn-
verses), the text might lead one to suppose that they only consist
of two, instead of the usual four parts (omitting the intermediate
Udgitha and Pratihâra, cf. part ii, p. 310 note). The sâman
being, however, sung by the Sacrificer himself, the usual distinction
into parts to be performed by different chanters was probably
dispensed with.

[1] That is, the Sacrificer bestows it on Agni; with probably,
however, the *double entente*, 'this Adhvaryu priest bestows it on the
Sacrificer.'

[2] See VII, 4, 1, 10 seq.; 15 seq.

is the sacrificer: as great as Agni is, as great as is his measure, with so much he thus bestows upon him immortality, that highest form. Five times (he strews),—five-layered is the altar, five seasons make a year, and Agni is the year: as great as Agni is, as great as is his measure, with so much he thus bestows upon him immortality, that highest form. With a thousand (chips he bestrews him),—a thousand means everything: with everything he thus confers upon him immortality, that highest form.

10. First (he scatters them) at the back whilst standing with his face towards the east; then on the left (north) side towards the south; then in front whilst facing the west; then, having gone round the back, from the south whilst facing the north: this is from left to right (sunwise), for that is (the way) with the gods. Then, having gone round, (he scatters chips) at the back whilst standing with his face to the east, for in this way that former performance of him [1] took place.

11. [He scatters, with, Vâg. S. XV, 65], 'The fore-measure of a thousand thou art,—The counter-measure of a thousand thou art,— The up-measure of a thousand thou art,— The thousandfold thou art,—For a thousand thee!'—a thousand, doubtless, means everything: thus, 'Everything thou art,—thee for everything!'

12. Now, then, the consideration of the layer-fillings. The first layer is this (terrestrial) world: and the filling of soil means cattle: thus, in

---

[1] Viz. of Agni (and the Sacrificer). The ceremony alluded to was the fivefold libation of ghee offered on the gold man (representing Agni and the Sacrificer), see VII, 4, 1, 34-35.

covering the first layer with a filling of soil he covers this (terrestrial) world with cattle.

13. The second layer is the air, and the filling of soil means birds : thus, in covering the second layer with a filling of soil, he covers (fills) the air with birds.

14. The third layer is the sky, and the filling of soil means stars ; thus, in covering the third layer with a filling of soil, he covers the sky with stars.

15. The fourth layer is the sacrifice, and the filling of soil means sacrificial gifts : thus, in covering the fourth layer with a filling of soil, he covers the sacrifice with sacrificial gifts (to the priests).

16. The fifth layer is the Sacrificer, and the filling of soil means progeny (or subjects) : thus, in covering the fifth layer with a filling of soil, he covers (abundantly supplies) the Sacrificer with progeny (or subjects).

17. The sixth layer is the heavenly world, and the filling of soil means the gods : thus in covering the sixth layer with a filling of soil, he fills the heavenly world with gods.

18. The seventh layer is immortality,—that is the last (layer) he lays down, and thus bestows immortality as the highest thing of all this (universe) : therefore immortality is the highest thing of all this (universe) ; therefore the gods are not separated therefrom ; and therefore they are immortal. Thus much as to the deity [1].

19. Now, as to the Self (body). The first layer is the legs, and the downward flowing vital air ; and

---

[1] That is, so much as to the objects to which the different parts of the altar are sacred or dedicated.

the filling of soil is the flesh: thus, in covering the first layer with a filling of soil, he covers that (part) of his (Agni's) body with flesh. [He does so] after laying down bricks, and bricks mean bone: he thus covers the bone with flesh. He does not cover (the altar-site) below (the first layer), whence these vital airs are not closed up below; but he covers it above, and thereby covers that (part) of his body above with flesh; and hence that (part) of his body above, being covered with flesh, is not visible.

20. The second layer is that (part of the body) which is above the legs and below the waist; and the filling of soil is flesh: thus, in covering the second layer with a filling of soil, he covers that (part) of his body with flesh. [He does so] after laying down bricks, and bricks mean bone: he thus covers the bone with flesh. He places them on a filling of soil, and covers them with a filling of soil: he thus covers that (part) of his body on both sides with flesh; whence that part of his body, being on both sides covered with flesh, is not visible.

21. The third layer is the waist itself; the fourth layer is that (part of the body) which is above the waist and below the neck; the fifth layer is the neck, the sixth layer is the head, and the seventh layer is the vital airs. This he lays down as the last (or highest): he thus makes the vital airs the highest of all this (universe), and hence the vital airs are the highest thing of all this (universe). He places it on a filling of soil; and the filling of soil means flesh; he thus covers (the channels of) the vital airs with flesh. He does not cover it above, whence these (channels of the) vital airs are not closed up above.

NINTH KÂNDA.

THE BUILDING OF THE SACRED FIRE-ALTAR
(continued).

SATARUDRIYA LUSTRATION, INSTALMENT AND CONSECRATION OF FIRE, AND SOMA-SACRIFICE.

FIRST ADHYÂYA. FIRST BRÂHMANA.

THE SATARUDRIYA.

THIS solemn and awful ceremony consists of 425 oblations to Rudra, the representative of the fearful aspects of life and nature, accompanied by appropriate formulas addressed to the various forms of the terrible god, and his associates, with a view to appeasing their wrath. These formulas make up a complete kânda (XVI) of the Vâgasaneyi-samhitâ, and constitute a special Upanishad. Though only a few of the formulas are actually referred to in the text of the Brâhmana, the different portions of which this dismal litany consists are otherwise alluded to, and for this reason, as well as on account of its intrinsic interest, as doubtless reflecting, to a considerable extent, the popular belief in demoniac agencies to which man is constantly exposed, a complete translation of the Satarudriya formulas is here given. For a German translation of the Taittiriya recension of the text, with the various readings of the Kâthaka and Vâgasaneyin versions, see A. Weber, Ind. Stud. II, p. 14 seqq.

1. 1. Reverence, O Rudra, be to thy wrath; and to thine arrow be reverence; and to both thine arms be reverence! 2. What auspicious form there is of thine, free from terror and boding of evil, with that most propitious form look down upon us, O mountain-dweller! 3. The shaft thou bearest in thy hand to hurl, O mountain-dweller, make it harmless, O protector of mountains, injure not man nor beast! 4. With auspicious speech we call upon thee, O mountain-dweller, that all these living beings of ours may

be healthy and of good cheer! 5. May he plead for us as our intercessor, the first divine physician; crushing all serpents, turn thou aside all practices of witchcraft! 6. That tawny one, and the ruddy and the brown one, the auspicious—the Rudras that hover around him by thousands in the quarters: their wrath do we deprecate. 7. That one who glideth downwards (the sun) blood-red and blue-necked—the cowherds have seen him and the water-bearers (f. the clouds) have seen him—be he gracious unto us, when seen! 8. Reverence be to the blue-necked, thousand-eyed showerer; and what henchmen there are of his, to them do I render homage. 9. Loose thou the string from the ends of thy bow; and cast away the arrows in thy hand, O holy one! 10. Stringless be the bow of the coil-braided one, and arrowless his quiver! may his arrows be futile, and empty his scabbard! 11. With that plague-repelling weapon in thy hand, with thy bow, protect us, O best of showerers, on all sides! 12. May the shaft of thy bow spare us on all sides, and far from us lay down that quiver of thine! 13. Unstringing the bow, and breaking off the points of thy shafts, be thou gracious and well-disposed unto us, O thousand-eyed lord of a hundred quivers! 14. Reverence be to thine unstrung weapon, the powerful one; and reverence be to thine arms and to thy bow! 15. Neither our full-grown, nor our little one, neither the virile, nor the unborn, neither our father strike thou, nor our mother: harm not our dear bodies, O Rudra! 16. Neither to our children, and our children's children, nor to our life, neither to our kine nor to our horses do thou injury! smite not our shining warriors; with offering we ever invoke thee, O Rudra!

II. 17. Reverence be to the golden-armed leader of hosts, and to the lord of regions be reverence! reverence be to the green-haired trees, and to the lord of beasts be reverence! reverence be to the grass-hued shining one, and to the lord of roads be reverence! reverence be to the gold-locked wearer of the sacred cord, and to the lord of the strong-bodied be reverence! 18. Reverence be to the dusky smiter, and to the lord of food be reverence! reverence be to Bhava's weapon, and to the lord of moving creatures be reverence! reverence be to the strung-bowed Rudra, and to the lord of fields be reverence! reverence be to the inviolable charioteer, and to the lord of forests be reverence! 19. Reverence be to the ruddy architect, and to the lord of trees be reverence! reverence be to the ubiquitous producer of wealth, and to the lord of plants be reverence! reverence be to the wise merchant, and to the lord of forest retreats be reverence! reverence be to the loud-noised crier,

and to the lord of wanderers be reverence! 20. Reverence be to
the onward-rushing one with his (weapon) levelled everywhere, and
to the lord of beings be reverence! reverence be to the victorious
smiter, and to the lord of victorious (hosts) be reverence! reverence
be to the matchless swordsman, and to the lord of thieves be reverence! reverence be to the prowling rover, and to the lord of the
forest be reverence! 21. Reverence be to the tricking arch-trickster,
and to the lord of pilferers be reverence! reverence be to the well-
quivered swordsman, and to the lord of robbers be reverence!
reverence be to the slaying spearmen, and to the lord of pillagers
be reverence! reverence be to the night-walking sword-wielders,
and to the lord of cut-throats be reverence!

III. 22. Reverence be to the turbaned mountaineer, and to the
lord of spoilers be reverence! reverence be to shooters of arrows, and
to ye bowmen be reverence! reverence be to the bow-stretching, and
to ye that fix the arrow be reverence! reverence be to ye that pull
(the bow), and to ye that hurl be reverence! 23. Reverence be to
ye that shoot, and to ye that pierce be reverence! reverence be
to ye that sleep, and to ye that wake be reverence! reverence be to
ye, the lying, and to ye, the sitting, be reverence! reverence be
to ye, the standing, and to ye, the running, be reverence! 24.
Reverence be to gatherings, and to ye, lords of the gathering,
be reverence! reverence be to horses, and to ye, masters of
horses, be reverence! reverence be to the victorious (armies), and
to ye that smite be reverence! reverence be to the serried (hosts),
and to ye that crush be reverence! 25. Reverence be to the
troops, and to ye, chiefs of troops, be reverence! reverence be to
the bands, and to ye, chiefs of bands, be reverence! reverence be
to sharpers, and to ye, chiefs of sharpers, be reverence! reverence
be to the unshapen, and to ye, the all-shaped, be reverence!
26. Reverence be to armies, and to ye, leaders of armies, be
reverence! reverence be to chariot-fighters, and to ye, the chariot-
less, be reverence! reverence be to car-fighters, and to ye, charioteers,
be reverence! reverence be to the adult, and to ye, children, be
reverence!

IV. 27. Reverence be to carpenters, and to ye, wheelwrights, be
reverence! reverence be to potters, and to ye, blacksmiths, be
reverence! reverence be to the jungle tribes, and to ye, fishermen,
be reverence! reverence be to dog-keepers, and to ye huntsmen be
reverence! 28. Reverence be to dogs, and to ye masters of dogs
be reverence! reverence be to Bhava and to Rudra! reverence be
to Sarva and to Pasupati (lord of beasts)! reverence be to Nilagriva

(the blue-necked) and to *Sitikantha* (the white-throated)!   29.
Reverence be to him of the coiled hair and to the shaven-haired
one! reverence be to the thousand-eyed and to the hundred-
bowed one! reverence be to the mountain-dweller and to the
bald one! reverence be to the chief of showerers and to the
arrow-shooter! 30. Reverence be to the short and the dwarfish
one! reverence be to the tall and the old one! reverence be to the
full-grown and the growing one! reverence be to the topmost and
first one! 31. Reverence be to the swift and agile one! reverence
be to the fast and nimble one! reverence be to the surging and
roaring one! reverence be to the river-dweller and the isle-dweller!

V. 32. Reverence be to the eldest and to the youngest! reverence be to the firstborn and to the afterborn! reverence be to the
middlemost and to the abortive (?) one! reverence be to the hindmost and to the bottommost one! 33. Reverence be to him dwelling
in the air-castles, and to him in the magic cord-ring! reverence
be to him who is in Yama's (death's) power, and to him who
liveth in safety! reverence be to him in (the height of his) fame,
and to him who is at his end! reverence be to him on the tilled
land, and to him on the threshing-floor! 34. Reverence be to him
dwelling in the wood, and to him in the jungle! reverence be to
the sound and to the echo! reverence be to him of the swift army,
and to him of the swift chariot! reverence be to the hero and the
shatterer! 35. Reverence be to the helmeted and the armoured
one! reverence be to the mailed and the cuirassed one! reverence
be to the famous one, and to the leader of the famous army!
reverence be to him dwelling in the drum, and to him in the drum-
stick! 36. Reverence be to the bold, and the deliberate one!
reverence be to the swordsman, and to the quiver-bearer! reverence be to the sharp-shafted and the armed one! reverence be to
the well-armed one, and to the wielder of a goodly bow!

VI. 37. Reverence be to him dwelling in the stream, and to him
on the road! reverence be to him in the mere (?), and to him in the
pool! reverence be to him in the ditch, and to him in the lake!
reverence be to him in the river, and to him in the pond! 38.
Reverence be to him dwelling in the well, and to him in the bank!
reverence be to him in the clouded sky (?), and to him in the heat
of the sun! reverence be to him in the cloud, and to him in the
lightning! reverence be to him in the rain, and to him in the
drought! 39. Reverence be to him dwelling in the wind, and to
him in the storm-cloud (?)! reverence be to him dwelling in the
house, and to the guardian of the house! reverence be to Soma

and Rudra! reverence be to the dusky and the ruddy one! 40. Reverence be to the propitious one, and to the lord of beasts! reverence be to the terrible and fearful one! reverence be to the near-hitter and the far-hitter! reverence be to the slayer and the slaughterer! reverence be to the gold-haired trees! reverence be to the deliverer!

VII. 41. Reverence be to the gentle and the friendly one! reverence be to the peaceful and pleasing one! reverence be to the kindly and the kindliest!

VIII. 42. Reverence be to him who is on the further shore, and to him on the near shore! reverence be to him who ferrieth over, and to him who bringeth ashore! reverence be to him dwelling in the ford, and to him on the bank! reverence be to him dwelling in the sward, and to him in the foam! 43. Reverence be to him dwelling in the sand, and to him in the current! reverence be to him dwelling in the stony and to him in habitable places! reverence be to the coil-haired and to the straight-haired (?) one! reverence be to him dwelling in barren land, and to him on the beaten track! 44. Reverence be to him dwelling in the cow-pen, and to him in the cattle-shed! reverence be to him dwelling in the couch, and to him in the house! reverence be to him dwelling in the heart, and to him in the whirlpool! reverence be to him dwelling in the well, and to him in the abyss! 45. Reverence be to him dwelling in what is dried up, and to him in what is green! reverence be to him dwelling in the dust, and to him in the mist! reverence be to him dwelling in the copse, and to him in the shrub! reverence be to him in the ground, and to him in the gully! 46. Reverence be to him dwelling in the leaf, and to him in the leaf-fall (sere leaf)! reverence be to the growler, and to the smiter! reverence be to the snatcher, and to the repeller (?)! reverence be to the arrow-makers, and to ye bow-makers!—Reverence be to ye, the sparkling hearts of the gods! reverence be to the discriminating, reverence to the destructive, reverence to the irremovable!

IX. 47. Chaser, lord of the (Soma) plant! blue-red cleaver! fright and hurt not these people and these cattle: let none of us sicken! 48. These prayers we bring before the mighty Rudra, the coil-braided smiter of heroes, that there may be safety for the two-footed and the four-footed, and that everything in this village may be healthy and thriving. 49. That friendly form of thine, O Rudra, friendly and ever healing, friendly and healing to the stricken: therewith be gracious unto us that we may live! 50. May the shaft of Rudra spare us, and the ill-will of the violent and malevo-

lent one : unstring the strong (bow) from (hurting) our patrons,
O showerer (of gifts), and be gracious unto our children and our
children's children!   51. Be thou kindly *and* well-disposed towards
us, O kindliest chief of showerers, lay down thy weapon on the
highest tree, and putting on the hide come and join us, bearing
the spear!   52. O blood-red scatterer, reverence be unto thee, holy
one, let those thousand shafts of thine lay low another than us!
53. The thousandfold thousand shafts of thine arms—turn thou
away their heads from us, O holy lord!   54. What countless thousands of Rudras there are upon earth, their bows do we unstring
(and cast away) at a thousand leagues.   55. The Bhavas in this
great sea, the air : their bows do we unstring at a thousand leagues.
56. The blue-necked, white-throated Rudras seated in the sky :
their bows do we unstring at a thousand leagues.   57. The blue-
necked, white-throated Sarvas dwelling below the earth : their bows
do we unstring at a thousand leagues.   58. The grass-green in the
trees, the blue-necked, blood-red ones : their bows do we unstring
at a thousand leagues.   59. They who are the chiefs of spirits,
hairless and coil-braided : their bows do we unstring at a thousand
leagues.   60. They who are the guardians of roads, food-bearers,
life-fighters (?) : their bows do we unstring at a thousand leagues.
61. They who haunt the bathing-places, wielders of spear and
sword : their bows do we unstring at a thousand leagues.   62.
They who strike men at their meals, and in their cups those that
drink : their bows do we unstring at a thousand leagues.   63. What
Rudras are scattered over the regions, so many and more : their
bows do we unstring at a thousand leagues.—64. Reverence be to
the Rudras dwelling in the sky, whose arrows the rain is! to them
(I stretch) ten (fingers) eastward, ten southward, ten westward, ten
northward, ten upward : to them be reverence! may they be
gracious unto us and help us : whomsoever we hate, and whosoever hateth us, him we cast into their jaws!   65. Reverence be to
the Rudras dwelling in the air, whose arrows the wind is! to them
(I stretch) ten (fingers) eastward, ten southward, ten westward, ten
northward, ten upward : to them be reverence! may they be gracious
unto us and help us : whomsoever we hate, and whosoever hateth
us, him we cast into their jaws!   66. Reverence be to the Rudras
dwelling upon earth, whose arrows food is! to them (I stretch) ten
(fingers) eastward, ten southward, ten westward, ten northward,
ten upward : to them be reverence! may they be gracious unto us
and help us : whomsoever we hate, and whosoever hateth us, him
we cast into their jaws!

1. He then performs the Satarudriya offering.
This whole Agni has now[1] been completed: he
now is the deity Rudra. Upon him the gods
bestowed that highest form, immortality. Flaming
he there stood longing for food. The gods were
afraid of him lest he should hurt them.

2. They spake, 'Let us gather together food for
him: therewith we will appease him!' They
gathered for him that food, the Sàntadevatya[2], and
thereby appeased him; and inasmuch as they
thereby appeased (sam) the god (deva), it is called
Sàntadevatya:—Sàntadevatya, doubtless, is here
called mystically 'Satarudriya[3],' for the gods love
the mystic. And in like manner does this Sacrificer now bestow upon him that highest form,
immortality. Flaming he there stands, longing for
food. He gathers for him that food, the Sàntadevatya, and thereby appeases him.

3. He offers wild sesamum seeds. He (Agni)
grows when he is being built up: he grows for
(the consumption) of every kind of food. And wild
sesamum seeds represent both kinds of food, the
cultivated as well as the wild-growing: inasmuch as
they are sesamum seeds they are a cultivated (kind
of food), and inasmuch as they ripen on unploughed
land they are wild-growing: he thus satisfies him
with both kinds of food, the cultivated as well as
the wild-growing.

---

[1] Or, here, in this (atra), in the shape of this (altar) on which the
fire is to be deposited.

[2] That is, that whereby the deity is propitiated or appeased.

[3] A fanciful etymology of Sata-rudriya, as if it were sànta (propitiated) + rudriya, instead of 'that which relates to a hundred
Rudras'; cf. paragraph 7.

4. He offers by means of an arka-leaf[1],—the Arka-tree (Calotropis gigantea) is food: he thus gratifies him with food.

5. He offers on (three) enclosing-stones:—these enclosing-stones are the (three) Agnis; and thus it is over Agni himself that these oblations of his become offered.

6. And as to why he performs the Satarudriya offering. When Pragâpati had become disjointed, the deities departed from him. Only one god did not leave him, to wit, Manyu (wrath): extended he remained within. He (Pragâpati) cried, and the tears of him that fell down settled on Manyu. He became the hundred-headed, thousand-eyed, hundred-quivered Rudra. And the other drops that fell down, spread over these worlds in countless numbers, by thousands; and inasmuch as they originated from crying (rud), they were called Rudras (roarers). That hundred-headed, thousand-eyed, hundred-quivered Rudra, with his bow strung, and his arrow fitted to the string, was inspiring fear, being in quest of food. The gods were afraid of him.

7. They spake unto Pragâpati, 'We are afraid of this one, lest he should hurt us!' He spake, 'Gather food for him, and appease him therewith!' They gathered for him that food, the Satarudriya (offering), and thereby appeased him; and inasmuch as they thereby appeased (sam) the hundred-headed (sata-sirsha) Rudra, it is called Satasirsharudrasamaniya, —and satasirsharudrasamaniya, doubtless, is what

---

[1] That is to say, the leaf is used in lieu of the ordinary offering-spoon. Whilst making continual oblations on one of the three stones from this leaf, held in his right hand, the priest holds a piece of arka wood in his left hand. Mahidh. on Vâg. S. XVI, 1.

they mystically call *Satarudriya*, for the gods love
the mystic. And in like manner does this (Sacrificer)
now gather for him that food, the *Satarudriya*, and
appease him thereby.

8. He offers gavedhuká flour; for from the place
where that deity lay disjointed, gavedhuká plants
(coix barbata) sprang forth : he thus gratifies him
by his own portion, by his own life-sap.

9. He offers by means of an arka-leaf; for that
tree sprang from the resting-place of that god : he
thus gratifies him by his own portion, by his own
life-sap.

10. He offers on (three) enclosing-stones [1], for the
enclosing-stones are the hair, and neither poison nor
anything else injures one at the hair. He offers
whilst standing on the left (north) side of Agni
(the altar), with his face to the north : for in that
region lies the house of that god [2]: it is thus in his
own region that he gratifies him, in his own region
he contents him with offering.

11. The first Svâhâ ('hail') he utters on the
knee-high one,—what is knee-high is, as it were,
below, and below, as it were, is this (terrestrial)
world : he thus gratifies those Rudras who entered
this world.

12. Then on the navel-high one,—what is navel-

---

[1] The site of the altar is enclosed within a continuous line of
261 parisrits, about half a foot in width, running along its edge.
Their height is indeterminate, with the exception of three of them,
dug in at the back (west) corner of the left wing, of which one is
to reach up to the knee, the second up to the navel, and the third
up to the mouth ; each of the latter two standing to the left (north)
of the preceding one.

[2] See I, 7, 3, 20, with note. Agni, in the form of the formidable
Rudra (who is to be kept at a distance), is referred to.

high is, as it were, the middle; and the middle, as it were, is the air-world: he thus gratifies those Rudras who entered the air-world.

13. Then on the one reaching up to the mouth,—what reaches up to the mouth is, as it were, above, and above, as it were, is yonder world: he thus gratifies those Rudras who entered yonder world. [He does so] with Svâhâ,—the Svâhâ is food: with food he thus gratifies them.

14. [He offers, with, Vâg. S. XVI, 1], 'Reverence, O Rudra, be to thy wrath!' he thereby does reverence to that wrath which remained extended within him;—'And to thine arrow be reverence, and to both thine arms be reverence!' for it was by his arrow and his arms that he was inspiring fear.

15. That god who became the hundred-headed (Rudra) is the chief (kshatra [1]), and those others who originated from the drops are the peasants (clansmen): those peasants in the first place assigned to that chief this as his special share, to wit, this first chapter of formulas [2], and gratified him thereby. And in like manner does this (Sacrificer) now assign this to him as his special fore-share, and gratify him thereby. Hence this (section) is addressed to a single deity, to Rudra; for it is him he thereby gratifies.

16. There are here fourteen formulas,—thirteen months are a year, and Pragâpati is the fourteenth:

---

[1] Literally, the ruling power.

[2] The first anuvâka of kânda XVI of the Vâg. S. consists of sixteen verses; which of these the fourteen referred to in the next paragraph are is not clear to me.

and Pragâpati is Agni : as great as Agni is, as great
as is his measure, with so much food he thus gratifies
him. 'Reverence! reverence!' he says;—reverence
being sacrifice, it is by sacrifice, by reverence, that
he thus reveres him. Therefore he must not mention any one unworthy of sacrifice, for it would be just
as if he were to say to him, 'Sacrifice be to thee!'

17. He then makes offering to those forming
pairs[1]: ' Reverence to so and so ! reverence to so and
so!' It is as if he were to say, ' Thou, N. N., and
this one, do not ye two injure us!' for in no wise
does a man who is known and appealed to[2] injure us.

18. [Vâg. S. XVI, 17], ' Reverence be to the
golden-armed leader of hosts, and to the lord
of regions be reverence!' for he (Rudra-Agni) is
indeed the golden-armed[3] leader of hosts, and the
lord of regions. And in that everything in this
second chapter of formulas applies to one and the
same deity, thereby he gratifies that (god Rudra), and
makes the chief to have a share in the people (or
the clan) : hence whatever belongs to the people[4], in
that the chieftain has a share. And those (Rudras)
that spread over these worlds, countless, by thousands[5], they are the deities to whom he now offers.

19. He thus makes offering to the tribes (of
Rudras), for it was those tribes, those Rudras, that
spread, and wheresoever they are there he thereby
gratifies them. And thus, indeed, (he gratifies)
those tribes of Rudras; and, men being after the

---

[1] That is from Vâg. S. XVI, 17 seqq.

[2] Or, who is appealed to as being known to us, i.e. in terms
showing that he is known to us.

[3] That is, aureis brachiis instructus.

[4] Pragâyâ yad dhanam asti, Sây.   [5] See paragraph 28.

manner of the gods, therefore also these tribes of
men : tribe after tribe he thus gratifies them.

20. Now some of these (formulas) have 'reverence'
on both sides, and others on one side only ;—more
terrible and more unappeased, indeed, are those
(Rudras) that have 'reverence' on both sides : on
both sides he thereby appeases them by sacrifice,
by reverence.

21. With (each set of) eighty (formulas) he utters
the Svâhâ [1],—on the first anuvâka, and on eighty,
and on eighty ; and the formulas which follow as
far as the 'unstringing'-formulas (Vâg. S. XVI,
54-63),—eighties [2] mean food : by means of food he
thus gratifies them.

22. He thus mutters these formulas (the last four
of Vâg. S. XVI, 46), 'Reverence be to you, the
sparkling (hearts of the gods) !' for this is his
favourite resort, either as a dear son or the heart :
hence whenever he should be in fear of that god
(Rudra), let him offer with those mystic utterances,
for he draws nigh unto the favourite resort of that
god, and so that god does not injure him.

23. 'Reverence be to you, the sparkling [3],'

---

[1] The calculation here, as so often in regard to metres, is rather
a loose one. Anuvâka I, consisting of sixteen verses, is taken as
amounting to the first fourscore formulas ; anuvâkas II and III,
consisting of ten kandikâs (each of which is calculated to consist
of eight mantras), constitute the second fourscore ; anuvâkas IV
and V again form the third fourscore ; anuvâkas VI–VIII (save
the last four formulas, see parag. 22), the fourth fourscore ; and
from there to the 'unstringing'-formulas, that is, from within XVI,
46 to 53, the fifth fourscore. At the end of each eighty formulas
he is to utter one Svâhâ (sakrit svâhâkârah, Sây.).

[2] An etymological play on the word 'asîti,' as if derived from as,
to eat.

[3] ? Or, scatterers, sprinklers (kirika), root kri. The author of the

for those (Rudras) produce (kar) everything here,—
'hearts of the gods!'—Agni, Vâyu and Âditya
(fire, wind and sun), these truly are the hearts of the
gods;—'Reverence to the discriminating!'—
for those (gods) discriminate everything here;—
'Reverence to the destructive!'—for those
(gods) destroy whom they wish to destroy;—'Reverence to the irremovable!'—for those (gods)
are not (to be) removed from these worlds.

24. He then mutters those that follow (Vâg. S.
XVI, 47 seq.), 'Chaser! lord of the (Soma)
plant!'—that (god) is indeed a repeller, for he
chases away whom he wishes to chase away;—
'lord of the plant'—that is, 'lord of the Soma-
plant;'—'O blue-red cleaver[1];'—these are names
and forms of him: he thus gratifies him by calling
him by his names;—'frighten and hurt not these
people and these cattle! let none of us sicken!'
as the text, so the sense.

25. That god (Rudra) is the kshatra (ruling power;
chieftainship or chief); and for that chief these
peasants set apart this special fore-share, to wit, that
first section (of formulas); and now he (the Sacrificer)
sets apart for him that after-share, and thereby
gratifies him; and hence this (section) also belongs
to a single deity, to wit, to Rudra; for it is him he
thereby gratifies.

Brâhmana, on the other hand, evidently takes it in the sense of
'maker, producer.'

[1] Thus ('Zerspalter') daridra is probably correctly interpreted
(from root 'dar,' to split) by Prof. Weber; whilst the commentators
take it in its ordinary sense of 'poor' (i.e. without an assistant,
Mahîdh.); blue-red Rudra is called inasmuch as he is the 'nîla-
kantha' blue-necked, and red all over the rest of his body.

26. These are seven formulas,—of seven layers the fire-altar consists, and the year consists of seven months, and Agni is the year: as great as Agni is, as great as is his measure, by so much food he thus gratifies him. These two kinds (of formulas) amount to twenty-one,—the twelve months, the five seasons, these three worlds, and yonder sun as the twenty-first (make up) this amount.

27. He then offers (the libations of the) 'unstringing'-formulas[1]. For at that time the gods, having gratified those (Rudras) by that food, unstrung their bows by means of these 'unstringing'-formulas; and in like manner this (Sacrificer), having gratified them by that food, now unstrings their bows by means of these 'unstringing'-formulas; for with an unstrung bow one injures no one.

28. Here now he says 'at a thousand leagues,' for a thousand leagues is the farthest distance: and he thus unstrings their bows at what is the farthest distance.

29. And, again, as to why he says 'at a thousand leagues,'—a thousand leagues means this Agni (fire-altar), for neither this way nor that way is there any other thing greater than he; and it is when he makes offering in the fire that he unstrings their bows at a thousand leagues.

30. 'Countless thousands,—in this great sea,'—thus, wheresoever they are, there he unstrings their bows.

---

[1] Viz. Vâg. S. XVI, 54–63: 'What countless thousands of Rudras there are upon earth, their bows do we unstring at a thousand leagues.—The Bhavas that are in this great sea, in the air, their bow do we unstring at a thousand leagues.' Thus each formula ends with the 'unstringing' refrain.

31. There are ten of these 'unstringing'-offerings he makes,—the Virâg consists of ten syllables, and Agni is Virâg (widely-shining or ruling); there are ten regions, and Agni is the regions; there are ten vital airs, and Agni is the vital airs: as great as Agni is, as great as is his measure, by so much he thus unstrings their bows.

32. He then offers the descending[1] (series of oblations). For then (in the preceding oblations) he ascends these worlds upwards from hence: this is, as it were, an ascent away from here. But this (earth) is a firm resting-place : the gods returned to this resting-place; and in like manner does the Sacrificer now return to this resting-place.

33. And, again, as to why he descends. Then (in the preceding oblations) he goes after those (gods), gratifying (propitiating) them. From thence he now recovers his own self unto life; and so does he by that self of his attain all vital power.

34. And, again, as to why he descends. He then (in the preceding oblations) gratifies those Rudras from hence upwards; he now does so again from thence hitherwards.

35. [Vâg. S. XVI 64]. 'Reverence be to the Rudras dwelling in the sky,'—he thereby does reverence to those Rudras who are in yonder world; —'whose arrows the rain is,' for the rain is

---

[1] Vâg. S. XVI, 64–66. In making these three oblations to the Rudras in the sky, the air, and on earth respectively, the procedure is the reverse from that described in paragraphs 11–13, viz. first on the enclosing-stone which reaches up to his mouth, then on that reaching up to his navel, and lastly on that reaching up to his knee.

indeed their arrows, and by the rain they injure whom they wish to injure.

36. [Vâg. S. XVI, 65], 'Reverence be to the Rudras dwelling in the air,'—he thereby does reverence to those Rudras who are in the air;—'whose arrows the wind is,' for the wind is indeed their arrows, and by the wind they injure whom they wish to injure.

37. [Vâg. S. XVI, 66], 'Reverence be to the Rudras dwelling upon earth,'—he thereby does reverence to those Rudras who are in this (terrestrial) world;—'whose arrows food is,' for food is indeed their arrows, and by means of food they injure whom they wish to injure.

38. 'To them (I stretch) ten (fingers) forwards, ten to the right, ten backwards, ten to the left, ten upwards[1],'—of ten syllables consists the Virâg, and Agni is Virâg; there are ten seasons, and Agni is the seasons; there are ten vital airs, and Agni is the vital airs: as great as Agni is, as great as is his measure, with so much food he thus gratifies them.

39. And as to why he says 'ten-ten,'—there are ten fingers in the joined hands[2]: he thus makes reverence to them in each direction; and hence he who is frightened places his hands together;—'To them be reverence!'—he thus does reverence to them;—'May they be gracious unto us!'—they thus are gracious unto him;—'whomsoever we hate, and whosoever hateth us, him we cast into their jaws!'—thus he casts into their jaws

---

[1] These words, as well as the spaced words in the next paragraph, are added to each of the three formulas in paragraphs 35-37.

[2] The joining of the hollow of the hands, by placing the tips of the fingers together, is a sign of reverence.

whomsoever he hates, and whosoever hates him. He may say, 'So-and-so I cast into their jaws!' naming him whom he hates, and then he has no longer any hold upon him. But let him take no notice of this (injunction), for indicated of himself is he whom he who knows this hates.

40. In three turns he descends,—Agni is three-fold: as great as Agni is, as great as is his measure, by so much food he thus gratifies them. With 'Svâhâ' (he makes offering), for the Svâhâ is food: with food he thus gratifies them. Thrice (in three turns) he ascends from hence upwards,—that makes six: the significance of this has been explained[1].

41. And as to why he descends in three turns,— it is because he ascends in three turns: thus in as many turns as he ascends, in so many turns does he descend.

42. He then throws that arka-leaf[2] into the pit; for it is therewith that he performs that sacrificial work sacred to Rudra, and that same (leaf) is inaus-picious; he now puts it away, lest any one should tread on this inauspicious (leaf), and suffer injury thereby: hence (he throws it) into the pit. And, again, as to why (he throws it) into the pit,—the pit, doubtless, means the fire, and thus that fire consumes it. Now as to the (symbolic) correspondence.

43. As to this they say, 'How does this Sataru-driya of his attain to (conformity with) the year, and Agni? how does it correspond to the year, to

---

[1] Of objects numbering six, the seasons commonly occur, e. g. VI, 7, 1, 16.

[2] See paragraph 4. According to Kâty. Srautas. 18, 1, 6 both offering-utensils (the arka-leaf and the arka-stick) are thrown into the pit.

Agni?' Well, this Satarudriya includes three hundred and sixty (formulas); and (other) thirty, and thirty-five. Now, as to the three hundred and sixty which there are, so many are there days in the year: thereby it obtains the days of the year. And as to the thirty (formulas) which there are, they are the thirty nights of the month : thereby it obtains the nights of the month : thus it obtains both the days and nights of the year. And as to the thirty-five (formulas) there are, they are the thirteenth month[1], (Agni's) self,— the body (consists of) thirty (limbs[2]), the feet of two, the breath of two (in-breathing and off-breathing), and the head is the thirty-fifth: so much is the year. And in this way this Satarudriya of his attains to (conformity with) the year, Agni, and corresponds to the year, Agni. And, indeed, in the Sândila fire-altar as many bricks with formulas attached to them are placed in the middle, for these bricks are indeed the same as these different Agnis (invoked in the Satarudriya); and thus these Agnis of his come to have oblations offered to them separately by means of the Satarudriya.

44. As to this they say, 'How does this Satarudriya of his attain to (conformity with) the Great

---

[1] As Prof. Weber, ' Die vedischen Nachrichten von den Nakshatra,' p. 298, points out, this passage points to a six years' period of intercalation, since, in counting 360 days in the year, the remainder accumulates in six years to an intercalary month of thirty-five days (or thirty-six according to Sat. Br. X, 5, 4, 5); and accordingly in Vâg. S. XXX, 15, and Taitt. Âr. IV, 19, 1, the names of the six years of such a period of intercalation are mentioned; while a five years' period and the names of the respective years are more frequently referred to.

[2] Viz. twenty fingers and toes, the upper and lower arms, the thighs and shanks, and the hands.

Litany[1]?—how does it correspond to the Great Litany?' Well, those twenty-five formulas which there are on both sides of the eighties[2], they are the twenty-five-fold body[3]; and where the body (of the altar-bird) is, that (includes) the head, and the wings and tail. And what eighties (of formulas) there are (in the Satarudriya), thereby indeed the (corresponding) eighties (of the Mahad uktham) are obtained, for by eighties the Great Litany is recited. And what there is (in the Satarudriya) after the eighties that is for him the same as what there, in the Great Litany, is after the eighties[4]; and in this way this Satarudriya

---

[1] For the mahad uktham, or Great Litany, recited on the Mahâvrata day, see p. 110, note 3. According to Sâyana, however, this does not refer to the Mahad uktham, or Great Litany, itself, but to its Stotra, the Mahâvrata-sâman (cf. note on X, 1, 1, 5), by the chanting of which it is preceded, and which, like the Great Litany itself, is represented as being composed of the different parts of Agni-Pragâpati's bird-shaped body. Now, that part of the chant which corresponds to the god's trunk (âtman) is the only part of this Stotra which is chanted in the Pañkavimsa-stoma, or twenty-five-versed hymn-form, which, indeed, is the characteristic Stoma of the Mahâvrata day, all other Stotras of that rite being chanted in that form. It is, however, doubtful to me whether it is not rather the opening part of the Great Litany itself representing the trunk that is here referred to, and which, indeed, consists of twenty-five verses; cf. F. Max Müller, Upanishads, I, p. 183. Besides, it has always to be borne in mind that the particular arrangement of the Great Litany which the authors of the Brâhmana had before them, may have differed in some respects from those known to us.

[2] See p. 112, note 1.

[3] That is, the body with its twenty-four limbs, viz. the two arms, two legs, and the twenty fingers and toes.

[4] According to Sâyana, the Pañkavimsa-stotra, chanted after the Mahad uktham, is here referred to. See p. 111, note 1. Sâyana takes it to refer to the prose formulas at the end of the Sastra, which, he says, represent the mind (buddhi) of Pragâpati.

of his attains to (conformity with) the Great Litany; in this way it corresponds to the Great Litany.

SECOND BRÂHMANA.

1. He then sprinkles him (Agni-Rudra, the fire-altar). For the gods, having now appeased him by the Satarudriya, thereby appeased him still further; and in like manner does this (Sacrificer), now that he has appeased him by the Satarudriya, still further appease him thereby.

2. With water he sprinkles him[1],—water is a means of appeasing (soothing): he thus appeases him thereby. He sprinkles him all over; he thus appeases him all over. Thrice he sprinkles,—threefold is Agni: as great as Agni is, as great as is his measure, with so much he thus appeases him.

3. And, again, as to why he sprinkles him,—that Agni (the fire-altar), doubtless, is these worlds: by water he thus encompasses these worlds, by the ocean, indeed, he encompasses them. On every side (he sprinkles the altar): hence the ocean flows round these worlds on every side. From left to right (he sprinkles): hence the ocean flows round these worlds from left to right.

4. For safety from injury it is the Agnîdh who sprinkles, for the Agnîdh is the same as Agni, and no one injures his own self. From a stone (he sprinkles), for from the rock water springs forth:—from the arm-pit, for from the arm-pit water springs forth:—from the right arm-pit[2], for from the right arm-pit water springs forth.

---

[1] Or rather, he pours water on it (the altar).

[2] That is, from the lower (or hindmost) point where the right

5. [He sprinkles the stone, with, Vâg. S. XVII, 1], 'The food that is lying in the rock, in the mountain,'—for that food, water, is indeed contained in the rock, in the mountains;—'the drink that is gathered from waters, plants and trees,' —for from all that that drink is indeed gathered;— 'that sap and food bring ye unto us, O Maruts, as bountiful givers!'—for the Maruts are the rulers of the rain. With 'In the rock is thy hunger,' he (after watering the altar) sets down (the pitcher on the stone): he thus lays hunger into the stone, whence the stone is not fit for eating. But hard also is the stone, and hard is hunger: he thus puts the hard along with the hard. With, 'In me thy food!' he takes up (the pitcher): he thereby takes up the food into his own self. Thus (he does) a second and a third time.

6. Having (finally) set down the pitcher, he perambulates thrice (the altar); for when (in sprinkling) he walks all round it, he, as it were, makes light of him (Agni-Rudra). He now makes amends to him, for (his own) safety.

7. And, again, as to why he perambulates it,—he then (in sprinkling the altar) goes after him[1] (Agni-Rudra): thereupon he now recovers his own self unto life, and so does he by that self of his obtain all vital power.

8. Thrice he perambulates it, for thrice he walks round it (whilst sprinkling): thus as many times as he walks round it, so many times does he perambulate it.

---

wing joins the body of the altar. He there places a stone, from which he begins the sprinkling of the altar.

[1] See IX, 1, 1, 33.

9. Having thereupon put that stone into the water-pitcher, they throw it in that (south-western) direction, for that is Nirriti's region: he thus consigns pain [1] to Nirriti's region.

10. For at that time, the gods, having appeased him by the Satarudriya and the water, thereby drove out his pain, his evil; and in like manner does this (Sacrificer) now, after appeasing him by the Satarudriya and the water, cast away his pain, his evil.

11. Outside the fire-altar he throws it; for this fire-altar indeed is the same as these (three) worlds: he thus puts pain outside these worlds;—outside the sacrificial ground (vedi); for the Vedi is this (earth): he thus puts pain outside this earth.

12. Whilst standing at the right thigh of the Vedi, with his face to the east, he throws it southwards, with, 'Let thy pain enter him whom we hate!' and thus its pain enters whomsoever he hates. He may say, 'Let thy pain enter so-and-so!' naming him whom he hates, and then he has no longer any hold upon him; but let him take no notice of this, for indicated of himself is he whom he who knows this hates. If it [2] should remain unbroken, let him bid (the Pratiprasthâtri) to break it; for only when it is broken, the pain enters him whom he hates. They return (to the altar) without looking back: they thus leave pain and evil behind without looking back to them.

13. Having returned, he makes the bricks his own

---

[1] The burning heat of the fire, and all physical and mental suffering.

[2] Viz. the stone, or the pot, according to others; cf. Kâty. Srautas. XVIII, 2, 5–8. According to Prof. Weber the stone is meant to represent the hungry greed of the fire.

milch cows; for the gods, having now appeased him
(Agni-Rudra) by the Satarudriya and the water, and
having driven out his pain and evil, returned (to the
altar) and made the bricks their own milch cows;
and in like manner does this (Sacrificer) now, after
appeasing him by the Satarudriya and the water, and
casting off his pain and evil, return and make the
bricks his own milch cows.

14. And some say, 'Let him make them his own
whilst sitting, for sitting one milks the cow.' But
let him rather make them his own standing; for
that fire-altar is these worlds, and these worlds are,
as it were, standing. And, moreover, one is stronger
whilst standing.

15. [He does so], whilst standing (near the right
thigh of the altar) with his face towards the north-east;
in front stands that cow by the Sacrificer with her
face towards the west (back), for from the right
side they approach the cow which stands with its
face towards the back (west).

16. And wherever he reaches (whilst stretching
his arms over the altar), there he touches it and
mutters this formula (Vâg. S. XVII, 2), 'Let these
bricks be mine own milch cows, O Agni!' for
Agni rules over this making of cows, whence he
addresses Agni out of so many deities:—'One, and
ten[1] .... and a hundred thousand millions,
and a billion;'—for the one, to wit, one and ten,
is the lowest quantity, and the other, to wit, a hundred
thousand millions, and a billion, is the highest
quantity; thus, having comprehended them by the

---

[1] The intervening numbers here omitted increase by multiples
of ten.

lowest and the highest quantity, the gods made them their own milch cows; and in like manner does this (Sacrificer), having thus comprehended them by the lowest and the highest quantity, make them his own milch cows. Hence also he need not care to make many (cows) his own [1], for in yonder world that (Sacrificer), by means of the Brahman (holy writ), the Yagus, will make many (cows) his own. And in that he carries on (the numbers) uninterruptedly, thereby he carries on, without interruption, his objects of desire.

17. And as to why he makes the bricks his own milch cows,—this fire-altar is speech, for with speech it is built up; and when he says, ' One, and ten, . . . and a hundred thousand millions, and a billion,'—' one' is speech, and a hundred thousand millions is speech, and a billion is speech : it is Speech herself that the gods thereby made their own milch cow; and in like manner does the Sacrificer thereby make Speech herself his own milch cow. And in that he carries on (the numbers) uninterruptedly, thereby it is Speech herself that he carries on :—' Let these bricks be mine own milch cows, O Agni, hereafter in yonder world!' He thereby makes them his own milch cows in this world, and he also makes them his own milch cows in yonder world ; and thus they are profitable to him in both worlds, in this one and in the other.

18. [Vâg. S. XVII, 3], ' The seasons ye are,'— for these (bricks) are indeed the seasons ;—' law-sustaining,' that is, ' truth-sustaining ;'—' be ye season-abiding, law-sustaining !'—for the bricks

---

[1] ? That is to say, he need not touch the altar more than once.

are the days and nights, and the days and nights indeed abide in the seasons;—'fat-showering, honey-showering,'—he thereby makes them fat-showering and honey-showering for himself.

19. 'The widely-shining by name,'—for the gods then called those bricks to them by their names, and in the same way in which they called them, they turned unto them; but the 'space-fillers' alone stood with averted faces discharging water, having no names applied to them. They called them by the name 'the widely-shining,' and they turned unto them. Hence, each time he has laid down ten bricks, he addresses them with the 'space-filling[1] (verse)': he thereby makes them widely-shining (virâg), for the Virâg (metre) consists of ten syllables:—'wish-milking, never-failing,'—he thereby makes them wish-milking and never-failing.

20. He then draws a frog, a lotus-flower, and a bamboo-shoot across (the central part of the altar). For the gods having now appeased him by the Satarudriya and the water, and having driven out his pain and evil, thereby still further appeased him; and in like manner does this (Sacrificer), now that he has appeased him by the Satarudriya and the water, and driven out his pain and evil, still further appease him thereby. In every direction he draws them: he thus appeases him everywhere.

21. And, again, as to why he draws them across. Now, in the beginning, when the Rishis, the vital airs, made up that Agni[2], they sprinkled him with water: that water dripped off and became the frogs.

---

[1] That is with the verse Vâg. S. XII, 54, beginning 'Lokam prina.' 'Fill thou the space;' see part iii, p. 153 note.

[2] See VI, 1, 1, 1-5.

22. They (the waters) said to Pragâpati, 'Whatever moisture [1] we had, has gone down.' He said, 'This tree shall know it!'—he shall know (vettu), he shall taste it (sam vettu)—that one, indeed, they mystically call 'vetasa' (bamboo), for the gods love the mystic. And because they said, 'Down (avâk) has gone our moisture (ka),' they became avâkkâs;—'avâkkâs,' they mystically call 'avakâs (lotuses),' for the gods love the mystic. These, then, are those three kinds of water, to wit, the frog, the lotus-flower, and the bamboo-shoot: by means of these three kinds of water he appeases him.

23. And, again, why he draws them across it;—when he (Agni, the fire-altar) is built up, he is being born, and he is born for every kind of food; and these are every kind of food, to wit, the frog, the lotus-flower, and the bamboo-shoot, for these, indeed, are animals, water, and trees : with all this food he gratifies him.

24. With the frog, on the part of animals, whence, of animals, the frog is the one affording least subsistence, for he is used up ;—with the lotus-flower, on the part of water, whence of the kinds of water (plants), lotus-flowers are those affording least subsistence, for they are used up;—and with the bamboo-shoot, on the part of trees; whence, of trees, the bamboo is the one affording least subsistence, for it is used up.

25. Having tied them to a cane, he, in the first place, draws them eastwards along the right (south) part of the (body of the) altar inside the enclosing-

---

[1] Thus, or essence (rasa), according to Sâyana ; cf. X, 6, 5, 1. The word 'ka' has, however, also the meaning 'joy.'

stones, with (Vâg. S. XVII, 4), 'With the lotus-
flower of the ocean we encompass thee, O
Agni: be thou bright and propitious unto us!'
that is, 'With the waters of the ocean we appease
thee.'

26. Then northwards along the hind part (of the
altar), with (Vâg. S. XVII, 5), 'With an outer
vesture of cold we encompass thee, O Agni:
be thou bright and propitious unto us!'—that
part of the cold which is frozen hard is an outer
vesture of cold: thus, 'By the frozen part of cold
we appease thee!'

27. Then eastwards along the left (north) part,
with (Vâg. S. XVII, 6), 'Upon the earth, into
the reed, into the rivers descend thou, O Agni,
thou art the bile[1] of waters: with them, come
thou, O she-frog, and make the sacrifice bright-
coloured and propitious for us!' as the text, so
the meaning.

28. Then southwards along the forepart, with
(Vâg. S. XVII, 7), 'Thou art the receptacle of
waters, the abode of the ocean: let thy darts
burn others than us! unto us be thou bright
and propitious!' as the text, so the meaning.   He
first draws them thus[2], then thus, then thus, then
thus: that is from left to right, for so it is with the
gods.

29. Over the body (of the altar) he draws them

---

[1] That is, 'the heat' which is considered the chief property of
the bilious humour.

[2] The procedure in this case is an exact counterpart of the
ploughing of the altar-site, for which see VII, 2, 2, 8–12, with
notes.   Hence also the verbs expressive of the two actions are
closely analogous, viz. vikrishati and vikarshati.

first, for of (the bird, or Agni) that is born the body is born first, then the right wing, then the tail, then the left wing: that is from left to right, for so it is with the gods.

30. Over the wings and tail he draws them in the direction of the body (self): he thus lays calmness into his own self;—from the further end (he draws) hitherwards: he thus lays calmness into his own self from the further end hitherwards. The right wing, with (Vâg. S. XVII, 8), 'O bright Agni, with thy light, (with thy dainty tongue, O god, bring hither the gods, and worship them)!' The tail, with (Vâg. S. XVII, 9), 'O bright and shining Agni, (bring hither the gods to our sacrifice and our offering)!' The left wing, with (Vâg. S. XVII, 10), 'He who with bright and glittering light (shineth upon the earth, as the dawns with their glow, who, the ever young, speeding, as in the race, in the battle, of the steed, thirsteth not in the heat).' 'Bright,' he says each time, for whatever is kindly and propitious is bright: he thus propitiates him thereby.

31. With seven (formulas) he draws them across,— the altar consists of seven layers, and seven seasons are a year, and Agni is the year: as great as Agni is, as great as is his measure, with so much he thus crosses him. Having thrown the cane on the heap of rubbish:—

32. [The Adhvaryu] then sings hymns round it (the altar):—for therein that whole Agni is completed; and the gods laid into him that highest form, immortality; and in like manner does this (Sacrificer) thereby lay into him that highest form, immortality. Sâman-hymns are (used), for sâmans are vital airs,

[4.] N

and the vital airs are immortality : immortality, that highest form, he thus lays into him. On every side he sings around it : everywhere he thus lays immortality, that highest form, into him.

33. And, again, as to why he sings sâman-hymns round about it ;—the gods then desired, 'Let us make this body of ours boneless and immortal.' They spake, ' Think ye upon this, how we may make this body of ours boneless and immortal !' They spake, ' Meditate (*k*it) ye!' whereby indeed they meant to say, ' Seek ye a layer (*k*iti) ! seek ye how we may make this body of ours boneless and immortal !'

34. Whilst meditating, they saw those sâman-hymns, and sang them round about it, and by means of them they made that body of theirs boneless and immortal; and in like manner does the Sacrificer, when he sings the sâman-hymns round about it, make that body of his boneless and immortal. On every side he sings : everywhere he thus makes that body of his boneless and immortal. Standing he sings, for these worlds stand, as it were ; and whilst standing one doubtless is stronger. He sings, after uttering (the syllable) ' hi*m*,' for therein the sâman-hymn becomes whole and complete.

35. He first sings the Gâyatra hymn [1], for the Gâyatri metre is Agni : he thus makes Agni his

---

[1] The Gâyatra-sâman is the hymn-tune composed on the verse called ' the Gâyatri,' *par excellence*, or ' Sâvitrî ' (tat savitur vare*n*yam, Rig-veda III, 62, 10), which plays an important part in the religious life of the Hindu. The verse, as figured for chanting, is given, Sâma-v. Calc. ed. vol. v, p. 601. On the present occasion, according to Lâ*t*y. Sr. I, 5, 11, a different text, viz. Sâma-v. II, 8, 14 (Rig-veda IX, 66, 19, agna âyû*m*shi pavase), is to be sung to this tune.

head, and that head of his (or of him, Agni) he thus makes boneless and immortal.

36. The Rathantara[1] (hymn he sings) at the right wing; for the Rathantara is this (earth), and this (earth), doubtless, is the most essential (rasatama) of these worlds, for it is in her that all these essences (rasa) are contained, and 'rasantama,' indeed, they call mystically, 'rathantara,' for the gods love the mystic: he thus makes this (earth) his right wing, and that right wing of his he thus makes boneless and immortal.

37. The Brihat[1] (hymn he sings) at the left wing; the Brihat (great), doubtless, is the sky, for the sky is the greatest (of worlds): he thus makes the sky his (Agni's) left wing, and that left wing of his he thus makes boneless and immortal.

38. The Vâmadevya[1] (hymn he sings) on the body (of the altar); for the Vâmadevya is the breath, and the breath is air (vâyu, the wind), and he, Vâyu, doubtless, is the self (body) of all the gods: he thus makes the air (wind) his body, and that body of his he thus makes boneless and immortal.

39. The Yagñâyagñiya[1] (hymn he sings) near the tail;—the Yagñâyagñiya, doubtless, is the moon; for whenever a sacrifice becomes completed[2], the essence of its oblations goes up to him (the moon):

---

[1] The Rathantara, Brihat, Vâmadevya, and Yagñâyagñiya tunes are apparently to be sung here on their original texts (Sâma-v. II, 30, 31, abhi tvâ sûra nonumah; II, 159, 160, tvâm id dhi havâmahe; II, 32, 33, kayâ nas kitra â bhuvat; and II, 53, 54, yagñâ-yagñâ vo agnaye), though hardly in their elaborate setting, as performed in chanting.

[2] It should be remembered that the chanting of the Yagñâyagñiya (or Agnishtoma)-sâman marks the completion (samsthâ) of the ordinary (Agnishtoma) Soma-sacrifice.

and inasmuch as sacrifice after sacrifice (yag*n*a) goes up to him, the moon is the Yag*n*âyag*n*iya : he thus makes the moon his (Agni's) tail, and that tail of his he thus makes boneless and immortal.

40. He then sings the heart of Pragâpati[1];—the heart assuredly is yonder sun, for he (the sun) is smooth, and the heart is smooth ; he is round, and the heart is round. On the body (of the altar) he sings, for the heart is in the body ;—at the arm-pit[2], for the heart is in (the vicinity of) the armpit ;—

---

[1] The Pragâpati-h*r*idaya, or Pragâpater h*r*idayam, as figured for chanting, is given, Sâma-v. Calc. ed. vol. ii, p. 499. It consists of the words, imâ*h* pragâ*h* pragâpate(*r*) h*r*idayam pragârûpam agîgane, with inserted stobhas and modulations. It is followed by a simpler form, which is perhaps the one used on the present occasion.

[2] Viz. on the place where the right wing joins the body of the altar. According to other authorities, the *S*yaita hymn-tune is likewise to be sung near the left arm-pit (or, according to *S*ân*d*ilya, at the place where the Adhvaryu mounts the altar). For other variations, see Weber, Ind. Stud. XIII, p. 276. I do not think that the ritual of the White Yagus, in omitting the left arm-pit, shows any gap or inconsistency, since the right arm-pit is marked out, not for any bodily parallelism, but for the simple reason that it is supposed to indicate the position of the heart. Whilst all the other places on which hymns are sung are essential parts of the bird Agni, the arm-pit is not an essential part, but is merely indicative of the central organ of the body. Lâ*t*y. I, 5, 11 seqq. supplies the following directions, apparently implying a somewhat different order of procedure from that followed in our text : He passes along the south, and whilst standing (east of the altar) with his face towards the west, he sings the Gâyatra at the head. Returning, he sings the Rathantara at the right wing. Going round behind, he sings the B*r*ihat at the left wing. Going back, and standing behind the tail, with his face towards the east, he sings the Yag*n*âyag*n*iya. The Vâmadevya he sings at the right, and the Pragâpati-h*r*idaya at the left, arm-pit. Then follow different views held by different teachers.— With this ceremony, by which homage is paid to the different parts of Agni-Pragâpati's body, compare the similar, but more elaborate, ceremony of the Parimâda*h* at the Mahâvrata, X, 1, 2, 9 with note.

at the right armpit, for the heart is nearer thereto[1] ; he thus makes the sun his (Agni's) heart, and that heart of his he thus makes boneless and immortal.

41. He sings about offspring (pragâ) and Pragâpati (the lord of creatures and procreation) ;—when he sings about offspring, he lays the heart into offspring ; and when he sings about Pragâpati, he lays the heart into Agni.

42. And, again, as to why he sings about offspring and Pragâpati ;—this Agni, doubtless, is both offspring and the lord of offspring, and hence, when he sings about Agni, he lays the heart both into the offspring and into the lord of offspring.

43. These (hymns) are the immortal bricks ; he lays them down last (highest) of all :—he thereby makes immortality the highest thing of all this (universe), and hence immortality is the highest thing of all this (universe). Let none other but the Adhvaryu[2] sing ; for these (hymns) are bricks, and he (Agni, the fire-altar) would be built up in the wrong way[3], were any other than the Adhvaryu to sing.

SECOND ADHYÂYA.   FIRST BRÂHMANA.

DAY OF PREPARATION FOR SOMA-SACRIFICE.

1. On the day of preparation, early in the morning, when the sun has risen, he releases his speech.

---

[1] That is, by taking the auricles as parts of the heart.

[2] According to Lâty. I, 5. 1 seq., it is the Prastotri who sings these sâmans. A similar conflict of competence in this respect is referred to not only in regard to detached sâmans (cf. Kâty. IV, 9, 6–9), but even in regard to such solemn performances as the chanting of the Mahâvrata-sâman (cf. note on X, 1, 1, 5).

[3] Vi-kita, in this sense, appears to be a ἅπαξ λεγόμενον. Sâyana seems to have read vigita (parâbhûta, defeated) instead.

Having released his speech, he takes clarified butter, in five ladlings, and throws five chips of gold thereon. Then these three (materials), sour curds, honey and ghee, are poured together, either into a dish, or a pot with a wide mouth ; and he puts a handful of sacrificial grass thereon.

2. He then mounts the fire-altar, with (Vâg. S. XVII, 11), 'Homage be to thy heat, thy fire[1]! homage be to thy flame!'—for that Agni has now been completely restored, and he now is equal to injuring whomever he might wish to injure; and whomever he injures, he injures either by his heat, or by his fire, or by his flame ; in this way he does not injure him thereby (etaiₕ);— 'Let thy darts burn others than us! unto us be thou bright and propitious!' as the text, so the sense.

3. Having mounted the altar, he makes the libation of fivefold-taken ghee on the naturally-perforated (brick): the significance of this has been explained[2].

4. On the naturally-perforated (brick) he makes the libation—the naturally-perforated one is the breath : into (the channel of) the breath he thus puts food.

5. And, again, as to why he offers on the naturally-perforated one ;—this (brick) is an uttara-vedi (high-altar) of Agni (the fire-altar); and that former libation which he makes[3] belongs to the

---

[1] Or, 'Homage be to thy burning (consuming) fire!' as Mahî-dhara takes 'harase soᵏishe,' and perhaps also the Brâhmana, though 'etaiₕ,' used in reference to Agni's weapons, would rather seem to indicate a plurality of them.

[2] See VII, 2, 3, 4; VIII, 6, 3, 15.

[3] See III, 5, 2, 9-11 ; the libation of ghee there offered on the

Soma-sacrifice, but this one belongs to the fire-altar ; this he now offers.

6. On that (former) occasion he makes the libation whilst looking at the gold ; for distinct is what one sees, and distinct was that high-altar ; and thrown down [1], indeed, are (the gold chips) on this occasion, and indistinct is what is thrown down, and indistinct is this high-altar.

7. With the Svâhâ-call he makes the libation on that (high-altar), for distinct (manifest) is the Svâhâ, and distinct is that high-altar ; but with the Vet-call (he offers) on this (brick), for indistinct is the Vet-call, and indistinct is this high-altar. With ghee (they offer), for with ghee they offer on the high-altar :—with fivefold-taken (ghee), for with fivefold-taken (ghee) they offer on the high-altar ;— by turns (he makes the libations), for by turns [2] they make the libations on the high-altar.

8. [He offers, with, Vâg. S. XVII, 12, a–c resp.], 'To the man-seated, vet!'—the man-seated one, doubtless, is the breath, and men mean human beings: he thereby gratifies that fire (or Agni), the breath, which is in human beings ;—'To the water-seated, vet!'—he thereby gratifies the fire which is in the waters ;—'To the barhis-seated, vet!'—he

uttara-vedi being preparatory to the leading forward of the fire to the high-altar.

[1] Each time he has poured out some of the ghee on one of the corners, or in the centre, of the stone ; he throws one of the chips of gold thereon, without looking at it.

[2] That libation was made crosswise— first on the right shoulder, then on the left thigh, then on the right thigh, then on the left shoulder, and finally in the centre, of the (navel of the) high-altar. In the same way he offers crosswise on the svayamâtrinnâ brick.

thereby gratifies the fire which is in plants[1];—'To
the wood-seated, ve*t*!'—he thereby gratifies the
fire which is in trees;—'To the heaven-winning,
ve*t*!'—the heaven-winning one is this Agni (*k*itya):
it is this Agni he thereby gratifies.

9. And as to why he says, 'To the man-seated,
ve*t*! To the water-seated, ve*t*!' &c., these are names
of this Agni: these names he thereby pleases. By
means of the oblation he makes them a deity: for
whatever deity the oblation is prepared, that deity
(they are), not that deity for whom it is not prepared.
And, in calling them by their names, he also thereby
places those fires along with this fire.

10. These are five oblations he offers,—the fire-
altar consists of five layers, the year of five seasons,
and Agni is the year: as great as Agni is, as great
as is his measure, with so much food he thus gratifies him.

11. He then sprinkles him (Agni, the fire-altar)
with the sour curds, honey and ghee; when he is
built up, he is born, and he is born for every (kind
of) food; and these, to wit, sour curds, honey and
ghee, are every (kind of) food: with every (kind of)
food he thus gratifies him. Everywhere (he sprinkles
the altar): everywhere he thus gratifies him with
every (kind of) food.

12. And, again, as to why he sprinkles him;—
here that Agni has been built up complete: on him
the gods now bestowed the highest (or last) form;
and in like manner does this (Sacrificer) now bestow
on him the highest (or last) form; but form means

---

[1] Inasmuch as 'barhis' is the sacrificial grass spread over the
ve*d*i, or altar-ground.

food, and these, to wit, sour curds, honey and ghee,
are the most excellent kind of food: this, the
most excellent form he thus bestows upon him as
his highest (property). Everywhere he sprinkles,
even outside the enclosing-stones; everywhere he
thus bestows on him the highest form;—by means
of sacrificial grass-stalks (he sprinkles), for they are
pure and meet for sacrifice; by means of their
tops (he sprinkles), for the top (is sacred) to the
gods.

13. And, again, as to why he sprinkles them;—of
old, when the *Ri*shis, the vital airs, joined him
together, they made that 'sagûrabdîya' (oblation)[1] his
special fore-share, and, when he had been built up,
they made this (sprinkling) his after-share: thus, in
sprinkling him, he gratifies those *Ri*shis, the vital
airs, who, when he (Agni) had been built up, made
this his after-share. With sour curds, honey and
ghee (he sprinkles): the significance of this has been
explained.

14. [He sprinkles, with, Vâg. S. XVII, 13, 14],
'The gods of the gods, the worshipful of the
worshipful,'—for they (the vital airs) are indeed
the gods of (among) the gods, and the worshipful of
the worshipful;—'who draw nigh unto the year-
long share,' for they do indeed draw near to this
their year-long share;—'not eaters of oblations,
—at this offering of sacrificial food,'—for the
vital airs, indeed, are not eaters of oblations;—'may
themselves drink of the honey and the ghee!'

---

[1] That is, the oblation (made on the bunch of sacrificial grass
placed in the centre of the freshly ploughed altar-site, where the
furrows meet) with the formula (Vâg. S. XII, 74) beginning 'sagûr
abdo.' See VII, 2, 3, 8.

that is, 'should themselves drink of this honey and ghee.'

15. 'The gods who attained godhead over the gods,'—for these gods have indeed attained a divine state over the gods;—'who are the fore-runners of this holy work,'—the holy work is this fire-altar (and sacrifice), and they are the fore-runners thereof;—'without whom no dwelling-place becometh pure;' for without the vital airs no dwelling-place becomes pure[1];—'they are not on the backs of the sky and the earth,'—that is, 'they are neither in the sky nor on earth: what-ever breathes therein they are.'

16. With two (verses) he sprinkles,—two-footed is the Sacrificer, and the Sacrificer is Agni: as great as Agni is, as great as is his measure, with so much he thus sprinkles him.

17. He then descends again (from the altar), with (Vâg. S. XVII, 15), 'Givers of in-breathing, givers of off-breathing.'—for this Agni who has been built up is all these breathings; were he not to utter at this time this (declaration of) self-surrender, then that (Agni) would possess himself of those breathings of his (the Sacrificer's); but now that he gives utterance to this self-surrender, that (Agni) does not possess himself of those breathings of his;—'Givers of in-breathing, givers of off-breath-ing, givers of through-breathing, givers of lustre, givers of room,'—he thereby says, 'A giver of this thou art to me,'—'let thy darts burn

---

[1] It is doubtful in what sense the author understands this part of the verse. Mahidhara takes it to mean, 'without whom no body moves.'

others than us! unto us be thou bright and
propitious!'—as the text, so the meaning.

18. Having returned (to the hall-fire) he proceeds
with the (forenoon performance of the) Pravargya[1]
and Upasad[1]; and having performed the Pravargya
and Upasad, he hands to him (the Sacrificer) the
fast-food or semi-fast-food. He then (proceeds) with
the (afternoon performance of the) Pravargya and
Upasad, and having obtained the object for which
he puts the (Pravargya-) cauldron on the fire, he
sets out (the apparatus of) the Pravargya.

19. Let him set it out on an island; for, when
heated, that (cauldron) is suffering pain; and were
he to set it out on this (earth) its pain would enter
this (earth); and were he to set it out on water, its
pain would enter the water; but when he sets it out
on an island, then it does not injure either the water
or this (earth): in that he does not throw it into the
water, it does not injure the water; and in that the
water goes all round it—water being a means of
soothing—it does not injure this earth;—let him
therefore set it out on an island.

20. But let him rather set it out on the fire-altar;—
for that fire-altar is these worlds, and the enclosing-
stones are the waters;—so that when he sets it out
on the fire-altar, he indeed sets it out on an island.

21. And, again, as to why he sets it out on the
fire-altar;—that fire-altar is these worlds, and those
Pravargya (vessels) are Agni (fire), Vâyu (wind), and
Âditya (sun): hence, were he to set them out in any
other place than the fire-altar, he would place those
gods outside these worlds; but in that he sets them

---

[1] For the Pravargya, see part i, p. 44 note; and the Upasads,
part ii, p. 104 seq.

out on the fire-altar, he places those gods in these worlds.

22. And, again, as to why he sets it out on the fire-altar,—the Pravargya is the head of the sacrifice, and this built-up fire-altar is the body: hence were he to set it out in any other place than the fire-altar, he would place that head away from that (body), but in that he sets it out on the fire-altar, he, having put together that body of him (Agni), restores the head to it.

23. The first Pravargya (vessel) he sets out close to the naturally-perforated (brick);—the naturally-perforated one is the breath, and the Pravargya is the head, and this built-up Agni is the body: he thus connects and puts together the head and the body by means of (the channel of) the breath. Having set out the Pravargya as is the way of its setting out,—

SECOND BRÂHMANA.

LEADING FORWARD OF AGNI TO THE FIRE-ALTAR.

1. Having returned to the (Gârhapatya[1]) in order to take forward the fire, he offers oblations, and puts on pieces of firewood. For now that Agni was about to go forward (to the fire-altar), the gods regaled him with food, both with oblations and pieces of firewood; and in like manner does this (Sacrificer), now that he (Agni) is about to go forward, regale him with food, both with oblations and pieces of firewood. He takes (ghee) in five ladlings: the meaning of this has been explained.

---

[1] That is, the newly-built Gârhapatya-hearth (part iii, p. 302) on which the Ukhya fire has been deposited.

2. He then takes (ghee) in sixteen ladlings[1],—
Pragâpati consists of sixteen parts, and Pragâpati is
Agni: he thus regales him with food proportionate
to his body; and the food which is proportionate to
the body satisfies and does no injury; but that which
is excessive does injury, and that which is too little
does not satisfy. He takes (the oblations) in the
same offering-ladle, for one and the same (Agni) is
he whom he regales therewith. With two (verses)
addressed to Visvakarman he offers; for this Agni
is Visvakarman (the all-worker): it is him he thereby
gratifies. Three oblations he offers,—threefold is
Agni: as great as Agni is, as great as is his measure,
with so much food he thus regales him.

3. He then puts on the pieces of firewood: this is
as if, after regaling some one, one were to attend
upon him. They are of udumbara (ficus glomerata)
wood; for the Udumbara is food and sap: with food
and sap he thus regales him. They are fresh
(green), for that part of trees which is fresh is uninjured and living: he thus regales him with what is
uninjured and living in trees. They are soaked in
ghee; for ghee is sacred to Agni: with his own
portion, with his own sap he thus regales him.
They remain the whole night in it, for there they
become imbued with sap. Three pieces of wood he
puts on,—threefold is Agni: as great as Agni is, as
great as is his measure, with so much food he thus
regales him.

4. And, again, as to why he offers those oblations;—now that he (Agni) was about to go forward,

---

[1] That is, he ladles sixteen sruva-spoonfuls of ghee into the sruk
or offering-ladle.

the gods restored (recruited) him beforehand with
food, with these oblations; and in like manner does
this (Sacrificer), now that he (Agni) is about to go
forward, restore him beforehand with food, with
these oblations.

5. He takes (ghee) in five ladlings, for fivefold
divided is that vital air in the head,—the mind,
speech, the breath, the eye, and the ear,—he thus
lays that fivefold divided vital air into this head.
[He offers it, with, Vâg. S. XVII, 16], 'Agni, with
sharp flame, (may destroy every demon! Agni
gaineth wealth for us)' thus with a (verse) containing (the word) 'sharp': he therewith sharpens
his head so as to become sharp.

6. He then takes (ghee) in sixteen ladlings: eight
vital airs, and eight limbs[1],—this (the symbolical)
amount. He takes it in the same spoon, for, indeed,
the vital airs and the limbs are in the same body.
Separately[2] he offers: he thereby makes a distinction between the vital airs and the limbs. With two
(verses) addressed to Visvakarman he offers: Visvakarman is this Agni, it is him he thus puts together.
Three oblations he offers,—threefold is Agni: as
great as Agni is, as great as is his measure, with so
much food he thus restores him. With seventeen
verses (he offers)[3],—Pragâpati is seventeenfold, and
Pragâpati is Agni: as great as Agni is, as great as
is his measure, with so much he thus restores him.

---

[1] Viz. the upper and fore-arms, the thighs and legs.

[2] That is, he offers this ladleful (obtained by sixteen ladlings
with the dipping-spoon) in two separate libations (âhuti) or, according to Kâty., in two halves.

[3] Viz. Vâg. S. XVII, 17–32 (sixteen verses, eight for each oblation)
and verse 16 (given above) used with the oblation of five ladlings.

With (ghee) taken in twenty-one ladlings (he offers
the two oblations),—there are twelve months, five
seasons, these three worlds, and yonder sun as the
twenty-first: this is the (symbolical) amount (or,
correspondence).

7. And, again, as to why he puts the pieces of firewood on; the gods having set him up wholly and completely, now regaled him with this food, these pieces
of firewood; and in like manner does this (Sacrificer),
now that he has set him up wholly and completely,
regale him with this food, these pieces of firewood.
They are of udumbara wood, and fresh, and remain
for a whole night (being) soaked in ghee : the significance of this has been explained. [He puts them
on, with, Vâg. S. XVII, 50–52], 'Upwards lead
thou him, O Agni!... Forward lead thou him, O
Indra!... In whose house we make offering ...,'
as the text, so the meaning. Three pieces of firewood
he puts on,—threefold is Agni: as great as Agni is, as
great as is his measure, with so much food he thus
regales him. Three oblations he offers,—that makes
six : the significance of this has been explained.

THIRD BRÂHMANA.

1. He (the Adhvaryu) then gives orders (to his
assistant, the Pratiprasthâtri), 'Lift the log[1]! hold
up the underlayer!'—[To the Hotri], 'Recite for

---

[1] Viz. a burning piece of wood taken from the Gârhapatya hearth
to serve as the new Âhavanîya on the great fire-altar. The Gârhapatya fire, it will be remembered, was the Ukhya Agni, or the
sacred fire carried in a pan (ukhâ) by the Sacrificer during his time
of initiation (dikshâ) lasting for a year (or some other definite
period), till, at the end of that period, at the beginning of the
Prâyanîya, or opening-offering, it was transferred from the pan to
the newly-built Gârhapatya hearth.

Agni as he is taken forward!'—'Agnidh, follow up with the single sword (-line)!'—'Brahman, mutter the Apratiratha (hymn)!'

2. For at that time, as the gods were about to come up in order to perform this sacrifice, the Asuras, the mischievous fiends, tried to smite them from the south, saying, 'Ye shall not sacrifice! ye shall not perform the sacrifice!'

3. The gods said to Indra, 'Thou art the highest and mightiest, and strongest of us: do thou hold those fiends in check!'—'Let the Brahman (n.) be my ally!' he said.—'So be it!' They made Brihaspati his ally, for Brihaspati is the Brahman (the priesthood); and having had the Asuras, the mischievous fiends, chased away in the south by Brihaspati and Indra, they spread this sacrifice in a place free from danger and devilry.

4. Now what the gods did then, that is done on this occasion. Those fiends, it is true, have now been chased away by the gods themselves, but when he does this, he does so thinking, 'I will do what the gods did;' and having had the Asuras, the mischievous fiends, chased away in the south by Indra and Brihaspati, he performs this sacrifice in a place free from danger and devilry.

5. As to that Indra, he is that Apratiratha (irresistible hymn); and as to that Brihaspati, he is the Brahman (priest): thus, when the Brahman mutters the Apratiratha (hymn) he (the Sacrificer), having the Asuras, the mischievous fiends, chased away in the south, by Indra and Brihaspati, performs this sacrifice in a place free from danger and devilry. This is why the Brahman mutters the Apratiratha (hymn, Vâg. S. XVII, 33–44; Rigv. S. X, 103, 1–12).

6. 'The swift (Indra), sharpening (his weapon), like a terrible bull,'—these are twelve suitable (verses) relating to Indra,—a year consists of twelve months, and Agni (the fire-altar) is the year: as great as Agni is, as great as is his measure, by so much he drives off the Asuras, the mischievous fiends, in the south. With trish/ubh[1] (verses he does so),—the Trish/ubh is the thunderbolt: by the thunderbolt he thus drives off the Asuras, the mischievous fiends, in the south. They amount to twenty-two Gâyatris[1], and thus they relate to Agni, for this is Agni's performance.

7. He then takes him up (in the form of a burning piece of firewood), with [Vâg. S. XVII, 53], 'Upwards may the All-gods bear thee, O Agni, by their thoughts!...' the meaning of this has been explained[2].

8. They then go forward, with (Vâg. S. XVII, 54-58). 'May the divine regions, the goddesses, protect the sacrifice!'—The gods and the Asuras, both of them sprung from Pragâpati, were contending for the regions, and the gods wrested the regions from the Asuras; and in like manner does the Sacrificer now wrest the regions from his hateful rival. 'Divine' he says, and thereby makes them divine for himself;—'may the goddesses protect the sacrifice,' that is, 'may the goddesses protect this sacrifice!'—'keeping off want and ill-will,'— want is hunger: thus, 'keeping off hunger;'—'grant-

---

[1] The trish/ubh verse consists of 4 × 11 syllables, hence the twelve verses of together 528 syllables. The gâyatrî verse, on the other hand, consists of 3 × 8 syllables; and twenty-two such verses would thus consist of altogether 528 syllables.

[2] Viz. VI, 8, 1, 7.

ing to the lord of the sacrifice a share in wealth-affluence,' that is, 'granting to the lord of the sacrifice a share in wealth and in affluence;' 'may the sacrifice be founded on wealth-affluence!' —that is, 'may the sacrifice be founded on wealth and affluence!'

9. 'Glorifying on the kindled fire,'—the glorifying one is the Sacrificer;—'the hymn-winged,'—for hymns are his wings;—'taken,'—that is, 'held;' —'praiseworthy,'—that is, 'worthy of worship;'— '(when) they sacrificed, encircling the heated cauldron,'—for they did sacrifice, whilst encircling the heated (Pravargya) cauldron; 'when the gods offered the sacrifice with food,'—for the gods did offer this sacrifice with food.

10. 'To the divine, fostering upholder,'— for he, Agni, is the divine upholder, the most fostering;—'he, the approacher of gods, the well-disposed, of a hundred draughts,'—for he is indeed an approacher of the gods, and well-disposed, and possessed of a hundred draughts;—'encircling, the gods drew nigh unto the sacrifice,'—for encircling him (Agni), the gods drew nigh to the sacrifice;—'the gods stood ready to perform the cult unto the gods,'—the cult, doubtless, is the sacrifice, thus, 'the gods stood ready to perform the sacrifice to the gods.'

11. 'The welcome oblation slaughtered by the slaughterer[1] to sacrifice;'—that is, 'wished-for, much wished-for;'—'where the fourth sacrifice goeth to the offering,'—the Adhvaryu first mutters the formulas, the Hotri afterwards recites

---

[1] Mahidhara takes 'samitâ' to stand for 'samitrâ.'

the verses, the Brahman mutters the Apratiratha (hymn) on the south side; this (set of verses), then, is the fourth sacrifice;—'may the prayers, the blessings favour us[1]!'—that is, 'may both prayers and blessings favour us!'

12. 'The sun-rayed, golden-haired Savitri ever lifted up[2] the light in front,'—this Agni, doubtless, is yonder sun, and that sun-rayed, golden-haired Savitri in front ever lifts up that light;—'at his behest Pûshan goeth, the wise,'—Pûshan, doubtless, means cattle, and they indeed start forth at his (Agni-Sûrya's) behest;—'viewing all beings as their guardian,'—for he indeed views everything here, and he is the protector of all this world.

13. Now, the gods thereby (viz. by these five verses) wrested from the Asuras the five regions which are on this side of yonder sun, and then ascended them; and so does the Sacrificer now wrest them from his hateful rival, and then ascend them. And by means of them the gods reached this place, and in like manner does this (Sacrificer) by means of them reach this place[3].

14. He then sets up a variegated stone;—the

---

[1] ? Or, 'May they favour our prayers and blessings!' These verses are rather enigmatical.

[2] The author of the Brâhmana connects 'udayâm' with 'yam,' Mahîdhara with 'yâ' (udayân for udayât).

[3] ? Or, reach that place; Sâyana, in the first instance, takes it to mean 'as far as this place' (from beyond the sun down to the end of the air); but in the second instance, he takes it as referring to the particular spot on the sacrificial ground near which this part of the ceremonial is performed, viz. the Âgnîdhra's fire-shed (as representing the air), south of which the Adhvaryu lays down a variegated stone close to the 'spine.'

variegated stone, doubtless, is yonder sun : it is thus
yonder sun that is set up.   It is variegated, for by
means of its rays that disk is variegated.   He sets
it up between the Âhavaniya and the Gârhapatya ;
for the Gârhapatya is this (terrestrial) world, and
the Âhavaniya is the sky: he thus places him (the
sun) between these two worlds, whence he shines
between these two worlds.

15. On the Âgnidhra range[1] (he places it), for
the Âgnidhra's fire-shed is the air ; he thus places
it in the air, whence that (sun) has the air for his
seat.   Halfway (between the two fires he places it) ;
for that (sun) is halfway from this (earth).

16. This (stone) is the breath,—he thus puts the
breath into the body ; and it is the vital power,—he
thus puts vital power into the body ; it is food, for it
is vital power, and vital power is indeed food.   It is
a stone, for a stone is firm : he thus makes the vital
power firm.   It is variegated, for food is variegated
(varied).

17. He sets it up (with, Vâg. S. XVII, 59, 60),
'Measuring he keeps in the middle of the sky,'
—for that (sun) indeed keeps measuring in the middle
of the sky;—'filling the two worlds and the air,'
for even in rising he fills these (three) worlds ;—'he
scans the all-reaching, the butter-reaching,'—
he thereby means the offering-ladles and the offering-
grounds ;—'between the front and back lights,'
—that is, between this world and that one ; or that
(fire-altar) which is here at this moment being built,
and that which was there built at first.

---

[1] That is, where the Âgnidhra shed and hearth will afterwards
have to be erected (see IX, 4, 3, 5–6) on the northern edge of the
Vedi, midway between the Gârhapatya and Âhavaniya fire-places.

18. 'The showering ocean, the ruddy bird,'—
for he (the sun) is indeed a showering ocean, and
a ruddy bird,—'hath entered the seat of his
easterly father,'—for he indeed enters that seat of
his easterly[1] father;—'the many-hued rock set up
in the middle of the sky,'—for that variegated
stone is indeed set up in the middle of the sky;—
'hath traversed and guardeth the two ends
of the atmosphere;'—for in traversing he guards
the ends of these worlds.

19. With two (verses) he sets it up;—two-footed
is the Sacrificer, and the Sacrificer is Agni : as great
as Agni is, as great as is his measure, with so much
he thus sets him (the sun, Agni) up. With trishtubh
(verses he sets him up),—for that (sun) is related
to the Trishtubh. He does not 'settle' (the stone),
for unsettled is that (sun); nor does he pronounce
the Sûdadohas over it ;—the Sûdadohas means the
breath, and that (sun) is the breath, and why should
he put breath into (or on) the breath? Having
deposited it in such a way that it is not lost ;—

20. They now approach (the fire-altar, with, Vâg.
S. XVII, 61-64), 'They all have magnified
Indra,'—the meaning of this has been explained[2].
'Let the god-invoking sacrifice lead hither,
let the favour-invoking sacrifice lead hither
(the gods)!'—both god-invoking and favour-invoking
indeed is the sacrifice ;—'let Agni, the god, make
offering and lead hither the gods!' that is, 'may

---

[1] Thus Mahîdhara here takes 'pûrva,' and apparently also the
author of the Brâhmana ; the easterly father being the Âhavanîya,
and hence the sky. In the formula it would rather seem to mean
'former, old.'

[2] See VIII, 7, 3, 7.

Agni, the god, both make offering and bring hither the gods!'

21. 'The creation of strength hath upheaved me with upheaval, and Indra hath laid low mine enemies by subdual,'—as the text, so the meaning.

22. 'May the gods advance the Brahman both by upheaval and subdual; and may Indra and Agni scatter asunder mine enemies!'—as the text, so the meaning.

23. Now, the gods thereby (viz. by these four verses) wrested from the Asuras the four regions which are above yonder sun, and then ascended them; and in like manner does the Sacrificer thereby wrest them from his hateful enemy, and then ascend them. And by means of them the gods then attained to that place; and in like manner does this (Sacrificer) by means of them attain thither.

24. They then mount the fire-altar, with (Vâg. S. XVII, 65-69), 'By Agni ascend ye to the firmament!'—the firmament, doubtless, is the heavenly world: thus, 'by means of this Agni (fire-altar) ascend ye to that heavenly world!'—'holding the Ukhya in your hands,'—for the Ukhya (the fire in the pan) they do hold in their hands[1];—'having gone to the back of the sky, to heaven, keep ye mingling with the gods!'—that is, 'having gone to the back of the sky, to the heavenly world, keep ye mingling with the gods!'

---

[1] Viz. inasmuch as the firebrand now being carried forward to the great fire-altar, where it is henceforth to serve as Âhavanîya, was taken from the Gârhapatya fire, which itself is identical with the Ukhya Agni, or fire carried about by the Sacrificer in the Ukhâ, or pan, during his period of initiation. See p. 191, note 1.

25. 'Go thou forth to the eastern quarter, knowing!'—the eastern quarter, doubtless, is Agni's: thus, 'To thine own quarter go thou forth, knowing!' —'be thou Agni's fore-fire here, O Agni!'— that is, 'Of this Agni (kitya) be thou, O Agni, the fore-fire[1]!'—'Shine thou, illumining all regions!'—that is, 'shine thou, illuminating every region!'—'Grant thou food to our two-footed and four-footed one!' he thereby invokes a blessing.

26. 'From the earth have I ascended the air: from the air have I ascended the sky;'— for from the Gârhapatya they go to the Âgnîdhrîya, and from the Âgnîdhrîya to the Âhavanîya;—'from the sky, the back of the firmament, have I gone to heaven, to the light;'—that is, 'from the sky, the back of the firmament, have I gone to the heavenly world.'

27. 'The heaven-going look not round, they ascend the heaven, the two worlds,'—those who go to the heavenly world do not indeed look round[2]; 'the wise who performed the all-sustaining sacrifice,'—for that sacrifice is indeed all-sustaining[3], and they who perform it are indeed wise.

28. 'Go forward, Agni, first of the godward-going,'—he thereby says to this Agni (that is carried forward), 'Go thou forward, as the first of these godward-going ones;'—'the eye of the gods

---

[1] Mahîdhara takes 'puro'gni' in the sense of fore-goer (puras agre añgati gakkhati).

[2] That is, according to Mahîdhara, they think not of their sons, cattle, &c.

[3] Thus Mahîdhara takes 'visvatodhâra;' 'flowing in every direction' (visvato + dhârâ), St. Petersb. Dict.

and of mortals,'—for this (Agni) is indeed the eye
of both gods and men;—'they who love to sacrifice together with the Bh*ri*gus,'—that is, 'sacrificing together with the Bh*ri*gus,'—'let the offerers
go unto heaven, hail!'—that is, 'may the offerers
go to the heavenly world, hail!'

29. Now, the gods thereby (viz. by these five
verses) wrested from the Asuras the five regions
which are in yonder world, and then ascended them;
and so does the Sacrificer thereby wrest them from
his hateful enemy, and then ascend them. And by
means of them the gods attained thither, and so
also does this (Sacrificer) by means of them attain
thither.

30. He then makes offering on that (firebrand);—
for now that he (Agni) had arrived the gods thereupon gratified him with food, this oblation; and in
like manner does this (Sacrificer), now that he (Agni)
has arrived, thereupon gratify him with food, this
oblation. With milk from a black (cow) which has
a white calf (he makes offering); the black (cow)
with a white calf is the night, and her calf is yonder
sun: he thus regales him with his own share, with
his own relish. On it (the firebrand, he offers)
while it is held above (the naturally-perforated brick);
for above (everything) is he whom he thereby gratifies. By means of the milk-pail (he offers), for with
the milk-pail milk is given away.

31. And, again, as to why he makes offering upon
it. That (Âhavanîya) fire is the head of the sacrifice, and milk means breath: he thus puts breath
into the head. He should make the offering so that
it (the milk) flows on the naturally-perforated (brick);
—the naturally-perforated one is breath, and this

(milk) is vital sap: he thus connects and puts together the head and the breath by means of vital
sap. [He pours it out, with, Vâg. S. XVII, 70, 71],
'Night and Dawn, of one mind, unlike in form,'
—the meaning of this has been explained[1].

32. 'O Agni, thousand-eyed!—through the
chips of gold[2] Agni is indeed thousand-eyed;—
hundred-headed,'—inasmuch as, at that time[3], he
was created as the hundred-headed Rudra;—'thine
are a hundred out-breathings, and a thousand
through-breathings,'—his indeed are a hundred
out-breathings and a thousand through-breathings
who is hundred-headed and thousand-eyed;—'thou
art the master of wealth,'—that is, 'thou art the
master of all wealth:'—'to thee, our strength,
do we give honour!'—he (Agni) is indeed the
strength[4]: it is him he thereby gratifies.

33. With two (verses) he makes offering thereon.—
two-footed is the Sacrificer, and the Sacrificer is Agni:
as great as Agni is, as great as is his measure, with
so much he thus makes offering to him.

34. He then lays it (the firebrand) down, with
(Vâg. S. XVII, 72, 73), 'A well-winged bird
thou art,'—for on that former occasion he, by
means of the fashioning-formula, fashions him into
a well-winged bird[5]; that well-winged bird he builds
up, and having fashioned that well-winged bird, he
finally sets him down;—'seat thee on the back

---

[1] Viz. VI, 7, 2, 2.   [2] See IX, 2, 1, 1.

[3] See IX, 1, 1, 6.

[4] ? Or, that (firebrand) is indeed food (vâga). Mahîdhara interprets this part of the formula thus: To thee do we give food (vâgâya
for vâgam).

[5] See VI, 7, 2, 5 seq.

of the earth, fill the air with thy shine, prop
the sky with thy light, and uphold the quarters by thy lustre!'—for that one (Agni) indeed
does all this.

35. 'Receiving offering, kind-faced, in front,'
—that is, 'receiving offering, kind-faced for us, in
front;'—'seat thee, O Agni, aright in thine
own seat!'—for this (fire-altar) is his (Agni's) own
seat: thus, 'do thou rightly seat thee in it!'—'in
this higher abode,'—the higher abode, doubtless,
is the sky;—'sit ye down, the All-gods and
the Sacrificer!'—he thus establishes the Sacrificer
together with the All-gods. With two (verses) he
deposits it: the significance of this has been explained,—with the Vashat-call: the significance of
this (will be explained) farther on.

36. He then puts pieces of firewood thereon; for
now that he (Agni) had arrived, the gods thereupon
gratified him with food, both pieces of firewood
and oblations; and in like manner does this (Sacrificer), now that he has arrived, thereupon gratify him
with food, both pieces of wood and oblations.

37. He first puts on one of sami-wood (acacia
suma). For at that time, when this oblation had
been offered, he (Agni) was enkindled and blazed
up. The gods were afraid of him, lest he might
injure them. They saw this sami tree, and therewith
appeased him; and inasmuch as they appeased (sam)
him by that sami, it is (called) Sami; and in like
manner this (Sacrificer) now appeases him by means
of that sami (wood),—just with a view to appease-
ment, not for food.

38. [He puts it on, with, Vâg. S. XVII, 74], 'I
desire the manifest favour of the admirable

Savit*ri*, enjoyed by all men; that great cow of his, the thousand-streamed, teeming with milk, which Ka*n*va was wont to milk;'—for Ka*n*va indeed saw her, and she, the thousand-streamed, milked him all his wishes (objects of desire); and in like manner does the thousand-streamed one now milk to the Sacrificer all his objects of desire.

39. He then puts on one of vikankata (flacourtia sapida) wood—the significance whereof has been explained—with (Vâg. S. XVII, 75), 'To thee give we honour, O Agni, in the highest home;'—his highest home, doubtless, is the sky;—'to thee give we honour, in hymns of praise, in the lower abode;'—the lower abode, doubtless, is the air;—'the birth-place whence thou hast arisen do I worship,'—that is, 'this is his (Agni's) own birth-place: that I worship;'—'on thee, when kindled, offerings are poured forth;'—for when he (the fire) is kindled, they make offerings on him.

40. He then puts on one of udumbara (ficus glomerata) wood;—the Udumbara means strength and sap: with strength and sap he thus gratifies him. It has forking branches[1],—forking branches mean cattle: with cattle, as food, he thus gratifies him. If he cannot get one with bifurcate branches, let him take up a globule of sour curds and put it on (the wood): that globule of sour curds which supervenes is a form of cattle. With the virâg (verse, Vâg. S. XVII, 76; *Ri*g-veda VII, 1, 3),

---

[1] Weber, Ind. Stud. XIII, 281, takes 'kar*n*akavat' to mean 'one that has a knot-hole;' but Deva's explanation, 'kar*n*ako dvitiya-sâkhodbheda*h*,' probably means nothing else than 'showing the appearance of a second branch,' or 'one in which a second branch (side branch) has struck out.'

'Kindled, blaze forth, O Agni, before us, (with inexhaustible flame, O youngest! perpetual viands accrue unto thee!)'—he puts it on;—the Virâg means food: with food he thus gratifies him. Three pieces of wood he puts on,—threefold is Agni: as great as Agni is, as great as is his measure, with so much food he thus gratifies him.

41. He then offers oblations,—this is just as if, after serving food to some one, one gives him something to drink. With the dipping-spoon (sruva) he offers the first two, with the offering-ladle (sruk) the last (oblation); (the first) with (Vâg. S. XVII, 77), 'O Agni, may we, with hymns and thoughts, speed this day this (sacrifice) of thine, even as a steed, as a noble, heart-stirring deed!'—that is, 'whatever heart-stirring hymn is thine, may I speed (perform) that for thee.' With a pankti (verse) he offers,—of five feet consists the Pankti, of five layers the fire-altar, five seasons are a year, and Agni is the year: as great as Agni is, as great as is his measure, with so much food he thus gratifies him.

42. He then offers (the second oblation), the one for Visvakarman,—Visvakarman (the all-worker) is this Agni: it is him he thereby gratifies,—with (Vâg. S. XVII, 78), 'Thought I offer, with mind and ghee,'—that is, 'The thought of these (priests and Sacrificer) I offer with mind and ghee;'—'that the gods come hither,'—that is, 'that the gods may come hither;'—'enjoying their offering-meal, the holy-minded,'—that is, the true-minded;—'to Visvakarman, the lord of all existence, I offer,'—that is, 'to that Visvakarman who is the lord of all that here exists I offer;'—'every day the

unimpaired oblation,'—that is, 'always the uninjured oblation.'

43. He then offers a full (-spoon) oblation,—the
full means everything: with everything he thus
gratifies him.

44. [He offers, with, Vâg. S. XVII, 79], 'Thine,
O Agni, are seven logs,'—logs mean vital airs, for
the vital airs do kindle him;—'seven tongues,'—
this he says with regard to those seven persons which
they made into one person[1];—'seven *Ri*shis,'—for
seven *Ri*shis they indeed were;—'seven beloved
seats,'—this he says with regard to the metres,
for his seven beloved seats are the metres;—'sevenfold the seven priests worship thee,'—for in
a sevenfold way the seven priests indeed worship
him;—'the seven homes,'—he thereby means
the seven layers (of the altar);—'fill thou!'—that
is, 'generate thou;'—'with ghee,'—ghee means
seed: he thus lays seed into these worlds;—'svâhâ!'—the svâhâ (hail!) is the sacrifice; he thus
at once makes everything here fit for sacrifice.

45. 'Seven' he says each time,—of seven layers
the fire-altar consists, and of seven seasons the year,
and Agni is the year: as great as Agni is, as great
as is his measure, with so much he thus gratifies
him.   Three oblations he offers,—threefold is Agni:
as great as Agni is, as great as is his measure, with
so much food he thus gratifies him.   Three logs he
puts on,—that makes six: the significance of this
has been explained.

46. Standing he puts on the logs,—the logs are
bones, and bones stand, so to speak.   Sitting he

---

[1] See VI, 1, 1, 1 seq.

offers the oblations,—oblations are the flesh, and
the flesh sits (lies), so to speak. The logs are
inside (the fire), and the oblations outside, for the
bones are inside, and the flesh is outside.

47. Now, then, as to the (mystic) correspondence
(or, amount). Six he offers before (the leading
forward of the fire), and six afterwards; with six
(formulas) they proceed up to the variegated stone;
with two he lays down the variegated stone; with
four they proceed as far as the fire-altar; with
five they mount the fire-altar: that makes twenty-
nine, and the oblation itself is the thirtieth. With
two (verses) he deposits the fire,—that makes
thirty-two, and of thirty-two syllables consists the
Anush/ubh : such, then, is this Anush/ubh.

48. And this one (Anush/ubh) they bring hither
from those three Anush/ubhs which they make up
on the Gârhapatya[1] ; and inasmuch as they bring
this (therefrom) hither, thereby this whole Agni
(fire-altar) becomes completed. But now he was not
yet fit to eat food[2].

49. He said to Agni[3], 'By thee I will eat food!'—
'So be it!' Hence it is only when they bring him
hither, that this (Kityâgni) becomes fit to eat food,
to eat oblations.

50. Moreover, they say, 'It is Pragâpati himself
who takes this (Agni) as his dear son to his bosom;'
and verily, whosoever so knows this, takes thus
a dear son to his bosom.

---

[1] See VII, 1, 2, 16–19.

[2] Literally, he was not equal thereto that he should eat food.

[3] That is, the Kityâgni (fire-altar) said to the Agni (fire) about to
be led forward.

51. And, again, as to why they bring it here,—
the Agni (fire-altar) which is built up here is the
same as those seven persons which they made into
one person; and that excellence and life-sap of them
which they concentrated above, that is the fire which
they now bring here,—hence, when they now bring
it here, they concentrate above (in the head) that
excellence and life-sap which belonged to those
seven persons,—that is his (Agni's) head, and this
built-up fire-altar is the body: having thus completed his body, he restores the head to it.

THIRD ADHYÂYA. FIRST BRÂHMANA.

INSTALLATION AND CONSECRATION OF AGNI.

1. He then offers the Vaisvânara (cake).
That Agni has now been completely restored;
he now is that deity, (Agni) Vaisvânara (belonging
to all men): to him he offers this oblation, and by
the oblation he makes him a deity, for for whatever
deity an oblation is prepared that is a deity, but not
one for whom no (oblation) is prepared. It is one
of twelve potsherds: twelve months are a year,
and Vaisvânara is the year.

2. And, again, as to why he offers the Vaisvânara
(cake),—it is as the Vaisvânara that he is about to
produce that Agni: on that former occasion, at
the initiation-offering [1], he pours him out in the form
of seed; and what the seed is like that is poured

---

[1] Cp. VI, 6, 1, 6. Whilst the initiation-offering of the ordinary
Soma-sacrifice consists only of a cake on eleven potsherds to Agni
and Vishnu, that of the Agnikayana requires two further oblations,
viz. a cake on twelve potsherds to Vaisvânara, and a rice-pap with
ghee to the Âdityas; cf. part iii, p. 247 note.

into the womb, such like (is the child that) is born ;
and inasmuch as there he pours out Vaisvânara in the
form of seed, therefore he now is born as Vaisvânara.
Silently[1] it is (performed) there, for there seed (is
implied) in the sacrifice, and silently seed is infused ;
but distinctly on the present occasion, for distinct
(manifest) is the seed when born.

3. Now, that Vaisvânara is all these worlds : this
earth is the All (visva), and Agni is its man (nara) ;
the air is the All, and Vâyu (the wind) is its man
(ruler) ; the sky is the All, and Âditya (the sun) is
its man.

4. And these worlds are the same as this head,—
this (lower part of the head) is the earth, the plants
(being) the hair of its beard : this is the All, and Agni
is Speech, he is the man.   That (speech) is at the top
thereof, for Agni is on the top of this (earth).

5. This (central part of the face) is the air, whence
it is hairless, for hairless, as it were, is the air ; it is
this All, and Vâyu (the wind) is the breath, he is
the man ; he is in the middle thereof, for the wind
is in the middle of the air.

6. The sky is the (upper part of the) head, and
the stars are the hair ; it is the All, and Âditya
(the sun) is the eye, he is the man : it is in the
lower part of the (upper) head, for the sun is below
the sky. Vaisvânara is the head thereof, and this
built-up Agni (the altar) is the body : thus, having
completed his body, he restores the head thereto.

7. He then offers the (cakes) to the Maruts ;—

---

[1] Or, rather, in a low voice, the name of the deity being pronounced in an undertone while the oblation is poured into the fire ;
see VI, 6, 1, 11. No special formula is, however, used on either
occasion.

the Maruts' (cakes) are the vital airs : he thus puts
the vital airs into him (Agni). [He does so] after
offering the Vaisvânara ; for the Vaisvânara is the
head : he thus puts vital airs into the head.

8. That (Vaisvânara oblation) is a single one, for
single, as it were, is the head ; the others (viz. the
Mârutas) are seven in number, of seven potsherds
each ; and though 'seven-seven' means 'many
times,' here it is only seven [1] : he thus places seven
vital airs in the head.

9. That (Vaisvânara oblation) is (performed in a)
distinct (voice), for the head is distinct ; but indistinct the other (oblations), for indistinct, as it were,
are the vital airs. Standing he offers the former,
for the head stands, so to speak ; sitting the others,
for the vital airs are, so to speak, seated.

10. Now, the first two Mâruta (oblations) he offers
are these two vital airs (in the ears) : he offers them
in the middle [2] of the Vaisvânara (oblations), for
these two vital airs are in the middle of the head.

11. And the second pair are these two (vital airs

---

[1] See VIII, 1, 1, 2. Also VI, 5, 3, 11, where the translation
should be altered accordingly.

[2] In baking the cakes, the Vaisvânara is placed on the centre of
the fire, and the first two Mâruta cakes are placed north and south
of it, then the following pair of cakes behind the first, but more
closely together, and behind these the third pair, still more closely
together, and finally the last cake forming, as it were, the apex
of a phalanx of Mâruta cakes (or wind-deities) protecting (that of)
Agni Vaisvânara.   In offering the cakes a similar method is to be
followed ; except that the first pair of Mâruta cakes may be offered,
not in the fire itself, but on the previously flattened out Vaisvânara
cake lying on the fire. Whilst the Kâtiya-sûtra (XVIII, 4, 23)
admits this as an alternative mode (though not very clearly expressed), our passage seems to require it as the only possible mode.
Both the Vaisvânara and the Mâruta cakes are offered whole.

in the eyes); he offers them closer together, for closer together, as it were, are these two vital airs.

12. And the third pair are these two (vital airs in the nostrils). He offers them closer together, for closer together, as it were, are these two vital airs. The one to be recited in the forest [1] is speech: it is to be recited in the forest, for by speech one gets into much terrible (trouble).

13. And, again, as to why he offers the Vaisvânara and Mârutas,—the Vaisvânara is the ruling power (chieftaincy), and the Mârutas are the clan : he thus sets up both the chief and the clan. The Vaisvânara he offers first : thus, having set up the chief, he sets up the clan.

14. The former is a single (oblation) : he thus makes the ruling power (chieftaincy) to attach to a single (person), and (social) distinction to attach to a single (person). The others are numerous : he thus bestows multiplicity on the clan.

15. The former is (offered in a) distinct (voice), for the ruling power is something distinct, so to speak ; and the others are indistinct, for indistinct, so to speak, is the clan. Standing he offers the former, for the ruling power (the chief) stands, so to speak ; and sitting (he offers) the others, for the clan sits, so to speak.

16. The former he offers with the offering-ladle,

---

[1] 'Aranye+nûkya' is the technical term applied to the odd, or seventh, Mâruta oblation. According to Sâyana it is so called after an anuvâka of the Samhitâ, to be recited only in the forest. Possibly, however, it is to the particular formula (Vâg. S. XXXIX. 7), also called 'vimukha' (? to be pronounced 'with averted face'), and containing the names of the seven most terrible Maruts, that the name applies.

when the Vashaṭ is uttered, with both an invitatory
formula (anuvâkyâ) and an offering-formula (yâgyâ);
with the hand the others sitting, with the Svâhâ-call:
he thus makes the clan subservient and obedient to
the chieftain.

17. As to this they say, 'How do these (Mâruta
oblations) also come to be offered for him by the
offering-ladle, at the Vashaṭ-call, and with invitatory
and offering formulas?' Well, the first three feet
of those seven-footed Mâruta (verses), being a
three-footed Gâyatrî, are the invitatory formula,
and the last four, being a four-footed Trishṭubh, are
the offering-formula. The one is the bowl, and
the other the handle (of the offering-ladle), and the
Svâhâ-call is the Vashaṭ-call: in this way, then,
these (Mâruta oblations) also become offered for
him by the offering-ladle, at the Vashaṭ-call, and
with invitatory and offering-formulas.

18. And the first Mâruta (cake) which he offers
on the right (south) side, is the seven (rivers) which
flow eastwards. It is one of seven potsherds, for
there are seven of those (rivers) which flow eastwards.

19. And the first (cake) which he offers on the
left (north) side, is the seasons; it is one of seven
potsherds, for there are seven seasons.

20. And the second (cake) which he offers on the
right side, is animals; it is one of seven potsherds,
for there are seven domestic animals. He offers it
close to the preceding one (representing the rivers):
he thus settles animals near water.

21. And the second (cake) which he offers on the
left side, is the seven Ṛishis; it is one of seven
potsherds, for the seven Ṛishis are seven in number.

He offers it close to the preceding one : he thus establishes the seven *R*ishis in the seasons.

22. And the third (cake) which he offers on the right side, is the vital airs ; it is one of seven potsherds, for there are seven vital airs in the head. He offers it close to the preceding one : he thus puts the vital airs so as to be close to (not separated from) the head.

23. And the third (cake) which he offers on the left side, is the metres ; it is one of seven potsherds, for there are seven metres increasing by four (syllables respectively). He offers it close to the preceding one : he thus places the metres close to the *R*ishis.

24. And the Ara*n*ye·nû*k*ya is the seven (rivers) which flow westwards ; it is one of seven potsherds, for there are seven of those (rivers) which flow westwards. It is that downward vital air of his. That Ara*n*ye·nû*k*ya belongs to this Pra*g*âpati ; for the forest (ara*n*ya) is, as it were, concealed, and concealed, as it were, is that downward vital air ; whence those who drink of these (downward flowing) rivers become most vile, most blasphemous, most lascivious in their speech. Whenever he here speaks of them as belonging to the Maruts, he makes them food for him (Agni)[1] and offers it to him, and gratifies him thereby.

25. That Vaiśvânara (cake), doubtless, is yonder sun, and the Mâruta (cakes) are those rays. They are of seven potsherds each, for the troops of the Maruts consist of seven each.

---

[1] Probably, inasmuch as the Maruts (and the Mâruta oblations) represent the clansmen who are considered the legitimate 'food' of the chief, Agni Vaiśvânara.

26. He offers (the first Mâruta cake), with (Vâg. S. XVII, 80), 'The clear-lighted, and the bright-lighted, and the true-lighted, and the light, and the clear, and the law-observing, and the sinless one!'—these are their names: having completed that disk (of the sun, in the shape of the Vaisvânara), he bestows those rays on it by calling them by their names.

SECOND BRÂHMANA.

THE SHOWER OF WEALTH AND OTHER OBLATIONS.

1. Thereupon[1] he (the Sacrificer[2]) offers the Vasor dhârâ That whole Agni has now been completed, and he is here the Vasu (good one): to that Vasu the gods offered this shower (dhârâ), whence it is called 'Vasor dhârâ[3];' and in like manner this (Sacrificer) offers to him this shower, and gratifies him thereby.

2. And, again, as to why he offers the 'Vasor dhârâ;'—this is his (Agni's) Abhisheka[4]; for the

---

[1] That is, after offering all the seven Mâruta cakes, the formulas of the last six of which (Vâg. S. XVII, 81–85; XXXIX, 7) are not given in the Brâhmana. At the end the Adhvaryu mutters the verse XVII, 86, and thereupon he either makes the Sacrificer mutter (or mutters himself) verses 87–99 in praise of Agni. Kâty. Sr. XVIII, 4, 25; 26.

[2] Thus, according to Kâty. XVIII, 5, 1 (the Adhvaryu, according to Weber, Ind. Stud. XIII. p. 283).

[3] It would rather seem to mean 'stream, or shower, of wealth: cf. paragraph 4.

[4] That is, the consecration ceremony, in which the king is 'sprinkled' with sacred water, or, so to speak, anointed. The 'Vasor dhârâ,' or 'shower of wealth,' consisting of an uninter-rupted series of 401 libations to Agni (through which all the powers of the god are to be secured to the Sacrificer), is intended as the

gods, having now completed him wholly and entirely, showered upon him those wishes (or, objects of desire), this 'Vasor dhârâ;' and in like manner does this (Sacrificer), now that he has completed him wholly and entirely, shower upon him those wishes, this 'Vasor dhârâ.' With ghee taken in five ladlings, and an offering-ladle of udumbara wood (he offers): the significance of this has been explained.

3. [He offers it] after offering the Vaisvânara (cake)—for the Vaisvânara is the head, and food is taken in from the head (downwards); and, besides, it is from the head (downwards) that he who is anointed is anointed;—and after offering the Mâruta (cakes), for the Mârutas are the vital airs, and through (the channels of) the vital airs food is eaten; and, besides, it is at (the openings of) the vital airs that he who is anointed is anointed [1].

4. And, furthermore, (it is offered) upon the Aranye'nûkya [2]; for the Aranye'nûkya is speech, and it is through (the channel of) speech that food is eaten; and, besides, it is with speech that he who

equivalent of that ceremony for the consecration of Agni as king; and, indeed, as a kind of superior consecration ceremony for the (royal) Sacrificer himself, more potent than the Râgasûya and Vâgapeya. There is thus to be noticed here the same tendency as elsewhere of exalting the efficacy of the Agnikayana, and of making it take the place of the whole of the ordinary sacrificial ceremonial.

[1] When anointed, or consecrated, the king is first sprinkled from the front and then from behind, and finally rubbed all over, with the consecrated water; see V, 4, 2, 1 seq.

[2] That is, as soon as the Adhvaryu has put the Aranye'nûkya cake in the fire the Sacrificer begins to pour the ghee on it with a large offering-ladle of udumbara wood, and the Adhvaryu begins to mutter the formulas.

is anointed is anointed. And everything here is wealth (vasu), for all these (cake-offerings) are (connected with special) wishes [1]; and in order that this shower, be it of milk or of ghee, (may be) fraught with wealth, this oblation of ghee is thus offered for the beginning; and inasmuch as this shower is fraught with wealth, it is called 'shower of wealth.'

5. He (as it were) says, 'This is mine, and that is mine;'—that is, 'Herewith I gratify thee, and therewith;—herewith I anoint thee, and therewith;' or, 'Give me this, and that!' And as soon as that shower reaches the fire, that prayer is fulfilled.

6. Now the gods, having gratified him (Agni) by this food, or by these objects of desire [2], and having anointed him by this shower of wealth, solicited from him these objects of desire [3]; and having received offering, and being gratified and anointed, he granted them these objects of desire; and in like manner this (Sacrificer), having gratified him by this food, and by these offerings of desire, and anointed him with this shower of wealth, now solicits from him these objects of desire; and having received offering, and being gratified and anointed, he (Agni) grants him these objects of desire. In order to avoid discontinuance, he each time embraces two wishes,—even as one would connect those living away from one another,—thinking, 'In this way shall they prosper by sacrifice!'

7. The gods now spake, 'Through whom shall we receive these objects of desire?'—'By our own

---

[1] Or, all these (objects) for which offerings are made are objects of desire.

[2] Or, perhaps, 'for (prompted by) these objects of desire.'

[3] Or, asked him these wishes (boons).

self,' they said; for the sacrifice is the self of the gods, and so is the sacrifice that of the Sacrificer; and when he says, 'By the sacrifice they shall prosper!' he means to say, 'By my own self they shall prosper!'

8. In twelve (things) he causes them to prosper[1], the year consists of twelve months, and Agni is the year: as great as Agni is, as great as is his measure, by so much food he thus gratifies him, and by so much food he thus consecrates him. In fourteen he causes them to prosper; in eight he causes them to prosper; in ten he causes them to prosper; in thirteen he causes them to prosper.

9. He then offers the Ardhendra (libations)[2];— the ardhendras are everything here[3]: he thus gratifies him (Agni) with everything, and with everything he thus consecrates him.

10. He then offers (the libations relating to) the Grahas[4];—the grahas (cups of soma, offered to

---

[1] That is, he makes the objects of desire mentioned in the formulas used during the Vasor dhârâ, accrue to himself, or turn out well for himself. The formulas usually contain the names of twelve such objects (in six pairs), those in XVIII, 1 being—'(may) strength and gain, endeavour and attempt, thought and wisdom, sound and praise, fame and hearing, light and heaven, prosper for (or accrue to) me by sacrifice!' In XVIII, 4, however, fourteen objects are enumerated, in XVIII, 15 (and 27) eight, in XVIII, 23 (and 26) ten, in XVIII, 28 thirteen.

[2] Literally, 'the half-Indra ones,' the technical term for the formulas of three sets of libations (XVIII, 16–18), in which three sets of twelve deities are named, each pair of whom consists of Indra coupled with some other deity, thus 'May Agni and Indra, Soma and Indra, &c., prosper for (or accrue to) me by sacrifice!'

[3] Viz. inasmuch as Indra represents the ruling power, and everything submits to him (III, 9, 4, 15); or inasmuch as Indra and Agni are the whole universe (IV, 2, 2, 14).

[4] These are three sets of libations (still forming part of the con-

the deities), doubtless, are sacrifice: by sacrifice, by food, he thus gratifies him; and by sacrifice he thus consecrates him.

THIRD BRÂHMANA.

1. He then offers these Yag̃akratus[1] (sacrificial rites), with, 'May the Agni and the Gharma (prosper) for me!'—by these sacrificial rites he thus gratifies him, and by these sacrificial rites he thus consecrates him.

2. He then offers (the libations relating to) the Uneven Stomas[2];—for the gods, having now obtained their desires, by means of the uneven Stomas went up to heaven; and in like manner does the Sacrificer, now that he has obtained all his desires, by means of the uneven Stomas go up to heaven.

3. Now this (set runs) up to the thirty-three-versed (hymn-form), for the Trayastrimsa is the last of the uneven Stomas: at the last the gods thus

tinuous 'Vasor dhârâ,' or 'wealth-stream'), the formulas of which (XVIII, 19–21) enumerate each six pairs of cups of Soma (graha) and of sacrificial implements.

[1] These are two sets of libations in the formulas of which (XVIII, 22; 23) objects connected with 'special sacrifices' are enumerated. Thus, of the first pair, 'Agni and Gharma,' 'Agni,' according to Mahîdhara, represents either the Agnikayana or the Agnishtoma (ordinary Soma-sacrifice); whilst the 'Gharma (cauldron)' stands for the Pravargya offering (part i, p. 44 note).

[2] The formula of this set of libations (XVIII, 24) enumerates the seventeen uneven numbers (in the feminine gender) from 1 to 33, repeating the second number of each pair, so as to be the first number of the next pair (thus, 1 and 3, 3 and 5, &c.). These numbers are meant to represent the corresponding Stomas, consisting of an uneven number of verses, up to the Trayastrimsa, or thirty-three-versed hymn-form.

went up to heaven; and in like manner does the Sacrificer thereby at the last go up to heaven.

4. He then offers (those relating to) the Even (Stomas)[1];—for the metres then said, 'The uneven stomas are worn out, by means of the even ones we will go up to heaven!' By means of the even stomas they went up to heaven; and in like manner does the Sacrificer thus, by means of the even stomas, go up to heaven.

5. This (set runs) up to the forty-eight-versed (hymn-form), for the Ashṭâkatvâriṃśa is the last of the even stomas: at the last the metres thus went up to heaven; and in like manner does the Sacrificer thereby at the last go up to heaven.

6. He says, 'May the One and the Three (prosper) for me!'—'May the Four and the Eight (prosper) for me!'—even as one climbing a tree would climb up by taking hold of an ever higher branch, so is this. And as to why he offers the Stomas,—the stomas are food: it is with food he thus consecrates him.

7. He then offers (the libations relating to) the Age-grades[2] (of cattle),—age-grades mean cattle: it is by cattle, for his food, that he thus gratifies

---

[1] The formula of this set of libations (XVIII, 25) enumerates the twelve quadruples of 4 (in the feminine gender), from 4 to 48 (again repeating each number, except the first and last), as representing the Stomas consisting of an even number of verses, up to the Ashṭâkatvâriṃśa, or forty-eight-versed hymn-form.

[2] The two formulas relating to these two sets of libations (XVIII, 26; 27) contain respectively five and four pairs of teams of cattle of different ages, beginning with 'tryavi and tryavî,' 'an eighteen-months bull and an eighteen-months cow;' and ending with 'a bullock and a milch cow.'

him; and by cattle, for his food, he thus consecrates him.

8. He then offers whilst mentioning names[1];—for the gods, having obtained all their wishes, now gratified him directly; and in like manner does the Sacrificer, having obtained all his wishes, now gratify him directly. 'To Strength, hail! to Gain, hail!'—these are his (Agni's) names: it is by mentioning his names that he thus gratifies him.

9. There are thirteen of these names,—a year consists of thirteen months, and the layers and fillings of the fire-altar amount to thirteen: as great as Agni is, as great as is his measure, with so much he thus gratifies him. And as to why he offers while mentioning names,—it is thus in mentioning his (Agni's) names that he consecrates him.

10. He then says, 'This is thy realm; a supporter and sustainer art thou for the friend: for sustenance, for rain, for the lordship of creatures (do I consecrate) thee;'—sustenance, doubtless, means food, and rain means food: by food he thus gratifies him.

11. And when he says, 'This is thy realm; a supporter and sustainer art thou for the friend: for sustenance, for rain, for the lordship of creatures—thee!' this is to say, 'This is thy kingdom; thou art consecrated (anointed)! thou art thy friend's supporter and sustainer: for our sustenance art thou, for rain unto us art thou, for our lordship of

---

[1] This set of thirteen libations (XVIII, 28) is offered to the months Vâga, Prasava, &c., here apparently considered as manifestations of Agni (the year). Each name is followed by 'svâhâ (hail!);' and the last of these dedicatory formulas is followed by the special benedictory formula, referred to in paragraph 10.

creatures art thou!' They thereby entreat him,
'For all this art thou unto us: for all this have we
consecrated thee!' And therefore people thus
entreat a human king who has been consecrated.

12. He then offers the Prospering[1] (libations);—
the prospering (libations) are the vital airs: it is the
vital airs he thus puts into him.—'May the vital
strength prosper by sacrifice! may the vital
air prosper by sacrifice! . . .' He thus puts
proper vital airs into him.

13. Twelve prospering (libations) he offers,—a
year consists of twelve months, and Agni is the
year: as great as Agni is, as great as is his measure,
by so much he thus puts proper vital airs into him.
And as to why he offers the prospering (libations),—
the prospering (libations) are vital airs, and the vital
airs are the immortal element: with the immortal
element he thus consecrates him.

14. He then says, 'The Stoma, and the Yagus,
and the Rik, and the Sâman, and the Brihat,
and the Rathantara,'—this, doubtless, is the triple
science, and the triple science is food: it is with
food he thus gratifies him, and with food he thus
consecrates him;—'to the heavenly light we
gods have gone, we have become immortal,'—
for he indeed goes to the heavenly light, and becomes immortal;—'Pragâpati's children have
we become!'—for he indeed becomes Pragâpati's
child,—'vet! svâhâ!'—the Vet-call, doubtless, is

---

[1] This final set of twelve (? sixteen) libations is called thus (kalpa),
because, in the formulas used with them (Vâg. S. XVIII, 29), the
verb 'klip (to prosper, to be right and proper)' is repeated each
time. At the conclusion of these twelve formulas the priest mutters
the final benediction given in full in paragraph 14.

esoterically the same as the Vasha/-call, and either with the Vasha/-call, or the Svâhâ-call is food offered to the gods: he thus gratifies him by both the Vasha/ and the Svâhâ, and also consecrates him by both of them. He now throws the offering-ladle after (the ghee into the fire) lest what there is anointed with ghee should remain outside of the fire.

15. Now as to this same shower of wealth, the body (from which it flows) is the sky, the udder the cloud, the teat the lightning, and the shower (of ghee) is the (rain-) shower: from the sky it comes to the cow.

16. Its body is the cow, its udder the (cow's) udder, its teat the (cow's) teat, its shower the shower (of milk): from the cow (it comes) to the Sacrificer.

17. Its body is the Sacrificer, its udder his arm, its teat the offering-ladle, its shower (of milk) the shower of (ghee): from the Sacrificer (it goes) to the gods: from the gods to the cow, from the cow to the Sacrificer: thus circulates this perpetual, never-ending food of the gods. And, verily, for whosoever knows this, there will thus be perpetual, never-ending food. Now as to the (mystic) correspondence.

18. As to this they say, 'How does this wealth-shower of his obtain (conformity with) the year, and Agni? how does it correspond to the year, to Agni?' Well, this shower of wealth consists of three hundred and sixty (libations), and of (other) six, and of thirty-five. Now, the three hundred and sixty which there are,—so many being the days in the year,—thereby it obtains the days of the year. And what six there are,—the seasons being

six in number,—thereby it obtains the nights of the
seasons: thus it obtains both the days and nights
of the year. And what thirty-five there are, they
are the (intercalary) thirteenth month [1], and that is
the body,—the body (consists) of thirty (limbs), the
feet of two, the breath of two (in-breathing and
up-breathing), and the head is the thirty-fifth: so
much is the year; and thus that shower of wealth
of his obtains (conformity with) the year, and Agni:
and thus it corresponds to the year, to Agni. And
so many are the bricks with special formulas which
are placed in the centre of a Sândila fire-altar; for
these bricks indeed are the same as these different
Agnis [2]; and thus these Agnis of his come to have
oblations offered to them separately by means of the
shower of wealth.

19. As to this they say, 'How does this shower
of wealth of his attain to (conformity with) the
Great Litany, how does it correspond to the Great
Litany?' Well, the first nine formulas of this
shower of wealth are the threefold [3] head; and the
forty-eight which follow are the twenty-four-fold
wings [4]; and the twenty-five which follow are the
twenty-five-fold body [5]; and the twenty-one which
follow are the tail, as the twenty-first [6]; and the

---

[1] See p. 167, note 1.

[2] Viz. the different forms, or powers, of Agni, to which the 401
libations are offered. See IX, 1, 1. 43, where the very same calculations are applied to the Śatarudriya.

[3] See p. 114, note 1.

[4] Paksha, wing, also means half-month, fortnight, of which there
are twenty-four in the year.

[5] See p. 168, note 3.

[6] Apparently in addition to the fingers and toes (? of monkeys).

thirty-five which follow are the Vasa (hymn) : and
by the eighties (of verses) which follow those eighties
(of the mahad ukthama) are obtained, for by eighties
the Great Litany is counted; and what there is
after the eighties, that to him (corresponds to)
what, in the Great Litany, there is after the
eighties [1]; and thus this shower of wealth of his
attains to (conformity with) the Great Litany, and
corresponds to the Great Litany.

Fourth Brâhmana.

1. He then offers the Vâgaprasavîya [2] (set of
fourteen libations),—'vâga' (strength, sustenance)
means food (anna): it thus is an 'anna-prasavîya' for
him, and it is food he thereby raises (pra-sû) for
him (Agni).

2. For the gods, now that they had gratified him
by that food, and consecrated him by those objects
of desire, (to wit) by that stream of wealth [3], hereby
gratified him once more; and in like manner does
this (Sacrificer), now that he has gratified him by
that food, and consecrated him by those objects of
desire, that shower of wealth, hereby gratify him
once more.

---

[1] See pp. 110, note 3 ; 112, n. 1 ; 113, n. 1.

[2] That is, oblations capable of promoting or quickening strength
(or food.—vâga) ; see part iii, p. 37 (where read Vâgaprasavîya).
While the formulas of the first seven of these oblations are the same
as those used for those of the Vâgapeya (see V, 2, 2, 5–11), the
formulas of the last seven of these oblations are Vâg. S. XVIII,
30–36 (for the first of which, being the same as IX, 5, see VI,
1, 4, 4).

[3] This seems to be in apposition to both 'that food,' and 'those
objects of desire.'

3. And, again, as to why he offers the Vága-prasaviya. This, to be sure, is his (Agni's) Abhi-sheka. For, the gods, having gratified him by that food, and consecrated him by those objects of desire, (to wit) by that shower of wealth, then by this (offering) consecrated him once more; and in like manner does this (Sacrificer), having gratified him by that food, and consecrated him by those objects of desire, that shower of wealth, hereby consecrate him once more.

4. It consists of (seeds of) all (kinds of) plants,—that which consists of all plants is all food: he thus gratifies him with all food, and with all food he thus consecrates him. Let him set aside one of these kinds of food, and not eat thereof as long as he lives. With an udumbara (ficus glomerata) cup[1] and an udumbara dipping-spoon (he offers): the significance of these two has been explained. They are both four-cornered,—there are four quarters: he thus gratifies him with food from every quarter, and by means of food from every quarter he thus consecrates him.

5. And, again, as to why he performs the Vága-prasaviya;—he thereby gratifies those same deities who have been consecrated by this very rite of consecration by which he is now about to be con-secrated, and, thus gratified by offering, they grant him permission (to perform) this rite of consecration, and, permitted by them, he becomes consecrated; for only he becomes king whom the (other) kings allow to assume the royal dignity, but not he whom

---

[1] Or, pan. It has a handle, and serves on this occasion in place of the offering-ladle as well as for anointing the Sacrificer.

they do not (allow to do so). Thus when he offers
in the fire he consecrates Agni, and when he offers
to these deities, he gratifies those gods who rule
over this consecration ceremony.

6. And, indeed, he offers here also the Pârtha[1]
(oblations) ;—for the gods now desired, 'May we be
consecrated even on this occasion by all the rites of
consecration!' They were indeed consecrated on
this occasion by all the rites of consecration; and in
like manner is the Sacrificer on this occasion consecrated by all the rites of consecration.

7. Now these Pârtha (oblations) are the Vâgaprasavîya of the Râgasûya; and by offering these
(oblations) he is consecrated by the Râgasûya; and
the first seven of the succeeding fourteen (Vâgaprasavîya oblations) are the Vâgaprasavîya ceremony
of the Vâgapeya[2]: thus, by offering these he is
consecrated by the Vâgapeya. And what other
seven there are, they belong to Agni (or, the Agnikayana): by offering these, he is consecrated by the
Agni-consecration.

8. He first offers those of the Râgasûya, then
those of the Vâgapeya; for by performing the
Râgasûya one becomes king (râgâ) and by the
Vâgapeya emperor (samrâg), and the position of
king is (obtained) first, and thereafter that of

---

[1] In the same way as, at the Râgasûya, six Pârtha oblations were
offered before, and as many immediately after, the Consecration
ceremony, or 'anointment' (see part iii. p. 81 seq.), so also on the
present occasion, except that, between the first six Pârthas and
the consecration ceremony, the Vâgaprasavîya set, referred to
in the preceding paragraphs, is inserted.

[2] For these seven oblations, see V, 2, 2, 6-11. Only the second
set of seven thus is peculiar to the Agnikâyana.

emperor[1]: hence after performing the Vâgapeya, one could not perform the Râgasûya,—it would be a descent, just as if one who is emperor were to become king.

9. Those (seven Vâgaprasaviya oblations) of the fire-altar he offers last, for the Agni-consecration indeed is (equal to) all those rites of consecration, and he who is consecrated by the Agni-consecration rite becomes everything, king and emperor: therefore he offers those of the fire-altar last of all.

10. He then anoints him on a black antelope skin,—for the black antelope skin is (a symbol of) the sacrifice: it is thus at the sacrifice that he anoints him. On the hairy side (of the skin),—for the hairs are the metres: on the metres he thus anoints him. On the left (north) side (of the fire-altar he anoints him): the significance of this (will be explained) further on. On (the skin laid down) with the neck-part towards the front, for that (tends) godwards.

11. Some, however, anoint him on the right (south) side of the fire-altar, on the ground that it is from the right side that food is served, and that they thus anoint him from the food-side. But let him not do so, for that (southern) region belongs to the Fathers, and quickly he goes to that region whom they anoint in that way.

12. And some, indeed, anoint him on the Âhavaniya, on the ground that the Âhavaniya is the world of heaven, and that they thus anoint him in the world of heaven. But let him not do so, for that (Âhavaniya, the fire-altar,) is his (the Sacrificer's)

---

[1] See V, 1, 1, 12.

divine body, and this (Sacrificer, or Sacrificer's real body) is his human one: they thus attach that divine body of his to this his mortal body, if they anoint him in this way.

13. Let him anoint him on the left (north) side and nowhere else, for that north-eastern region belongs to both gods and men: they thus anoint him whilst seated and established in his own region, for he who is established in his own seat suffers no injury.

14. One who has gained a position in the world should be anointed sitting, for one who has gained a position is seated, so to speak;—and one who is striving to gain one standing, for one who wishes to gain a position, stands, so to speak. On a he-goat's skin should be anointed one desirous of prosperity, on a black-antelope skin one desirous of spiritual lustre, on both (kinds of skins) one desirous of both: that (skin) he spreads north of the tail (of the fire-altar) with its hair uppermost and its neck-part towards the east.

15. Close to the enclosing-stones[1]: inasmuch as the black-antelope skin is close to the enclosing-stones, so that divine body of his is consecrated on the black-antelope skin; and inasmuch as he is consecrated whilst keeping hold of the fire-altar he is not cut off from that divine consecration (of the Fire).

16. He anoints him after making offering on the fire-altar, for that (altar) is his divine body, and

---

[1] Sâyana takes 'âsprishtâm parishtitah' to mean 'lightly touched (just touched) by an enclosing-stone.' The participle would rather seem here to have an active meaning, like 'anvârabdha' in the same paragraph.

this (Sacrificer himself) is his human one; and the gods indeed were first, and thereafter the men: therefore, after making offering, he anoints him with what remains over of that same (offering-material) [1]. He then throws the dipping-spoon after (the oblations into the fire).

17. Placing himself near the (Sacrificer's) right arm, he then anoints him [2], with (Vâg. S. XVIII, 37), 'At the impulse of the divine Savit*ri*, I anoint thee, by the arms of the A*s*vins, by the hands of Pûshan, by the support of Sarasvatî Vâ*k*, the supporter, by the universal sovereignty of Agni!'—for Sarasvati is Vâ*k* (speech), and hers is all this support. Impelled by Savit*ri*, he thus anoints him by all this support of Sarasvatî Vâ*k*, the supporter, and by the universal sovereignty of Agni. Here he throws the cup (into the fire), lest what is anointed (with offering material) should remain outside the fire.

18. He anoints him in the middle of the Pârtha oblations, for the Pârtha oblations are the year: he thus places him in the middle of the year. Six he offers before, and six after (the consecration ceremony), for there are six seasons: by the seasons he thus encloses (guards) him who is consecrated on both sides. B*ri*haspati is the last of the first (six [3]), and Indra the first of the

---

[1] That is, with the remainder of the mess of different kinds of seed mixed with milk and water.

[2] That is, by sprinkling him with the liquid, or pouring it on him.

[3] The formulas of the twelve Pârtha oblations are the same as those used on the occasion of the Râgasûya (V, 3, 5, 8. 9), the sixth of which is 'To B*ri*haspati hail!' and the seventh 'To Indra hail!'

last (six),—Brzhaspati is the priesthood (or priestly office), and Indra is the nobility (or political power): by the priesthood and the nobility he thus encloses him who is consecrated on both sides.

FOURTH ADHYÂYA.   FIRST BRÂHMANA.

1. He then offers the Râshtrabhrzt (realm-sustaining) oblations ;—the realm-sustainers, doubtless, are the kings, for it is they that sustain realms. These deities, indeed, have been consecrated by this same consecration ceremony by which he (the Sacrificer) is now to be consecrated: it is them he thereby gratifies, and thus gratified by offering, they grant him permission (to perform) this consecration ceremony, and, permitted by them, he is consecrated ; for only he becomes king whom the (other) kings allow (to assume) the royal dignity, but not he whom they do not (allow to assume it). And inasmuch as the kings sustain realms, and these gods are kings, therefore Realm-sustaining (oblations are performed).

2. And, again, as to why he offers the Realm-sustaining (oblations). From Pragâpati, when dismembered, couples went forth, in the form of Gandharvas and Apsaras ; and he, having turned into a chariot, enclosed them, and having enclosed them, he took them to himself and made them his own ; and in like manner does this (Sacrificer), thereby enclosing them, take them to himself and make them his own.

3. Now that Pragâpati who was dismembered, is this very Agni who is here being built up ; and

those couples which went forth from him, are these same deities to whom he now makes offering.

4. He makes offering to the Gandharvas and Apsaras, for in the form of Gandharvas and Apsaras they went forth (from Pragâpati). But the Gandharvas and Apsaras also busy themselves with sweet scent (gandha) and beauteous form (rûpa[1]), whence if any one goes to his mate he cultivates sweet scent and a beautiful appearance.

5. He offers pairs (of oblations), for birth originates from a pair; and he alone is (ruler of) a kingdom who propagates offspring, but not he who does not propagate offspring. And inasmuch as couples sustain the realm, and these deities consist of couples, these (oblations are called) Realm-sustainers. With ghee taken in twelve ladlings (he offers), and there are twelve of these oblations: the significance of this has been explained.

6. To the male (deity) he makes offering first, then to the females: he thereby endows the male pre-eminently with power[2]. To a single male he makes offering, and to many females, whence even a single man has many wives. To the male (deity) he makes offering both with the Vasha/-call and the Svâhâ-call, to the female (deities) only with the Svâhâ: he thereby endows the male pre-eminently with power.

7. [He offers, with, Vâg. S. XVIII, 38–43], 'The

---

[1] This is apparently intended as an etymological explanation of the two names: Apsaras being taken as derived from 'apsas,' in the sense of 'beauty.' Cf. Weber, Ind. Stud. XIII, p. 135, note 3.

[2] Or, perhaps, 'he places the male above (the female) in respect of power;' see p. 133, note 1.

law-upholding, law-abiding,'—that is, the truth-upholding, truth-abiding,—'Agni is the Gandharva: his Apsaras are the plants,'—for as a Gandharva, Agni, indeed, went forth with the plants as the Asparas, his mates,—'Delights (mud) by name,'—the plants are indeed delights, for everything here delights in plants;—'may he protect this our priesthood and nobility: to him Hail! Vât! To them (fem.) Hail!' The meaning of this has been explained[1].

8. 'The Close-knit,'—yonder sun is indeed close-knit, for he knits together the days and nights;—'all-wealthy,'—for that (sun) indeed is every kind of wealth;—'Sûrya is the Gandharva: his Apsaras are the sun-motes;'—for as a Gandharva, the sun, indeed, went forth with the sun-motes as the Apsaras, his mates,—'Mobile (âyu) by name,'—for moving together[2], as it were, the sun-motes float;—'may he protect this our priesthood and nobility,'—the meaning of this has been explained.

9. 'The most blessed,'—that is, the most worthy of worship,—'sun-rayed,'—for like the sun's are the moon's rays;—'Kandramas (the

---

[1] In accordance with the preceding paragraph, that part of the formula which relates to the male deity, viz. 'The law-upholding, law-abiding Agni is the Gandharva—may he protect this our priesthood and nobility: to him Svâhâ! Vât!' is to be uttered first, and the first oblation to be offered at the call 'Vât,' i.e. Vashat, 'may he (Agni) carry it (to the gods)!' Then that part relating to the female deities is uttered, after which the second oblation is offered. In the same way the other five formulas are to be treated. See Mahîdhara's remarks on the present formula.

[2] Â-yuvânah, literally 'holding to each other,' a wrong etymology of 'âyu,' 'lively.'

moon) is the Gandharva: his Apsaras are the
stars;'—for as a Gandharva the moon, indeed, went
forth with the stars as the Apsaras, his mates;—
'Luminous (bhekuri) by name;'—light-giving
(bhâku*ri*[1]) these, indeed, are called, for the stars
give light;—'may he protect this our priesthood and nobility!' the meaning of this has been
explained.

10. 'The Agile,'—that is, the swift,—'all-ex-
pansive,'—for the wind (air), indeed, makes up all
this expanse;—'Vâta (the wind) is the Gandharva:
his Apsaras are the waters,'—for as a Gandharva the wind, indeed, went forth with the waters
as the Apsaras, his mates;—'Viands (ûrg) by
name,'—the waters, indeed, are called 'ûrga*h*,' for
food is produced from the waters;—'may he
protect this our priesthood and nobility!' the
meaning of this has been explained.

11. 'The beneficent, well-winged,'—beneficent
(bhugyu[2]) indeed is the sacrifice, for the sacrifice
benefits all beings,—'Yag*n*a (the sacrifice) is the
Gandharva: his Apsaras are the offering-
gifts,'—for as a Gandharva the sacrifice, indeed,
went forth, with the offering-gifts as the Apsaras,

---

[1] This etymological explanation of 'bhekuri' is doubtful.

[2] The real meaning of bhugyu in this passage is very doubtful;
while it usually means 'flexible,' the St. Petersburg Dictionary here
tentatively assigns to it the meaning 'adder.' Whether the author
of the Brâhma*n*a really connects it with 'bhug (bhunakti),' 'to
enjoy, benefit' (instead of with 'bhug,' 'to bend') or whether the
explanation is merely meant as an etymological play of words, is
not clear. Mahîdhara indeed derives it from the former root, in
the sense of 'to protect.' The order of the words 'yag*n*o vai
bhugyu*h*' would properly require to be rendered by—The 'bhugyu'
doubtless is the sacrifice.

his mates;—'Praises (stávà) by name,'—the
offering-gifts are indeed praises, for the sacrifice is
praised for offering-gifts ; and whosoever gives an
offering-gift (to priests) is praised;—'may he protect this our priesthood and nobility!' the
meaning of this has been explained.

12. 'The lord of creatures, the all-worker,'—
Pragâpati (lord of creatures) is indeed the all-worker,
for he has wrought all this (universe);—'Manas
(the mind) is the Gandharva : his Apsaras are
the hymn-verses and hymn-tunes,'—as a Gandharva, the Mind indeed went forth, with the hymn-
verses and hymn-tunes as the Apsaras, his mates :—
'Wishes (esh/i) by name,'—the hymn-verses and
hymn-tunes are indeed wishes, for by verses and
tunes people pray. 'May this accrue unto us! may
it fare thus with us!'—'may he protect this our
priest and nobility!' the meaning of this has
been explained.

13. He then makes an offering on the Head of
the Chariot;—this, indeed, is that very rite of
consecration,—and by that he is now consecrated,—
which this (Sacrificer) is permitted to perform by
those deities with whose permission he is consecrated[1]; for he alone becomes king whom the
(other) kings allow (to assume) the royal dignity,
and not he whom (they do) not (allow to assume it).
With ghee taken in five ladlings (he offers), and
this is offered as five oblations : the significance of
this has been explained.

14. On the head (or front part of the chariot the

---

[1] The construction of the text (occurring again at IX, 4, 4, 8) is
rather irregular.

offering is made), for it is from the head (downwards)
that he who is anointed is anointed,—whilst it is
held above (the Âhavanîya), for above (others) is he
who is thus anointed;—with the same formula
(repeated each time), for one and the same (person)
is he who is thus anointed;—whilst taking round
(the chariot-head) in every direction [1]: on every
side he thus is anointed.

15. And, again, as to why he makes offering on
the head of the chariot;—it is because this chariot
is yonder sun; for it was by assuming that form
that Pragâpati enclosed those couples, and took
them to himself, and made them his own; and in
like manner does this (Sacrificer) thereby enclose
them, and take them to himself, and make them his
own. Whilst it (the chariot-head) is held above
(the fire, he offers), for above (others) was he who,
enclosing those couples, took them to himself, and
made them his own;—and with the same formula,
for one and the same is he who, by enclosing those
couples, took them to himself, and made them his own.

16. [He offers each time, with, Vâg. S. XVIII,
44], 'O Lord of the world, Lord of creatures!'
—for this (Agni), indeed, is the lord of the world,
and the lord of creatures;—'thou whose dwellings
are on high, or here below,'—both on high and

---

[1] The body (or 'nest,' seat-part) of the chariot is shifted sunwise
round the fire on the great altar, so that the fore-part keeps over
the fire where the Adhvaryu's assistant holds it, and in each of the
four directions, as well as in the centre of the fire, the Adhvaryu
offers a libation of ghee, whilst facing the chariot-head. According
to a comment on the respective rules (Kâty. XVIII, 5, 17–20)
alluded to by Prof. Weber (Ind. Stud. XIII, p. 286), the fore-part
of the chariot would, however, seem to be taken off the seat-part;
the latter being carried round the fire as the oblations are made.

IX KÂNDA, 4 ADHYÂYA, 2 BRÂHMANA, 5.   235

here below, indeed, are his dwellings;—'to this priesthood and this nobility of ours,'—for this Agni is both the priesthood and the nobility, 'grant thou mighty protection, hail!'—that is, 'grant thou powerful protection!'

SECOND BRÂHMANA.

1. He then offers (three) oblations of air;—this fire-altar is these (three) worlds, and the oblations of air are wind: he thus places the wind into these worlds, and hence there is wind here in these worlds.

2. He takes (the air) from outside the Vedi; for that wind which is in these worlds is already contained in this (fire-altar), and he now puts into it that wind which is beyond these worlds.

3. From outside the Vedi (he takes it),—for the Vedi is this (earth), and the wind which is on this (earth) is already contained in this (fire-altar): he now puts into it the wind which is beyond this (earth).

4. By his two hollow hands (he takes it), for only in this way is the catching of that (wind brought about). With the Svâhâ-call (he offers), for he offers just under the shafts (of the chariot),—this chariot is yonder sun: he thus places the wind on this side of the sun, and hence that one blows on this side thereof.

5. [He offers, with, Vâg. S. XVIII, 45], 'Thou art the cloudy ocean,'—the cloudy ocean, doubtless, is yonder world (of the sky),—'the giver of moisture,'—for that (wind) indeed gives moisture: he thus bestows on this (fire-altar) the wind which is in yonder world; 'blow thou kindly and propitiously upon me, hail!'—that is, 'blow favourably and gently upon me!'

6. 'Thou art the stormy (region), the troop of the Maruts,'—the stormy (region), the troop of the Maruts, doubtless, is the air-world: he thus bestows on this (fire-altar) the wind which is in the air-world;—'blow thou kindly and propitiously upon me, hail!'—that is, 'blow favourably and gently upon me!'

7. 'Thou art the one affording protection and worship,'—the one that affords protection and worship, doubtless, is this (terrestrial) world : he thus bestows upon this (fire-altar) the wind which is in this world;—'blow thou kindly and propitiously upon me, hail!'—that is, 'blow favourably and gently upon me!'

8. With three (formulas) he offers,—three are these worlds, and threefold is Agni: as great as Agni is, as great as is his measure, with so much he thus puts air into these worlds.

9. And as to why he offers the oblations of air : he thereby yokes that chariot of his ; for it was thereby that the gods yoked that chariot for (the obtainment of) all their wishes, thinking, ' By it, when yoked, we shall obtain them;' and by that yoked (chariot) they indeed obtained their wishes ; and in like manner does the Sacrificer thereby yoke that chariot of his for (the obtainment of) all his wishes, thinking, ' By it, when yoked, I shall obtain them;' and by that yoked (chariot) he indeed obtains all his wishes.

10. He yokes it with the oblations of air [1],—the oblations of air are the vital airs: it is thus with the

---

[1] That is, these oblations are, as it were, to represent the team of the chariot.

vital airs he yokes it[1]. With three (oblations) he yokes it,—there are three vital airs, the out-breathing, up-breathing, and through-breathing: it is with these he thus yokes it. Just below the shaft (he offers), for just below the shaft the horse is yoked;—with his hands, for by the hands the horse is yoked;—in moving round[2], for in moving round the horse is yoked.

11. The right yoke-horse he puts to first, then the left yoke-horse, then the right side-horse: for thus it is (done) among the gods, otherwise in human (practice). Let him not yoke that (chariot[3]) again, lest he should yoke again the yoked one: but let him give away the vehicle, thinking, 'I shall reap the benefit of the yoking of it[4].' They carry it as far as the Adhvaryu's dwelling, holding it right upwards, for above is that (Agni). He presents it to the Adhvaryu, for it is he that performs therewith. Let him, however, (not) assign it to him (till) the time of the offering-gifts.

12. He then offers the 'Lightsome[5]' oblations.

---

[1] Or, he supplies him (Agni).

[2] According to Kâty. Sr. XVIII, 6, 1, 2, the Adhvaryu first takes a double handful of air from beyond the east side of the Vedi, and offers it below the right (south) shaft; then from beyond the north side to be offered up below the left shaft, and lastly from beyond the south side to be offered below the shaft where the right side-horse would be yoked. In each case the girth (or yoke-tie) is to be carried round in the same way as if a real horse were yoked.

[3] Sâyana takes it to mean 'that horse'; and according to Kâty. Sr. XVIII, 6, 3–5, the carriage is to be carried to the Adhvaryu's house, and, at the time when the dakshinâs are presented to the priests, it is to be given to that priest along with three horses. The Brâhmana, however, does not seem to mention the horses.

[4] Literally, of the yoked one.

[5] These oblations are here called 'ruhmati,' because the three

For now the whole Agni was completed; he now wished for brilliance (ru*k*), and the gods, by means of these lightsome (oblations), endowed him with brilliance; and in like manner does this (Sacrificer) now endow him therewith.

13. And, again, as to why he offers the lightsome oblations. When Pragâpati was dismembered, his brilliance departed from him. When the gods restored him, they, by means of these lightsome oblations, endowed him with brilliance; and in like manner does this (Sacrificer) endow him therewith.

14. [He offers, with, Vâg. S. XVIII, 46–48], 'O Agni, what lights of thine in the sun[1] . . . ,' 'O ye gods, what lights of yours are in the sun . . .[1]'—'Bestow thou light upon our priests, (work thou light in our kings, light in our people and *S*ûdras, bestow light upon me by thy light)!' He thus says 'light' each time,—light is immortality: it is immortality he thus bestows upon him.

15. He then offers one relating to Varu*n*a. That whole Agni has now been completed, and he now is the deity Varu*n*a: it is to him that he offers this oblation, and by the oblation he makes him (Agni) a deity, for that one alone is a deity to whom offering is made, but not that one to whom (offering is) not (made). With a verse addressed to Varu*n*a (he offers): he thus gratifies him by his own self, by his own deity.

16. And, again, as to why he offers one relating

verses used with them contain the word 'ru*k*,' being prayers for the bestowal of light.

[1] These two verses had already been used in laying down the Dvi*y*agus bricks; see VII, 4, 2, 21.

to Varuna. When Pragâpati was dismembered, his strength departed from him. When the gods restored him they, by this (oblation), bestowed strength upon him; and in like manner does this (Sacrificer) bestow it upon him. With a verse addressed to Varuna (he offers),—Varuna is the ruling power, and ruling power means strength : it is thus by strength that he bestows strength upon him.

17. [He offers, with, Vâg. S. XVIII, 49], 'For this I appeal to thee, worshipping thee with prayer,'—that is, 'For that I beseech thee, worshipping thee with prayer;'—'for this the Sacrificer imploreth thee with offerings,'—that is,'for this, this Sacrificer implores thee with offerings;'—'without wrath listen thou here, O Varuna!' —that is, 'without anger listen thou here to us, O Varuna!'—'take not our life from us, O far-ruler!'—he thereby gives utterance to a surrender of his own self.

18. He then offers the Arkâsvamedha-santati[1] oblations. The light (arka), doubtless, is this fire (Agni), and the Asvamedha (horse-sacrifice) is yonder sun,—when created, these two were separate: by means of these oblations the gods drew them together and connected them; and in like manner does this (Sacrificer), by means of these oblations, now draw them together and connect them.

19. [He offers, with, Vâg. S. XVIII, 50], 'Heaven-like heat, hail!'—the heat, doubtless, is yonder sun ; he thus establishes yonder sun in Agni.

20. 'Heaven-like flame, hail!'—the flame is

---

[1] That is, the joining together of the fire and the horse-sacrifice.

this Agni: he thus establishes this Agni in yonder sun.

21. 'The Heaven-like shining one, hail!'— the shining one, doubtless, is yonder sun: he places him again up there.

22. 'Heaven-like light, hail!'—the light is this Agni: he places him again here (on the fire-altar).

23. 'The heaven-like Sûrya, hail!'—Sûrya, doubtless, is yonder sun: he thus places yonder sun highest of all this (universe), whence he is the highest of all this (universe).

24. These are five oblations he offers,—the fire-altar consists of five layers, a year of five seasons, and Agni is the year: as great as Agni is, as great as is his measure, with so much he thus draws together and connects those two.

25. And as to why he says, 'Heaven-like heat, hail! heaven-like flame, hail!'—these indeed are names of this fire: he thereby gratifies these, and by the offering he makes them a deity; for only that one is a deity to whom an oblation is offered, but not that to whom it is not offered. Moreover, by naming them, he thus places them on this fire-altar.

26. These are five oblations he offers,—the fire-altar consists of five layers, and the year of five seasons, and Agni is the year: as great as Agni is, as great as is his measure, by so much food he thus gratifies him.

27. Now as to the insertion [1] of (any other) oblations. If he should know any oblation supplied with a brâhmana (dogmatic explanation) let him offer it at

---

[1] Or, location, proper place; cf. p. 138, note 1.

this time; for it is for (the obtainment of his) wishes that he yokes this chariot, and whatsoever oblation he offers on this occasion he offers as one that is (to be) fulfilled.

28. As to this they say, 'Let him not offer (any additional oblations), lest he should do what is excessive.' Let him, nevertheless, offer them; for it is for (special) wishes that these oblations are offered, and in wishes there is nothing excessive.

THIRD BRÂHMANA.

PREPARATORY RITES OF THE SOMA-SACRIFICE.

1. Having now returned (to the hall), he, at the proper time, throws up the Dhishnyas[1] (fire-hearths)—these hearths are fires: he thus builds up fire-altars. They are the clansmen, and the built-up fire-altar is the chieftaincy: he thus sets up both the chieftaincy and the clan. The former (altar) he builds up first, then these (hearths): thus he sets up the clan after setting up the chieftaincy.

2. That (fire-altar) is a single one: he thus makes the chieftaincy to attach to a single (person), and (social) distinction to attach to a single (person). The others are numerous: he thus bestows multiplicity on the clan.

---

[1] A Soma-sacrifice being about to be performed on the newly erected fire-altar, now properly consecrated, all the necessary preparatory business and ceremonial enjoined for such a sacrifice have now to be gone through in the way detailed in part ii of this translation. The author here only alludes to those points in the Soma-ritual in regard to which the present performance offers any special feature either additional to, or modificatory of, the ordinary ceremonial. The construction of the Dhishnyas, or fire-hearths of the different priests (for which see part ii, p. 148, note 4), is one of these points.

3. That (fire-altar) consists of five layers, the others of a single layer : he thus endows the chieftain (or, ruler) pre-eminently with power, and makes the chieftain more powerful than the clan (or people). Upwards he builds that one : he thus builds the ruling power upward by (social) layers ; sideways the others : he thus makes the clan obedient to the chieftain from below.

4. That one he builds up both with the Yagush-mati (bricks laid down with a special formula), and with the Lokamprinâ (or space-filling ones, laid down with a common formula) ; the others with the space-filling one alone : he thus endows the chieftain pre-eminently with power, and makes the chieftain more powerful than the clan, and the clan less powerful than the chieftain.

5. And when he builds up these (hearths) only with the space-filling one, the Lokamprinâ being the nobility[1]—he thereby places the chieftain, as the eater, among the clan. He builds up (dhishnya-hearths) both of the Soma-sacrifice[2], and of the fire-altar ; first those of the Soma-sacrifice, and then those of the fire-altar : the significance of this has been explained. Whatever Soma-hearth he (merely) throws up (at the Soma-sacrifice), that he (now) builds up. The Âgnidhriya he builds first, for that

---

[1] See p. 132, note 2.

[2] There are eight dhishnya-hearths at the Soma-sacrifice, two of which, the Âgnidhriya and Mârgâlîya, were raised north and south of the cart-shed (havirdhâna), whilst the others (viz. those of the Hotri, &c.) were raised inside the Sadas along its eastern side. They were merely mounds of earth covered with sand, whilst the additional hearths (of the fire-altar) now to be erected are partly built of bricks.

one he throws up first (at the Soma-sacrifice) ; (he does so) whilst sitting to the right (south) of it : the significance of this has been explained [1].

6. On this (Âgnîdhriya) he puts eight bricks,—the Gâyatrî consists of eight syllables, and Agni is of Gâyatra nature : as great as Agni is, as great as is his measure, so great he thus builds him up. The variegated stone [2] is the ninth of them : there are nine vital airs—seven in the head and two downward ones—it is these he thus puts into it. The fire which is placed on the erected (hearth) is the tenth ;—there are ten vital airs [3], and the Âgnîdhra is the middle (between the Gârhapatya and Âhavanîya fires) : he thus puts the vital airs in the middle of it : for the vital airs, being in the middle of the body, move along it in this direction, and in that direction.

7. Twenty-one he places on the Hotriya (hearth), and there are twenty-one enclosing-stones [4] : the significance of this has been explained.

8. Six (he places) on the Mârgâlîya,—these are the six seasons, the Fathers ; for the seasons, the

[1] See VII, 1, 1, 21 seq., where the way in which the bricks of the Gârhapatya hearth are laid down is described in detail.

[2] When Agni was led forwards from the Gârhapatya to be installed on his newly built altar, as the Âhavanîya or offering fire, a variegated stone, meant to represent the sun, was deposited near the place (on the northern edge of the Vedi) where the Âgnîdhra shed and hearth would afterwards have to be erected ; see IX, 2, 3, 14–19.

[3] That is, including the central one, the outlet of which is the navel ; cf. VIII, 1, 3, 10.

[4] The numbers of bricks and enclosing-stones are the same as for the Gârhapatya hearth, for which (with their symbolic meaning) see VII, 1, 1, 32–35.

Fathers[1], indeed, heaped up (a rampart) round that (fire) from the south. This one lies to the south of those (other hearths)[2],—this (Âgnîdhrîya) he lays down in this way (direction), and these (other hearths) in this way, and that one (the Fire-altar) in this way: he thereby makes the peasantry look towards the chieftain.

9. He then encloses these (hearths) by enclosing-stones;—the enclosing-stones are the waters: it is thus by water that he surrounds them[3]. He merely lays them down all round, for those of the waters which flow in a hollow (channel) are the chieftain, and these stray waters are the clansmen; thus, when he encloses that (great fire-altar) by a dug-in (row of stones), he thereby adds power to power, and surrounds (protects) power by power; and when he merely lays down those (enclosing-stones of the hearths) all round, he thereby adds clansman (or clan) to clansman, and surrounds (protects) clansman by clansman[4]. As many bricks with special formulas as

---

[1] Sâyana refers to a passage in the Taittirîyaka, according to which a dying man is changed to whatever season he dies in, whence the six seasons are the representatives of all the deceased ancestors. Since the Fathers reside in the southern region it is from that quarter that, by laying down the bricks, they are supposed to raise a rampart for the Mârgâlîya fire.

[2] Viz. on the southern edge of the Vedi, exactly south of the Âgnîdhrîya, whilst the other dhishnyas run in a line from north to south to the left of the space between the Âgnîdhrîya and Mârgâlîya. The other hearths, together with the great fire-altar occupying the eastern part of the Vedi, would thus, as it were, face the Mârgâlîya in a semicircle. See the plan of the Sacrificial ground, part ii, p. 475.

[3] That is, as the earth is surrounded by the ocean (VII, 1, 1, 13), or a stronghold by a moat.

[4] Viz. inasmuch as the fire-altar and the Âhavanîya fire on it, as

there are (in each hearth) so many enclosing-stones
there are (in each); for with that (fire-altar) there
are as many enclosing-stones as there are such
bricks in it [1]: he thus makes the clan obedient
and subservient to the chief.

10. He then scatters a layer of earth on (each of)
these (hearths): the significance of this has been
explained [2]. Silently [3] (he scatters it), for indistinct
is the clan (or people). Then, after the cake-offering of the Agnishomîya (animal sacrifice) [4], he
prepares the propitiatory oblations to the
Regions;—that fire-altar is the regions: it is to
them he offers these oblations, and thus by offering
makes them a deity, for only that one is a deity to
whom an oblation is offered, but not that to whom
it is not offered. There are five (such oblations),
for there are five regions.

11. As to this they say,—Let him prepare this

---

well as the dug-in circle of enclosing-stones, are identified with the
ruling power; whilst the dhishnyas as well as the circles of stones
lying loosely around them represent the clan.

[1] This is not clear to me: whilst there are 395 such bricks with
special formulas in the five layers of the great altar, it is enclosed
by only 261 parisrits; see p. 158, note 1. Besides there are no
'yagushmatî' bricks in these hearths, but only 'lokamprinâs';
one would therefore expect 'ish/akâs' (bricks) for 'yagushmatyas'
the first time (cf. comm. on Kâty. Sr. XVIII, 7, 13). The Hotri's
hearth contains twenty-one bricks, the Brâhmanâkkhamsin's eleven,
the Mârgâliya six, and the others eight bricks: and in each case
the common formula, 'Lokam prina, &c.' (see VIII, 7, 2, 6), is
pronounced once after every ten bricks, and after any odd bricks
remaining over at the end. Cf. Kâty. Sr. XVIII, 6, 8 seq.

[2] See VIII, 7, 3, 1 seq.

[3] He does not use any such formula as that used in covering
each layer of the great altar with earth; see VIII, 7, 3, 7.

[4] See part ii, p. 109, note 2 (where the reference at the end should
be to IV, 2, 5, 22).

offering (ish/i) so as to consist of material for ten
oblations ;—this (offering) is (performed) with all the
stomas and all the prishtha (sàmans)[1]; and there are
(used in it) all the metres, all the regions, all the
seasons—and this Agni (the fire-altar) is all this:
he thus, by the (amount of) offering material (taken
out for the ish/i), makes (Agni) the deity[2]; for only
that one is the deity for whom the oblation is
prepared, not one for whom it is not prepared.
There are (in that case) ten (oblations),—the Virâg
(metre) consists of ten syllables, and Agni is virâg
(far-shining, or far-ruling) ; there are ten regions,
and Agni (the fire-altar) is the regions; ten vital
airs, and Agni is the vital airs : as great as Agni is,
as great as is his measure, with so much food he
thus gratifies him.

12. But, indeed, he may also take out these
oblations for the Divine Quickeners[3]; for these are
the deities which become consecrated by this consecration ceremony by which he is now to be consecrated : it is them he thus gratifies, and gratified by
offering they permit him (to perform) this consecration ceremony, and with their permission he is

---

[1] See part iii, introduction. p. xx seq.

[2] As Sâyana points out, the Taittiriyas make Agni the deity of
this ish/i, the invitatory formulas (puro-nuvâkyâ) of the different
havis (oblations) naming him each time with different epithets
relating to different metres, stomas, prishthas, and seasons. Cf.
Taitt. S. I, 8, 4 : Taitt. Br. I, 8, 19.

[3] For these eight deities (Savit/i Satyaprasava, Agni Grihapati,
&c.), to whom offering is made at the Abhishekanîya or Consecration ceremony of the Râgasûya, between the chief oblation of the
animal cake-offering (Pasupurodâsa) and its Svish/akrit, whilst the
whole of the Pasupurodâsa is again performed in the middle of
the animal sacrifice, see part iii, p. 69 seq.

consecrated; for only he becomes king whom the
(other) kings allow (to assume) the royal dignity, but
not he whom they do not (allow to assume it). And
inasmuch as these deities are consecrated (quickened) by this consecration ceremony and quicken
him for this consecration, they are (called) the
Divine Quickeners.

13. These (deities) come to have two names, as
he who is consecrated by the rite of consecration
comes to have two names: for the very rite of
consecration for which he is quickened, and by which
he is consecrated (quickened), is his second name[1].

14. There are eight (such deities),—the Gâyatrî
consists of eight syllables, and Agni is of Gâyatra
nature: as great as Agni is, as great as is his
measure, by so much food he thus gratifies him.

15. As to this they say,—He ought not to offer
(any of) these oblations, lest he should do what is excessive. Let him nevertheless offer them: for these
oblations are offered for (the obtainment of special)
wishes, and in wishes there is nothing excessive.
And whatsoever oblation he offers after the Pasupurodâsa (the cake-offering connected with the animal
sacrifice), that is placed inside the animal victim
itself as its sacrificial sap[2]. He offers both kinds
(of oblations), those of the Soma-sacrifice and those
of the fire-altar (or Agnikayana), first those of the

---

[1] That is to say, for example, he who has performed the Vâgapeya is called Vâgapeya-yâgin, Sây.

[2] These oblations, as well as those of the Pasupurodâsa, inserted
as they are in the middle of the animal offering,—just after the
offering of the omentum of the victim,—are supposed to supply to
the victim its sacrificial sap or essence which was taken out of it in
the shape of the omentum. See III, 8, 3, 2.

Soma-sacrifice, and afterwards those of the fire-altar : the purport of this has been explained. In a loud voice[1] the Paśupuroḍâsa offering (is performed), in a low voice these (additional oblations), for they are an ishṭi[2]. With the Paśupuroḍâsa he (the Adhvaryu) says, 'Recite!—Urge!' and with these (oblations), 'Recite!—Worship[3]' for they are an ishṭi. There is the same Svishṭakṛit and the same iḍâ[4] (for these oblations). The (Devasû) deities have received offering, and the Svishṭakṛit (of the Paśupuroḍâsa) has not yet been attended to[5],—

---

[1] That is, in the formulas the name of the deity to whom the oblation is offered is pronounced in a loud voice.

[2] That is, a 'kâmyeshṭi,' or offering for the obtainment of some special object, which has to be performed in a low voice; see I, 3, 5. 10.

[3] Or, 'Pronounce the offering-prayer!' For these two latter calls (anubrûhi!—yaga!), by which the Adhvaryu calls on the Hotṛi to pronounce the invitatory prayer (anuvâkyâ or puro-nuvâkyâ) and the offering-prayer (yâgyâ) respectively, at ishṭis, see I, 5, 2, 8-10 and I, 5, 3. 8; and for the first two (anubrûhi!—preshya!), by the former of which the Adhvaryu calls on the Hotṛi to recite the invitatory prayer; whilst by the latter he calls on the Maitrâvaruṇa to 'urge' (or 'prompt') the Hotṛi to pronounce the offering-prayer at the animal sacrifice, see III, 8, 1, 4 with note (where attention might have been called to the difference that exists between the ishṭi and the animal sacrifice in regard to the formula by which the Adhvaryu calls for the recitation of the offering-prayer). In regard to this point there is, however, a difference of opinion between the Mâdhyandina and the Kâṇva schools, the latter using for the Paśupuroḍâsa on this occasion, as well as on that of the Râgasûya, the same calls as those of the inserted ishṭis; cf. Kâty. Sr. XV, 4, 18-20.

[4] For the Svishṭakṛit, or oblation to Agni, 'the maker of good offering,' offered after the chief oblations, see I, 7, 3, 1 seq.; for the iḍâ-oblation (and invocation of Iḍâ), I, 8, 1, 1 seq.

[5] The tentative meaning assigned to 'asamavahitam,' 'not in immediate connection with (the Svishṭakṛit),' can scarcely be right. The clause seems simply to mean that the (pûrvâbhisheka) touching

16. He then touches it (the fire-altar) with (the formula of) the preliminary consecration (Vâg. S. IX, 39. 40), 'May Savit*ri* quicken thee for (powers of) quickening[1]! . . . This (man), O ye (people), is your king; Soma is the king of us Brâhma*n*as!'— he thereby excludes the Brâhma*n*as (from the power of the king) and makes them such as are not to be fed upon (by the king).

Fourth Brâhma*n*a.

Agni*y*ogana, or Yoking of the Fire-altar ; and Soma-sacrifice.

1. Then, early next morning[2], when about to bespeak the morning prayer[3], he yokes the Fire-altar, thinking, 'With it, when yoked, I shall obtain :' and by it, when yoked, he obtains all wishes. He

of the altar is to take place, as in the case of the (preliminary) consecration at the Râgasûya, immediately after the oblations to the Divine Quickeners, and before the Svish*t*ak*ri*t oblation of the Pasu-puro*d*âsa has been performed. See V, 3, 3, 10, where a somewhat similar expression is used. One might have some doubt as to whether, both here and at the Râgasûya, there is any Svish*t*ak*ri*t at all to these Devasû-havim*s*hi, or whether the statement, ' There is the same svish*t*ak*ri*t and the same i*d*â,' applies not to them merely, but to them and the Pasupuro*d*âsa. If this latter alternative were the correct one, we should, however, expect that something had been said on this point in connection with the Devasû oblations of the Râgasûya ; and moreover the nature of the two oblations seems too different for such a partial identification, requiring as they do different ' praishas,' or calls, in the Svish*t*ak*ri*t (viz. ' yaga' the one, and ' preshya' the other) ; see also IX, 5, 1, 40, and note 3, p. 248 ; also Kâty. *S*r. V, 11, 23-24.

[1] For the complete formulas, see V, 3, 3, 11, 12.

[2] That is, on the first Sutyâ, or pressing-day.

[3] That is, by calling on the Ho*tri* to ' Recite to the gods, the early coming!' see III, 9, 3, 10, with note thereto giving particulars regarding the Prâtaranuvâka.

yokes it prior to the whole performance, so that
all that is done thereafter is laden on that yoked
(altar-cart).

2. He yokes it on the enclosing-sticks, for those
enclosing-sticks are fires[1]: it is with fires he thus
yokes the fire-altar.

3. Having touched the middle enclosing-stick[2],
he mutters this formula (Vâg. S. XVIII, 51). 'The
Fire I yoke with might, with ghee!'—might
means strength: thus, 'The fire I yoke (furnish) with
strength, with ghee;'—'the heavenly bird, great
in vigour,'—for that (fire-altar) is indeed a heavenly
bird, and great in vigour, in smoke[3];—'Thereby
we will go to the region of the bay, rising unto
the light, beyond the highest firmament!'—
The firmament, doubtless, is the heavenly world:
thus, 'Thereby we will go to the region, of the bay
(horse, the sun) mounting up to the heavenly world,
beyond the highest firmament.'

4. Then on the southern (right) one, with (Vâg. S.
XVIII, 52), 'By these never-decaying, feathered
wings of thine wherewith thou repellest the
demons, O Agni, may we fly to the world of
the righteous whither the erst-born seers went
of old!' he thereby alludes to those Rishis[4].

---

[1] See the ritual legend, I, 3, 3. 13 seq.

[2] That is, the one along the hind (or west) side of the Âhavanîya
fire on the great altar, being the base of the triangle formed by the
three enclosing-sticks. The order in which they are touched is
the same as that in which they were laid down.

[3] Mahidhara actually takes 'smoke (dhûma)' here to be intended
as the literal meaning of 'vayas.'

[4] Viz. the seven Rishis, identified with the seven vital airs which
came to constitute the first Purusha (Agni-Pragâpati), and hence
the bird-shaped fire-altar. See VI, 1, 1, 1 seq.

5. Then on the northern (left) one, with (Vâg. S. XVIII, 53), 'The potent drop, the faithful eagle, the golden-winged bird, the active (bhuranyu),'—golden means immortal: thus, 'the immortal-winged bird, the bearer (bhartri);'— 'the mighty is seated in the firm seat: homage be to thee, injure me not!'—he thereby gives utterance to a surrender of his own self.

6. Now that middle formula is the body, and the two on both sides thereof are the wings (of the bird-shaped altar) : hence these two allude to 'wings[1],' for these two are the wings.

7. With three (formulas) he yokes it,—threefold is Agni: as great as Agni is, as great as is his measure, with so much he thus yokes him.

8. And when he has pressed the king (Soma) he offers in the fire[2]. This, indeed, is that very rite of consecration (or pressing)—and by that he is now consecrated (or pressed)—which this (Sacrificer) is permitted to perform by those deities with whose permission he is consecrated[3]; for he alone becomes king whom the (other) kings allow (to assume) the royal dignity, and not he whom (they do) not (allow to assume it). Now when he offers in the fire he thereby consecrates (anoints) Agni, and that divine body of his, being consecrated by Soma, becomes consecrated by the nectar of immortality. And he himself drinks (thereof) : he thereby conse-

---

[1] In the first formula the word for 'bird (eagle)' is 'suparna,' literally 'the well-winged (well-feathered) one.'

[2] This refers to the libations made from the several cups (grahas), the contents of which are afterwards consumed by the priests (and Sacrificer) ; cf. part ii, p. 316, note 1.

[3] For the same irregular construction, see IX, 4, 1, 13.

crates himself, and this self (body) of his, being
consecrated by Soma, becomes consecrated by the
nectar of immortality.

9. Having offered in the fire (or, on the fire-altar),
he drinks (Soma), for that (fire-altar) is his (the
Sacrificer's) divine body[1], and this (Sacrificer's real
body) is his human one; and the gods indeed were
first, and afterwards men : therefore, having offered
(Soma) in the fire, he drinks (thereof).

10. Having now obtained the wish for (the
accomplishment of) which he yokes it (the altar), he
unyokes it when about to bespeak the Yagñâyagñiya stotra[2],— for the Yagñâyagñiya is the
heavenly world, and it is for the attainment of that
(world) that he yokes it : thus (he unyokes it) after
obtaining the wish for which he yoked it.

11. It is prior to the Stotra that he unyokes it :--
were he to unyoke after the Stotra, he would pass
beyond that world[3] and lose it ; but when he unyokes prior to the Stotra, he unyokes forthwith
after reaching the world of heaven.

12. He unyokes it on the enclosing-sticks, for it

---

[1] See IX. 3, 4. 12.

[2] The Yagñâyagñiya (or Yagñâyagñiya) stotra is the last and
characteristic chant of the Agnish/oma mode of Soma-sacrifice,
whence it is more properly called Agnish/oma-sâman ; the Yagñâyagñiya, properly speaking, being the verses, Sâma-v. II. 53, 54,
chanted to a particular tune, and generally (though not always)
used for the closing chant of the Agnish/oma.

[3] That is, because the Yagñâyagñiya marks, as it were, the end
of the (Agnish/oma) Soma-sacrifice, and anything performed thereafter is, so to speak, outside the sacrifice, or beyond it. Kâty. Sr.
XVIII, 6, 17 calls it Âgnimâruta stotra, i.e. the chant belonging
to the Âgnimâruta-sastra (which has to be recited by the Hotri
after that chant) ; cf. part ii, p. 369 note.

is on the enclosing-sticks that he yokes it, and at whatever place (of the body) people yoke a horse there they also unyoke it.

13. Having touched it (the fire) at the two joints [1], he mutters these two formulas,—thus two formulas equal in power three enclosing-sticks,—with (Vâg. S. XVIII, 54), 'The sky's head thou art, the earth's navel, [the essence of the waters and plants, the life of all, the ample refuge (?): homage be to the path!]' on the right, and with (55), 'On the head of the Ail dost thou keep standing, [in the (aerial) ocean is thy heart, in the waters thy life: bestow water, send the water-store (cloud),—from the sky, from the cloud, from the air, from the earth, favour us with rain!]' on the left (joint),—thus with two (verses) containing (the word) 'head,' for this is indeed its head; and containing (the words) 'in the waters [2]': that Yagñâyagñiya doubtless is Agni Vaisvânara's chant of praise, and water is (a means of) appeasing,—therefore (he touches them) with two (verses) containing (the words)—'the waters.'

14. With two (verses) he unyokes it,—two-footed is the Sacrificer, and Agni is the Sacrificer: as great as Agni is, as great as is his measure, with so much he thus unyokes him. With three (verses) he yokes,—that (makes) five,—the fire-altar consists of five layers, the year (of) five seasons, and Agni is

---

[1] That is, at the two points where the right (southern) and left (northern) enclosing-sticks (forming the two sides of the triangle, the apex of which lies east of the centre of the fire) meet the western enclosing-stick (as the base of the triangle).

[2] The first verse, in point of fact, contains the genitive case 'of the waters.'

the year: as great as Agni is, as great as is his
measure, so great is this.

15. Now, some yoke it (the fire-altar) at a Práyaníya [1] Atirâtra, and unyoke it at an Udayaniya,
saying, 'The unyoking, surely, is a certain form
of completion, and why should we perform a form
of completion prior to the completion (of the sacrifice)?' But let him not do this, for day by day this
sacrifice is performed, and day by day it comes to
completion; day by day he yokes that (altar) for the
attainment of the heavenly world, and day by day
he thereby attains the heavenly world: let him therefore yoke it day by day, and unyoke it day by day.

16. And, indeed, it would be just as if, at the
Práyaníya Atirâtra, after reciting the kindling-
verses, he were to say, 'Hereafter [2], at the Udayaniya, I shall recite (them again)!' Let him therefore yoke (the altar) day by day, and unyoke it day
by day.

17. And on this point, Sândilya, indeed, having
enjoined on the Kankatîyas the day-by-day per-

---

[1] For the Práyaníyâ ishti (to five deities) of the ordinary Agnishtoma, see part ii, pp. 47, 48, note. In the present case a special
Soma-sacrifice of the Atirâtra type would seem to take its place,
just as the Pavitra, an Agnishtoma Soma-sacrifice, at the Râgasûya,
took the place of the ordinary Anvârambhaníyâ ishti (or opening
offering); see part iii, p. 42. In the same way there would
apparently be a special Udayaniya Soma-sacrifice; whilst our
author would have the ceremonies of yoking and unyoking of
the fire-altar performed on the very day (or days) of the Soma-
sacrifice, that is to say, he would have the ordinary Práyaníyeshti
and Udayaniyeshti performed as parts of the principal Soma-day
(or days, if there are to be more than one).

[2] Or, therefore, as Sâyana takes it. If the Udayaniya were
a special Soma-sacrifice, the Sâmidhenîs (part i, p. 102 seq.; ii.
p. 13, note 3) would have to be recited anew.

formance, went on his way, saying, 'Day by day
they shall yoke for you, and day by day they shall
unyoke!' Let him therefore yoke day by day, and
unyoke day by day.

FIFTH ADHYÂYA. FIRST BRÂHMANA.

1. Now, then, as to the taking of milk as fast-
food: the initiated should take milk for his fast-
food. Once upon a time the nectar of immortality
departed from the gods.

2. They said, 'Let us seek for it here by toil and
penance!' They sought for it by toil and penance.
Having become initiated, they were living on fast-
milk, for penance it is when, after becoming initiated,
one lives on fast-milk. They heard the sound of it.

3. They said, 'It is indeed coming nearer: let
us practise penance still further!' They resorted
to three teats: they saw it.

4. They said, 'It is indeed coming nearer: let us
practise penance still further!' They resorted to
two teats: they saw it still nearer.

5. They said, 'It is indeed coming nearer: let us
practise penance still further!' They resorted to
one teat: it came nigh unto them, but they could
not lay hold of it.

6. They said, 'It has indeed come nigh unto us,
but we cannot lay hold of it: let us undergo the
whole (practice of) penance!' On the day of preparation they underwent entire abstention from
food: for the whole (practice of) penance it is when
one abstains from food: let him therefore eat nothing
on the day of preparation.

7. On the morrow, having laid hold of it and
pressed it (the Soma), they offered (of it) in the fire,

and thereby bestowed immortality upon Agni. And he, Agni (the fire-altar), indeed, is the body of all the gods; and hence, when they bestowed immortality on Agni (the fire-altar), they bestowed immortality on their own selves, and thereby the gods became immortal.

8. Now that same nectar of immortality is Soma. And even to this day the Sacrificer seeks for it by toil and penance; having become initiated he lives on fast-milk; for penance it is when, after being initiated, one lives on fast-milk; he hears the sound of it, saying, 'On such and such a day the buying (will take place [1])!'

9. He resorts to three teats (of the cow): he sees it. He resorts to two teats: he sees it nearer by. He resorts to one teat: it comes nigh to him, but he cannot lay hold of it. He undergoes entire abstinence from food; for the whole (practice of) penance it is when one abstains from food: let him therefore eat nothing on the day of preparation.

10. And, on the morrow, having laid hold of it, and pressed it, he offers (of it) in the fire, and thereby bestows immortality on Agni. He then drinks (of it), and thereby bestows immortality on his own self, and becomes immortal; for this, assuredly, is immortality to man when he attains the whole (perfect) life: and so, in truth, he attains the whole life by this self of his.

11. When he has offered in the fire, he drinks (Soma); for that (fire-altar) is his divine body, and this (Sacrificer's own body) is his human one; and

---

[1] That is, the buying of the Soma plants, for which see part ii, p. 69 seq.

the gods were first, and then men : therefore he drinks (Soma), after offering in the fire.

12. Now, then, the discussion of the Samish/ayagus (oblations). The gods and the Asuras, both of them sprung from Pragâpati, entered upon their father Pragâpati's inheritance, to wit, speech—truth and untruth, both truth and untruth : they, both of them, spake the truth, and they both spake untruth ; and, indeed, speaking alike, they were alike.

13. The gods relinquished untruth, and held fast to truth, and the Asuras relinquished truth, and held fast to untruth.

14. The truth which was in the Asuras beheld this, and said, 'Verily, the gods have relinquished untruth, and held fast to truth : well, then, I will go thither !' Thus it went over to the gods.

15. And the untruth which was in the gods beheld this, and said, 'Verily, the Asuras have relinquished truth, and held fast to untruth : well, then, I will go thither !' Thus it went over to the Asuras.

16. The gods spake nothing but truth, and the Asuras nothing but untruth. And the gods, speaking the truth diligently, were very contemptible, and very poor : whence he who speaks the truth diligently, becomes indeed very contemptible, and very poor ; but in the end he assuredly prospers, for the gods indeed prospered.

17. And the Asuras, speaking untruth diligently, throve even as salt soil [1], and were very prosperous : whence he who speaks untruth diligently, thrives indeed, even as salt soil, and becomes very pros-

---

[1] Both salt (V, 2, 1, 16 ; VII, 1, 1, 6) and saline soil (VII, 3, 1, 8) mean cattle.

perous; but in the end he assuredly comes to naught, for the Asuras indeed came to naught.

18. Now that same truth, indeed, is this threefold lore [1]. The gods said, 'Now that we have made up the sacrifice, let us spread out [2] this truth!'

19. They prepared the Initiation-offering. But the Asuras became aware of it, and said, 'Having made up the sacrifice, the gods are now spreading out that truth: come, let us fetch hither what was ours!' The Samish/ayagus of that (offering) was not yet performed, when they arrived: whence people offer no Samish/ayagus [3] for that sacrifice. The gods, espying the Asuras, snatched up the sacrifice, and began doing something else [4]. They (the Asuras) went away again, thinking, 'It is something else they are doing.'

20. When they had gone away, they (the gods) prepared the Opening-offering. But the Asuras

---

[1] That is, the Veda, and hence the sacrificial ritual as the sole end for which the three collections of hymn-verses (rik), hymn-tunes (sâman), and sacrificial formulas (yagus) were made.

[2] The verb 'tan,' 'to spread,' is the regular expression for the 'performing' of the sacrifice,—a figure of speech taken from the spreading out of a web, in which literal sense it has to be taken here.

[3] See III. 1, 3, 6, where the injunction is given that no Samish/ayagus should be performed for the Dikshaniyesh/i, 'lest he who has put on the garment of initiation should reach the end of the sacrifice before its completion; for the Samish/ayagus is the end of the sacrifice.' It should be remembered that the initiation-offering, however essential, is merely a preliminary ceremony of the Soma-sacrifice, at the end of which latter sacrifice nine Samish/ayagus oblations are offered (IV, 4, 4, 1 seq.) instead of the single one offered at the ordinary haviryagña. The term signifies 'the formula (yagus) of the completed offering (samish/a).'

[4] Prof. Delbrück. Altind. Syntax, p. 429, makes this last clause part of the Asuras' speech or thoughts,—'one thing they have undertaken to do, and another they are doing.' This can hardly be right.

became aware of this also. The Samyos (formula)
of that (offering) had been pronounced, when they
arrived; whence that sacrifice ends with the Samyos[1].
The gods, espying the Asuras, snatched up the
sacrifice, and began doing something else. They
went away again, thinking, 'It is something else
they are doing.'

21. When they had gone away, they (the gods),
having bought and driven about the king (Soma),
prepared the guest-offering for him. But the Asuras
became aware of this also. The Idâ of that (offering)
had been invoked, when they arrived: whence that
sacrifice ends with the Idâ[2]. The gods, espying
the Asuras, snatched up the sacrifice, and began
doing something else. They went away again,
thinking, 'It is something else they are doing.'

22. When they had gone away, they (the gods)
spread out (performed) the Upasads[3]. When they
had recited three kindling-verses, and no more,
they made offering to the deities, but laid out[4] no
fore-offerings and no after-offerings on either side
of the sacrifice, for they were in too great haste
at that time; whence at the Upasads, when he has
recited three kindling-verses, and no more, he

---

[1] See III. 2, 3, 23, where it is stated that the Prâyanîya of the
Soma-sacrifice is to end with the Samyos (or Samyuvâka, for
which see part i. p. 254 seq.); the Patnîsamyâgas (and Samishtayagus) of the ordinary ishti being thus omitted.

[2] For the Âtithya, see part ii. p. 85 seq. It is shorn of the
after-offerings (in addition to the Patnîsamyâgas and Samishtayagus).

[3] For the Upasads, see part ii, p. 104 seq.

[4] That is, performed; but the verb (ut-sâdaya, 'to set out, or in
order') is used purposely, as if laying out for display,—so as to be
in keeping with the 'spreading out' of the sacrifice.

makes offering to the deities, but lays out no fore-
offerings and no after-offerings on either side of the
sacrifice.

23. On the day of preparation they slaughtered
the Agnishomiya victim. But the Asuras became
aware of this also. The Samish*t*ayag*us oblations of
this (offering) had not yet been offered, when they
arrived ; whence people offer no Samish*t*ayag*us for
this animal(-offering). The gods, espying the
Asuras, snatched up the sacrifice, and began doing
something else. They went away again, thinking,
' It is something else they are doing.'

24. On the next morning after they had gone
away, they (the gods) spread out (performed) the
morning-service (of the Soma-sacrifice). But the
Asuras became aware of this also. As much as
the morning-service had been performed of it, when
they arrived. The gods, espying the Asuras,
snatched up the sacrifice, and began doing something else. They went away, thinking,' It is something else they are doing.'

25. When they had gone, they (the gods) spread
out the midday-service. But the Asuras became
aware of this also. As much as the midday-service
had been performed of it, when they arrived. The
gods, espying the Asuras, snatched up the sacrifice,
and began doing something else. They went away,
thinking, ' It is something else they are doing.'

26. When they had gone, (the gods) went on
with the animal-offering of the Soma-sacrifice[1].

---

[1] The portions from the Savanîya pasu, which is slain during
the morning-service, continue being cooked until the evening-
service, when they are offered. See IV, 2, 5, 13; and part ii,
p. 357, note.

But the Asuras became aware of this also. As
much of this animal-offering as is done (at the
evening-service) had been done, when they arrived.
The gods, espying them, snatched up the sacrifice,
and began doing something else. They went away,
thinking, 'It is something else they are doing.'

27. When they had gone away, they (the gods)
spread the evening-service and completed it; and
by completing it they obtained that whole truth.
Then the Asuras went down[1]. Then the gods
prevailed, and the Asuras came to naught. And,
indeed, he who knows this, himself prevails, and his
spiteful enemy comes to naught.

28. The gods said, 'Those sacrifices of ours which
are half-completed, and leaving behind which we
went off[2],—think ye upon this, how we may complete them!' They said, 'Meditate ye!' whereby,
indeed, they meant to say, 'Seek ye how we may
complete these sacrifices!'

29. Whilst meditating, they saw these Samish/a-
yagus (oblations), and offered them, and thereby
completed those sacrifices; and inasmuch as thereby
they completed (samsthâpaya) them, they are 'sam-
sthitayagus'; and inasmuch as thereby they sacrificed completely (sam-yag[3]), they are 'samish/a-
yagus.'

30. Now there are nine such (incomplete) sacri-

---

[1] Literally, leapt down (from their high station).

[2] That is, which we left behind us when we went off.

[3] Cf. IV, 4. 4. 6. For whatever deities this sacrifice is performed,
they all are thereby 'sacrificed-to together' (sam-ish/a); and because,
after all those (deities) have been 'sacrificed-to together,' he now
offers those (libations), therefore they are called Samish/ayagus.
See also I, 9, 2, 26, with note thereto.

fices, and there are nine samish/ayagus-oblations [1];
and by offering these, he completes those sacrifices.
He offers both kinds, those of the Soma-sacrifice,
and those of the Agni(-ⁱayana),—first those of the
Soma-sacrifice, and afterwards those of the fire-altar:
the significance of this has been explained.

31. Two he offers of the fire-altar,—two-footed is
the Sacrificer, and Agni is the Sacrificer: as great
as Agni is, as great as is his measure, with so much
he thus completes the sacrifice. [He offers them,
with, Vâg. S. XVIII, 56, 57]. 'Sacrifice hath
been offered up by the Bhrigus . . .;'—'May
Agni who hath received sacrifice and oblation
speed our offered meat!'

32. These two amount to eleven,—the Trish/ubh
consists of eleven syllables, and the Trish/ubh
means strength : it is strength he thus imparts to the
Sacrificer.

33. And, again, as to why there are eleven,—the
Trish/ubh consists of eleven syllables, and Indra is
of trish/ubh nature, Indra is the self (soul) of the
sacrifice, Indra is the deity [2]: he thus finally establishes the sacrifice in him who is the self, the deity
of the sacrifice.

34. Having performed the Samish/ayagus-obla-
tions, they betake themselves to the expiatory bath
(avabhrïtha [3]). Having come out from the bath,

_____

[1] That is to say, the same nine Samish/ayagus-oblations which
are performed at the end of the Soma-sacrifice (IV, 4, 4, 1 seq.).
At the end of these, however, two additional such oblations are
offered on the present occasion.

[2] See I, 4, 5, 4, 'Indra is the deity of (this?) sacrifice;' IV, 4,
2, 16, 'Indra is the leader of the sacrifice.' The first of the nine
Samish/ayagus-oblations of the Soma-sacrifice is offered to Indra.

[3] See IV, 4, 5, 1 seq.

and performed the Udayanîya (concluding oblation)[1], he, after the animal cake of the offering
of the barren cow[2], prepares oblations for the
goddesses.

35. For now Pragâpati, having gained his end,
thought himself quite perfect. Establishing himself
in the quarters he went on ordering (or creating)
and disposing everything here; and inasmuch as he
went on ordering and disposing, he is the Orderer.
And in like manner does the Sacrificer, establishing
himself in the quarters, order and dispose everything
here.

36. And, again, as to why he prepares these
oblations. This Agni (the fire-altar) is the quarters
(regions), and these he lays down beforehand (in
the shape of) the bunch of Darbha grass[3] and the
clod-bricks[4]: the Prânabhrits[5] in the first layer,
the whole of the second, the whole of the third, and
the whole of the fourth (layers[6]); and of the fifth

---

[1] See IV, 5, 1, 1 seq.

[2] For this offering to Mitra and Varuna, see IV, 5, 1, 5.

[3] The bunch of Darbha grass is placed in the centre of the newly
ploughed altar-site; see VII, 2, 3, 1 seq.

[4] The four logeshtakâs (clods of earth), being placed at the ends
of the two 'spines,' represent the four quarters, marking as they do
the centre of the east, south, west, and north sides of the altar-site,
sown with seeds of all kinds; see VII, 3, 1, 13 seq. The bunch
of Darbha grass, placed in the centre, would thus represent the
fifth region, viz. the one above.

[5] Though the Prânabhrits are said to represent, not the regions,
but the (channels of the) vital airs, they are placed in rows along
the diagonals of the square body of the altar, thus marking, as it
were, the intermediate regions; whilst the fifth set is placed in
a circle round the centre. See VIII, 1, 1, 1 seq.

[6] The bricks of these layers are all of them supposed to be
marked by their position to relate to the regions or quarters.

layer the Asapatnâs, Nâkasads and Pañka*k*ûd*as* [1], —
these kept going out upwards [2] (from Pragâpati,
the altar). Pragâpati was afraid of them, thinking,
'Whilst moving away, these will go beyond this
universe.' Having become the Orderer, he went
round them and established himself in them.

37. Now the same as that Orderer is yonder sun;
and that which was the farthest gone of the regions
is that in which that (sun) shines firmly established.

38. And the same as that Orderer is this cake
to the Orderer on twelve potsherds. On twelve
potsherds (it is),—the year is (of) twelve months,
Pragâpati is the year, and Pragâpati is the Orderer.
And that one which was the farthest gone of the
regions is the same as these previous oblations,—
a pap to Anumati, a pap to Râkâ, a pap to
Sinivali, and a pap to Kuhû [3]: when he prepares
these oblations, he thereby establishes him (Pragâpati) in that which was the farthest gone of the
regions. That (cake) he offers whole, for the completeness of that (Pragâpati).

39. These are goddesses, for they are the regions,

---

[1] For the Asapatnâs, laid down near the ends of the spines, to
drive off evil in all four quarters, see VIII, 5, 1, 1; for the other
two kinds of bricks, expressly identified with the regions, see VIII,
6, 1, 1 seq.

[2] That is, the altar was so full of regions that they escaped at
the top.

[3] These deities are supposed to be personifications of the four
phases of the moon; whilst Prof. Weber (Ind. Stud. XIII, p. 290)
would also take the Orderer (dhâtr*i*)—by the Brâhma*n*a identified
with the sun—to represent the moon. On Sinivalî (identified with
Vâ*k*, VI, 5, 1, 9), see also A. Kuhn, Zeitschr. f. v. Sprachf. II,
p. 120; Weber, Ind. Stud. V, 230. Anumati is identified with the
earth, V, 2, 3, 4.

the regions are the metres, and the metres are deities; and that Ka is Pragâpati; and inasmuch as they are goddesses (devi) and Ka, they are 'devikâh¹.' There are five of them, for there are five regions.

40. As to this they say, 'He should not offer these oblations, lest he should do what is excessive.' Let him nevertheless offer them; for these oblations are offered for (the fulfilment) of (special) wishes, and in wishes there is nothing excessive. And whatever oblation is offered after the cake of the animal-offering that is placed inside the victim itself as its sacrificial sap. He offers both kinds (of oblations), those of the Soma-sacrifice and those of the Agni(-kayana), to wit, first those of the Soma-sacrifice, and then those of the fire-altar: the significance of this has been explained. The cake-offering of the animal sacrifice is (performed) in a loud voice, and these (five oblations) in a low voice, for they are an ishti². With the Pasupurodâsa he (the Adhvaryu) says, 'Recite!—Urge!' and with these (oblations), 'Recite!—Worship!' for they are an ishti³. There is the same Svishtakrit, and the same Idâ⁴.

41. Of that same animal-offering (of the barren cow) they perform the Samishtayagus-oblations; they enter the expiatory bath with the heart-spit⁵:

---

¹ This is an etymological quibble resorted to in order to account for the oblation to Pragâpati as one of the oblations of the goddesses (devikâ).

² See p. 248, note 1.   ³ See ibid., note 2.

⁴ That is, for these five oblations which are inserted between the chief oblations and the Svishtakrit of the Pasupurodâsa; as above, IX, 4, 3, 12 seq.

⁵ For this expiatory ceremony, called the Sûlâvabhritha (spit-

for this animal-offering is the end. Having proceeded with the heart-spit;—

42. And having returned (to the fire-altar), he performs the oblations to Viśvakarman:—This Agni(-kayana) indeed (includes) all sacrificial rites (viśvâni karmâṇi); and all these its rites have been performed in this (agnikayana): he now gratifies them, and makes them a deity by means of an offering of sacrificial food; for only that one is a deity, for whom an oblation is prepared, but not one for whom it is not (prepared). Moreover, this Agni is Viśvakarman (the all-worker): it is him he thereby gratifies.

43. And, again, as to why he offers the Vaiśvakarmaṇa (oblations)[1]. For the fire-altar there is both a beginning and an end: the Sâvitra[2] (formulas) are the beginning, and the Vaiśvakarmaṇa (oblations) the end. Were he to offer only those to Savitṛi, and not those to Viśvakarman, it would be as if he made only a beginning and no end; and were he to offer only those to Viśvakarman, and not those to Savitṛi, it would be as if he made only an end and no beginning. He offers both of them, and thus makes both a beginning and an end.

44. There are eight of those (Sâvitra), and so (there are eight of) these: thus he makes the end

bath), and marking the conclusion of an ordinary (nirûdha) animal sacrifice—not one belonging to the Soma-sacrifice—as well as of the offering of a sterile cow, see part ii. p. 215.

[1] Or, perhaps, formulas; the verses used along with the oblations being ascribed to Viśvakarman. In any case, however, these oblations are offered to Agni, as the Viśvakarman, or all-worker (viśvakartṛi), or (in the case of Agni=Agnikayana) as including all works (or sacrificial performances).

[2] See VI. 3. 1, 1 seq.; part iii, p. 190 seq.

(the same) as the beginning. The Svâhâ-call is the ninth of those [1], and so it is of these: thus he makes the end as the beginning. The oblation (âhuti) is the tenth of those [2], and so it is of these: thus he makes the end as the beginning. On that occasion he offers the oblation continuously so as not to stop the seed, the sacrifice there being seed;—on this occasion (he offers) with the dipping-spoon at the Svâhâ-call, for manifest is the seed when it is born.

45. [He offers, with, Vâg. S. XVII, 58 65], 'What hath flowed from out of the will, or the heart, or was gathered from the mind, or the eye, after that go ye forward,—to the world of the righteous whither the first-born seers went of old!' he thereby means those Rishis [3].

46. 'Unto thee, O (heavenly) seat, I commit this treasure which the knower of beings shall bring thither [4]! Here the lord of the sacrifice will go after you: acknowledge ye [5] him in the highest heaven!'—as the text, so the meaning.

47. 'Acknowledge him, O ye gods, seated

---

[1] See VI, 3. 1. 21.

[2] The Sâvitra formulas accompany eight libations, which form, however, only one single continuous offering (âhuti) with one svâhâ-call.

[3] For the seven Rishis, identified with the vital airs, the first existing beings, see VI. 1. 1. 1 seq.

[4] Mahîdhara (and apparently Sâyana) seems to supply 'yagamânam' to 'etam,' and construe thus: 'Unto thee, O heavenly seat, I commit this (Sacrificer), which treasure Gâtavedas shall bring thither.'

[5] 'O gods, honour ye him (the Sacrificer)!' Mahîdhara; but perhaps the Rishis are addressed in this second line. Mahîdhara takes 'atra' ('here') along with 'parame vyoman'—'in this highest heaven.'

in the highest heaven, know ye his form!
When he cometh by the godward paths,
reveal ye unto him the fulfilment of his
wishes!'—as the text, so the meaning.—'Awake,
O Agni, and be watchful! . . .'—'Whereby
thou carriest a thousand, . . .'—the meaning of
these two has been explained [1].

48. 'With grass-bunch and enclosing-stick,
with spoon, altar-ground and grass-cover,
with verse of praise, lead thou this our sacrifice unto heaven, to go unto the gods!' that is,
'with these outward forms of our sacrifice make
it go to the heavenly world!'

49. 'What gift, what bounty, what fulfilment, what offering-presents there are of ours,
—Agni Vaisvakarmana shall deposit them in
heaven with the gods!'— that is, 'whatever we
give, seasonably or unseasonably, that this fire-
altar of Visvakarman shall place in the heavenly
world!'

50. 'Where the streams of honey and ghee
are never-failing,—there, in heaven, Agni Vaisvakarmana shall place us with the gods!'—
as the text, so the meaning [2].

51. Eight Vaisvakarmana (oblations) he offers,—
the Gâyatrî consists of eight syllables, and Agni
is of Gâyatra nature: as great as Agni is, as great

---

[1] See VIII, 6, 3, 23, 24.

[2] The meaning of the verse is, however, far from certain. The
above is Mahîdhara's interpretation, except that he takes 'yâ/' to
mean 'and what (other) streams there are.' It might, however, also
mean—'What streams of honey and ghee of ours are never-failing
anywhere—Agni Vaisvakarmana shall deposit them in heaven with
the gods!'—in which case due reward for sacrifice would be
prayed for.

as is his measure, by so much food he thus gratifies
him.

52. When he has performed the Vaisvakarmana
(oblations), he gives a name [1] (to the fire of the
altar); for when any one has been born sound and
safe, they give a name to him, and now this (Agni)
has indeed been born sound and safe.

53. Having given a name to him, he reverently
approaches him; for this (Sacrificer) builds him
with his (own) whole self, and were he not to give
utterance now to this surrender of his own self,
he (Agni) would now take away his (the Sacrificer's)
self; but when he now gives utterance to this
surrender of his own self, he (Agni) does not take
away his self. [He approaches the fire] with the
Anushtubh verse (Vâg. S. XVIII, 67), 'What fires
of the five races of men there are upon this
earth,—thou art the chiefest of them: quicken
us unto life!'—the Anushtubh, doubtless, is speech,
and all the metres are speech [2]: he thus makes
amends to him (Agni) by all the metres. Having
stood by the fire, and lifted [3] it, and churned it out,
he offers the completing oblation [4].

---

[1] According to VI, 1, 3, 20, the newly built Agni is to be called
'Kitra,' the Bright one.

[2] Or, are Vâk, the Veda, cf. IV, 6, 7, 1 seq.

[3] Or, 'having mounted it;'—that is to say, he heats the churning-
sticks (arani) at the altar-fire, betakes himself with them to the old
(Gârhapatya) fire-place; 'churns out' the fire, and offers on the
fire thus produced.

[4] The Udavasânîyâ-ishti, consisting of a cake on five potsherds
for Agni (or a libation of ghee taken in five ladlings for Vishnu), is
the same as for the Soma-sacrifice, IV, 5, 1, 13. But whilst there
it is followed at once by the (evening) Agnihotra, or oblation of
milk regularly performed twice a day; on the present occasion an
additional oblation is performed.

54. He then offers a dish of clotted curds to
Mitra and Varuna [1]. Now he who performs this
(Agni-kayana) rite comes to be with the gods; and
these two, Mitra and Varuna, are a divine pair.
Now, were he to have intercourse with a human
woman without having offered this (oblation), it
would be a descent, as if one who is divine would become human; but when he offers this dish of clotted
curds to Mitra and Varuna, he thereby approaches
a divine mate [2]: having offered it, he may freely
have intercourse in a befitting way.

55. And, again, as to why he offers this dish of
clotted curds to Mitra and Varuna. When Pragâpati was released, the seed fell from him. When the
gods restored him, they, by means of this dish of
clotted curds, put seed into him; and in like
manner does this (Sacrificer) thereby put seed into
him.

56. Now that Pragâpati who became released is
this very fire-altar which is here being built; and
the seed which fell from him is this dish of clotted
curds of Mitra and Varuna; for Mitra and Varuna
are the in-breathing and up-breathing, and the in-
breathing and up-breathing fashion the infused seed.
A dish of clotted curds it is, because seed is milk;
and sacrifice it is, because sacrifice is the seed of
sacrifice. In a low voice it is (offered), for silently
seed is shed. At the end (of the sacrifice) it is
(offered), for from the end seed is introduced.

---

[1] The same payasyâ-oblation is performed at the Dâkshâyana
modification of the new and full-moon sacrifice (II, 4, 4, 10 seq.);
see also the Sânnâyya of the new-moon sacrifice (part i, p. 178,
note 4) which is the same dish.

[2] Or, he enters into a divine union.

57. They proceed with the whey [1] of that (dish of clotted curds). At this (oblation of whey) he gives a dakshinâ (sacrificial gift): 'Let him give a pair of hornless he-goats,' so (they say);—' Only by assignment, I think [2]:' said Mâhitthi. And, verily, this libation of the fire-builder flows away as a libation of Soma which one offers on a (fire) without bricks.

58. He need only lay down the naturally-perforated (bricks) [3]; for the naturally-perforated ones are these worlds; and this built fire-altar is the same as these worlds.

59. He need only lay down the seasonal (bricks); for the seasonal ones are the year, and this built fire-altar is the year.

60. He need only lay down the all-light (bricks); for the all-light (bricks) are those deities [4], and this built fire-altar is those deities.

61. He need only lay down the Punaskiti; for this is a repeated sacrifice (punar-yagña), it is a later (higher) worship of the gods: it is thus a repeated sacrifice and the higher worship of the gods he thereby arranges, and the repeated sacrifice inclines to him [5]!—so (they say), but let him not do this,

---

[1] The whey (vâgina) is offered to the (divine) Coursers, i.e. the regions or quarters; see II, 4, 4, 22–25.

[2] The meaning of this passage is not quite clear to me.

[3] The three Svayamâtrinnis in the centre of the first, third, and fifth layers represent the three worlds. These, and the subsequent injunctions, refer to one who, subsequent to the Agnikayana, wishes to perform a Soma-sacrifice, without being able to repeat the Agnikayana itself. Kâty. Sr. XVIII, 6, 33.

[4] See VI, 3, 3, 16; 5, 3, where the three Visvagyotis bricks are said to represent Agni, Vâyu (wind), and Âditya (sun) respectively.

[5] Though there is nothing in the text to show where this quota-

for, indeed, whenever Agni is placed on the built
(altar), this whole Agni passes into that very brick [1]:
thus whenever he offers in the fire, then these
oblations of his will be offered even as would be his
oblations, when offered on a complete Sândila fire-
altar built up with wings and tail.

62. And, indeed, he who carries about Agni [2]
becomes pregnant with all beings, and with all the
gods; and he who builds him when he has not been
carried about for a year kills all beings in the form
of an embryo. But, surely, he who kills a human
embryo, is despised, how much more then he who kills
him (Agni), for he is a god: 'Let no one become
an officiating priest for an (Agni) who has not been
carried about for a year,' said Vâtsya, 'lest he
should be a participator in the killing of this,
a god's seed [3]!'

---

tion begins, it would seem, from Kâtyâyana's rules, that it runs
from the beginning of paragraph 58,—XVIII, 6, 33. In case of
inability (to perform a second) kityâ, at a repeated Soma-sacrifice,
(he may lay down) one or other kind of the Svayamâtrinnâs,
Visvagyotishas, or Kîtavyâs; 34. The Punaskiti; 35. Or no building (at all a second time); 36. Because the (Agni) Kîtya has
become the Âhavanîya.

[1] That is (as would seem from Sâyana's interpretation), into the
Âhavanîya fire, considered as the last brick of the altar; and hence
the Sacrificer's offering-fire will for ever thereafter remain for him
the Kîtya Agni.

[2] During the time of initiation (dikshâ), which, if at all possible,
is to last for a year, the Ukhya Agni has to be carried about by the
intending Sacrificer, for at least part of each day, in the fire-pan
(ukhâ), suspended in a sling from his neck; the pan-fire being
afterwards transferred to the newly built Gârhapatya and thence
to the great fire-altar, to serve as the Kîtya Agni, or the Âhavanîya
fire. See VI, 7, 1, 12 seq.

[3] In the original this last clause is in the first person, or in the
oratio directa, from the point of view of him who is asked to officiate

63. 'A six-month (Agni) is the last [1] he may build,' they say, 'for six-month embryos are the last [1] that live when born.' If he were to recite the Great Litany on one not carried for a year, he should recite (only) the eighties of verses; for something incomplete is (the Agni) not carried for a year, and something incomplete are the eighties of verses [2]. But, indeed, he would only still further pull asunder that (Agni, already) pulled asunder [3]; and, indeed, whether he (Agni) be carried for a year, or not carried for a year, he (the Hotri) should recite the whole of the Great Litany.

64. Now Sândilyâyana was once upon a time sojourning in the eastern region. Daiyâmpâti said to him, 'Sândilyâyana, how is Agni to be built? For, indeed, we are loth to carry him for a year, and yet we wish to build him.'

65. He said, 'Let him by all means build him by whom he has previously been carried for a year; for that, that (Agni) alone he builds as one that has been carried [4] (as a child in the womb).'

66. And, indeed, let him by all means build who

as a priest, hence—Let no one become an officiating priest . . . . thinking, 'Lest I should be a participator . . . .'

[1] That is to say, he must have been carried about for at least six months; and embryos less than six months old cannot live.

[2] This is so for the reason that the Mahad uktham consists of more than the eighties of verses; see IX, 3, 3. 19. One might feel inclined to include this whole sentence in the preceding quotation.

[3] That is, already too much attenuated, by being made as large as one a year old (?).

[4] Sâyana remarks, that this reply does not restrict the building of the fire-altar to one who has carried the fire for a full year, but only discountenances the building in the case of one who has only carried it for a few days (?).

intends to press Soma for a year, for he, manifestly, supports him by food (in the shape of) those libations.

67. And, indeed, let him by all means build who offers the Agnihotra for a year, for he who offers the Agnihotra indeed supports him (Agni, the fire).

68. And, indeed, let him by all means build who was born a year (after conception); for Agni is the breath: it is thus him (Agni) he holds. And, indeed, as the breath, he enters into the infused seed, and takes possession of it; and inasmuch as he takes possession (vid) of every one that is born (gâta), he is Gâtavedas. Wherefore by all means let even one who knows this build him as one ever carried (within him). And, indeed, if one who knows this either drinks (Soma), or offers drink to any one else, these libations of his will be offered even as would be his libations, when offered on a complete Sândila fire-altar built up with wings and tail.

Second Brâhmana.

1. Indra saw this seven-versed (hymn, suitable) for making good what is deficient[1], for reducing what is redundant, and for perfecting what is imperfect. And, indeed, after building the fire-altar, one is (still) apt to get into trouble, or to stumble, or what not. Now, when Syâparna Sâyakâyana heard this, he ventured upon this performance.

2. Now, there is here a perfecting of three things,—the perfecting of the fire-altar, the perfecting of

---

[1] Viz. in the building of the fire-altar; literally, for the obtainment of the deficient.

him who has it built for him, and the perfecting
of him who builds it.

3. Thus, when he reverently stands by (the altar)
with this (hymn), everything is thereby made good[1]
for him that, knowing or unknowing, he either does
in excess, or does not carry to the end, in this
building of the altar—in short, whatever was not
secured for him. And whatever wish there is in
that anush/ubh verse[2], that he secures even now;
and, moreover, he thereby keeps off the fiends, the
Rakshas, from this sacred work, and they do not
wreck him, whilst uttering imprecations. Wherefore
one who knows this may readily build a fire-altar
even for an enemy, for he is able to gain the better
of him.

4. [He approaches reverently the fire-altar[3], with,
Vâg. S. XVIII, 68–74], 'For mighty strength
that smiteth Vritra, and for victory in battle,
we call thee hither, O Indra!' 'O much-in-
voked Indra, crush thou the handless Kunâru,
lurking here, together with the Dânus; and
with might smite thou the footless Vritra,
the ever-growing mocker!' thus he reverently
stands by (the fire) with the first two (verses) relating
to the slaying of Vritra. For now the gods, having
warded off Vritra, evil, performed this rite freed
from evil; and in like manner does the Sacrificer,
having warded off Vritra, evil, now perform this rite
freed from evil.

---

[1] Literally, obtained.

[2] Viz. the first of the seven verses (Rig-veda III, 37, 1).

[3] According to Kâty. Sr. XVII, 7, 1, this ceremony should take
place on the completion of each layer, after it has been covered
with loose earth; cf. paragraph 11.

5. 'Scatter thou our scorners, O Indra[1]!'—
'Like a terrible, creeping beast, dwelling in
the mountains, hast thou come from the
farthest distance: having sharpened thy
pointed, piercing thunderbolt[2], O Indra, beat
thou off the foes, and scatter the spurners!'
thus with the second two (verses) relating to (Indra)
Vimridh[3]. For now the gods, having warded off
the spurners, evil, performed this rite freed from evil;
and in like manner does the Sacrificer now, having
warded off the spurners, evil, now perform this rite
freed from evil.

6. 'May Agni Vaisvânara come forward
from afar to our help, to hear our hymns of
praise!'—'Sought after in the sky, sought
after on earth, Agni, sought after, hath entered all the plants: Agni Vaisvânara, sought
after, may guard us from injury by day and by
night!' thus with the third two (verses) relating to
(Agni) Vaisvânara. For now the gods, having, by
Vaisvânara, burnt out evil, performed this rite, freed
from evil; and in like manner does the Sacrificer
now, by Vaisvânara, burn out evil, and perform this
rite freed from evil.

7. 'May we obtain this wish, O Agni, with
thy help! may we obtain, O wealthy one,
wealth with abundant heroes! striving for
strength, may we obtain strength; may we
obtain undecaying glory, O thou ever-young!'
thus with one (verse) containing wishes. For now

---

[1] For the complete verse, see IV, 6, 4, 4.

[2] Thus Mahídhara.

[3] That is, the repeller of spurners, or enemies.

the gods, having, by the six-versed (hymn), warded
off evil, made once for all, by the one wish-holding
(verse), all (objects of) wishes their own ; and in like
manner does the Sacrificer now, having, by the six-
versed (hymn), warded off evil, make once for all,
by the one wish-holding (verse), all wishes his own.

8. It is (a hymn) of seven verses,—the fire-altar
consists of seven layers, (and there are) seven
seasons, seven regions, seven worlds of the gods,
seven stomas, seven prishtha (sâmans), seven metres,
seven domestic animals, seven wild ones, seven vital
airs in the head, and whatever else there is of seven
kinds, relating to deities and relating to the self,—
all that he thereby secures. They become equal to
the Anushtubh[1], for the Anushtubh is speech, and it
is by speech that he secures for him (Agni) all that
which is not yet secured for him.

9. ' Let him approach (the fire-altar) with an eight-
versed (hymn)!' say some ;—'with (Vâg. S. XVIII.
75), "We thereby offer unto thee thy wish,
reverently approaching thee with open hands:
with holiest mind and peaceful thought offer
thou sacrifice unto the gods as priest, O
Agni!" thus with a second wish-holding one,—and
the seven foregoing ones, that makes eight,—the
Gâyatri consists of eight syllables, and Agni is of
Gâyatra nature: as great as Agni is, as great as is
his measure, by so much he thus secures for him

---

[1] The seven verses consist of two Gâyatris (twenty-four syllables
each), four Trishtubhs (forty-four each), and one Anushtubh (thirty-
two syllables). Whilst the two Gâyatris are sixteen syllables short
of two Anushtubhs, the four Trishtubhs have forty-eight syllables
in excess of four Anushtubhs. Hence the seven verses consist of
8 × 32 syllables, or eight Anushtubhs.

whatsoever is not yet secured for him; and thus, moreover, the two deities[1] receive the same (amount) for their share.' Let him, however, not do so, for surely those seven (verses) are (equal to) eight anush/ubh (verses), and thus he even therein obtains whatever wished-for object there is in the eight-versed (hymn).

10. With (verses) addressed to Indra and Agni he approaches (the fire):—the fire-altar belongs to Indra and Agni: as great as Agni is, as great as is his measure, by so much he thus gains for him whatever has not been gained for him. And Indra and Agni are all the gods, and the fire-altar belongs to (or Agni is) all the deities: as great as Agni is, as great as is his measure, by so much he thus gains for him whatever has not been gained for him.

11. Now some make this (hymn) the opening rite of every performance, saying, 'Freed from evil, we must perform this sacred work!' And others, indeed, say, 'Let him approach reverently (each) layer when it is covered with soil, for therein that (layer) becomes whole and complete.' Let him, then, do as he chooses. So much as to the building; now as to the non-building.

12. Verily, there are three oceans,—the Fire-altar (being the ocean) of Yagus-formulas, the Mahâvrata (-sâman)[2] that of Sâmans (hymn-tunes), and the Mahad uktham (Great Litany[3]) that of Rik (verses). Whoever performs these (three rites) for another

[1] Viz. Indra and Agni, having each four verses addressed to them.

[2] See p. 282, note 5.

[3] See p. 110, note 3; p. 111, note 1.

person causes these oceans to dry up for himself,
and after them, thus drying up, the metres[1] dry up
for him; and after the metres the world; and after
the world his own self; and after his own self his
children and cattle: indeed, he who performs these
for another person becomes poorer day after day.

13. And he who, not having performed these
(rites) for another person, were to officiate in the
performance even of all other sacrifices, for him the
metres again replenish themselves from out of those
oceans, and after the metres the world, and after the
world his own self, and after his own self his children and cattle: indeed, he who does not perform
those rites for another person, becomes more prosperous day after day. For, indeed, these (rites) are
his divine, immortal body; and he who performs
them for another person, makes over to another
his divine body, and a withered trunk is all that
remains.

14. Now, some (say), 'Having performed them
for another person, they either perform them for
themselves or cause them to be performed again:
this is the atonement.' But let him not do this,
for it would be as if one were to water a withered
trunk: it would rot and die: let him know that
there is no atonement for such an one.

15. And Sândilya once upon a time said—Tura
Kâvasheya once built a fire-altar for the gods at
Kâroti. The gods asked him, 'Sage, seeing that
they declare the building of the fire-altar not to be
conducive to heaven, why then hast thou built one?'

16. He said, 'What is conducive to heaven,

---

[1] That is, the Vedic texts.

and what is not conducive thereto? The Sacrificer is the body of the sacrifice, and the officiating priests are the limbs; and, surely, where the body is there are the limbs; and where the limbs are there is the body. And, verily, if the priests have no place in heaven, then the Sacrificer has none, for both are of the same world. But let there be no bargaining as to sacrificial fees, for by bargaining the priests are deprived of their place in heaven.'

TENTH KÂNDA.

THE MYSTERY OF AGNI, THE FIRE-ALTAR.

First Adhyâya.   First Brâhmana.

1. In the first place that Agni (the Fire-altar), the year, is built[1]; thereafter the Great Litany (mahad uktham) is recited[2]. When Pragâpati became relaxed, the vital fluid flowed upwards[3].

2. Now, that Pragâpati who became relaxed is the year; and those joints of his which became relaxed are the days and nights.

3. And that Pragâpati who became relaxed is this very Fire-altar which here is built; and those joints of his, the days and nights, which became relaxed are no other than the bricks;—thus, when he lays down these (in the layers of the altar), he thereby restores to him those joints of his, the days and nights, which had become relaxed: and thus

---

[1] Or, possibly, 'that Agni is built in a year,' as paragraph 4 might seem to suggest. Sâyana, however, takes it in the above sense,—esho'gnih Samvatsarâtmakah purastât pûrvam kiyate. The Agnikayana, when properly performed, requires a full year, whence Agni-Pragâpati is constantly identified with the year and the seasons.

[2] According to Sâyana, the intermediate Mahâvrata-sâman (see note 1, p. 283), chanted prior to the recitation of the Mahad uktham, is likewise implied here.

[3] Thus—ûrdhvalokam agakkhat—Sâyana takes 'agram.'

it is even in this (building of the altar) that this Yagus is built up[1] and secured (for Pragâpati).

4. And that vital fluid (essence) of his which flowed upwards (became) the Great Litany: it is in quest of that vital fluid that (the priests) go by means of the *Rik* and Sâman. And when the Yagus marches in front in this (quest)[2], it is in order to fetch something that that (Veda) goes— even as (one might say), 'That one thing there is mine, I will fetch it,' so does that Yagus go in front (or forward). That (vital fluid) they obtain in the course of a year[3].

5. The Adhvaryu takes (draws) it by means of the Graha (Soma-cup); and inasmuch as he thereby takes (grah) it, it is (called) Graha[4]. The Udgâtri puts the vital fluid into it by means of the (sâman of the) Great Rite (mahâvrata[5]); but, indeed, the

---

[1] Viz. inasmuch as yagus-formulas have to be used with the laying down of many of the bricks (the so-called 'yagushmatîs'). Whilst, in the case of the *Rik* and Sâman, other rites are necessary to secure them for the restored Pragâpati, the Yagus is secured for him in the very act of building up his body, the fire-altar.

[2] The Adhvaryu priest has to do all the practical work connected with the sacrificial performance, the building of the altar, &c.; and inasmuch as it is with yagus-formulas he does so throughout, the Yagus is said here to take the lead; cf. X, 3. 5. 3.

[3] Viz. by means of the sacrificial session of sacrificing, chanting, and reciting, called 'Gavâm ayanam' (procession of the cows), lasting for one year, on the last day but one of which the Mahâvrata, or Great Rite, is performed.

[4] The particular cup of Soma here referred to is the Mahâvratîya-graha, the special cup of the Great Rite; cf. X, 4, 1, 12 seq.

[5] The central feature of the Mahâvrata consists in the chanting, at the mid-day service—as the Hotri's *Prishtha*-stotra—of the so-called Mahâvrata-sâman. It consists of five different parts which,—like those of which the Mahad uktham, recited after it, is

(sâman of the) Great Rite is (equivalent to) all these
(other) sâmans (hymn-tunes) : it is thus by means
of all the hymn-tunes that he puts the vital fluid
therein. The Hotri puts the vital fluid therein
by means of the Great Litany; but, indeed, the
Great Litany is the same as all these rik (hymn-
verses) [1] : it is thus by means of all the hymn-verses
that he puts the vital fluid into it (the Soma-cup).

composed,—are considered as representing different parts of Agni-
Pragâpati's body, viz.: 1. Gâyatra-sâman, representing the head;
it is chanted in the trivrit-stoma (nine-versed hymn-form) and consists of the triplets, Sâma-v. II, 146–8 (= Rig-veda I, 7, 1–3;
indram id gâthino brihat), II, 263–5 (indro dadhiko asthabbir),
and II, 800–2 (ud ghed abhi srutâmagham); though, according
to others, the Sâma-triplets corresponding to Rig-veda I, 7, 1–9
may be chanted instead.   2. Rathantara-sâman (Sâma-v. II,
30–1), representing the right wing, chanted in the Pañkadasa-
stoma, or fifteen-versed form.   3. Brihat-sâman (II, 159–60,
the left wing, in the Saptadasa-stoma, or seventeen-versed form.
4. Bhadra-sâman (on II, 460–2; cf. Calc. ed., vol. v, p. 402), the
tail, in the Ekavimsa, or twenty-one-versed form.   5. Râgana-
sâman (on II, 833–5; cf. Calc. ed., vol. v, p. 449), the body (âtman), in the Pañkavimsa-stoma, or twenty-five-versed form; instead
of this the Vâmadevya-sâman (on II, 32–4) may be chanted in
the pañkanidhana form (Calc. ed., vol. v, p. 451).—The chanting of
this Stotra is preceded by the singing of thirteen sâmans, called parimâdah (see X, 1, 2, 8), followed by certain ceremonies—buckling
armour on a nobleman, driving in a sunwise direction round the
sacrificial ground, shooting arrows at two ox-hides, beating of drums,
&c.—apparently symbolising the driving off of evil spirits from the
sacrifice, or a combat for the possession of (the light of) the sun.
The chanting itself is, according to some authorities, performed by
the Udgâtris, whilst, according to others, all the priests (except the
Hotri, for whom the Maitrâvaruna acts), as well as the Grihapati,
or Sacrificer, take part in turn in the singing of the sâmans; the
Prastotri and Pratihartri, assistants of the Udgâtri, joining in with
the successive performers in the Nidhanas, or finales.

[1] See p. 110, note 3; p. 112, note 1.   During his recitation
of the Great Litany, the Hotri is seated on a swing, the Adhvaryu

6. When those (Udgât*ri*s) chant (the stotra), and when he (the Hot*ri*) recites (the *s*astra) afterwards, then he (the Adhvaryu) offers that (vital fluid, in the form of Soma) unto him (Agni-Pragâpati) at the Vasha*t*-call; and thus this vital fluid enters him. For, indeed, they do not see it to be the Great Rite that lies there being praised, nor the Great Litany, but it is Agni alone they see; for Agni is the self (body), and thus those two, the *Rik* and the Sâman, enter him in the form of the vital fluid; and thus they both enter (join) the Ya*g*us.

7. Now, that Agni (fire-altar) consists of pairs—the first layer and the second, and the third and fourth; and of the fifth layer the fire which is placed on the built (altar) is the mate. And, indeed, this body consists of pairs.

8. The thumbs (and great toes, 'angush*th*a,' m.) are males, and the fingers and toes ('anguli,' f.) females; the ears ('kar*n*a,' m.) are males, and the eyebrows ('bhrû,' f.) females; the lips ('osh*th*a,' m.) are males, and the nostrils ('nâsikâ,' f.) females; the teeth ('danta,' m.) are males, and the tongue ('*g*ihvâ,' f.) is a female: indeed the whole (body) consists of pairs, and with this body, consisting of pairs, that (vital fluid) enters this Agni (the fire-altar), consisting of pairs [1].

9. This, then, is the entering therein;—even thus, indeed, he (Agni) consists of pairs [2]; but in this

making his responses whilst standing on a plank, and the Hot*ri*'s assistants being seated on bundles of grass.

[1] Or, with this body as a mate it thus enters this Agni, its mate; literally, with this body forming one of a (productive) pair, it thus enters this Agni, forming one (i.e. the other) of a pair.

[2] That is, he has in him the generative energy. Apparently

way also he consists of pairs :—the fire-altar here built up is no other than this speech, for with speech it is built up; and the fire which is placed on the built (altar) is the breath; and the breath ('prâna,' m.) is the male, the mate, of speech ('vâk,' f.). And, indeed, this body is speech; and the breath which is in the body is its mate : with this mated body that (vital fluid) thus enters into the mated Agni.

10. This also is the entering therein;—there is indeed no fear of him (Agni) being without offspring to whosoever thus knows these two, the body and Agni, to be a pair; but, indeed, this body is food, as is said by the *Ri*shi (*Ri*g-veda X, 107, 7), 'The Dakshinâ winneth food which is our own self (breath).'

11. Now, this food, when eaten, becomes of two kinds,—that part of it which is immortal (remains) above the navel : by the upward vital airs it moves upwards and enters the air; but that part of it which is mortal tends to move away : it passes beyond the navel, and, having become twofold, enters this (earth), as urine and faeces. Now that which enters this (earth) enters the fire-altar [1] built here; and that which enters the air enters that fire which is placed on the built (altar). This also is the entering therein.

SECOND BRÂHMANA.

1. Pragâpati was desirous of gaining these worlds. He saw this bird-like body, the Fire-altar : he

'mithuna,' m. has also the sense of 'paired,' 'mated,' i.e. 'one who has his complement or mate,' and so perhaps here.

[1] Viz. inasmuch as the altar is built on the earth, and the latter forms its foundation. Comm.

fashioned it, and thereby gained this (terrestrial) world. He saw a second bird-like body, the (chant of the) Great Rite[1]: he fashioned it, and thereby gained the air. He saw a third bird-like body, the Great Litany[1]: he fashioned it, and thereby gained the sky.

2. This built Fire-altar, doubtless, is this (terrestrial) world, the Great Rite the air, and the Great Litany the sky: all these, the Fire-altar, the Great Rite, and the Great Litany, one ought therefore to undertake together, for these worlds were created together; and as to why the Fire-altar is built first, it is because of these worlds this (terrestrial) one was created first. Thus with regard to the deity.

3. Now with regard to the body. The Fire-altar is the mind, the (chant of the) Great Rite the breath, and the Great Litany speech: all these one ought therefore to undertake together, for mind, breath, and speech belong together; as to why the Fire-altar is built first, it is because the mind is prior to the breathings.

4. The Fire-altar, indeed, is the body (trunk), the Great Rite the breath, and the Great Litany speech: all these one ought therefore to undertake together, for body, breath, and speech belong together; and as to why the Fire-altar is built first, it is because of him who is produced the trunk is produced first.

5. The Fire-altar, indeed, is the head, the Great Rite the breath, and the Great Litany the body:

---

[1] The Mahâvrata-sâman and the Mahad ukthaṃ, as we have seen (p. 282, note 5; p. 111, note 1), are constructed so as to correspond to the different parts of the bird-like Agni-Pragâpati.

one ought therefore to undertake all these together, for head, breath, and body belong together; and as to why the Fire-altar is built first, it is because of him who is born the head is born first; and hence, whenever all these are undertaken together the Great Litany, indeed, is accounted the highest (âtamâm)[1], for the Great Litany is the body (or self, âtman).

6. As to this they say, ' If all these are difficult to obtain together, what (means of) obtaining them is there?'—In the Gyotish/oma (form of the) Agnish/oma[2]: let him perform offering with the Gyotish/oma Agnish/oma.

7. In this Gyotish/oma Agnish/oma the Bahish-pavamâna (stotra) is (in) the Trivr̍t (stoma)—that is the head of the rite; the two other Pava-mânas are (in) the Pañ/kadasa and Saptadasa (stomas)—they are the two wings; the Hotr̍i's

---

[1] The combination 'âtamâm khyâyate' is, as it were, the super-lative of 'â-khyâyate;' cf. anutamâm gopâyati, X, 5, 2, 10; and Delbrück, Altind. Syntax, p. 194.

[2] The Agnish/oma may be performed in three different modes, according to the variation of stomas (or hymn-forms) employed for the stotras (or chants). In the Gyotish/oma the order of stomas is that set forth in paragraph 7, viz.: a. Bahishpavamâna-stotra in the Trivr̍t (nine-versed); b. Âgya-stotras, and c. Mâ-dhyandina-pavamâna-stotra, in the Pañ/kadasa (fifteen-versed); d. Prˢish/tha-stotras, and e. Ârbhava-pavamâna-stotra, in the Saptadasa (seventeen-versed); and f. Agnish/oma-sâman (Yagñâyagñiya) in the Ekavimsa (twenty-one-versed) stoma, or hymn-form. In the Gosh/oma, on the other hand, the succession of stomas is a. Pañ/kadasa, b. Trivr̍t, c. d. Saptadasa, e. f. Ekavimsa; and in the Âyush/oma: a. Trivr̍t, b. Pañ/kadasa, (c. d.) Sap-tadasa, (e. f.) Ekavimsa. Cf. part ii, p. 402, note 4; for the scheme of Stotras (and Sastras), ib. p. 325, note 2. The Agnish/oma is singled out here for the reason that the Mahâvrata-day takes the form of an Agnish/oma sacrifice.

Âgya (stotra) is (in) the Pañkadasa, the Prishtha (stotra in) the Saptadasa, and the Yagñâyagñiya (stotra in) the Ekavimsa (stoma)—they are the tail.

8. Now these two, the Pañkadasa and Saptadasa, have thirty-two hymn-verses : twenty-five of these are the twenty-five-fold body [1] ; and the seven which remain over are the Parimâd (sâmans), for these are the cattle (or animals), (for) cattle are sporting all around us (pari-mâd [2])—thus much, then, is the

---

[1] See p. 168, note 3.

[2] Sâyana takes 'parimâd' here in the sense of 'a source of pleasure all around'—parito harshahetavah.—The Parimâdah are thirteen Sâmans sung (not chanted, in the proper sense of the word) by the Udgâtri, his two assistants joining merely in the Nidhanas or chorus-like passages. They are given, figured for chanting, in the Aranyagâna of the Sâma-veda (Calc. ed., ii, p. 387 seq.). This performance takes place immediately after the Adhvaryu has given the sign for, and the Udgâtri 'yoked,' the Mahâvrata-stotra or sâman (i.e. the Hotri's Prishtha-stotra of the Great Rite),—or, according to some authorities, before either the 'yoking,' or the Adhvaryu's summons,—and thus serves as an introduction to the central and chief element of the Great Rite, the Mahâvrata-sâman. According to the ritual symbolism, these preliminary sâmans are intended to supply the newly completed Pragâpati with hair (feathers) and nails ; but the performance would rather seem to be a solemn mode of doing homage (upasthânam) to the different parts of the bird-like altar and the sacrificial ground ; thus corresponding to a similar, though simpler, ceremony performed on the completion of the fire-altar in its simplest form, as described at IX, 1, 2, 35-43. On the present occasion the ceremony is performed in the following order : 1. near the head of the altar (the Âhavanîya fire) he sings the Prâna ('breath ;' Sâma-v., vol. ii, p. 436) ; 2. near the tail the Apâna (downward-breathing, ii, p. 437) ; 3. 4. near the right and left wing the two Vratapakshau (ii, p. 438) ; 5. near the left armpit the Pragâpati-hridaya ('heart of Prag.,' ii, p. 499) ; 6. near the Kâtvâla or pit, the Vasishthasya Nihava (Sâma-v., vol. v, p. 602) ; 7. near the Âgnîdhra hearth the Satrasyarddhi ('success of the sacrificial session,' ii, p. 465) ; 8. 9. in front and behind the Havirdhâna carts, the Sloka and Anusloka (i, pp.

Great Rite: thereby he obtains the Great Rite even in this (Agnish/oma).

9. And the Hot/i recites seven metres—each subsequent one-versed (metre) increasing by four (syllables)—with the Virâg as an eighth: these (eight) consist of three eighties and forty-five syllables. Now by the eighties thereof the eighties (of the mahad ukpham) [1] are obtained, for the Great Litany is counted (or recited) by eighties (of triplets); and of the forty-five (syllables which remain) twenty-five are this twenty-five-fold body [2]; and where the body is there, indeed, are (included) the head, and the wings and tail: and the twenty (syllables which remain) are the insertion [3];—thus much, then, is the Great Litany: thereby he obtains the Great Litany even in this (Agnish/oma). All these (three) are indeed obtained in the Gyotish/oma Agnish/oma: let him, therefore, perform offering with the Gyotish/oma Agnish/oma.

THIRD BRÂHMANA.

1. Pragâpati created living beings. From the out- (and in-) breathings he created the gods, and from the downward breathings the mortal beings; and

---

887-9); 10. towards the Mârgâliya the Yâma (ii, p. 461); 11. 12. in front and behind the Sadas, the Âyus, and Nava-stobha (ii, pp. 450–51); 13. in front of the Gârhapatya the Ris-yasya sâman (ii, p. 324).

[1] See p. 112, note 1.

[2] Viz. the body, as consisting of the ten fingers, the ten toes, the arms and legs, and the trunk.

[3] Towards the end of the Mahad Ukpham, in the portion representing the thighs, nine trish/ubh verses (Rig-veda III, 43, 1–8, and X, 55, 5) are inserted as an 'âvapanam.'

above the (mortal) beings he created Death as their consumer.

2. Now, one half of that Pragâpati was mortal, and the other half immortal : with that part of him which was mortal he was afraid of death ; and, being afraid, he became twofold, clay and water, and entered this (earth).

3. Death spake unto the gods saying, ' What has become of him who has created us ? '—' Being afraid of thee, he has entered this (earth),' they said. He spake, ' Let us search for him, let us gather him up for I shall not injure him.' The gods gathered him from out of this (earth) : that part of him which was in the water, they gathered as water, and that which was in this (earth, they gathered) as clay. Having gathered together both clay and water, they made a brick, whence a brick consists of both clay and water.

4. And, indeed, these five forms (bodily parts) of him are mortal—the hair on the mouth, the skin, the flesh, the bone, and the marrow ; and these are immortal—the mind, the voice, the vital air, the eye, and the ear.

5. Now, that Pragâpati is no other than the Fire-altar which is here built up, and what five mortal parts there were of him, they are these layers of earth ; and those which were immortal they are these layers of bricks.

6. The gods spake, ' Let us make him immortal !' Having encompassed that mortal form by those immortal forms of his, they made it immortal—the layer of earth by means of two layers of bricks : in like manner the second, the third, and the fourth (layers of earth).

7. And having laid down the fifth layer (of bricks), he (the Adhvaryu) scatters earth on it; thereon he lays the Vikarnî and the Svayamâtrinnâ, scatters chips of gold, and places the fire: that is the seventh layer, and that (part) is immortal; and in this way, having encompassed that mortal form of his by those two immortal forms, they made it immortal,—the layer of earth by means of two layers of bricks. Thereby, then, Pragâpati became immortal; and in like manner does the Sacrificer become immortal by making that body (of the altar) immortal.

8. But the gods knew not whether they had made him complete, or not; whether they had made him too large, or left him defective. They saw this verse (Vâg. S. XVIII, 76), 'The seat-hiding Agni, Indra, god Brahman, Brihaspati, and the wise All-gods may speed our sacrifice unto bliss!'

9. Of this (verse) one part is Agni's, one part Indra's, and one part the All-gods';—with that part thereof which is Agni's they made up that part of him (Pragâpati) which is Agni's, and with Indra's (part) that which is Indra's, and with the All-gods' (part) that which is the All-gods': in this very (fire-altar) they thus made him up wholly and completely.

10. And when he stands by (the altar, worshipping it) with this (verse), he thereby secures (makes good) all that part of him (Pragâpati) which, whether he knows it or not, he either does in excess or insufficiently in this (fire-altar),—whatever has not been secured for him. The 'seat-hiding' (verse) is an Anushtubh, for the Anushtubh is speech, and the seat-hider is speech: it is by speech that he

secures for him what was not secured for him.
'Let him approach (the altar with this verse) when
he has covered a layer with earth,' say some, 'for
then that (layer) becomes whole and complete.'

FOURTH BRÂHMANA.

1. Now, at the beginning, Pragâpati was (composed of) both these, the mortal and the immortal—
his vital airs alone were immortal, his body mortal:
by this sacrificial performance, and by this order
of proceeding, he made his body uniformly undecaying and immortal. And in like manner is the
Sacrificer (composed of) both the mortal and the
immortal—his vital airs alone are immortal, his
body mortal: by this sacrificial performance, and
by this order of proceeding, he makes his body
uniformly undecaying and immortal.

2. He lays down the first layer,—this, doubtless,
is his out- (and in-) breathing[1], and it is an immortal (element), for the out-breathing is something
immortal: this, then, is an immortal layer. He
then scatters loose soil thereon,—this, doubtless, is
his marrow, and it is a mortal (element), for the
marrow is mortal: he establishes it on that immortal (element), and thereby this part of him
becomes immortal.

3. He lays down the second layer,—this, doubtless, is his downward breathing, and it is an immortal
(element), for the downward breathing is something
immortal: this, then, is an immortal layer. He
thus encompasses that mortal (element) on both

---

[1] That is, the breath-proper, of the mouth and nose, passing
upward into the air from the middle of the body.

sides by an immortal one, and thereby that part
of him becomes immortal. He then scatters loose
soil thereon,—this, doubtless, is his bones, and it is
a mortal (element), for the bone is mortal: he
establishes it on that immortal (element), and thereby
this part of him becomes immortal.

4. He lays down the third layer,—this, doubtless,
is his through-breathing[1], and it is an immortal
(element), for the through-breathing is something
immortal: this, then, is an immortal layer. He
thus encompasses that mortal (element) on both
sides by an immortal one, and thereby that part
of him becomes immortal. He then scatters loose
soil thereon,—this, doubtless, is his sinews, and it
is a mortal (element), for the sinew is mortal: he
establishes it on that immortal (element), and thereby
this part of him becomes immortal.

5. He lays down the fourth layer,—this, doubtless,
is his upward breathing[2], and it is an immortal
(element), for the upward breathing is something
immortal: this, then, is an immortal layer. He thus
encompasses that mortal (element) on both sides
by an immortal one, and thereby that part of him
becomes immortal. He then scatters loose soil
thereon,—this, doubtless, is his flesh, and it is a
mortal (element), for flesh is mortal: he establishes
it on that immortal (element), and thereby this part
of him becomes immortal.

6. He lays down the fifth layer,—this, doubtless,

---

[1] The Vyâna, through-breathing, or circulating air, is the vital
air which serves the upward air (or out- and in-breathing, prâna) and
downward air (apâna). Maitryup. II, 6 (Cowell).

[2] Or, outward breathing.—'That which belches forth or keeps
downwards the food eaten or drunken, this is the udâna;' Cowell. ib.

is his central (or pervading) breathing[1], and it is
an immortal (element), for the central breathing is
something immortal : this, then, is an immortal
layer. He thus encompasses that mortal (element)
on both sides by an immortal one, and thereby that
part of him becomes immortal. He then scatters
loose soil thereon,— this, doubtless, is his fat, and
it is a mortal (element), for the fat is mortal : he
establishes it on that immortal (element), and thereby
this part of him becomes immortal.

7. He lays down the sixth layer,—this, doubtless,
is his voice, and it is an immortal (element), for the
voice is something immortal : this, then, is an immortal layer. He thus encompasses that mortal
(element) on both sides by an immortal one, and
thereby that part of him becomes immortal. He
then scatters loose soil thereon,—this, doubtless, is
his blood and his skin, and it is a mortal (element),
for blood is mortal, and skin is mortal : he establishes
it on that immortal (element), and thereby this part
of him becomes immortal.

8. These, then, are six layers of bricks, and six
layers of earth, that makes twelve,—the year (consists of) twelve months, and Agni is the year : as
great as Agni is, as great as is his measure, with
so much did Pragâpati then make his body uniformly undecaying and immortal ; and in like manner
does the Sacrificer now make his body uniformly
undecaying and immortal.

9. Having then laid down the Vikarnî and Svayamâtrinnâ, he scatters chips of gold, and places

---

[1] 'The Samâna (equalizing air) distributes the digested pieces
through the limbs.' Maitryup. II, 6 (Cowell).

the fire thereon: Pragâpati then finally made a
golden form for his body; and inasmuch as (he did
so) finally, this was the final form of his body;
whence people speak of 'the golden Pragâpati[1].'
And in like manner does the Sacrificer now finally
make a golden form for his body; and inasmuch as
(he does so) finally, this is the final form of his
body; and hence, whether they know this or not,
people say that the Agnikit (he who has built an
altar) is born in yonder world as one made of gold[2].

10. Now, on this point, Sândilya and Sâptarathavâhani, teacher and pupil, were once disputing
with one another: ' This is his form,' said Sândilya;
'his hair,' said Sâptarathavâhani.

11. Sândilya said, ' Surely, there is a hairy form
(as well as) a hairless form: his form it certainly
is;' and this, indeed, is as Sândilya has said: when
it (the altar) is completely built, Agni is led forward;
and after he has been led forward, logs of wood[3]
are offered as 'oblations.'

12. By means of (the channel of) the out- (and in-)
breathing the gods eat food, and Agni (the sacrificial fire) is the out-breathing of the gods; whence
it is in front (of the sacrificial ground) that offering
is made to the gods, for by means of the (channel of
the) out-breathing the gods eat food. By means
of the down-breathing men eat food, whence food

---

[1] Apparently an allusion to Hiranyagarbha, the golden germ, or
the golden egg (XI, 1, 6, 1), from which the Puru-ha, creator of
the universe, arose. Cf. also Aitareyâr. II, 1, 3, with Sâyana's
commentary.

[2] Sâyana assigns to 'hiranmaya' the meaning ' of a colour
resembling gold' (hiranyasamânavarnah).

[3] See IX, 2, 3, 36 seq.

is introduced into men (from the front) towards the back, for by their down-breathing men eat food.

13. Here, now, they say, 'He who has built an altar must not eat of any bird, for he who builds a fire-altar becomes of a bird's form; he would be apt to incur sickness: the Agni*k*it therefore must not eat of any bird.' Nevertheless, one who knows this may safely eat thereof; for he who builds an altar becomes of Agni's form, and, indeed, all food here belongs to Agni: whosoever knows this will know that all food belongs to him.

14. Here, now, they say, 'What is done here in (the building of) the altar, whereby the Sacrificer conquers recurring death?' Well, he who builds an altar becomes the deity Agni; and Agni (the fire), indeed, is the immortal (element);—the gods are splendour: he enters splendour; the gods are glory: he becomes glorious whosoever knows this.

Fifth Brâhmana.

1. This built fire-altar, in truth, (includes) all these sacrifices :—when he slaughters an animal victim, that is the Agnyâdheya (establishment of the sacred fires)[1]; when he collects (the materials for) the fire-pan, that constitutes the oblations of the Agnyâdheya; when he performs the initiation,

---

[1] Though no animal sacrifice takes place at the Agnyâdhâna, the latter, as the fundamental ceremony pre-supposed by all subsequent sacrificial performances, is here compared with the immolation of five victims (VI, 2, 1, 15 seq.) which, taking place as it does on the Upasavatha, or day of preparation, i.e. the day before the Soma-sacrifice on the newly built fire-altar, is, as it were, a preliminary ceremony.

that is the Agnihotra; and when the initiated puts
two logs on (the fire)[1], these are the two oblations
of the Agnihotra.

2. He puts them on in the evening and in the
morning, for in the evening and in the morning
the Agnihotra oblations are offered;—with one
and the same formula, for with one and the same
formula the two Agnihotra oblations are offered[2].
Then the driving about (of the fire in the pan[3]),
and the taking down (to the water) of the ashes,
these two (constitute) the New and Full-moon
offerings; and when he builds the Gârhapatya
hearth[4], that is the Kâturmâsya (seasonal offerings);
and what takes place from (the building of) the
Gârhapatya up to the (sowing of) all-herb (seed[5],
that constitutes) the ishtis[6], and what takes place
after the all-herb (sowing) and prior to (the building

---

[1] This refers to the two samidhs (kindling-sticks) put on the
Ukhya Agni,—one in the evening, and one in the morning,—after
the ashes had been cleared out of the fire-pan (ukhâ); see VI,
6, 4, 1 seq.

[2] Both in the evening and in the morning two libations of milk
are offered (the pûrvâhuti and the uttarâhuti), but only the first is
offered with a formula, the evening formula being, 'Agni is the
light, the light is Agni, hail!' whilst the morning formula is, 'Sûrya
is the light, the light is Sûrya, hail!' See II, 3, 1, 30. For
alternative formulas—'With the divine Savitri, with the Night
(or Dawn, respectively) wedded to Indra, may Agni (or Indra,
respectively) graciously accept, hail!' see II, 3, 1, 37, 38.

[3] See VI, 8, 1, 1 seq. Sâyana takes it to refer to the Agni-
pranayana, or leading forward of the fire to the fire-altar; but that
would not fit in well with the ceremony next referred to, viz. the
removal of the ashes of the Ukhyâgni, or fire in the pan; for which
see VI, 8, 2, 1 seq.

[4] VII, 1, 1, 1 seq.

[5] Viz. on the newly ploughed altar-site, see VII, 2, 4, 13 seq.

[6] That is, offerings for the fulfilment of some special wishes.

of) the layers, that is the animal sacrifices [1]; and the Vishnu-strides [2] which are (performed) at these sacrifices are just these Vishnu-strides; and what muttering of formulas there is that is the Vâtsapra [3].

3. The first layer is the Soma-sacrifice; the second the Râgasûya as prior to the consecrations [4]; the third the Vâgapeya; the fourth the Asvamedha (horse-sacrifice); and the fifth the Agnisava [5]. Then the sâmans he sings around the built (altar) are the Mahâvrata(-sâman); the Udgâtri's preliminary muttering (of the text of his chants) on that occasion is the Satarudriya; the 'shower of wealth' the Great Litany; and what takes place subsequent to (the singing of) the sâmans, and prior to the shower of wealth, that is the Hotri's preliminary muttering on that occasion; and what takes place after the shower of wealth is the Grihamedhas [6] (house-sacrifices). Such are all the sacrifices: these he secures by (building) the fire-altar.

---

[1] That is, animal sacrifices performed independently of other ceremonies.

[2] See VI. 7. 2, 12 seq

[3] See VI. 7. 4. 1 seq.

[4] That is, the ceremonies connected with the Vâgaprasavîya oblations, V, 2, 2, 4 seq.; and the devasû-havîmshi, or oblations to the Divine Quickeners (by whom the king is supposed to be first consecrated), V, 3, 3. 1 seq.

[5] See IX, 3, 4, 7. 9. It is strange that the Agnisava should be mentioned here, as it is said to be confined to the Agnikâyana. It would seem that some independent ceremony, such as the Brihaspatisava (consecration of Brihaspati, cf. V, 2, 1, 19; and part iii, introd. p. xxiv seq.), may be referred to.

[6] Sâyana identifies these with the offerings of sacrificial sessions (sattra), during which the Sacrificer is indeed called the Grihapati, or master of the house; see IV, 6, 3, 5 seq.; and part ii, p. 97, note 1.

4. Now, then, as to the powers (conferred by the performance) of sacrifices. Verily, he who (regularly) performs the Agnihotra eats food in the evening and in the morning (when he comes to be) in yonder world, for so much sustenance is there in that sacrifice. And he who performs the New and Full-moon sacrifice (eats food) every half-month; and he who performs the Seasonal sacrifice (does so) every four months; and he who performs the animal sacrifice (twice a year, eats food) every six months; and the Soma-sacrificer once a year; and the builder of the fire-altar at his pleasure eats food every hundred years, or abstains therefrom[1]; for a hundred years is as much as immortality[2], unending and everlasting : and, verily, for him who knows this, there shall thus be immortality, unending and everlasting; and whatever he as much as touches, as it were, with a reed, shall be for him immortal, unending and everlasting.

SECOND ADHYÂYA.   FIRST BRÂHMANA.

1. Pragâpati was desirous of going up to the world of heaven; but Pragâpati, indeed, is all the (sacrificial) animals[3]—man, horse, bull, ram, and

---

[1] That is to say, the food eaten the first time will sustain him for a hundred years, after which time he may, or may not, take food, being sure of everlasting life and a godlike nature.

[2] Or, perhaps, for so long lasts the Amrita (the food of the immortals):—agnim kitavân purushas tu satasamkhyâkeshu samvatsareshu teshu kâmam aparimitam asnâti yato yâvantah satam samvatsarâs tâvad amritam devatvaprâpakam anantam aparimitam annam bhavati. Sây.

[3] See VI, 2, 1, 15 seq.

he-goat:—by means of these forms he could not do so. He saw this bird-like body, the fire-altar, and constructed it. He attempted to fly up, without contracting and expanding (the wings), but could not do so. By contracting and expanding (the wings) he did fly up: whence even to this day birds can only fly up when they contract their wings and spread their feathers.

2. He measures it (the fire-altar) by finger-breadths; for the sacrifice being a man [1], it is by means of him that everything is measured here. Now these, to wit, the fingers, are his lowest measure: he thus secures for him (the sacrificial man [2]) that lowest measure of his, and therewith he thus measures him.

3. He measures by twenty-four finger-breadths [3],— the Gâyatrî (verse) consists of twenty-four syllables, and Agni is of Gâyatra nature [4]: as great as Agni is, as great as is his measure, by so much he thus measures him.

4. He contracts [5] (the right wing) inside on both

---

[1] The sacrifice, being the substitute of (the sacrificing) man, is represented as identical with the Sacrificer, its measurements being taken from his body and stature; see part i. p. 78. note 1.

[2] Or,—for it, viz. the fire-altar, representing both Agni-Pragâpati and the Sacrificer: hence this assumed identity has to be borne in mind to understand the symbolic speculations of the Brâhmana.

[3] This measure (24 aṅguli) is equal to one 'aratni' or cubit: 12 aṅguli being equal to a 'vitasti' or span (of thumb and little finger, or from wrist to tip of middle finger).

[4] See VI, 1, 1, 15; 1, 3, 19.

[5] Or, he draws in, draws together (upasamûhati).

sides[1] by just four finger-breadths, and expands[2] it
outside on both sides[1] by four finger-breadths: he
thus expands it by just as much as he contracts it;
and thus, indeed, he neither exceeds (its proper
size) nor does he make it too small. In the same
way in regard to the tail, and in the same way in
regard to the left wing.

5. He then makes two bending-limbs[3] in the
wings, for there are two bending-limbs in a bird's

---

[1] That is, on both sides of that part of the wing which joins the
body of the altar he draws in by four finger-breadths the two long
sides of the wing, thus changing the parallelogram into a trapezium,
without altering the superficial area of the wing. On the plan of
the altar given in part ii, p. 419, the effect of this manipulation on
the wings and tail is indicated by pointed lines.—Sâyana remarks,
—ubhayatah pakshasya pârsvadvaye, antaratah kityâgner madhyadese
katurangulam upasamûhati samkarshati pravesayatîty arthah:
bâhyatah agnimadhyâd bâhyadese katurangulam vyudûhati, ante
vivardhayati.

[2] Or, he draws out, or draws asunder (vyudûhati).

[3] Literally 'outbendings' (nirnâma)—'Schwunggelenke' (spring-
limbs), St. Petersb. Dict.—This 'bending-limb' would seem to
include the two inner segments of the (solid part of the) wing—
those corresponding to the upper and fore-arm of man—as well as
the adjoining and connecting joints or articulations, which portions
may be taken roughly as forming the inner third of the wing when
covered with feathers. The 'bending-limb' would thus derive its
name from its 'bending,' or drawing, the wing 'out' from the body.
Sâyana, however, explains it by 'nitarâm namati,' 'that which
bends down,' as if it were formed from the prep. 'ni' instead
of 'nis.' The manipulation to which this part of the wing is to be
subjected is, however, not quite easy to understand from the
description, and the commentary affords very little assistance—
viznîya iti pakshabhâgam tredhâ vibhagya antare trtîyabhâge
nirnâmakaranam . . .; etâm srutim apekshyaivâpastambenoktam,
'vakrapaksho vyastapukkho bhavati, paskât prân (!) udûhati, purastât pratyudûhati, evam eva hi vayasâm madhye pakshanirnâmo
bhavatîti vignâyate' iti.

wings. In one-third (of each wing he makes them),
for the bending-limbs are in one-third of the bird's
wings ;—in the inner third[1], for the bending-limbs
are in the inner third of a bird's wings. He
expands (each of these limbs) in front[2] by just
four finger-breadths, and contracts it behind by
four finger-breadths; he thus expands it by just
as much as he contracts it; and thus, indeed, he
neither exceeds (its size), nor does he make it
too small.

6. On that bending-limb he places one brick : he
thereby gives to it that single tube (tubular organ)
which joins on to[3] (the body) from the bending-
limb of the flying bird. Then here (on the left wing).

7. He then makes the wings crooked, for a bird's
wings are crooked ; he expands them behind by just
four finger-breadths, and contracts them in front by
four finger-breadths[4] : he thus draws them out by

---

[1] That is, the third part of the wing adjoining the body.

[2] That is, at the front edge of the wing of the flying bird, that
which cuts through the air. The joint between the second and
third segments of the wing, when expanded, would protrude, whilst
on the opposite side of the wing the tops of the feathers would
somewhat recede ; but I am not sure whether this is what is
referred to in these indications.

[3] Literally, which lies beside, or close to (upasete, viz. the body,
as it would seem) from the bending-limb. The brick is apparently
meant to represent symbolically the bone of the upper segment, or
some tubular organ by which the vital air is supposed to enter the
wing from the body. Sâyana remarks,—pakshipakshamadhyaga-
tanâdîtvena prasamsati, . . kityâgneh pakshamadhye ekâm nâdim
eva nihitavân bhavati.

[4] Comm.—katurangulamâtram paskâdbhâge udûhati vikarshati,
purastâdbhâge katurangulamâtram samûhati samkarshati ; evam
krite vakratvam bhavati. Cf. Âpastamba's directions in note 3 of
last page. I fail to see, however, in what respect this manipulation
differs from that referred to in paragraph 5; and whether the

just as much as he draws them in ; and thus, indeed, he neither exceeds (its size) nor does he make it too small.

8. He now gives to it (the altar) the highest form[1]. This Agni had now been completely restored, and the gods conferred upon him this highest form : and in like manner does this (Sacrificer) confer upon him this highest form : he makes a thousand bricks marked with straight lines, a thousand marked this way (from left to right), and a thousand marked that way (from right to left).

9. And when he has laid down the fifth layer, he measures out the altar in three parts, and on the central part he places the one thousand bricks marked with straight lines : he thereby gives to it those straight plumes of the bird pointing backwards (with their tops, and covering it) from head to tail.

10. On the right side he then lays down the one thousand (bricks) marked *thus* (from left to right) : he thereby gives to it those curved plumes on the right side of the bird [2].

11. On the left side he then lays down the one thousand (bricks) marked *thus* (from right to left) : he thereby gives to it those curved plumes on the left side of the bird. With a thousand (bricks he does it each time)—a thousand means everything :

'vakratvam' refers to the irregular shape, or to the curved nature, of the wings.

[1] That is, he gives to it the last finish.

[2] Or, perhaps, those soft feathers of the bird curved towards the right. Sâyana as above—dakshinatah dakshinapakshe ityâlikhitâ dakshinâvritta ishtakâh ; uttaratah uttarasmin pakshe ityâlikhitâh savyâvritta ishtakâ upadadhyât.

with everything (required) he thus confers that highest form upon him (Agni);—with three thousand —Agni is threefold: as great as Agni is, as great as is his measure, with so much he thus confers the highest form upon him.

SECOND BRÂHMANA.

1. Now the one person which they made out of those seven persons[1] became this Pragâpati. He produced living beings (or offspring), and having produced living beings he went upwards,—he went to that world where that (sun) now shines. And, indeed, there was then no other (victim) meet for sacrifice but that one (Pragâpati), and the gods set about offering him up in sacrifice.

2. Wherefore it is with reference to this that the Rishi has said (Vâg. S. XXXI, 16, Rig-veda X, 90, 16), 'The gods offered up sacrifice by sacrifice,'—for by sacrifice they did offer up him (Pragâpati), the sacrifice;—'these were the first ordinances:'—for these laws were instituted first;— 'these powers clung unto the firmament,'—the firmament is the world of heaven, and the powers are the gods: thus, 'Those gods who offered up that sacrifice shall cling to the world of heaven;'--

3. 'Where first the perfect gods were,'—the perfect[2] gods, doubtless, are the vital airs, for it is they that perfected him in the beginning[3] when they

---

[1] Literally, those seven persons which they made into one person. See VI, 1, 1, 1 seq.

[2] It is difficult to see what meaning the author assigns to 'sâdhya' applied to minor classes of deities.

[3] See VI, 1, 1, 1.

were desirous of becoming that (body of Pragâpati [1]); and even now, indeed, they do perfect
(him).—[Rig-veda X, 149, 3]—'Thereafter this
other became meet for sacrifice by the abun-
dance of the immortal world,'—for thereafter,
indeed, other things here—whatsoever is immortal—
became fit for sacrifice.

4. 'Savitri's well-winged eagle verily was
first born, and he was according to his
ordinance,'—the well-winged eagle, doubtless, is
Pragâpati, and Savitri is that (sun): thus, 'In
accordance with his (the sun's) law he indeed
(comported himself).'

5. He indeed consists of seven persons, for that
Person [2] consisted of seven persons:—to wit, the
body of four, and the wings and tail of three, for of
four the body of that Person consisted, and of three
his wings and tail.

6. He measures it (the altar) by the man with
upstretched arms [3]; for the sacrifice is a man, and
by him everything here is measured; and that is
his highest measure when he stands with upstretched arms: he thus secures for him what is
his highest measure, and therewith he then measures
it. And what (space) there is over and above that
when he is raised on the forepart of his foot, that
he secures by the enclosing-stones; and hence he

---

[1] Tad eva bubhûshanta iti, prânâh svayam api | igâpatyât-
manâ (? prâgâpatyâtmâno) bhavitum ikkhantah.   Sây.

[2] See VI, 1, 1, 3–6.

[3] That is to say, wherever he speaks of man's lengths, the height
to which a man reaches with his upstretched arms is understood;
the particular man who supplies this (relative) standard of measure
being the Sacrificer.

should dig a line for the enclosing-stones outside
(the altar-ground).

7. Two cubits he gives to the two wings: he
thereby lays strength into the wings. And the
wings are (the bird's) arms, and by means of the
arms food is eaten: it is thus for the sake of food
that he gives them that space; and when he gives
two cubits to the two wings, it is because food is
taken from the distance of a cubit.

8. To the tail he gives a span: he thus lays
strength into the support, for the tail is the support.
The span means the hand [1], and by means of the
hand food is eaten: it is thus for the sake of food
that he gives it that space; and when he gives
a span to the tail, he thereby settles him (Agni)
in (the midst of) food; and when he gives less
(space) to this (part of the body), it is because he
thereby settles him in (the midst of) food [2]. But,
indeed, so much does this (the bird's wing) measure,
and so much this (the bird's tail), and hence when
he thus measures them, it is for the sake of securing
for him that (natural measure).

Third Brâhmaņa.

1. Now this Vedi (altar-ground, viz. the Mahâvedi of the Soma-sacrifice) is just that (right)
measure for the Vedi of the sevenfold [3] (fire-altar).

---

[1] The span of thumb and little finger is taken to be equal to
the distance from the wrist to the tip of the middle finger.

[2] That is to say, he makes him so as to occupy but small space,
and to be surrounded by abundant food.

[3] That is, measuring seven times the length of a man standing
with upstretched arms.

Having fixed upon (the place for) the sacrificial
ground, he enters the Patnisâla [1] by the front (east)
door, and having thrown up (the ground) for the
Gârhapatya, he sprinkles it with water. From
the raised (site) of the Gârhapatya he strides
seven steps eastward. From there he measures
off a fathom [2] towards the east, and having, in the
middle thereof, thrown up (the ground) for the
Âhavanîya, he sprinkles it with water. From
the front part of the fathom he strides three steps
eastward : that is the end of the Vedi [3].

2. Now, there are here, including the fathom (as
one), eleven steps [4] between the end of the Vedi and
the (original) Gârhapatya ;—the Trish/ubh consists

---

[1] That is, 'the wife's hall,'—the sacrificial hall or shed, usually
called Prâkînavamsa or Prâgvamsa, measuring 20 cubits by 10
(part ii. p. 3, note 2), in which the original fires and vedi of ish/is are
enclosed at the Soma-sacrifice : see the plan, part ii, p. 475.

[2] A fathom (vyâma) is the space between the tips of the two
middle fingers of a man standing with outstretched arms, this being
considered the man's height. In this paragraph, the author roughly
recapitulates the main dimensions of the sacrificial ground used for
ish/is, which will also be required for the present purpose. The
dimensions here supplied will give about the distance of eight steps
between (the centres of) the Gârhapatya and Âhavanîya fires required
by I, 7, 3, 23. In the middle of the space of a fathom here alluded
to as the easternmost space of the hall, the (original square)
Âhavanîya is laid down, but this ultimately makes way for the new
circular Gârhapatya hearth built of bricks and having the whole of
this 'fathom' for its diameter.

[3] That is, the hindmost (western) point of the (easterly line of
the) Mahâvedi of the Soma-sacrifice, where the peg, called 'anta/-
pâtya,' is driven in, being three steps east from the post of the
front door of the Prâkînavamsa (and hence three steps from the
future circular Gârhapatya hearth built of bricks).

[4] Literally, these are (ten) steps, having the fathom as an eleventh
(space or step).

of eleven syllables, and the Trish/ubh is a thunderbolt, and the Trish/ubh means strength : it is thus
by the thunderbolt, and by strength, that the
Sacrificer from the very first drives off the fiends,
the Rakshas, from the mouth of the sacrifice.

3. This is the womb of the Vedi, for it was from
that womb that the gods begat the Vedi. And
that (space of a) fathom which was (marked off),
is the womb of the Gârhapatya [1], for it was from
that womb that the gods begat the Gârhapatya; and
from the Gârhapatya the Âhavaniya.

4. From the (western) end of the Vedi he measures
off the Vedi [2] thirty-six steps long eastward, thirty
(steps) broad behind, and twenty-four (steps broad)
in front,—that makes ninety. This, then, is the
Vedi measuring ninety steps : thereon he lays out
the sevenfold Fire-altar.

5. As to this they say, 'How does this sevenfold
(Person, the fire-altar,) correspond to this Vedi
(measuring ninety steps)?' Well, there are these

---

[1] That is, the brick-built Gârhapatya of the Agni/ayana on
which the Ukhya Agni, having been carried about by the Sacrificer
for a year, is transferred from the fire-pan (ukhá), and from which
afterwards the fire of the great altar is derived. This new Gârhapatya has been raised on the site of the old (square) Âhavaniya
(the so-called 'sâlâdvârya' or hall-door fire), on which the fire in
the pan, the Ukhya Agni, was kindled (esha âhavaniyo vakshya-
mânâyâs kayanamahâveder gârhapatyo bhavati; Sây.). The pan
containing this fire was then placed half a fathom south of (the
centre of) the old Âhavaniya, and hence so as to stand quite close
to the brick-built Gârhapatya raised in its place, and forming
a circle with a diameter of one fathom. Thus this 'space of a
fathom' is here quite correctly referred to as the original source
of the fires of the Agni/ayana.

[2] For the dimensions of the Mahâvedi here referred to, see
part ii, p. 111 seq.

ten vital airs in a man[1], four limbs, and the trunk as the fifteenth; in the same way in the second, and in the same way in the third (man),—in six men this makes ninety; and one man remains over. Now, (that seventh) man is fivefold—hair, skin, flesh, bone, and marrow (fat), and this Vedi also is fivefold—the four regions (quarters), and the body (of the altar) as the fifth[2]: thus this sevenfold (altar) does indeed correspond to this Vedi.

6. Now, some, intending to construct higher forms (of altars), increase (the number of) these steps and this fathom accordingly, saying, 'We enlarge the womb in accordance therewith;'—but let him not do so; for the womb does not enlarge along with the child that has been born[3], but, indeed, only as long as the child is within the womb, does the womb enlarge, and so long, indeed, the growth of the (unborn) child here (lasts)[4].

7. Indeed, those who do it in that way, deprive this Father Pragâpati of his due proportions; and they will become the worse for sacrificing, for they deprive Father Pragâpati of his due proportions.

---

[1] That is, in the first of these seven persons or men, making up the sacrificial man (yagña-purusha), Pragâpati; that first man being the Sacrificer himself, as supplying the standard for these measures.

[2] That is, the fifth region, situated in a vertical direction, this being represented by the fire-altar which rises upwards.

[3] Somewhat differently Professor Delbrück, Altind. Syntax, p. 444, 'The womb does not grow in proportion with the embryo produced therein.'

[4] The argument of the author apparently is, that the planned enlargement of the fire-altar is an enlargement of the child Agni, after he has been born, and does not involve an increased size of the original sacrificial ground of the Prâkinavamsa.

As large as this Vedi[1] of the sevenfold (fire-altar) is, fourteen times as large he measures out the Vedi of the one hundred and one-fold (altar).

8. He now measures off a cord thirty-six steps[2] (yards) long, and folds it up into seven (equal) parts: of this he covers (the space of) the three front (eastern) parts (with bricks), and leaves four (parts)[3] free.

9. He then measures (a cord) thirty steps long, and lays it sevenfold: of this he covers three parts (with bricks) behind, and leaves four (parts) free[4].

---

[1] That is, of course, the Mahâvedi on which the (ordinary) fire-altar is raised, and which is enlarged in proportion to the size of the altar. The intermediate sizes of the fire-altar between the two extremes here alluded to increase each by four square 'man's lengths' (the man being measured with upstretched arms), or by one man's length on each side of the body of the altar; the largest possible altar thus measuring 101 man's lengths on each side.

[2] A step, or pace (prakrama) is equal to 3 feet (pada), a foot measuring 12 finger-breadths (aṅgula),-- these measures being, however (at least theoretically), relative to the Sacrificer's height.

[3] That is to say, he stretches the cord along the ground from the (western) 'end of the Vedi' eastwards, and marks off on the ground three-sevenths of the cord on the eastern side, that part of the Vedi being afterwards covered by the brick-built altar, whilst the remaining space behind is required for the Sadas and Havir-dhâna sheds, &c. If we take the Mahâvedi to be 108 feet long (= 36 prakramas) this would allow 15⅜ feet for each part, or some 46 feet for the length of the part to be covered with bricks, and this measure, being equal to seven man's lengths, would allow 6½ feet for a man's length (including the upstretched arms). Between the altar and the front (eastern) edge of the Vedi a space of one foot is, however, to be left.

[4] That is, he stretches the cord across (north to south) and marks off the three central divisions of it as forming the hind side of the altar (leaving two-sevenths of the string free on either side). This gives 12⁶⁄₇ (out of 90) feet for each part, or 38½ feet for the back, or western, side of the altar.

10. He then measures (a cord) twenty-four steps long, and lays it sevenfold : of this he covers three parts in front (with bricks), and leaves four (parts) free[1]. This, then, is the measuring out of the Vedi.

11. Now as to the (other) forms of the fire-altar. Twenty-eight man's lengths long (from west to east) and twenty-eight man's lengths across is the body (of the altar), fourteen man's lengths the right, and fourteen the left wing, and fourteen the tail. Fourteen cubits (aratni) he covers (with bricks) on the right, and fourteen on the left wing, and fourteen spans (vitasti) on the tail. Such is the measure of (an altar of) ninety-eight man's lengths with the additional space (for wings and tail).

12. He now measures a cord of three man's lengths, and lays it sevenfold : of this he covers (the space of) four parts (with bricks) on the body (of the altar), and three parts on the wings and tail.

13. He then measures one three cubits long, and lays it sevenfold : of this he covers (the space of) three parts on the right, and three on the left wing, and leaves four (parts) free.

14. He then measures one a span long, and lays it sevenfold : of this he covers (the space of) three parts on the tail, and leaves four (parts) free. In this way does this one hundred and one-fold (Agni) correspond to this Vedi.

15. As to this they say, 'When thirteen man's lengths are over, how is it that these do not deviate

---

[1] This gives 10⅔ (out of 72) feet for each part, or 30⅔ feet for the front, or eastern, side of the altar. The measurements here given are intended as a refinement on the usual square shape of the fire-altar.

from the right proportions (of the altar)[1]?' Well,
what right proportions there were in the case of
that seventh man's length[2], these same proportions (also apply) to all these (redundant man's
lengths).

16. And they also say, 'When Pragâpati had
formed the body he filled it up with these (redundant
lengths) wherever there was anything defective in
it; and therefore also it is rightly proportioned.

17. As to this some say, 'The first time they
construct a simple (altar[3]), then the one higher by
one (man's length), up to the one of unlimited size.'
Let him not do so.

18. Sevenfold, indeed, Pragâpati was created in
the beginning. He went on constructing (developing) his body, and stopped at the one hundred and
one-fold one. He who constructs one lower than
a sevenfold one cuts this Father Pragâpati in twain:
he will be the worse for sacrificing as one would be
by doing injury to his better. And he who constructs one exceeding the one hundred and one-fold
one steps beyond this universe, for Pragâpati is
this universe. Hence he should first construct the
sevenfold (altar), then the next higher up to the
one hundred and one-fold one, but he should not
construct one exceeding the one hundred and one-

---

[1] Or, from the right total (sampad) which the altar ought to
obtain. By paragraph 7, the altar is to be made fourteen times as
large as the sevenfold one; and the latter being said to be in exact
proportion with Pragâpati (in paragraph 3), the larger altar would
thus show an excess of thirteen man's lengths over the rightly
proportioned altar.

[2] Viz. in paragraph 5.

[3] That is, one of a single man's length on each side.

fold one, and thus, indeed, he neither cuts this Father Pragâpati in twain, nor does he step beyond this universe.

FOURTH BRÂHMANA.

1. Pragâpati, indeed, is the year, and Agni is all objects of desire. This Pragâpati, the year, desired, 'May I build up for myself a body so as to contain[1] Agni, all objects of desire.' He constructed a body one hundred and one-fold; and in constructing a body one hundred and one-fold, he built up for himself a body so as to contain Agni, all objects of desire, and himself became all objects of desire; there was not one object of desire outside of him: whence they say, 'The year (includes) all objects of desire;' for, indeed, outside the year there is no object of desire whatever.

2. And in like manner does the Sacrificer now, by constructing a body (of the altar) one hundred and one-fold, build for himself a body so as to contain Agni, all objects of desire: he becomes all objects of desire, and not one object of (his) desire is outside of him.

3. Now this year is the same as yonder sun; and he is this one hundred and one-fold (Agni):—his rays are a hundredfold, and he himself who shines

---

[1] Literally, May I build for myself a body (self) with a view to (abhi) Agni; or, perhaps, 'He builds (a body) so as to become (Agni;' in which case 'abhi' of 'abhisamkinute' would have the same force as in 'abhisampadyate.' See, however, X, 2, 5, 9–12, where Sâyana explains it by 'yo yah kâmah tam sarvam âtmânam abhilakshya sampâditavân bhavati'—'He brings about (accomplishes) all that desire for his body.'

yonder, being the one hundred and first, is firmly
established in this universe; and in like manner
does the Sacrificer now establish himself in this
universe by constructing for himself a body a hundred and one-fold.

4. And, indeed, the one hundred and one-fold
passes into (becomes equal to) the sevenfold one;
for yonder sun, whilst composed a hundred and
one-fold, is established in the seven worlds of the
gods, for, indeed, there are seven worlds of the
gods,—the four quarters and these three worlds:
these are the seven worlds of the gods, and in
them that (sun) is established. And in like manner
does the Sacrificer now establish himself in the
seven worlds of the gods by constructing for himself
a body a hundred and one-fold.

5. And, again, as to how the one hundred and
one-fold (altar) passes into the sevenfold one:—
yonder sun, composed of a hundred and one parts,
is established in the seven seasons, in the seven
stomas (hymn-forms), in the seven pr ish*t*ha (-sâmans),
in the seven metres, in the seven vital airs, and in
the seven regions; and in like manner does the
Sacrificer now establish himself in this universe (or,
on everything here) by constructing for himself
a body one hundred and one-fold.

6. And, again, as to how the one hundred and
one-fold passes into the sevenfold one:—yonder
sun, composed of a hundred and one parts, is established in the seven-syllabled Brahman, for the
Brahman (holy writ or prayer) indeed consists of
seven syllables,—' *ri*k ' is one syllable, ' yagu*h* ' two,
and ' sâma ' two; and what other Brahman there
is that is just the ' brahman ' of two syllables—this

seven-syllabled Brahman is the universe[1]: therein that (sun) is established; and in like manner does the Sacrificer now establish himself in the seven-syllabled Brahman by constructing for himself a body one hundred and one-fold.

7. Therefore, also, they lay down around (the altar) sets of seven (bricks) each time, and hence the one hundred and one-fold passes into the sevenfold one; and, indeed, the sevenfold one passes into the one hundred and one-fold.

8. Sevenfold, indeed, Pragâpati was created in the beginning. He saw this body composed of a hundred and one parts—fifty bricks in the Prâna-bhrıts[2], and fifty sacrificial formulas, that makes a hundred, and the 'settling' and sûdadohas-formula are the two one hundred and first—these two are one and the same, for when he has 'settled' (a brick), he pronounces the sûdadohas-formula over it: by means of this one hundred and one-fold body he gained that conquest and obtained that success; and in like manner does the Sacrificer, by means of this one hundred and one-fold body, gain that conquest and obtain that success. And thus, indeed, the sevenfold (altar) passes into the one hundred and one-fold: that which is a hundred and one-fold is sevenfold, and that which is sevenfold is a hundred and one-fold. So much as to the forms (of altars).

---

[1] Or, perhaps, 'all this (taken together) is the sevenfold Brahman.'

[2] In the first layer ten Prânabhrıt bricks were placed along the diagonals in each of the four corners of the body of the altar (or in the intermediate quarters), and as many round the centre.

FIFTH BRÂHMAṆA.

1. Now as to the building itself. He builds between the two (performances of the) Upasads[1]. For at that time the gods were afraid lest the fiends, the Rakshas, should destroy that (Agni's body) of theirs (built) there[2]. They saw these strongholds, the Upasads, to wit, these worlds, for these worlds are indeed strongholds. They entered them, and having entered them, they completed that body in a place free from danger and devilry; and in like manner does the Sacrificer now, after entering these strongholds, complete this body in a place free from danger and devilry.

2. And, again, as to why he builds between the Upasads. At this time the gods were afraid lest the fiends, the Rakshas, should destroy that (Agni's body) of theirs (built) there. They saw these thunderbolts, the Upasads, for the Upasads indeed are thunderbolts: they entered them[3], and, having entered them, they completed that body in a place free from danger and devilry; and in like manner does the Sacrificer now, after entering those thunder-

---

[1] The Upasads (or sieges) are performed twice a day on at least three days (the regular number for ordinary one day's Soma-sacrifices) intervening between the end of the Dîkshâ (initiation) and the day of the Soma-sacrifice; see part ii. p. 105. note 1. On the first day the first layer is built between the two performances (whilst the final preparation of the altar-site, as well as the building of the Gârhapatya altar and the installation of the Ukhya Agni thereon, takes place before the morning performance of the Upasads), and on the second day the remaining layers are built.

[2] For the construction in the *oratio directa*, see part iii, p. 34, note 2.

[3] Or, they went into their shelter (pra-pad).

bolts, complete this body (of Agni) in a place free
from danger and devilry.

3. And the Upasads also are the fervour[1] in the
sacrifice, for they are indeed fervour ; and inasmuch
as it is built (ki) in fervour (tapas) it is called
'Tâpaskita[2].' As long as they perform the Upasads
so long (do they perform) the Pravargya[3]: (if) it
is for a year that they perform the Upasads, it is
for a year (they perform) the Pravargya.

4. The Upasads, indeed, are the days and nights,
and the Pravargya is the sun: he thus establishes
yonder sun on the days and nights, whence he is
established on the days and nights.

5. And if there are twenty-four (Upasad-days[4]),
there being twenty-four half moons—the Upasads

[1] Or, austere devotion, see III, 4, 4, 27, where fasting during the
Upasad days is recommended as calculated to promote religious
fervour. There is also, however, the primary meaning 'heat' implied, whence the 'heating' of the cauldron (gharma = θερμός) at the
Pravargya (representing the sun) is connected with the Upasads.

[2] That is, the fire-altar used at the sacrificial period (ayana)
called Tâpaskita, which generally requires a full year (360 days)
for the performance of the Upasads (as do also the Dîkshâ
before them, and the performance of the Soma-sacrifice after
them); cf. XII, 3, 3, 10 seq.; Kâty. XIV, 5, 1.—Âsval. XII,
5, 9; Kâty. XXIV, 5, 7, however, mention a Tâpaskita which
only requires four months for each of the three periods, or
a year altogether, whilst the maximum duration is by Âsv. fixed
at thirty-six years (twelve for each period); and by Kâty. at three
years for the Upasads and a year for each of the two other
ceremonies.

[3] See part ii, p. 104.

[4] Sâyana does not specify what sacrificial performance is intended as requiring twenty-four Upasad-days, but merely says that
they are required 'kratuviseshe,' at some special kind of sacrifice.
At all events, the Sacrificer would be at liberty to adopt that
number of Upasad-days instead of the minimum of days prescribed,
if he hoped to derive special benefit therefrom.

are the half-moons, and the Pravargya is the sun : he thus establishes yonder sun on the half-moons, whence he is established on the half-moons.

6. And if there are twelve (Upasad-days)[1]— there being twelve months—the Upasads are the months, and the Pravargya is the sun : he thus establishes yonder sun on the months, whence he is established on the months.

7. And if there are six (Upasad-days)—there being six seasons—the Upasads are the seasons, and the Pravargya is the sun : he thus establishes yonder sun in the seasons, whence he is established in the seasons.

8. And if there are three (Upasad-days)—there being these three worlds—the Upasads are these three worlds, and the Pravargya is the sun : he thus establishes yonder sun in these worlds, whence he is established in these worlds.

9. Now, then, the inquiry as to the earth-layers of the altar-pile. One month (the building of) the first layer (of bricks takes), and one month the layer of earth [2],—so long desire (lasts) in the spring season (of two months) : he thus [3] builds for himself a body so as to obtain all of whatever desire there is in the spring season [4].

---

[1] For an ordinary Ekâha, or one day's Soma-sacrifice, the Upasads may be performed for twelve days instead of the usual three days (Kâty. VIII, 2, 40). It is also the regular number of days for Ahînas (ib. XIII, 1, 1 ; Âsv. IV, 8, 15) and for most sattras.

[2] That is, when the Upasads last for a whole year, as at the Tâpaskita.

[3] That is, by building for his Soma-sacrifice an altar the body of which requires a whole year in being laid down, as it does in the Tâpaskita.

[4] Translated literally, the sentence would run thus : 'Thus as

10. One month the second (layer of bricks takes), and one month the layer of earth,—so long desire (lasts) in the summer season: he thus builds for himself a body so as to obtain all of whatever desire there is in the summer season.

11. One month the third (layer of bricks takes), and one month the layer of earth,—so long desire (lasts) in the rainy season: he thus builds for himself a body so as to obtain all of whatever desire there is in the rainy reason.

12. One month the fourth (layer of bricks takes), and one month the layer of earth,—so long desire (lasts) in the autumn season: he thus builds for himself a body so as to obtain all of whatever desire there is in the autumn season.

13. And of the fifth layer (of bricks) he lays down the Asapatnâ and Virâg (bricks) on the first day, and of the Stomabhâgâs one each day: these he 'settles' together once, and pronounces once the sûdadohas-formula over them[1]. For a month they silently apply the earth-layer for the Stomabhâgâs, for so long desire (lasts) in the winter season: thus he builds for himself a body so as to obtain all of whatever desire there is in the winter season.

14. One month the sixth (layer of bricks takes),

_____

much desire as there is in the spring season—he builds for himself a body so as to obtain all that (desire).' Only the building of an altar (body) for a whole year ensures the full fruition of sensual pleasures supplied during the year.

[1] That is, these three kinds of bricks—the five Asapatnâs, and forty Virâgs being laid down on the first day, and of the twenty-nine Stomabhâgâs one each day,—the three kinds of bricks thus take one month in being laid down, after which the 'sâdanam' and 'Sûdadohas' (cf. part iii, p. 301, note 3) are performed upon them.

and one month the layer of earth,—so long desire
(lasts) in the dewy season : he thus builds for himself
a body so as to obtain all of whatever desire there
is in the dewy season. So long, indeed, desire (lasts)
in the twelve months and the six seasons : he thus
builds for himself a body so as to obtain all of
whatever desire there is in the twelve months and
the six seasons.

15. And in addition to these there are three days [1],
to wit, the day on which he performs the Satarudriya
offering, the day of preparation, and the day on
which the Soma is pressed. When they perform
the Upasad on these days, these (days) are the days
and nights of that (thirteenth, or intercalary) month :
and when (they perform) the Pravargya, he thereby
establishes yonder sun also in that (seventh) season,
—so long, indeed, desire (lasts) in the thirteen
months and the seven seasons : he thus builds for
himself a body so as to obtain all of whatever desire
there is in thirteen months and seven seasons.

16. For a year Soma should be pressed,—the
year is everything, and the one hundred and
one-fold (altar) is everything : by means of everything he thus gains everything. Should he be
unable (to press Soma) for a year, he should
perform the Visvagit Atirâtra [2] with all the Pri-

---

[1] Viz. after the twenty-eight days of the twelfth month two days
remain to make up the year, so that the (first) Sutyâ day (pressing
day) takes place after the expiry of a full year.

[2] The Visvagit, as usually performed, is an Agnish/oma sacrifice,
the twelve Stotras of which are chanted in three different stomas or
hymn-forms, viz. the first four in the trivr/i (nine-versed), the next
four in the pañ/adasa (fifteen-versed), and the last four in the
saptadasa (seventeen-versed) stoma. For the stotriya-texts see

shthas [1], and at that (sacrifice) he should give away all his property [2]; for the Visvagit (all-conquering) Atirâtra with all the Prishthas means everything, and all one's property means everything, and the one hundred and one-fold (altar) means everything: by means of everything he thus gains everything.

Sixth Brâhmana.

1. The one hundred and one-fold Pragâpati, doubtless, is the year, and thereto belong days and

Tândya-Br. XVI, 5, 1 seq. It is closely united with the Abhigit Soma-day—the stotras of which are performed in four stomas, viz. three in each of those used for the Visvagit, and the last three in the ekavimsa, or twenty-one-versed, stoma—with which it may, indeed, be combined in one and the same performance; and both form part of the sacrificial session called Gavâm ayanam (part ii, p. 427). The Visvagit (as well as the Abhigit) may, however, also be performed as an Atirâtra instead of Agnishtoma, and in that case the sequence of Stomas is entirely different, their order being as follows: the first four stotras are performed in the first four stomas (trivrt, pañkadasa, saptadasa, ekavimsa); the next four stotras in the four stomas beginning with the second stoma (up to trinava), and the next four stotras in the four stomas beginning with the third stoma (up to trayastrimsa). Of the three Ukthastotras, the first is performed in the trinava, and the two others in the ekavimsa; the Shodasin in its own (ekavimsa) form; the night-chants in the pañkadasa; and the twilight-chant in the trivrt-stoma. See Tândya-Br. XX, 9.

[1] On 'sarvaprishtha' Soma-days, see part iii, introduction, pp. xx seq.

[2] As an equivalent for one's 'whole property (sarvavedasa, sarvasva),' Kâtyâyana (XXII, 2, 26, 27) enumerates 'cows, oxen, ploughs, sacks of corn (or corn-sacks), pairs of slaves, waggons, animals for riding, houses (or sheds), and couches.' For other similar enumerations, see A. Weber, Omina and Portenta (Abh. of Berl. Acad. 1858), p. 398.

nights, half-months, months, and seasons. The
days and nights of a month are sixty, and in the
month, doubtless, the days and nights of the year
are obtained ; and there are twenty-four half-months,
thirteen months, and three seasons (of four months)
—that makes a hundred parts, and the year itself
is the one hundred and first part.

2. By the seasons it is sevenfold,—six seasons
(of two months), and the year itself as the seventh
part. And he who shines yonder is the light of that
year : his rays are a hundredfold, and the (sun's)
disk itself is the one hundred and first part.

3. By the regions it is sevenfold,—the rays which
are in the eastern region are one part, and those in the
southern are one, and those in the western are one,
and those in the northern are one, and those in the
upper (region) are one, and those in the lower (region)
are one, and the disk itself is the seventh part.

4. Beyond this (year) lies the wish-granting world ;
but the wish-granting one is the immortal (element) :
it is thus the immortal that lies beyond this (year,
temporal existence) : and that same immortal (element) is that very light which shines yonder.

5. Now that same boon (the immortal light), bright
with wealth, he, Savit*ri* (the sun), distributes among
the distributed creatures, and among plants and
trees, too ; and to some, indeed, he gives more of it,
and to some less ; and they to whom he gives more
of it live longest, and they to whom he gives less
live less long.

6. It is regarding this that it is said in the *Rik*
(I, 22, 7 ; Vâg. S. XXX, 4). 'The distributer of
wealth, the bright boon, we invoke, Savit*ri*,
the beholder of men.' And that is the full

(measure of) life, for it is long, it is unending [1]; and when people here say, 'May thy life be long! mayest thou reach the full (extent of) life!' it is as much as to say, 'May that world, may that (immortal light) be thine!'

7. It is Vâk (Speech) that, seeing it, speaks (thus). That same (immortal light), indeed, is to be obtained either by the one hundred and one-fold (altar), or by a life of a hundred years: whosoever builds a one hundred and one-fold (altar), or whosoever lives a hundred years, he, indeed, obtains that immortality. Therefore, whether they know it, or whether they do not, people say, 'The life of a hundred years makes for heaven.' Hence one ought not to yield to his own desire and pass away before (he has attained) the full extent of life, for (such shortening of one's life) does not make for the heavenly world [2]; and these are indeed the worlds, to wit, the days and nights, the half-moons, moons, and seasons, and the year.

8. Those who pass away in the years below twenty are consigned to the days and nights as their worlds; and those who (pass away) in the years above twenty and below forty, to the half-moons; and those who (pass away) in the (years) above forty and below sixty, to the months; and those who (pass away) in the (years) above sixty and below

---

[1] Thus Sâyana—tad etat sarvam âyur iti sarvapadasyârtham aba dîrgham anantam hi.

[2] Literally, 'conducive to the world,' or, perhaps, 'conducive to a place (in yonder world).' Sâyana interprets it by—his death is 'alokyam,' that is, not procuring the world consisting of immortality. Some such meaning as '(such conduct) is not world-winning' seems to be implied by the words which follow.

eighty, to the seasons ; and those who (pass away)
in the (years) above eighty and below a hundred (are
consigned) to the year; and he alone who lives
a hundred years or more attains to that immortal
(life).

9. Only by many sacrifices, indeed, is a single
day, or a single night (of life) gained ; and only he
who builds the one hundred and one-fold (altar), or
he who lives a hundred years, is certain of his
attaining to that immortal (life). But he, indeed,
builds a one hundred and one-fold (altar) who
carries him (Ukhya Agni) for a year: hence one
should only build (an altar for) such an (Agni) who
has been carried for a year. Thus much as to the
deity.

10. Now as to the sacrifice. When he measures
out those one hundred and one men (man's lengths)
with upstretched arms, that is a one hundred and
one-fold (altar) in form, and a sevenfold one in
respect of its layers : the layers contain six seasonal[1]
(bricks) and the fire (or altar) itself is the seventh
form.

11. And, indeed, it is a hundred and one-fold in
respect of bricks,—the first fifty bricks and the last
fifty[2] which are (laid down) make a hundred forms
(parts) ; and the bricks which are laid down between
(those two sets) are the one hundred and first form.

---

[1] The five layers contain five sets of two such bricks, each
representing the two months of the respective season; except the
third layer, which contains four such bricks, only, however, of half
the thickness of the others.

[2] According to Sâyana, this refers to the fifty Prânabhrzts in the
first, and to the forty Virâgs, five Nâkasads, and five Pankakûdâs in
the fifth layer.

12. And, having the Yagus for its light, it is a hundred and one-fold in respect of the Yagus (formulas),—the first fifty and the last fifty which are (used) make a hundred forms; and the Yagus which are used between them are the one hundred and first form. In this way also the sevenfold one becomes a hundred and one-fold, and whosoever knows this obtains even by the sevenfold one whatever wish there is both in a life of a hundred years and in the one hundred and one-fold (altar).

13. In this way, indeed, all sacrifices [1] up to the Agnihotra are a hundred and one-fold by way of verses, formulas, words, syllables, rites, and hymn-tunes; and whosoever knows this obtains by every sacrifice whatever wish there is either in a life of a hundred years, or in the one hundred and one-fold (altar), or in the sevenfold one. Thus much as to the sacrifice.

14. Now as to the body. There are these four sets of five fingers and toes, the two—wrist and elbow [2],—the arm, the shoulder-blade, and the collarbone,—that makes twenty-five; and in the same way (each of) these other limbs,—that makes a hundred parts, and the trunk itself is the one hundred and first part. As regards the sevenfold state this has been explained [3].

---

[1] That is, according to Sâyana, all Soma-sacrifices,—ekâhas, ahînas, sattras, &c. In this case we should perhaps translate, 'down to the Agnihotra,' that being the simplest kind of Soma-sacrifice.

[2] This meaning is assigned by Sâyana to 'kalkushî' (= mani-bandhâratnî); it cannot mean here 'the two wrists' (? 'kalyusha,' Mon. Will. Dict.), as both must be parts of the same limb.

[3] Viz. X, 2, 2, 1, 5 (VI, 1, 1, 1 seq.).

15. And, having the vital air for its light, it is a hundred and one-fold by the vital airs limb by limb, for there is vital air in each limb : whosoever knows this obtains, even by his knowledge, whatever wish there is in a life of a hundred years, or in the one hundred and one-fold (altar), or in the sevenfold one, or in all sacrifices; for he has obtained a body perfected by all the sacrifices.

16. Now, there are these three fivefold (objects), the year, the fire, and man : their five forms are food, drink, well-being [1], light, and immortality. Whatever food there is in the year, that is its food ; whatever water, that is its drink ; its well-being is the night, for in the night, as in well-being (contentment or goodness), all beings dwell together [2]; its light is the day, and its immortal element the sun. Thus much as to the deity.

17. Now as to the sacrifice. Whatever food is placed on the fire, that is its food, and whatever water, that is its water ; its well-being is the enclosing-stones, for they are of the nature of nights [3]; its light the (bricks) with special formulas, for they are of the nature of days ; and its immortal

---

[1] Or, perhaps, goodness, excellence (srî).

[2] According to Sâyana, this is an etymological play on the word 'srî' (well-being, contentment, peace), as connected with the verb 'sri'—sriyanti nivasanty asmin kâla iti râtrih srisabdavâkyâ. Cf. II, 3, 1, 3, where, with the Kânva, we have to read, 'ilitâ hi sere (serate, K.) samgânâh'—'for (when the sun has set) those who are at variance with one another lie quiet (together).'

[3] Viz. inasmuch as they enclose the altar, and protect it on all sides. Cf. VII, 1, 1, 12 seq., where the enclosing-stones are said to represent the womb in which the embryo Agni is contained; and are also compared with the ocean which flows round the earth like a protecting moat.

element the fire, for that is of the nature of the sun.
Thus much as to the sacrifice.

18. Now as to the body. Whatever food there
is in man, that is his food; whatever water, that is
his water; his well-being (safety, strength) is the
bones, for they are of the nature of enclosing-stones:
his light the marrow, for that is of the nature of the
yagushmati (bricks); his immortal element the
breath, for that is of the nature of fire;—and,
indeed, people say, 'The breath is fire, the breath
is the immortal.'

19. Now, hunger ceases through food, thirst
through drink, evil through well-being (goodness),
darkness through light, and death through immortality; and, in truth, whosoever knows this
from him all these pass away, and he conquers
recurring death, and attains the whole (perfect) life.
And let him hold this to be immortality in yonder
world and life here below. Some, indeed, hold it
to be breath, saying, 'The breath is fire, the breath
is the immortal;' but let him not believe this, for
something uncertain is breath. And regarding this
it has also been said in the Yagus (Vâg. S. XII, 65),
'That (bond) of thine I unloose, as from the middle
of Âyus (life):' let him therefore hold it to be
immortality in yonder world, and life here below,
and thus, indeed, he attains the whole life.

THIRD ADHYÂYA. FIRST BRÂHMANA.

1. The Gâyatri is the breath (of Pragâpati, the
altar), the Ushnih the eye, the Anushtubh the voice,
the Brihati the mind, the Pankti the ear; the
Trishtubh is that generative breath; and the Gagati

that downward breathing:—these are the seven metres increasing by four (syllables) each [1], which are produced in Agni (the fire-altar).

2. 'The Gâyatrî is the breath,'—thus, whatever power, whatever vigour there is in the breath that is this one thousand; and to the breath, indeed, this vigour belongs; for were the breath of him who builds it to pass away, this fire-altar, assuredly, would not be built: by this its form that (altar) becomes built (so as to contain) a thousand Gâyatrîs.

3. 'The Ushnih is the eye,'—thus, whatever power, whatever vigour there is in the eye that is this one thousand; and to the eye, indeed, this vigour belongs, for were the eye-sight of him who builds it to pass away, this fire-altar, assuredly, would not be built: by this its form that (altar) becomes built (so as to contain) a thousand Ushnihs.

4. 'The Anushtubh is the voice,'—thus, whatever power, whatever vigour there is in the voice that is this one thousand; and to the voice, indeed, this vigour belongs, for were the voice of him who builds it to pass away, this fire-altar, assuredly, would not be built: by this its form that (altar) becomes built (so as to contain) a thousand Anushtubhs.

5. 'The Brihatî is the mind,'—thus, whatever power, whatever vigour there is in the mind that is this one thousand; and to the mind, indeed, this vigour belongs, for were the mind of him who builds it to pass away, this fire-altar, assuredly,

---

[1] The Gâyatrî verse consists of twenty-four syllables; and each of the following increases by four syllables, the Gagatî consisting of 4 × 12, or forty-eight syllables.

would not be built: by this its form that (altar)
becomes built (so as to contain) a thousand
Br*i*hatis.

6. 'The Pankti is the ear,'—thus, whatever
power, whatever vigour there is in the ear that
is this one thousand; and to the ear, indeed, this
vigour belongs, for were the power of hearing
of him who builds it to pass away, this fire-altar,
assuredly, would not be built: by this its form that
(altar) becomes built (so as to contain) a thousand
Panktis.

7. 'The Trish*t*ubh is that generative (life-giving)
breath,'—thus, whatever power, whatever vigour
there is in that breath, that is this one thousand;
and to that breath, indeed, this vigour belongs,
for were that breath of him who builds it to become
disordered, this fire-altar, assuredly, would not be
built: by this its form that (altar) becomes built
(so as to contain) a thousand Trish*t*ubhs.

8. 'And the *G*agati is that downward breathing,'—
thus, whatever power, whatever vigour there is in
that breathing, that is this one thousand; and to
that breathing, indeed, this vigour belongs, for
were that breathing of him who builds it to
become disordered, this fire-altar, assuredly, would
not be built: by this its form that (altar) becomes
built (so as to include) a thousand *G*agatis.

9. Now, these seven metres which increase by
four (syllables) successively, and are firmly established in one another, are those seven vital airs [1] in
man, firmly established in one another: thus, by

---

[1] Viz. those enumerated in the preceding paragraphs, including
those passing through the eye, ear, &c.

as much as the number of metres he utters has
that (altar) of him who knows this, prayers uttered
upon it in metre after metre, or hymns chanted, or
sastras recited, or (bricks) laid down upon it.

SECOND BRÂHMANA.

1. As to this they say, 'What metre and what
deity are the head of the fire-altar?' The metre
Gâyatrî and the deity Agni are its head.

2. 'What metre and what deity are its neck?'
The metre Ushnih and the deity Savitri are its
neck.

3. 'What metre and what deity are its spine?'
The metre Brihatî and the deity Brihaspati are
its spine.

4. 'What metre and what deity are its wings?'
The metres Brihat and Rathantara and the deities
Heaven and Earth are its wings.

5. 'What metre and what deity are its waist?'
The metre Trishtubh and the deity Indra are its
waist.

6. 'What metre and what deity are its hips?'
The metre Gagatî and the deity Âditya (the sun)
are its hips.

7. 'What metre and what deity are the vital air
whence the seed flows?' The metre Atikhandas
and the deity Pragâpati.

8. 'What metre and what deity are that downward
vital air?' The metre Yagñâyagñiya and the deity
Vaisvânara.

9. 'What metre and what deity are the thighs?'
The metre Anushtubh and that deity, the Visve-
devâh, are the thighs.

10. 'What metre and what deity are the knees?' The metre Pankti and that deity, the Maruts, are the knees.

11. 'What metre and what deity are the feet?' The metre Dvipadâ and the deity Vishnu are the feet.

12. 'What metre and what deity are the vital airs?' The metre Vikhandas and the deity Vâyu (the wind) are the vital airs.

13. 'What metre and what deity are the defective and redundant parts?' The metre (of the verse) wanting a syllable (or syllables) and that deity, the waters, are the defective and redundant parts. This, then, is the knowledge of the body (of the altar), and suchlike is the deity that enters into this body; and, indeed, there is in this (sacrificial performance) no other prayer for the obtainment of heavenly bliss[1].

THIRD BRÂHMANA.

1. Dhira Sâtaparneya once on a time repaired to Mahâsâla[2] Gâbâla. He said to him, 'Knowing what[3], hast thou come to me?'—'Agni (the fire) I know.'—'What Agni knowest thou?'—'Speech.'—'What becomes of him who knows that Agni?'—'He becomes eloquent[4],' he said, 'speech does not fail him.'

---

[1] Atrâgnau lokyatâyai punyalokâvâptaye anyâ uktavyatiriktâ âsih prârthanâ nâsti. Sâyana.

[2] Literally, one who keeps a large house, a lord. Sâyana, however, treats it as a proper name.

[3] That is, 'with what knowledge.'

[4] Or, perhaps, possessed of a good voice. To be 'vâgmin' is

2. 'Thou knowest Agni,' he said; 'knowing what (else) hast thou come to me?'—'Agni I know.'—'What Agni knowest thou?'—'The Eye.'—'What becomes of him who knows that Agni?'—'He becomes seeing,' he said; 'his eye does not fail him.'

3. 'Thou knowest Agni,' he said; 'knowing what hast thou come to me?'—'Agni I know.'—'What Agni knowest thou?'—'The Mind.'—'What becomes of him who knows that Agni?'—'He becomes thoughtful,' he said; 'his mind does not fail him.'

4. 'Thou knowest Agni,' he said; 'knowing what hast thou come to me?'—'Agni I know.'—'What Agni knowest thou?'—'The Ear.'—'What becomes of him who knows that Agni?'—'He becomes hearing,' he said; 'his ear does not fail him.'

5. 'Thou knowest Agni,' he said; 'knowing what hast thou come to me?'—'Agni I know.'—'What Agni knowest thou?'—'The Agni who is everything here, him I know.'—On (hearing) this said, he stepped down to him and said, 'Teach me that Agni, sir!'

6. He said,—Verily, that Agni is the breath: for when man sleeps, speech passes into the breath, and so do the eye, the mind, and the ear; and when he awakes, they again issue from the breath. Thus much as to the body.

7. Now as to the deity. That speech verily is Agni himself; and that eye is yonder sun; and that

enumerated among the necessary qualifications of the officiating priest by Lât́y. I, 1, 6, where the commentator, however, explains the term either as 'ready of speech (vaktum samarthah),' or as 'using correct, or elegant, speech (samskritavâk).'

mind is that moon; and that ear is the quarters:
and that breath is the wind that blows here.

8. Now, when that fire goes out, it is wafted up
in the wind (air), whence people say of it, 'It has
expired[1], for it is wafted up in the wind. And
when the sun sets it enters the wind, and so does
the moon; and the quarters are established in the
wind, and from out of the wind they issue again.
And when he who knows this passes away from
this world, he passes into the fire by his speech,
into the sun by his eye, into the moon by his mind,
into the quarters by his ear, and into the wind by
his breath; and being composed thereof, he becomes
whichever of these deities he chooses, and is at
rest.

FOURTH BRÂHMANA.

1. Svetaketu Âruneya[2], once upon a time, was
about to offer sacrifice. His father said to him,
'What priests hast thou chosen to officiate?' He
said, 'This Vaisvâvasavya here is my Hotri.'
He asked him, 'Knowest thou, Brâhmana Vaisvâvasavya,—

2. The four great (things)?'—'I know them, sir,'
he said.—'Knowest thou the four great ones of the
great?'—'I know them, sir,' he said.—'Knowest
thou the four rites (vrata)?'—'I know them, sir,'
he said.—'Knowest thou the four rites of rites?'—
'I know them, sir,' he said.—'Knowest thou the

---

[1] Literally, 'it has blown out, or up.'

[2] That is, grandson of Aruna (Aupavesi), and son of (Uddâlaka)
Âruni (II, 3, 1, 3t, 34; IV, 5, 7, 9).

four relating to Ka [1] ?'—' I know them, sir,' he said.
—' Knowest thou the four deepest of those relating
to Ka [2]?'—' I know them, sir,' he said.—' Knowest
thou the four flames [3]?'—' I know them, sir,' he
said.—' Knowest thou the four flames of flames?'—
' I know them, sir,' he said.

3. ' Knowest thou the Arka [4]?'—' Nay, but thou
wilt teach us [5], sir!'—' Knowest thou the two Arka-
leaves?'—' Nay, but thou wilt teach us, sir!'—
' Knowest thou the two Arka-flowers?'—' Nay, but
thou wilt teach us, sir!'—' Knowest thou the two
pod-leaves [6] of the Arka?'—' Nay, but thou wilt
teach us, sir!'—' Knowest thou the two coops [7] of
the Arka?'—' Nay, but thou wilt teach us, sir!'—
' Knowest thou the Arka-grains?'—' Nay, but thou
wilt teach us, sir!'—' Knowest thou the bulge [8] of

[1] Sâyana takes 'kya' to mean 'those useful to, or pleasing to
(hita), Ka, i.e. Pragâpati.'

[2] Literally, 'the four Kya of the Kya.' For more symbolical
speculation on these terms, see X, 4, 1, 4.

[3] Or, fires (arka), used of the sun, the fire and the lightning, as
well as of the Arka plant. Sâyana, however, here explains 'arkâh'
by 'arkaniyâh,' 'worthy of being praised, or honoured.'

[4] That is, the Arka plant (Calotropis gigantea), apparently so
called (= 'arka,' lightning) from the wedge-like shape of its leaves.
Cf. IX, 1, 1, 4, where the leaf is used in offering the Satarudriya
oblations. The other meanings of 'arka,' especially that of 'flame,
fire,' however, are likewise implied in these mystic speculations.

[5] Or, simply, 'Thou wilt tell us, then (atha vai), sir.'

[6] ? Or, the pods, sheaths; arkakosyau kosyâkâre phale (or pu/ake).
Sâyana.

[7] ? Or, 'seas' (samudra). Sâyana explains it as two opened
'lip-parts' at the top of the Arka-pod (arkakosâgre vidalitaush//a-
bhâgau).

[8] That is, according to the St. Petersb. Dict., 'the globular, cake-
shaped, hardened cicatrix of the Calotropis gigantea,' Sâyana

the Arka?'—' Nay, but thou wilt teach us, sir!'—
'Knowest thou the root of the Arka?'—'Nay, but
thou wilt teach us, sir!'

4. Now, when he said, 'Knowest thou the four
great (things)? Knowest thou the four great of
the great?'—the great one is Agni (the fire), and
the great (thing) of that great one are the plants
and trees, for they are his food; and the great one
is Vâyu (the wind), and the great (thing) of that
great one are the waters, for they are his (the wind's)
food; and the great one is Âditya (the sun), and
the great (thing) of that great one is the moon, for
that is his food; and the great one is Man, and the
great (thing) of that great one is cattle, for they are
his food:— these are the four great things, these the
four great of the great;—these are the four rites,
these the four rites of rites;—these are the four
relating to Ka, these the four deepest relating to
Ka;—these are the four flames, these the four
flames of flames.

5. And when he said, 'Knowest thou the Arka?'
he thereby meant man;—'Knowest thou the two
Arka-leaves?' he thereby meant his ears:—
'Knowest thou the two Arka-flowers?' he thereby
meant his eyes;—'Knowest thou the pod-leaves
of the Arka?' he thereby meant his nostrils:—
'Knowest thou the two coops of the Arka?' he
thereby meant his lips;—'Knowest thou the Arka-
grains?' he thereby meant his teeth;—'Knowest
thou the bulge of the Arka?' he thereby meant his
tongue;—'Knowest thou the root of the Arka?'

---

explains it by, 'arkakosamadhye vistarena (? v. l. gihvâstârana-)
vartamânâ tûlî.'

he thereby meant his food. Now that Arka, to wit,
man, is Agni; and verily, whoso regards Agni as
the Arka and the man, in his (altar-) body that Agni,
the Arka, will be built up even through the knowledge that ' I here am Agni, the Arka.'

Fifth Brâhmana.

1. Now, the Yagus, indeed, is he who blows here,
for even whilst passing along he (Vâyu, the wind)
generates (vivifies) everything here, and after him
passing along everything is generated : this is why
the Yagus is no other than Vâyu.

2. And the course[1] (gûh) is this space, to wit,
this air[2], for along this space it (the wind) courses ;
and the Yagus is both the wind and the air—the
'yat' and the 'gûh'—whence (the name) Yagus.
And the 'yat' (that which goes) is this (Adhvaryu)[3],
for when he 'goes' on (performing), the Rik and
Sâman carry that Yagus established on the Rik and
Sâman. Hence the Adhvaryu performs his work
with the very same Grahas (cups of Soma), (while)
there are each time[4] different stotras (chants) and
sastras (recitations) : it is just as if, after driving
with a first pair (of horses), one drives with a second
pair.

---

[1] 'Gûh' would rather seem to mean ' the urger, or speeder.'

[2] 'Yad idam antariksham,' perhaps, with the double sense—
'this air is the "yat (the going, moving thing)"'—made use of
in the sequel. The construction, however, is not quite clear.
Sâyana explains: ayam evâkâso gûr iti; gu iti sautro dhâtur
gatyarthah ; yad idam pratiyamânam antariksham asti tad eva gûr
iti ; yad evokyate—etam âkâsam anulakshya gavate, vâyur gakkhati,
vâyugavamâdakarana—tvâg gûr âkâsah.

[3] Or, whence (the name) Yagus, to wit, this (Adhvaryu).

[4] That is, in different Soma-sacrifices.

3. Now Agni is in front[1] (puras), for placing Agni in front (of them) these creatures attend upon him ; and the sun is motion (karana), for as soon as he rises everything here moves about. Such is the Yagus with the preparatory performance (puras-karana[2]) as regards the deities.

4. Now as regards the body. The Yagus is the breath, for whilst moving (yat) it generates (vivifies) everything here, and along with the moving breath birth takes place here : hence the Yagus is the breath.

5. And this course (gûh) is space—this space which is inside the body—for along this space it (the breath) courses ; and the Yagus is both the breath and space, —the ' yat ' and the ' gûh ': hence ' yagus.' And the ' yat ' (moving) is the breath, for the breath moves.

6. The Yagus, indeed, is food, for by food one is produced, and by food one moves. And food carries along that Yagus established on food, whence even different food is introduced into the same (channel of the) breath.

7. And the Mind is in front (puras), for the mind is the first of vital airs ; and the eye is motion (karana), for it is in accordance with the eye that this

---

[1] Literally, apparently, 'The in-front is Agni.'

[2] This term, literally, ' moving in front,' seems virtually to imply the entire manual work connected with the sacrifice, and which, along with the muttering of the Yagus-formulas, forms the official duty of the Adhvaryu. It would thus include all the sacrificial performances prior to the muttering of a Yagus, as the finishing or consecratory rite. For a somewhat similar discussion, see IV, 6, 7, 20, 21. The commentary introduces the present discussion thus : atha brâhmanâparanâmadheyasya puraskaranasabdasya pûrvavan nirvakanapurahsaram adhidaivam artham âha.

body moves. Such is the Yagus with the preparatory performance, firmly established both as regards
the deity and the body; and, indeed, whosoever thus
knows this Yagus with the preparatory performance
to be firmly established both as regards the deity
and the body,—

8. He, indeed, reaches successfully the end of the
sacrifice, unscathed and uninjured : he who knows
this becomes the first, the leader (pura-etri), of his
own people, an eater of food (i.e. prosperous), and
a ruler.

9. And if any one strives to become a rival [1]
among his own people to one who knows this, he
does not satisfy his dependants ; but, indeed, only
he satisfies his dependants, who is faithful [2] to that
one and who, along with him, strives to support his
dependants.

10. And this is the greatest Brahman (n., mystic
science), for than this there is no thing greater;
and, he who knows this, being himself the greatest,
becomes the highest among his own people.

11. This Brahman has nothing before it and
nothing after it [3]; and whosoever thus knows this
Brahman to have nothing before it and nothing

---

[1] Or, tries to make opposition, as Sâyana takes it—yah purushah
sveshu madhye evamvidam uktavidyâm gânânam purusham prati-
bubhûshati (!) prâtikûlyam âkaritum ikkhati.

[2] Thus 'anu-bhû' is taken by the St. Petersb. Dict. ('to serve,
be helpful to'), and by Sâyana—'yas tv evamvidam anukûlayet sa
poshyân poshayitum saknoti.'

[3] Sâyana seems to take 'aparavat' in the sense of 'it has (only)
something after it'—srashtavyagagadrûpâparavat—and the use of
the word 'aparapurushâh (descendants)' immediately after might
indeed seem to favour that interpretation.

after it, than he there is no one higher among his
equals in station; and ever higher will be the
descendants that spring from him. Wherefore, if
any one would be greater than he, let him rever-
entially approach the regions in front (to the eastward) of that one in this way, and he will do him
no injury [1].

12. But, indeed, the mystic import (upanishad) is
the essence of this Yagus; and thus, if, with ever so
small a yagus-formula, the Adhvaryu draws a cup
of Soma, that (essence) is equal to both the Stotra
and the Sastra, and comes up to both the Stotra
and the Sastra: hence, however small the essence
(flavour) of food, it benefits (renders palatable)
the whole food, and pervades the whole food.

13. Satiation (contentment), doubtless, is the
successful issue thereof (to wit, of food, and the
Yagus): hence when one is satiated by food he
feels like one who has succeeded. And joy, the
knowledge thereof (viz. of the essence, the mystic
import), is its soul (self); and, assuredly, all the
gods are of joyful soul: and this, the true knowledge, belongs to the gods alone,—and, indeed,
whosoever knows this is not a man, but one of
the gods.

---

[1] The MSS. of the commentary (I. O. 613, 149) are unfortunately
not in a very satisfactory condition:—sa yo haitad iti, evam upâsitety
artha*h*; yadi veditu*h* sakâsât gyâyasa*h* purushasya sadbhâve tadâ
svayam bâdhyo bhavatity âsankya tasmâd adhikapurushâd adhikam
(a*hh*idikât B) vastu davopâsitavyam (!) ity âha. yo smâg gyâyân
iti; yadi asmâd upâsakât yo dhika*h* syât tarhi tasmâd adhikât, om.
B disa*h* pûrvâ ity upâsita; tata*h* gyâyaso pi gyâya-upâsane svasyâ-
dhikvât bâdhako nâstity artha*h*. The commentary would thus seem
to take it to mean that by showing reverence to something before,
or higher than, his rival, he would turn aside his schemes.

14. And Priyavrata Rauhiṇâyana, knowing this (truth), once spake unto the blowing wind, 'Thy soul[1] is joy: blow thou either hither or thither!' and so, indeed, it now blows. Wherefore, if one desire to invoke any blessing from the gods, let him approach them with this, 'Your soul is joy,—my wish is such and such: let it be fulfilled unto me!' and whatever the wish he entertains, it will be fulfilled to him; for, assuredly, he who knows this attains this contentment, this successful issue, this joy, this soul.

15. This Yagus is silent[2], indistinct; for the Yagus is the breath, and the breath is of silent (secret) abode; and if any one were to say of that (Adhvaryu) who pronounces (the Yagus) distinctly, 'He has uttered distinctly the indistinct deity: his breath shall fail him!' then that would, indeed, come to pass.

16. And, assuredly, he who knows the indistinct (secret) manifestation of this (Yagus) becomes manifest in fame and glory. Silently the Adhvaryu draws the cup of Soma with the (muttered) Yagus, and, when drawn and deposited, it becomes manifest;—silently he builds the fire-altar with the Yagus, and, when built and completed, it becomes manifest;—silently he takes out (material for) the oblation with the Yagus, and, when cooked and ready (for offering), it becomes manifest: thus, whatever he performs silently, when performed and completed, it becomes manifest. And, assuredly, he who thus knows this secret manifestation of this

---

[1] Or, thine own self, thy nature—tavâtmâ svarûpam. Sâyana.

[2] That is, pronounced in an undertone, muttered.

(Yagus) becomes manifest in fame, and glory, and sanctity; and quickly, indeed, he becomes known: he becomes the Yagus itself, and by the Yagus people call him [1].

FOURTH ADHYÂYA. FIRST BRÂHMANA.

1. When the gods restored the relaxed Pragâpati, they poured him, as seed, into the fire-pan (ukhâ) as the womb, for the fire-pan is a womb. In the course of a year they prepared for him this food, to wit, the fire-altar built here, and enclosed it in a body; and, being enclosed in a body, it became the body itself; whence food, when enclosed in a body, becomes the body itself.

2. In like manner does the Sacrificer now pour his own self (or body), as seed, into the fire-pan as the womb, for the fire-pan is a womb. In the course of a year he prepares for it (his self) this food, to wit, the fire-altar here built, and encloses it in a body, and, being enclosed in a body, it becomes the body itself; whence food, when enclosed in a body, becomes the body itself.

3. He places him (the Ukhya Agni, on the fire-altar) with 'Vaushat [2]!' for 'vauk' is he (Agni),

---

[1] Yagushaivainam âkakshata iti gñâtrigñeyayor abhedopakârena tasya vidusha eva yaguh tasya vyavahâryatvam bhavatity arthah. Sâyana.

[2] See IX. 2. 3. 35. where it was stated that the fire should be laid down with the Vashat-call ('vaushat!') uttered after the two verses, Vâg. S. XVII. 72. 73. Here, as at 1, 7. 2. 21, the sacrificial call, 'vaushat'—for 'vashat,' apparently an irregular subjunctive aorist of 'vah': 'may he bear (the oblation to the gods)!'— is fancifully explained as composed of 'vauk' (i.e. vâk, speech), and 'shat,' six.

and 'sha*t* (six)' is this six-layered food: having
prepared it, he offers it to him as proportionate
to this body, for food which is proportionate to the
body satisfies, and does not injure it; but when
there is too much, it does injure it, and when there
is too little, it does not satisfy it.

4. Now that Arka[1] (flame) is this very fire which
they bring here; and the Kya[1] is this his food,
to wit, the fire-altar built here: that (combined)
makes the Arkya[2] in respect of the Yagus. And
the Great one (mahân) is this (Agni), and this vrata[3]
(rite) is his food: that makes the Mahávrata
(sâman) in respect of the Sâman. And 'uk' is
this (Agni), and 'tha' his food,—that (combined)
makes the Uktha (*s*astra, recitation)[4] in respect
of the *R*/k. Thus, whilst being only one, this is
accounted threefold.

5. Now Indra and Agni were created as the
Brahman (priesthood) and the Kshatra (nobility):
the Brahman was Agni and the Kshatra Indra.
When created, the two were separate. They spake,
'Whilst being thus, we shall be unable to produce
creatures (people): let us both become one form!'
The two became one form.

6. Now those two, Indra and Agni, are the same
as these two, to wit, the gold plate and the (gold)
man[5]: Indra is the gold plate, and Agni the man.

---

[1] See X, 3, 4, 2 seq.

[2] That is, what relates to the Arka (the Fire, or Agni*k*ayana).

[3] That is, here, the Mahad uktham, or Great Recitation of the
Mahâvrata day.

[4] Perhaps with the implied sense of 'fast-food,' 'fast-milk,' the
milk taken by the Sacrificer during the initiation as his only food.

[5] For the gold plate worn by the Sacrificer whilst carrying about

They are made of gold: gold means light, and Indra and Agni are the light; gold means immortal life, and Indra and Agni mean immortal life.

7. It is these two, Indra and Agni, that they build up. Whatever is of brick that is Agni: whence they bake that (part) by fire, and all that is baked by fire is Agni. And what filling of earth there is (in the altar) that is Indra: whence they do not bake that (part) by fire, lest it should be Agni, and not Indra. Thus it is these two, Indra and Agni, that are built up.

8. And the two become that one form, to wit, the fire which is placed on the built (altar), and hence those two, by means of that form, produce creatures. Now Agni, indeed, is this single brick[1], and into this the whole Agni passes: this, indeed, is the perfection of bricks,—it is that one syllable (akshara) 'vauk,' it is this into which the whole Agni passes, and which is the perfection of syllables.

9. It is this that the Rishi saw when he said, 'I praise what hath been and what will be, the Great Brahman, the one Akshara,—the manifold Brahman, the one Akshara; for, indeed, all the gods, all beings pass into that Akshara (imperish-

the Ukhya Agni, and ultimately deposited on the lotus-leaf in the centre of the altar-site before the first layer is laid down, see VI, 7, 1, 1 seq.; VII, 4, 1, 10 seq. For the gold man placed on the gold plate, VII, 4, 1, 15 seq. Whilst the gold man was indeed identified with Agni-Pragâpati, as well as with the Sacrificer, the gold plate was taken throughout as representing the sun.

[1] According to Sâyana, this one brick is the syllable ('akshara,' which also means 'the imperishable, indestructible') 'vauk' contained in the 'Vaushat,' uttered when the sacred fire is placed on the newly-built altar.

able element[1]) : it is both the Brahman and the
Kshatra ; and the Brahman is Agni, and the
Kshatra Indra ; and the Viśve Devâḥ (all the gods)
are Indra and Agni. But the Viśve Devâḥ (the
All-gods) are also the peasantry : hence it is Priest-
hood, Nobility, and Peasantry.

10. And, indeed, Syâparña Sâyakâyana, know-
ing this, once said, ' If this my sacrificial performance
were complete, my own race would become the
kings (nobles), Brâhmañas, and peasants of the
Salvas ; but even by that much of my work which
has been completed[2] my race will surpass the
Salvas in both ways ; '—for this (Agni, the fire-
altar), indeed, is (social) eminence and fame, and an
eater of food[3].

---

[1] Aksharam avinaśvaraṃ sarvagataṃ vâ brahma saḱḱidânandai-
karasam. Sâyaña.

[2] Or, perhaps—but since so much of my work has been completed, my race will thereby surpass the Salvas. Cf. Delbrück,
Altind. Syntax, p. 266.

[3] Sâyaña takes this as intended to explain the ' in both ways ' of
the quotation, viz. in regard to ' śrî ' (social distinction) on the one
hand, and to ' yaśas ' (fame) and food (material prosperity) on the
other. There is, however, nothing in the text to favour any such
grouping of the distinctive objects of aspiration associated with the
three classes (varñatrayâtmakatvam upagîvya karmañaḥ, śriya-
soṣnnâdalakshañam phalam. Sâyaña), or with men generally (cf.
Aitareyâr. I, 4, 2, 10). Perhaps it means both in an intellectual
and material point of view. The Syâparñas seem to have been
a rather self-assertive family of priests. The Aitareya Brâhmaña
tells the following story about them (VII, 27):—Viśvantara Sau-
shadmana, setting aside the Syâparñas, got up a sacrifice without
them. The Syâparñas, becoming aware of this, came to the sacrifice and sat them down inside the sacrificial ground. On seeing
them, Viśvantara said, ' There sit those doers of evil deeds, those
speakers of foul language, the Syâparñas : turn them out ; let them
not sit inside my sacrificial ground !'—' So be it !' they said, and

11. And regarding this, Sâ*n*dilya, having instructed Vâmakakshâya*na*[1], said, 'Thou wilt become eminent, famous, and an eater of food (rich);' and, indeed, he who knows this becomes eminent, famous, and an eater of food.

12. And this Agni is no other than Pra*g*âp*a*ti.

---

turned them out. In being turned out, they cried aloud, 'At a sacrifice of *G*anamegaya, son of Parikshit, performed without the Ka*s*yapas, the Asitam*ri*gas from amongst the Ka*s*yapas won the Soma-drink from the Bhûtavîras (who were officiating). In them they had heroic men on their side: what hero is there amongst us who will win that Soma-drink?'—'Here is that hero of yours,' said Râma Mârga*v*eya. Râma Mârga*v*eya was a *S*yâpar*n*a, learned in sacred lore. When they rose to leave, he said, 'O king, will they turn out of the sacrificial ground even one so learned as me?'—'Whoever thou art, what knowest thou, vile Brâhman?'— 'When the gods turned Indra away because he had outraged Tvash*tri*'s son Vi*s*varûpa, and laid low V*ri*tra, and thrown devotees before the jackals, and slain the Arurmaghas, and retorted on B*ri*haspati (the teacher of the gods)—then Indra was deprived of the Soma-cup; and along with him the Kshatriyas were deprived of the Soma-cup. By stealing the Soma from Tvash*tri*, Indra obtained a share in the Soma-cup, but to this day the Kshatriyas are deprived of the Soma-cup: how can they turn out from the sacrificial ground one who knows how the Kshatriya race can be put in possession of the Soma-cup from which they are deprived?' —'Knowest thou (how to procure) that drink, O Brâhman?'— 'I know it indeed.'—'Tell us then, O Brâhman?'—'To thee, O king, I will tell it,' he said. Ultimately the *S*yâpar*n*as are reinstated in their sacrificial duties. Cf. R. Roth, Zur Litteratur und Geschichte des Weda, p. 118. At VI, 2, 1, 39, *S*yâpar*n*a Sâyakâyana was stated to have been the last who was in the habit of immolating five victims instead of two, as became afterwards the custom.

[1] In the succession of teachers of the doctrine of the fire-altar, given at the end of the present Kâ*n*da, Vâmakakshâya*na* is said to have received his instruction from Vâtsya, and the latter from Sâ*n*dilya, who, in his turn, received it from Ku*s*ri. Cf. Weber, Ind. Stud. I, p. 259.

The gods, having restored this Agni-Pragâpati, in the course of a year prepared this food for him, to wit, this Mahâvratîya cup of Soma.

13. The Adhvaryu draws it by means of a cup, and inasmuch as he draws (grah) it it is (called) a draught (graha, cup of Soma). The Udgâtri (chanter), by the Mahâvrata (sâman), puts flavour (vital sap) into it; and the Mahâvrata (sâman) being (composed of) all those (five) sâmans, he thus puts flavour into it by means of all sâmans (hymn-tunes). The Hotri puts flavour into it by means of the Great Recitation ; and the Great Recitation being (composed of) all those Rik-verses : he thus puts flavour into it by all the Rik-verses.

14. And when they chant the hymn, and he (the Hotri) afterwards recites (the sastra) [1], he (the Adhvaryu) offers that (cup of Soma) to him (Agni-Pragâpati) as the Vashat-call is uttered. Now 'vauk' is this (Agni), and 'shat' this sixfold food [2]: having prepared it, he offers it to him as proportionate to his body ; for food which is proportionate to the body satisfies, and does not injure it ; but when there is too much, it does injure it, and when there is too little, it does not satisfy it.

15. Now that Arka (flame) is this very fire-altar

---

[1] Viz. the Mahad ukthani (see p. 110, note 3), preceded by the chanting of the Mahâvrata-sâman (see p. 382, note 5).

[2] That is, according as it is flavoured by the six different 'rasas' (flavours or tastes)—sweet (madhura), sour (amla), salt (lavana), pungent (katuka), bitter (tikta), and astringent (kashâya). Thus according to Sâyana; but see also paragraph 3, where the sixfold nature of the food is identified with the six-layered altar. Perhaps both explanations are intended to apply.

built here; and the Kya is this his food, to wit, the
Mahâvratiya-graha: that (combined) makes the
Arkya in respect of the Yagus. And the Great
one (mahân) is this (Agni), and this rite (vrata)
is his food: that makes the Mahâvrata in respect
of the Sâman. And 'uk' is this (Agni), and 'tha'
his food: that makes the (Mahad) Uktha in respect
of the Rik. Thus, whilst being only one, this is
accounted threefold.

16. And this Agni is Pragâpati, the year[1]: the
Sâvitra (oblations) are one half thereof, and the
Vaisva-karmana (oblations)[2] the (other) half; the
Sâvitra are eight digits (kalâ[3]) thereof, and the
Vaisvakarmana (the other) eight; and that which
is performed between them is the seventeenfold
Pragâpati. Now what a digit is to men that
a syllable (akshara) is to the gods.

17. And 'loma (hair)' is two syllables, 'tvak'
(skin)' two, 'asrik (blood)' two, 'medas (fat)' two,
'mâmsam (flesh)' two, 'snâva (sinew)' two, 'asthi
(bone)' two, 'maggâ (marrow)[5]' two,—that makes
sixteen digits; and the vital air which circulates
therein, is the seventeenfold Pragâpati.

18. These sixteen digits convey the food to that
vital air; and when they take to conveying no food
to it, then it consumes them and departs (from the
body): hence he who is hungry here, feels very

---

[1] Or, perhaps, this Pragâpati-Agni is the year.

[2] For these two sets of formulas and oblations, see IX. 5, 1, 43
and note.

[3] A 'kalâ' is the sixteenth part of the moon's diameter, and then
a sixteenth part generally.

[4] Pronounce 'tu-ak.'

[5] For five of these parts of the body, see X. 1, 3, 4.

restless, consumed as he is by his vital airs ; and
hence he who suffers from fever becomes very thin,
for he is consumed by his vital airs.

19. Now for that seventeenfold Pragâpati they
prepared this seventeenfold food, the Soma-sacrifice :
those sixteen digits of his are these sixteen officiating
priests,—one should not, therefore, take a seventeenth
priest [1] lest one should do what is excessive ;—and
what vital sap there is here—the oblations that
are offered—that is the seventeenfold food.

20. And when they chant the hymn, and when he
(the Hotri) afterwards recites (the sastra), he (the
Adhvaryu) offers to him that food as the Vashat-
call is uttered. Now 'vauk' is this (Agni), and
'shat' this sixfold food : having prepared it, he
offers it to him as proportionate to his body ; for
food which is proportionate to the body satisfies,
and does not injure it ; but when there is too much
it does injure it, and when there is too little, it does
not satisfy it.

21. Now that Arka (flame) is this very fire-altar
built here ; and the Kya is this his food, to wit, the
Soma-sacrifice : that (combined) makes the Arkya
in respect of the Yagus. And the Great one (mahân) is this (Agni), and this rite (vrata) is his food :
that makes the Mahâvrata in respect of the Sâman.
And 'uk' is this (Agni), and 'tha' his food : that
makes the (Mahad) Uktha in respect of the Rik.
Thus, whilst being only one, this is accounted threefold. With this food he went upwards ; and he who

---

[1] This prohibition is probably directed against the Kaushîtakins,
who recognise a seventeenth officiating priest, the Sadasya, who
seems to have taken no other part in the sacrificial performance
except sitting in the Sadas as the permanent custodian thereof.

went upwards is yonder sun, and that food wherewith
he went up is that moon.

22. He who shines yonder is indeed that Arka
(flame), and that moon is his food, the Kya : that
(combined) makes the Arkya in respect of the
Yagus. And the Great one (mahân) is this (Agni),
and this rite (vrata) is his food : that makes the
Mahâvrata in respect of the Sâman. And 'uk'
is this (Agni), and 'tha' his food : that makes the
(Mahad) Uktha in respect of the R*i*k. Thus, whilst
being only one, this is accounted threefold. Thus
much as to the deity.

23. Now as to the body. The Arka (flame),
doubtless, is the breath (vital air), and the Kya is
its food : that makes the Arkya in respect of the
Yagus. And the Great one (mahân) is this (Agni),
and this rite (vrata) is his food : that makes the
Mahâvrata in respect of the Sâman. And 'uk' is
this (Agni), and 'tha' his food : that makes the
(Mahad) Uktha in respect of the R*i*k. Thus, whilst
being only one, this is accounted threefold. And,
indeed, that (Agni) is that (sun) as to the deity, and
this (breath) as to the body.

SECOND BRÂHMANA.

1. Verily, Pragâpati, the year, is Agni, and King
Soma, the moon. He himself, indeed, proclaimed
(taught) his own self to Yag*n*ava*k*as Râgastambâyana, saying, 'As many lights as there are of
mine, so many are my bricks.'

2. Now in this Pragâpati, the year, there are
seven hundred and twenty days and nights, his
lights, (being) those bricks ; three hundred and sixty

enclosing-stones [1], and three hundred and sixty bricks with (special) formulas. This Pragâpati, the year, has created all existing things, both what breathes and the breathless, both gods and men. Having created all existing things, he felt like one emptied out, and was afraid of death.

3. He bethought himself, ' How can I get these beings back into my body? how can I put them back into my body? how can I be again the body of all these beings?'

4. He divided his body into two; there were three hundred and sixty bricks in the one, and as many in the other: he did not succeed [2].

5. He made himself three bodies,—in each of them there were three eighties of bricks: he did not succeed.

6. He made himself four bodies of a hundred and eighty bricks each: he did not succeed.

7. He made himself five bodies,—in each of them there were a hundred and forty-four bricks: he did not succeed.

8. He made himself six bodies of a hundred and twenty bricks each: he did not succeed. He did not develop himself sevenfold [3].

9. He made himself eight bodies of ninety bricks each: he did not succeed.

10. He made himself nine bodies of eighty bricks each: he did not succeed.

---

[1] See X, 4, 2, 27 with note.

[2] Na vyâpnot, intrans., ' he did not attain (his object),' cf. vyâpti, in the sense of 'success';—(svayam teshâm âtmâ bhavitum) asamartho bhavat. Sâyana.

[3] Or, did not divide sevenfold, na saptadhâ vyabhavat,—saptadhâ-vibhâgam na kritavân. Sâyana.

11. He made himself ten bodies of seventy-two bricks each : he did not succeed. He did not develop elevenfold.

12. He made himself twelve bodies of sixty bricks each : he did not succeed. He did not develop either thirteenfold or fourteenfold.

13. He made himself fifteen bodies of forty-eight bricks each : he did not succeed.

14. He made himself sixteen bodies of forty-five bricks each : he did not succeed. He did not develop seventeenfold.

15. He made himself eighteen bodies of forty bricks each : he did not succeed. He did not develop nineteenfold.

16. He made himself twenty bodies of thirty-six bricks each : he did not succeed. He did not develop either twenty-one-fold, or twenty-two-fold, or twenty-three-fold.

17. He made himself twenty-four bodies of thirty bricks each. There he stopped, at the fifteenth ; and because he stopped at the fifteenth arrangement [1] there are fifteen forms of the waxing, and fifteen of the waning (moon).

18. And because he made himself twenty-four bodies, therefore the year consists of twenty-four half-months. With these twenty-four bodies of thirty bricks each he had not developed (sufficiently). He saw the fifteen parts of the day, the muhûrtas [2],

---

[1] Literally, shifting (about of the bricks of the altar), development.

[2] The day and night consists of thirty muhûrtas, a muhûrta being thus equal to about forty-eight minutes or four-fifths of an hour.

as forms for his body, as space-fillers (Lokamprinâs[1]), as well as fifteen of the night; and inasmuch as they straightway (muhu) save (trai), they are (called) 'muhûrtâh'; and inasmuch as, whilst being small, they fill (pûr) these worlds (or spaces, 'loka') they are (called) 'lokamprinâh.'

19. That one (the sun) bakes everything here, by means of the days and nights, the half-moons, the months, the seasons, and the year; and this (Agni, the fire) bakes what is baked by that one: 'A baker of the baked (he is),' said Bhâradvâga of Agni; 'for he bakes what has been baked by that (sun).'

20. In the year these (muhûrtas) amounted to ten thousand and eight hundred: he stopped at the ten thousand and eight hundred.

21. He then looked round over all existing things, and beheld all existing things in the threefold lore (the Veda), for therein is the body of all metres, of all stomas, of all vital airs, and of all the gods: this, indeed, exists, for it is immortal, and what is immortal exists; and this (contains also) that which is mortal.

22. Pragâpati bethought himself, 'Truly, all existing things are in the threefold lore: well, then, I will construct for myself a body so as to contain the whole threefold lore.'

23. He arranged the Rik-verses into twelve thousand of Brihatis[2], for of that extent are the

---

[1] The Lokamprinâ bricks contained in the whole fire-altar amount to as many as there are muhûrtas in the year, viz. 10,800; see X, 4, 3, 20.

[2] The Brihatî verse, consisting of 36 syllables, this calculation makes the hymns of the Rig-veda to consist of 36 × 12,000 = 432,000 syllables.

verses created by Pragâpati.   At the thirtieth arrangement they came to an end in the Pânktis; and
because it was at the thirtieth arrangement that they
came to an end, there are thirty nights in the month;
and because it was in the Pânktis, therefore Pragâpati
is ' pânkta ' (fivefold) [1].   There are one hundred-and-
eight hundred [2] Pânktis.

24. He then arranged the two other Vedas into
twelve thousand Brihatis,— eight (thousand) of
the Yagus (formulas), and four of the Sâman (hymns)
—for of that extent is what was created by Pragâpati
in these two Vedas.   At the thirtieth arrangement
these two came to an end in the Pânktis; and
because it was at the thirtieth arrangement that
they came to an end, there are thirty nights in the
month; and because it was in the Pânktis, therefore
Pragâpati is 'pânkta.'   There were one hundred-
and-eight hundred [2] Pânktis.

25. All the three Vedas amounted to ten thousand
eight hundred eighties (of syllables) [3]; muhûrta by
muhûrta he gained a fourscore (of syllables), and
muhûrta by muhûrta a fourscore was completed [4].

26. Into these three worlds, (in the form of) the

---

[1] The Pânkti consists of five pâdas (feet) of eight syllables each.

[2] That is to say, 10.800 Pânktis, which, as the Pânkti verse has
40 syllables, again amount to 432,000 syllables.

[3] The three Vedas, according to the calculations in paragraphs
23 and 24, contain $2 \times 432,000 = 864,000$ syllables, which is
equal to 80×10.800.   On the predilection to calculate by four-
scores, see p. 112, note 1.

[4] That is, within the year, for the year has $360 \times 30 = 10,800$
muhûrtas, which is just the amount of eighties of which the three
Vedas were said to consist.   I do not see how any division of the
'muhûrta' itself into eighty parts (as supposed by Professor Weber,
Ind. Streifen, I, p. 92, note 1) can be implied here.

fire-pan [1], he (Pragâpati) poured, as seed into the womb, his own self made up of the metres, stomas, vital airs, and deities. In the course of a half-moon the first body was made up, in a further (half-moon) the next (body), in a further one the next,—in a year he is made up whole and complete.

27. Whenever he laid down an enclosing-stone [2], he laid down a night, and along with that fifteen muhûrtas, and along with the muhûrtas fifteen eighties (of syllables of the sacred texts) [3]. And whenever he laid down a brick with a formula (yagushmatî), he laid down a day [4], and along with that fifteen muhûrtas, and along with the muhûrtas fifteen eighties (of syllables). In this manner he put this threefold lore into his own self, and made it his own; and in this very (performance) he became the body of all existing things, (a body) composed of the metres, stomas, vital airs, and deities; and having become composed of all that, he ascended upwards; and he who thus ascended is that moon yonder.

28. He who shines yonder (the sun) is his founda-

---

[1] On the construction of the Ukhâ, as representing the universe, see VI, 5, 2 seq.

[2] The number of 'parisrits' by which the great altar is enclosed is only 261; but to these are usually added those of the other brick-built hearths, viz. the Gârhapatya (21) and the eight Dhishnyas (78),—the whole amounting to 360 enclosing-stones, or one for each day (or night) in the year.

[3] According to paragraph 25, a fourscore of syllables was completed in each muhûrta; and day and night consist of fifteen muhûrtas each.

[4] See IX, 4, 3, 6, where the number of Yagushmatî bricks is said to be equal to that of the parisrits, or enclosing-stones—with, however, 35 (36) added for the intercalary month, hence altogether 395 (396); cf. X, 4, 3, 14-19.

tion, (for) over him he was built up [1], on him he was
built up : from out of his own self he thus fashioned
him, from out of his own self he generated him.

29. Now when he (the Sacrificer), being about to
build an altar, undergoes the initiation-rite,—even
as Pragâpati poured his own self, as seed, into the
fire-pan as the womb,—so does he pour into the fire-
pan, as seed into the womb, his own self composed
of the metres, stomas, vital airs, and deities. In the
course of a half-moon, his first body is made up, in
a further (half-moon) the next (body), in a further
one the next,—in a year he is made up whole and
complete.

30. And whenever he lays down an enclosing-
stone, he lays down a night, and along with that
fifteen muhûrtas, and along with the muhûrtas
fifteen eighties (of syllables). And whenever he lays
down a Yagushmati (brick), he lays down a day, and
along with that fifteen muhûrtas, and along with the
muhûrtas fifteen eighties (of syllables of the sacred
texts). In this manner he puts this threefold lore
into his own self, and makes it his own ; and in this
very (performance) he becomes the body of all existing things, (a body) composed of the metres, stomas,
vital airs, and deities ; and having become composed
of all that, he ascends upwards.

31. And he who shines yonder is his foundation,
for over him he is built up, on him he is built up :
from out of his own self he thus fashions him, from
out of his own self he generates him. And when

---

[1] Viz. inasmuch as the round gold plate, representing the sun,
was laid down in the centre of the altar-site, before the first layer
was built. Sâyana.

he who knows this departs from this world, then he passes into that body composed of the metres, stomas, vital airs, and deities ; and verily having become composed of all that, he who, knowing this, performs this sacrificial work, or he who even knows it, ascends upwards.

THIRD BRÂHMANA.

1. The Year, doubtless, is the same as Death, for he[1] it is who, by means of day and night, destroys the life of mortal beings, and then they die : therefore the Year is the same as Death ; and whosoever knows this Year (to be) Death, his life that (year) does not destroy, by day and night, before old age, and he attains his full (extent of) life.

2. And he, indeed, is the Ender, for it is he who, by day and night, reaches the end of the life of mortals, and then they die : therefore he is the Ender, and whosoever knows this Year, Death, the Ender, the end of his life that (Year) does not reach, by day and night, before old age, and he attains his full (extent of) life.

3. The gods were afraid of this Pragâpati, the Year, Death, the Ender, lest he, by day and night, should reach the end of their life.

4. They performed these sacrificial rites—the Agnihotra, the New and Full-moon sacrifices, the Seasonal offerings, the animal sacrifice, and the Soma-sacrifice : by offering these sacrifices they did not attain immortality.

5. They also built a fire-altar,—they laid down

---

[1] Father Time, Pragâpati.

unlimited enclosing-stones, unlimited Yagushmati
(bricks), unlimited Lokamprinâ (bricks), even as
some lay them down to this day, saying, 'The gods
did so.' They did not attain immortality.

6. They went on praising and toiling, striving to
win immortality. Pragâpati then spake unto them,
'Ye do not lay down (put on me) all my forms:
but ye either make (me) too large or leave (me) defective: therefore ye do not become immortal.'

7. They spake, 'Tell thou us thyself, then, in
what manner we may lay down all thy forms!'

8. He spake, 'Lay ye down three hundred and
sixty enclosing-stones, three hundred and sixty
Yagushmati (bricks), and thirty-six thereunto; and
of Lokamprinâ (bricks) lay ye down ten thousand
and eight hundred; and ye will be laying down
all my forms, and will become immortal.' And the
gods laid down accordingly, and thereafter became
immortal.

9. Death spake unto the gods, 'Surely, on this
wise all men will become immortal, and what share
will then be mine?' They spake, 'Henceforward
no one shall be immortal with the body: only when
thou shalt have taken that (body) as thy share, he
who is to become immortal either through knowledge, or through holy work, shall become immortal
after separating from the body.' Now when they
said, 'either through knowledge or through holy
work,' it is this fire-altar that is the knowledge, and
this fire-altar that is the holy work.

10. And they who so know this, or they who do
this holy work, come to life again when they have
died, and, coming to life, they come to immortal life.
But they who do not know this, or do not do this

holy work, come to life again when they die, and
they become the food of him (Death) time after time.

11. But when he builds the fire-altar, he thereby
gains Agni, Pragâpati, the Year, Death, the Ender,
whom the gods gained; it is him he lays down,
even as the gods thus laid him down.

12. By the enclosing-stones he gains his nights;
by the Yagushmatî (bricks) his days, half-moons,
months, and seasons; and by the Lokamprinâs
the muhûrtas (hours).

13. Thus the enclosing-stones, supplying the place
of nights, are made the (means of) gaining the
nights, they are the counterpart of the nights: there
are three hundred and sixty of them, for there are
three hundred and sixty nights in the year. Of these,
he lays twenty-one round the Gârhapatya, seventy-
eight round the Dhishnya hearths, and two hundred
and sixty-one round the Âhavanîya.

14. Then the Yagushmatî (bricks with special
formulas):—the grass-bunch, the (four) clod-bricks,
the lotus-leaf, the gold plate and man, the two spoons,
the naturally-perforated (brick), the dûrvâ-brick, the
(one) dviyagus, two retahsik, a visvagyotis, two
seasonal ones, an ashâdhâ, the tortoise, the mortar
and pestle, the fire-pan, the five victims' heads,
fifteen apasyâs, five khandasyâs, fifty prânabhrits—
these ninety-eight are (in) the first layer.

15. Then the second (layer):—five asvinis, two
seasonal ones, five vaisvadevis, five prânabhrits, five
apasyâs, nineteen vayasyâs—these forty-one are
(in) the second layer.

16. Then the third (layer):—the naturally-perforated one, five regional ones, a visvagyotis, four
seasonal ones, ten prânabhrits, thirty-six khandasyâs,

fourteen vâlakhilyas—these seventy-one are (in) the
third layer.

17. Then the fourth (layer):—first eighteen, then
twelve, then seventeen—these forty-seven are (in)
the fourth layer.

18. Then the fifth (layer):—five asapatnâs, forty
virâgs, twenty-nine stomabhâgâs, five nâkasads, five
pañkakûdâs, thirty-one khandasyâs, eight (of) the
Gârhapatya hearth, eight (of) the Punaskiti, two
seasonal ones, a visvagyotis, a vikarni, a naturally-
perforated one, the variegated stone, the fire which
is placed on the altar—these one hundred and
thirty-eight are (in) the fifth layer.

19. All these make three hundred and ninety-five.
Of these, three hundred and sixty, supplying the
place of days, are made the (means of) gaining the
days, they are the counterpart of the days: There
are three hundred and sixty of them, for there are
three hundred and sixty days in the year.   And for
the thirty-six (additional days) which there are [1] the
filling of earth (counts as) the thirty-sixth; and
twenty-four thereof, supplying the place of half-
moons, are made the (means of) gaining the half-
moons, they are the counterpart of the half-moons.
And the (remaining) twelve, supplying the place of
months, are made the (means of) gaining the months,
they are the counterpart of the months.   And, lest
the seasons should be wanting, these (twelve bricks),
by two and two (taken) together, supply the place
of seasons.

---

[1] Namely, in an intercalary month.   The layers of loose soil
have to be counted in for the reason that only 35 yagushmatis
remain after taking away the 360.

20. And as to the Lokamprinâ (space-filling bricks), supplying the place of muhûrtas (hours), they are made the (means) of gaining the muhûrtas, they are the counterpart of the muhûrtas: there are ten thousand and eight hundred of them, for so many muhûrtas there are in the year. Of these, he lays down twenty-one in the Gârhapatya (altar), seventy-eight in the Dhishnya-hearths, and the others in the Âhavanîya. So many, indeed, are the (different) forms of the year: it is these that are here secured for him (Pragâpati, the Year), and are put on him.

21. Now, some wish to get this total amount[1] in the Âhavanîya itself, arguing, 'Those are different brick-built fire-altars: why should we here (in the Âhavanîya altar) take into account those laid down there (in the Gârhapatya and Dhishnyas)?' But let him not do so. There are, indeed, ten of these fire-altars he builds—eight Dhishnyas, the Âhavanîya and the Gârhapatya—whence they say, 'Agni is Virâg (wide shining or ruling),' for the Virâg (metre) consists of ten syllables: but, surely, all these (altars and hearths) are looked upon as only one, as Agni; for it is merely forms of him that they all are,—even as the days and nights, the half-moons, the months, and the seasons (are forms) of the year, so are they all forms of him (Agni).

22. And, assuredly, they who do this put those forms of his[2] outside of him, and produce confusion between the better and the worse; they make the peasantry equal and refractory to the nobility. Surely, on the Âgnîdhrîya he places the variegated

---

[1] Viz. of 10,800 Lokamprinâs.
[2] Viz. the Gârhapatya and Dhishnya hearths.

stone[1], and that he takes into account: why, then, taking that into account, should he not take others into account? That (altar) by which they ward off Nirriti[2], evil, is the eleventh.

23. As to this they say, 'Why, then, do they not take into account here those (of Nirriti's altar)?' Because he makes no offering on them, for it is by offering that a brick becomes whole and complete.

24. As to this they say, 'How are these (bricks) of his laid down so as not to be excessive?' Well, these (bricks) are his (Agni's) vital power, and man's vital power is not excessive. Thus whosoever, knowing this, performs this holy work, or he who but knows this, makes up this Pragâpati whole and complete.

FOURTH BRÂHMANA.

1. When Pragâpati was creating living beings, Death, that evil, overpowered him. He practised austerities for a thousand years, striving to leave evil behind him.

2. Whilst he was practising austerities, lights went upwards from those hair-pits[3] of his; and those lights are those stars: as many stars as there are, so many hair-pits there are; and as many hair-pits as there are, so many muhûrtas there are in a (sacrificial performance) of a thousand years.

3. In the one-thousandth year, he cleansed himself all through; and he that cleansed all through is this wind which here cleanses by blowing; and that evil which he cleansed all through is this body.

---

[1] See IX, 2, 3, 14-17; 4, 3, 6.   [2] See VII, 2, 1, 1 seq.
[3] That is, the pores from which the hairs spring.

But what is man that he could secure for himself
a (life) of a thousand years[1]? By knowledge,
assuredly, he who knows secures for himself (the
benefits of a performance) of a thousand years.

4. Let him look upon all these bricks as a thousandfold: let him look upon each enclosing-stone
as charged with a thousand nights, each day-holder[2]
with a thousand days, each half-moon-holder with
a thousand half-moons, each month-holder with a
thousand months, each season-holder with a thousand seasons, each muhûrta-holder[3] with a thousand
muhûrtas, and the year with a thousand years.
They who thus know this Agni as being endowed
with a thousand, know his one-thousandth digit; but
they who do not thus know him, do not even know
a one-thousandth digit of him. And he alone who
so knows this, or who performs this sacred work,
obtains this whole and complete Pragâpatean Agni
whom Pragâpati obtained. Wherefore let him who
knows this by all means practise austerities[4]; for,
indeed, when he who knows this practises austerities,
even to (abstention from) sexual intercourse, every
(part) of him will share in the world of heaven[5].

---

[1] Tasmai sahasrasamvatsaragîvanâya ko vâ manushyah saknuyât;
manushyâvadhih satam ato gîvato manushyena sahasrasamvatsarâh
prâptum asakyât. Sây.

[2] That is, the majority of Yagushmatî bricks, viz. 360 of them,
whilst the remaining ones are supposed to stand in lieu of half-
moons, months, and seasons; see X, 4, 3, 19.

[3] Viz. the Lokamprinâ bricks; see X, 4, 3, 20.

[4] Or, religious fervour (meditation).

[5] Or, as Sâyana seems to interpret it, 'that austerity will gain
for him all his (Agni's thousandfold perfection) and the heavenly
world (?),'—etat tapah agnes tadavayavânâm ka sahasrâtmakatva-
rûpam karoti tasmâk ka svargalokaprâptir bhavatity arthah.

5. It is regarding this that it is said in the *Rik*
(I. 179, 3), 'Not in vain is the labour which the
gods favour;' for, in truth, for him who knows
there is no labouring in vain, and so, indeed, the
gods favour this every (action) of his [1].

FIFTH BRÂHMANA.

1. Now the doctrines of mystic imports [2]. The
Sâkâyanins hold that 'Agni is Vâyu (the wind);'
but some say that 'Agni is Âditya (the sun).' And
either Sraumatya, or Hâlingava, said, 'Agni is
no other than Vâyu : wherefore the Adhvaryu, when
he performs the last work [3], passes into that (wind).'

2. And Sâlyâyani said, 'Agni is no other than
the Year; his head is the spring, his right wing the
summer, his left wing the rainy season, his middle
body (trunk) the autumn season, and his tail and
feet the winter and dewy seasons—Agni is speech,
Vâyu breath, the sun the eye, the moon the mind,
the quarters the ear, the generative power water [4],
the feet (and tail) fervour, the joints the months, the
veins the half-moons, the silver and gold feathers

---

[1] Evam vidvân yat kurute tat sarvam yad yasmâd devâ avanti. Sây.

[2] Adhânantaram upanishadâm rahasyârthânâm âdesâ upadesâ
vakshyante. Sây. — Prof. Oldenberg (Zeitsch. of G. Or. S., 50,
p. 457 seq.) takes 'upanishad' in the sense of 'worship.'

[3] That is, the concluding rites of the sacrifice,—tasmâd adhvar-
yuh yadâ uttamam yagñasamâptilakshanam karma karoti, tadaitam
eva vâyum apyeti, tathâ hi, samishtayagurhome devâ gâtuvido gâtum
vittvâ gâtum ita manasâspata iti mantre vâki, svâhâ vâte dhâh
svâhâ, iti vâyau dhâranam uktam. Sây. See IV, 4, 4, 13, where the
sacrifice (though not the Adhvaryu priest) is consigned to the
wind by means of the Samishtayagus formulas.

[4] Note the change in the relative position of subject and predicate
from here.

the days and nights: thus he passes over to the gods.' Let him know, then, that Agni is the Year; and let him know that it is thereof [1] he consists.

3. And *Kelaka Sândilyâyana* said, 'Let him know that the three layers containing the naturally-perforated (bricks) [2] are these worlds, that the fourth (layer) is the Sacrificer, and the fifth all objects of desire; and that it is these worlds, and his own self and all his objects of desire he compasses.'

FIFTH ADHYÂYA. FIRST BRÂHMANA.

1. The mystic import of this Fire-altar, doubtless, is Speech; for it is with speech that it is built: with the *Rik*, the Yagus and the Sâman as the divine (speech); and when he (the Adhvaryu) speaks with human speech, 'Do ye this! do ye that!' then also it (the altar) is built therewith.

2. Now, this speech is threefold—the *Rik*-verses, the Yagus-formulas, and the Sâman-tunes;—thereby the Fire-altar is threefold, inasmuch as it is built with that triad. Even thus, then, it is threefold; but in this respect also it is threefold, inasmuch as three kinds of bricks are put into it—those with masculine names, those with feminine names, and those with neuter names; and these limbs of men also are of three kinds—those with masculine names, those with feminine names, and those with neuter names.

---

[1] That is, of the objects enumerated before.

[2] That is, the first, third, and fifth layers. By the fourth and fifth layers mentioned immediately after, we have not of course to understand the real fourth and fifth layers, but the two making up the five layers (viz. the second and fourth).

3. This body (of the altar), indeed, is threefold; and with this threefold body he obtains the threefold divine Amrita (nectar, immortality). Now all these (bricks) are called 'ish/akâ (f.),' not 'ish/akah (m.),' nor 'ish/akam (n.):' thus (they are called) after the form of speech (vâk, f.), for everything here is speech—whether feminine (female), masculine (male), or neuter—for by speech everything here is obtained. Therefore he 'settles' all (the bricks)[1] with, 'Angiras-like lie thou steady (dhruvâ, f.)!' not with, 'Angiras-like lie thou steady (dhruvah, m.)!' or with, 'Angiras-like lie thou steady (dhruvam, n.)!' for it is that Speech he is constructing.

4. Now, this speech is yonder sun, and this (Agni, the Fire-altar) is Death: hence whatsoever is on this side of the sun all that is held by Death; and he who builds it (the Fire-altar) on this side thereof, builds it as one held by Death, and he surrenders his own self unto Death; but he who builds it thereabove, conquers recurring Death, for by his knowledge that (altar) of his is built thereabove.

5. This speech, indeed, is threefold—the Rik-verses, the Yagus-formulas, and the Sâman-tunes: the Rik-verses are the orb, the Sâman-tunes the light, and the Yagus-formulas the man (in the sun); and that immortal element, the shining light, is this lotus-leaf[2]: thus, when he builds up the Fire-altar

---

[1] See VI. 1, 2, 28; VII. 1, 1, 30.

[2] Viz. the lotus-leaf deposited in the centre of the altar-site, before the first layer is laid down, see VII, 4, 1, 7 seqq., where, however, it is represented as symbolising the womb whence Agni (the fire-altar) is to be born.

after laying down the lotus-leaf, it is on that immortal element that he builds for himself a body consisting of the *Rik*, the Yagus, and the Sâman ; and he becomes immortal.

SECOND BRÂHMANA.

1. Now, that shining orb is the Great Litany, the *Rik*-verses: this is the world of the *Rik*. And that glowing light is (the hymn of) the Great Rite, the Sâman-tunes : this is the world of the Sâman. And the man in yonder orb is the Fire-altar, the Yagus-formulas : this is the world of the Yagus.

2. It is this threefold lore that shines, and even they who do not know this say, 'This threefold lore does indeed shine;' for it is Speech that, seeing it, speaks thus.

3. And that man in yonder (sun's) orb is no other than Death ; and that glowing light is that immortal element : therefore Death does not die, for he is within the immortal ; and therefore he is not seen, for he is within the immortal [1].

4. There is this verse :—'Within Death is immortality,'—for below death is immortality ;— 'founded on Death is immortality,'— for established on that man (in the sun) the immortal shines [2];—' Death putteth on the radiant,'—the

---

[1] Mrityurûpah purusho mritarûpe rkishy antar vartate, . . . mrityoh purushasya amritam amritarûpârkir adhikaranam mandalam âhitam pratishthitam. Sâyana.

[2] 'Antaram mrityor amritam ity avaram hy etan mrityor amritam' ity âdinâ, avaram adhastâdbhâvam amritam purushah

radiant one (vivasvant), doubtless, is yonder sun, for
he irradiates (vi-vas) day and night; and it is him that
(Death) puts on, for on every side he is surrounded
by him;—'Death's self is in the radiant,'—for
the self (body) of that man indeed is in that orb:
such, then, is that verse.

5. Now, that orb is the foundation (foothold) of
both that light and that man; whence one must not
recite the Great Litany for another [1], lest he should
cut away that foothold from beneath his own self;
for he who recites the Mahad Uktham for another,
indeed cuts away that foothold from beneath his own
self: wherefore the (professional) singer of praises
(sastra) is greatly despised, for he is cut off from his
foothold. Thus in regard to the deity.

6. Now as to the sacrifice. That shining orb
is the same as this gold plate (under the altar) [2],
and that glowing light is the same as this lotus-
leaf (under the altar); for there are those (divine)

---

parastâd ity arthasiddhah; anena amritamadhyavartitvam uktam
ity arthah; dvitîyapâdagatâmritapadenârkir adhikaranam mandalam
ukyate, tat purushe pratishthitam tapati, tena hi tasya mandalasya
gagatprakâsakatvam asti. Sây. But for this interpretation, one
might have rendered the first pâda by, ' Close unto death is immortality,' for after death comes immortality.

[1] Cf. Aitareyâr. V, 3, 3, 1, 'No one but a dîkshita (initiated)
should recite the Mahâvrata (sastra); and he should not recite it at
a (Mahâvrata) unless it be combined with (the building of) a fire-
altar; neither should he do so for another person, nor at a
(sacrificial session lasting) less than a year,' so say some; but he
may recite it for his father or for his teacher, for in that case it is
recited on his own behalf.

[2] In these symbolical identifications, one might also take the
relative clause to be the predicate, not the subject, of the sentence;
the former usually preceding the latter.

waters [1], and the lotus-leaf is water [2]; and that man in yonder orb is no other than this gold man (in the altar): thus, by laying down these (in the fire-altar), it is that (divine) triad he constructs. And after the consummation of the sacrifice it rises upwards and enters that shining (sun): one need not therefore mind destroying Agni, for he is then in yonder (world) [3]. Thus, then, in regard to the sacrifice.

7. Now as to the self (body). That shining orb and that gold plate are the same as the white here in the eye; and that glowing light and that lotus-leaf are the same as the black here in the eye; and that man in yonder orb and that gold man are the same as this man in the right eye.

---

[1] Though the sun itself does not consist of water, he at any rate floats along a sea of water; cf. VII, 5, 1, 8, 'For that indeed is the deepest of waters where yonder sun shines;' and there are waters above and below the sun, VII, 1, 1, 24; and the sun is encircled by 360 navigable streams, and as many flow towards it, X, 5, 4, 14.— Sâyana, on the other hand, takes it to mean, 'for that (light) is water,' inasmuch as the sun's rays produce the rain,—arkisho hy âpah sûryakiranânâm eva vrîshtikartrîkatvât kâryakâranayor abhedena arkir vâ âpa ity uktam. Possibly this may be the right interpretation.

[2] See VII, 4, 1, 8, where the lotus-plant is said to represent the (cosmic) waters, whilst the earth is a lotus-leaf floating on the waters.

[3] According to Sâyana, he is so in the shape of both the sun and the Sacrificer's body or self,—yato ʼsminn agnim kitavân parâ-trâdityo bhavati, ato ʼgnim parihantum nâdriyeta, kilam agnim ishtakâviseshena nâsayitam âdaram na kuryât, kutah, esho ʼgnir amutra bhavati, paraloke yagamânasarirâtmanotpadyate; yad vâ parihantum prâptum sprashtum ity arthah, kityâgnisparsane dosha-sravanât. Sâyana, thus, is doubtful as to how 'Agnim parihantum' is to be taken, whether it means 'to injure the altar (? or extinguish the fire) by some brick,' or to 'knock against (touch) the altar.' The St. Petersb. Dict. takes it in the sense of 'to extinguish the fire,'

8. The Lokampriñâ (space-filling brick) is the same as that (gold man in the sun)[1]: it is that (brick) which this entire Agni finally results in[2]. Moreover, this man (or person) in the left eye is the mate of that one (in the right eye and in the sun); and a mate is one half of one's own self[3], for when one is with a mate he is whole and complete: thus it (the second man) is for the sake of completeness. And as to there being two of these (persons in the eyes), a pair means a productive couple: hence two Lokampriñâs are laid down each time[4], and hence they set up the layer by two (kinds of bricks).

9. Now, that person in the right eye is the same as Indra, and (that other person is) the same as Indrânî: it is for the sake of these two that the gods made that partition (between the eyes), the nose; whence he (the husband) should not eat food in the presence of his wife[5]; for from him (who

but it might also, perhaps, mean 'to destroy the fire-altar' by taking it to pieces.

[1] On the identification of the sun with the Lokampriñâ on the ground that the former fills these worlds (lokân pûrayati), see VIII, 7, 2, 1.

[2] Or, finally comes to; viz. inasmuch as it is by the placing of the Lokampriñâ bricks that the altar is completed (Sây.); and inasmuch as Agni passes into the sun.

[3] Purusho mithunam yoshid ity etasmin mithunam hy âtmano ꞓrdham ardhabhâgah, ardho vâ esha âtmano yat patnîti taittirîya-sruteh. Sây.

[4] When the layers are filled up with 'space-fillers,' two Lokampriñâs are first laid down in one of the four corners, and from them the available spaces are then filled up, in two turns, in the sunwise direction: cf. p. 22, note 1.

[5] Cf. I, 9, 2, 12, 'whenever women here eat, they do so apart from men;' where the use of the 'gighatsanti' (swallow their

does not do so) a vigorous son is born, and she in
whose presence (the husband) does not eat food
bears a vigorous (son) :—

10. Such, indeed, is the divine ordinance ;—amongst
men princes keep most aloof [1], and for that reason
a vigorous (son) is born to them ; and of birds the
Amṛitavâkâ (does so, and she) produces the Kshi-
prasyena [2].

11. Those two (persons in the eyes) descend to the
cavity of the heart [3], and enter into union with each
other ; and when they reach the end of their union,
then the man sleeps,—even as here on reaching the
end of a human union he becomes, as it were,
insensible [4], so does he then become, as it were,

---

food)—as against asniyât in our passage—is not meant disrespect-
fully, but as the regular desiderative of 'ad' (Pân. II, 4, 37), for
which no doubt 'asisishanti' (Sat. Br. III, 1, 2, 1) might have
been used.

[1] Or, 'act most in secrecy.' Sâyana explains it: manushyânâm
madhye râganyabandhavo ⸳ nutamâm gopâyanti atyartham rahasyat-
vena kurvanti tasmât teshu vîryavân putro gâyate. The St. Petersb.
Dict., on the other hand, takes it in the sense of 'they protect
most of all;' though it is difficult to see how the 'protection'
afforded by princes or rulers could have any bearing on men taking
their food apart from their wives. If the above interpretation is
right we may compare 'anu-gup' in the sense of 'to conceal.'
See, however, the next note, where Sâyana takes 'gopâyati' in
the sense of 'observes (that law),' which might also have suited
here. Princes, having their seraglio, would naturally have less
occasion for coming into contact with their wives at mealtime than
men of lower stations of life. On the superlative of the preposition,
see p. 287, note 1.

[2] ? The swift eagle,—vayasâm pakshinâm madhye amṛitavâkâ
nâma pakshigâtir etad vratam gopâyati, atah sâ kshipram sîghra-
gâminam syenam nâma pakshinam ganayati. Sây.

[3] Hṛidayasyâkâsam daharam prâpya. Sây.

[4] That is, 'unconscious,' with something of 'indifferent, apa-
thetic,' implied:—Loke mânushasya maithunasyântam gatvâ ⸳ sam-

insensible; for this is a divine union [1], and that is
the highest bliss.

12. Therefore let him, who knows this, sleep, for
it makes for heaven [2]: he thereby, indeed, makes
those two deities enjoy their dear wish, union. And
one should not therefore forcibly [3] awaken him who
sleeps, lest he should hurt those two deities whilst
enjoying their union; and hence the mouth of him
who has been asleep is, as it were, clammy, for those
two deities are then shedding seed, and from that
seed everything here originates, whatsoever exists.

13. Now, that man in yonder orb (of the sun),
and that man in the right eye truly are no other than
Death;—his feet have stuck fast in the heart,
and having pulled them out he comes forth; and
when he comes forth then that man dies: whence
they say of him who has passed away, 'he has been
cut off [4].'

14. And, indeed, he is the breath (prâna), for it
is he (the man in the eye) that leads forward (pra-
nayati) all these creatures. These vital airs (prâna)
are his own (sva); and when he sleeps (svapiti) then

vidâ agânâmeva nrâ strî bhavati (marg. corr. agânânâv eva stripu-
rushau bhavatah) evam tadâ tayor mithunabhâve (? mithunâbhâve)
purusho samvida iva bhavati. Sây.

[1] Viz. because it is the union of Indra and Indrânî.

[2] Or, perhaps, it is the usual practice (lokyam), as the St. Petersb.
Dict. takes it.

[3] Dhureva pîdayaiva ma bodhayet, na prabuddham kuryât, dhûr-
vater himsârthat kvipi âblope rûpam. Sây.

[4] ? His (life) has been cut off; or, his (life-string) has been
severed. Sâyana (unless there is an omission in the MS.) does
not explain 'kikhedy asya,' but seems to take 'pretam' (passed
away) as the word on which the stress lies:—tasmâd imam pretam
ity âhuh, prapûrvâd eteh ktapratyaye rûpam; katham, akshipurusha-
nirgame purushasya maranam.

these vital airs take possession of him[1] as his own
(svâ api-yanti) : hence (the term) 'svâpyaya (being
taken possession of by one's own people),' 'svâpyaya' doubtless being what they mystically call
'svapna (sleep),' for the gods love the mystic.

15. And when he is asleep, he does not, by
means of them, know of anything whatever, nor does
he form any resolution with his mind, or distinguish
the taste of food with (the channel of) his speech,
or distinguish any smell with (the channel of) his
breath ; neither does he see with his eye, nor hear
with his ear, for those (vital airs) have taken possession of him. Whilst being one only, he (the
man in the eye) is numerously distributed among
living beings : whence the Lokamprinâ (representing
the man in the sun), whilst being one only (in kind),
extends over the whole altar ; and because he (the
man in the eye) is one only, therefore (the Lokamprinâ) is one.

16. As to this they say, 'One death, or many?'
Let him say, 'Both one and many;' for inasmuch
as he is that (man in the sun) in yonder world he is
one, and inasmuch as he is numerously distributed
here on earth among living beings, there are also
many of them.

17. As to this they say, 'Is Death near or far
away?' Let him say, 'Both near and far away;'
for inasmuch as he is here on earth in the body
he is near, and inasmuch as he is that one in yonder
world he also is far away.

18. Regarding this there is the verse,—'Con-

---

[1] Or, they keep within him, they nestle in him,—apiyanti prâp-
nuvanti, âliyanta ity arthah. Sây.

cealed in food he, the immortal, shineth at the
flowing together of vital saps;'—yonder shining
orb is food, and the man in that orb is the eater:
being concealed in that food, he shines. Thus
much as to the deity.

10. Now as to the body. This body indeed
is food, and that man in the right eye is the eater:
being concealed in that food he shines.

20. That same (divine person), the Adhvaryus
(Yagur-veda priests) serve under the name of 'Agni'
(fire-altar) and 'Yagus,' because he holds together
(yug) all this (universe)[1]; the Khandogas (Sâma-veda
priests, chanters) under that of 'Sâman,' because
in him all this (universe) is one and the same
(samâna)[2]; the Bahvrikas (Rig-veda priests, Hotars)
under that of 'Uktham,' because he originates
(utthâp) everything here; those skilled in sorcery,
under that of 'sorcery (yâtu),' because everything
here is held in check (yata) by him; the serpents
under that of 'poison;' the snake-charmers under
that of 'snake;' the gods under that of 'ûrg (strengthening food);' men under that of 'wealth;' demons
under that of 'mâyâ (magic power);' the deceased
Fathers under that of 'svadhâ (invigorating
draught);' those knowing the divine host under
that of 'divine host;' the Gandharvas under that of
'form (rûpa[3]);' the Apsaras under that of 'fragrance
(gandha),'—thus, in whatsoever form they serve him
that indeed he becomes, and, having become that,

[1] Esha purusha idam sarvam gagad yunakti sarvatra svayam
samgata iti. Sây.

[2] Etasmin paramâtmani kârane sarvam kâryagâtam samânam
iti. Sây.

[3] The characteristic attributes of the Gandharvas and Apsaras
are evidently exchanged in the text as it stands; cf. IX, 4, 1, 4.

he is helpful to them ; whence he who knows should
serve him in all these (forms), for he becomes all that,
and, having become all that, he is helpful to him.

21. Now this Agni (fire-altar) consists of three
bricks,—the *Rik* being one, the *Yagus* another,
and the Sâman another : whatever (brick) he lays
down here with a *rik* (verse) that has the gold plate
for its foundation[1] ; whatever (brick he lays down)
with a *yagus* (formula) that has the (gold) man for
its foundation ; and whatever (brick he lays down)
with a sâman (hymn-tune) that has the lotus-leaf for
its foundation. Thus he consists of three bricks.

22. And, indeed, these two, to wit, that gold plate
and that lotus-leaf join that (gold) man, for both
the *Rik* and the Sâman join the Yagus ; and so he
also consists of a single brick.

23. Now, that man in yonder orb (of the sun),
and this man in the right eye, are no other than
Death[2] ; and he becomes the body (self) of him
who knows this : whenever he who knows departs
this world he passes into that body, and becomes
immortal, for Death is his own self.

THIRD BRÂHMANA.

1. Verily, in the beginning this (universe) was,
as it were[3], neither non-existent nor existent ; in

---

[1] Viz. inasmuch as the (round) gold plate (representing the sun)
is deposited in the centre of the altar-site, before the first layer is
constructed. In the same way the other two objects.

[2] Sâyana seems to construe this somewhat differently : sa esho
'gnir yagurâtmako 'dhidaivam mandalamadhyavartî adhyâtmam
dakshinâkshivartî purusho mrityurûpah.

[3] Sâyana seems to take 'iva' here in the sense of 'eva,' as indeed
it often has to be taken, especially in negative sentences.

the beginning this (universe), indeed, as it were, existed and did not exist: there was then only that Mind.

2. Wherefore it has been said by the *Ri*shi (*Ri*g-veda X, 129, 1), 'There was then neither the non-existent nor the existent;' for Mind was, as it were, neither existent nor non-existent.

3. This Mind, when created, wished to become manifest,—more defined [1], more substantial: it sought after a self (body) [2]. It practised austerity [3]: it acquired consistency [4]. It then beheld thirty-six thousand Arka-fires [5] of its own self, composed of mind, built up of mind: mentally [6] alone they were established (on sacrificial hearths) and mentally

---

[1] Niruktatara*m* nirukta*m* sabdanirvâkyam. Sây.

[2] Sâya*na* also allows the interpretation, 'after (its source, or cause,) the (supreme) self,'—âtmâna*m* svakâra*nam* paramâtmâna*m* svasvarûpa*m* vâ ₊ nvai*kkh*at. What seems, indeed, implied in these esoteric lucubrations, is that meditation on the infinite is equivalent to all ceremonial rites which are supposed to be incessantly performed for one so engaged, even during his sleep (paragraph 12).

[3] I. e. intense meditation (paryâlokanam), Sây. ? 'it became heated.'

[4] Sâya*na* apparently takes 'prâmûr*kh*at' in the sense of 'became great, or important,'— samu*kkh*ritam babhûva.

[5] Sâya*na* here takes 'arka' in the sense of 'arkanîya (worthy of veneration), as, indeed, he did several times before: though once he seems to call them 'agnyarkâ*h*,' as being the highest, merely speculative or immaterial form of sacrificial fires or fire-altars (dhyeyâ agnaya*h*); cf. X, 3, 4, 3 seq.—The 36,000 fires are calculated so as to be equal to the number of days in the life of the perfect man living a hundred years (X, 2, 6, 9): there being thus for each day of his life a (spiritual) sacrificial fire, a mental exercise or discipline, as Sâya*na* expresses it,—tatraikasmin dine (âgneyâ?) mano*vri*tti*h*.

[6] The text has everywhere the instrumental 'manasâ,' which would imply either the agent, the instrument, or the material, as the case might be.

built up [1]; mentally the cups (of Soma) were drawn
thereat; mentally they chanted, and mentally they
recited on (near) them,—whatever rite is performed
at the sacrifice, whatever sacrificial rite there is,
that was performed mentally only, as a mental performance, on those (fires or fire-altars) composed of
mind, and built up of mind. And whatever it is that
(living) beings here conceive in their mind that was
done regarding those (mental Agnis [2]):—they establish
them (on the hearths) and build them up (as fire-
altars); they draw the cups for them; they chant on
(near) them and recite hymns on them,—of that
extent was the development of Mind, of that extent
its creation,—so great is Mind: thirty-six thousand
Arka-fires; and each of these as great as that
former (fire-altar) was.

4. That Mind created Speech. This Speech,
when created, wished to become manifest,—more
defined, more substantial: it sought after a self.
It practised austerity: it acquired consistency. It
beheld thirty-six thousand Arka-fires of its own self,
composed of speech, built up of speech: with speech
they were established, and with speech built up;
with speech the cups were drawn thereat; with
speech they chanted, and with speech they recited
on them—whatever rite is performed at the sacrifice, whatever sacrificial rite there is, that was

---

[1] That is, the ceremonies of Agnyâdhâna (establishment of the
sacrificial fire) and Agnikayana (building of the fire-altar) were
performed by means of these fires. Sâyana remarks that these rites
were performed by the same 'beings (bhûtâni),' which are mentioned immediately after, as would, indeed, appear to be the case
from paragraph 12.

[2] Yat kim ka bhûtâni manasâ dhyâyanti vâkâ vadanti taih sam-
kalpavadanâdibhir eva teshâm agnînâm karanam. Sây.

performed by speech alone, as a vocal performance,
on those (fires) composed of speech, and built up of
speech. And whatever beings here speak by speech
that was done regarding those (fires): they establish
them and build them up; they draw the cups for
them; they chant on them and recite hymns on
them,—of that extent was the development of
Speech, of that extent its creation,—so great is
Speech: thirty-six thousand Arka-fires; and each
of these as great as that former (fire-altar) was.

5. That Speech created the Breath. This Breath,
when created, wished to become manifest.—more
defined, more substantial: it sought after a self.
It practised austerity: it acquired consistency. It
beheld thirty-six thousand Arka-fires of its own self,
composed of breath, built up of breath: with breath
they were established, and with breath built up;
with breath the cups were drawn thereat; with
breath they chanted and with breath they recited
on them,—whatever rite is performed at the sacrifice, whatever sacrificial rite there is, that was
performed by breath alone, as a breathing-per-
formance, on those (fires) composed of breath, and
built up of breath. And whatever beings here
breathe with breath that was done regarding those
(fires):—they establish them, and build them up:
they draw the cups for them; they chant on them
and recite hymns on them,—of that extent was the
development of Breath, of that extent was its
creation,—so great is Breath: thirty-six thousand
Arka-fires; and each of these as great as that
former (fire-altar) was.

6. That Breath created the Eye. This Eye,
when created, wished to become manifest,—more

defined, more substantial: it sought after a self.
It practised austerity: it acquired consistency. It
beheld thirty-six thousand Arka-fires of its own self,
composed of the eye, built up of the eye : by means
of the eye they were established, and by means of
the eye built up; by the eye the cups were drawn
thereat; by means of the eye they chanted and
recited hymns on them,—whatever rite is performed
as the sacrifice, whatever sacrificial rite there is,
that was performed by the eye alone, as an eye-
performance, on those (fires) composed of eye, and
built up of the eye. And whatever beings here see
with the eye that was done regarding those (fires) :—
they establish them and build them up; they draw
the cups for them; they chant on them and recite
hymns on them,—of that extent was the development of the Eye, of that extent its creation,—so
great is the Eye : thirty-six thousand Arka-fires;
and each of these as great as that former (fire-
altar) was.

7. That Eye created the Ear. This Ear, when
created, wished to become manifest,—more defined,
more substantial : it sought after a self. It practised
austerity : it acquired consistency. It beheld thirty-
six thousand Arka-fires of its own self, composed of
the ear, built up of the ear : by means of the ear
they were established, and by means of the ear
built up; by the ear the cups were drawn thereat;
by means of the ear they chanted and recited hymns
on them,—whatever rite is performed at the sacrifice, whatever sacrificial rite there is, that was
performed by the ear alone, as an ear-performance,
on those (fires) composed of ear, and built up of the
ear. And whatever beings here hear with the ear

that was done regarding those (fires) :—they establish
them and build them up ; they draw the cups for
them ; they chant on them and recite hymns on
them,—of that extent was the development of the
Ear, of that extent its creation,—so great is the
Ear : thirty-six thousand Arka-fires ; and each of
these as great as that former (fire-altar) was.

8. That Ear created Work, and this condensed
itself into the vital airs, into this compound, this
composition of food[1]; for incomplete is work without
the vital airs, and incomplete are the vital airs
without work.

9. This Work, when created, wished to become
manifest,—more defined, more substantial : it sought
after a self. It practised austerity : it acquired
consistency. It beheld thirty-six thousand Arka-
fires of its own self, composed of work, built up of
(or by) work : by work they were established, and
by work built up ; by work the cups were drawn
thereat ; by work they chanted and recited hymns
on them,—whatever rite is performed at the sacrifice,
whatever sacrificial rite there is, that was performed
by work alone, as a work-performance, on those
(fires) composed of work, and built up of work.
And whatever beings here work by work that was
done regarding those (fires) :—they establish them
and build them up ; they draw the cups for them ;
they chant on them and recite hymns on them,—of
that extent was the development of Work, of that

---

[1] Sâyana explains 'samdegham annasamdeham' by 'annaprânâ-
srayam sariram,'—svayam asamdeham asariram sat karma prânin-
mayor anyonyasâhakaryâd abhivriddhim vyatirekam makhyenâha,
akrisnam &c. Sâyana would thus take 'samdegha' as equivalent
to the later 'deha' (body), and in no depreciatory sense.

extent its creation,—so great is Work : thirty-six thousand Arka-fires ; and each of these as great as that former (fire-altar) was.

10. That Work created the Fire,—Fire, doubtless, is more manifest than Work, for by work (sacrificial performance) they produce it, and by work they kindle it.

11. This Fire, when created, wished to become manifest,—more defined, more substantial : it sought after a self. It practised austerity [1] : it acquired consistency. It beheld thirty-six thousand Arka-fires of its own self, composed of fire, built up of fire : with fire they were established, and with fire built up ; with fire the cups were drawn thereat ; with fire they chanted and recited hymns on them ;— whatever rite is performed at the sacrifice, whatever sacrificial rite there is, that was performed with fire alone, as a fire-performance, on those (fires) composed of fire, and built up of fire. And whatever fire beings here kindle that was done regarding those (fires) :—they establish them and build them up ; they draw the cups for them ; they chant on them and recite hymns on them,—of that extent was the development of Fire, of that extent its creation,—so great is Fire : thirty-six thousand Arka-fires ; and each of these as great as that former (fire-altar) was.

12. These fires (altars), in truth, are knowledge-built ; and all beings at all times build them for him who knows this, even whilst he is asleep : by knowledge alone these fires (altars) are indeed built for him who knows this.

---

[1] Or, fervid devotion ; though perhaps the physical sense of ' it became heated ' would suit better here.

Fourth Brâhmana.

1. Verily, this (brick-)built Fire-altar (Agni) is this (terrestrial) world:—the waters (of the encircling ocean) are its (circle of) enclosing-stones; the men its Yagushmatis (bricks with special formulas); the cattle its Sûdadohas[1]; the plants and trees its earth-fillings (between the layers of bricks), its oblations and fire-logs[2]; Agni (the terrestrial fire) its Lokamprinâ (space-filling brick);—thus this comes to make up the whole Agni, and the whole Agni comes to be the space-filler[3]; and, verily, whosoever knows this, thus comes to be that whole (Agni) who is the space-filler[4].

2. But, indeed, that Fire-altar also is the air:—the junction of heaven and earth (the horizon) is its (circle of) enclosing-stones, for it is beyond the air that heaven and earth meet, and that (junction) is the (circle of) enclosing-stones; the birds are its Yagushmati bricks, the rain its Sûdadohas, the rays

---

[1] That is, either the food obtained by the milking of the drink of immortality (amritadohânnam), or the verse Rig-veda VIII, 69, 3 (tâ asya sûdadohasah, &c.) pronounced over the 'settled' brick, and supposed to supply vital air to the different parts of Agni-Pragâpati's body (whence it is also repeated in the Brihad Uktham between the different parts of the bird-like body; cf. p. 112, note 1). Sây.

[2] Sâyana seems to interpret this in two different ways,—oshadhi-vanaspataya eva purishâhutisamittrayarûpâ etasya purishâhutisamit-trayarûpatvam uttaratra spashtikarishyate; atha (vâ) yad dikshu ka rasmishu kânnam tat puri-ham tâ ahutayas tâh samidhah.

[3] See X, 5, 2, 8. Viz. 'inasmuch as all become fit for their work by being provided with fire.' Sây.

[4] Or, the word-filler, the ruler of the world (lokâdhishthâtri). Sây.

of light its earth-fillings, oblations and fire-logs;
Vâyu (the wind) is its space-filler; thus this comes
to make up the whole Agni, and the whole Agni
comes to be the space-filler; and, verily, whosoever
knows this, thus comes to be that whole (Agni) who
is the space-filler.

3. But, indeed, that Fire-altar also is the sky:—
the (heavenly) waters are its enclosing-stones, for
even as a case [1] here is closed up so are these
worlds (enclosed) within the waters; and the waters
beyond these worlds are the enclosing-stones;—the
gods are the Yagushmatî bricks; what food there is
in that world is its Sûdadohas; the Nakshatras
(lunar mansions) are the earth-fillings, the oblations
and the fire-logs; and Âditya (the sun) is the space-
filler;—thus this comes to make up the whole Agni;
and the whole Agni comes to be the space-filler;
and, verily, whosoever knows this, thus comes to be
that whole (Agni) who is the space-filler.

4. But, indeed, that Fire-altar also is the sun:—
the regions are its enclosing-stones, and there are
three hundred and sixty of these [2], because three
hundred and sixty regions encircle the sun on all
sides;—the rays are its Yagushmatî bricks, for there
are three hundred and sixty of these [3], and three
hundred and sixty rays of the sun; and in that
he establishes the Yagushmatîs within the enclosing-
stones thereby he establishes the rays in the regions.
And what is between the regions and the rays, is its
Sûdadohas; and what food there is in the regions
and rays that is the earth-fillings, the oblations and

<hr>

[1] Or, as (the valves, or shells, of) a pod are closed up.
[2] See p. 354, note 2.   [3] See IX, 4, 3, 6.

the fire-logs ; and that which is called both 'regions'
and 'rays' is the space-filling (brick) :—thus this
comes to make up the whole Agni ; and the whole
Agni comes to be the space-filler ; and, verily,
whosoever knows this, thus comes to be that whole
(Agni) who is the space-filler.

5. But, indeed, that Fire-altar also is the Nakshatras :—for there are twenty-seven of these
Nakshatras, and twenty-seven secondary stars
accompany each Nakshatra,—this makes seven
hundred and twenty [1], and thirty-six in addition
thereto. Now what seven hundred and twenty
bricks [2] there are of these, they are the three
hundred and sixty enclosing-stones and the three
hundred and sixty Yagushmatî bricks ; and what
thirty-six there are in addition, they are the
thirteenth (intercalary) month, the body (of the
altar) ; the trunk [3] (consisting of) thirty, the feet
of two, the (channels of the) vital airs of two [4],
and the head itself being the (thirty-fifth and)
thirty-sixth,—and as to there being two of these,
it is because 'siras' (head) consists of two syllables ;
—and what (space) there is between (each) two

[1] On this inaccurate calculation (the real product being 729),
resorted to in order to get a total amount equal to the number of
Yagushmatî bricks (756), see A. Weber, Nakshatra, II, p. 298.

[2] That is, Nakshatras considered as the bricks of which the fire-
altar is constructed. The latter being identical with the year, the
720 bricks represent the days and nights of the year.

[3] Thus Sâyana (madhyadeha),—the âtman (in that case, however, the whole body) is usually represented as consisting of twenty-
five parts. Here the thirty parts would probably be the trunk, the
head, the upper and fore-arms, the thighs and shanks, and the
fingers and toes.

[4] Viz. inasmuch as eyes, ears, and nostrils are in pairs. Say.

Nakshatras that is the Sûdadohas; and what food
there is in the Nakshatras that is the earth-fillings
(between the layers of bricks), the oblations and
the fire-logs; and what is called 'nakshatras' that
is the space-filling (brick):—thus this comes to
make up the whole Agni, and the whole Agni
comes to be the space-filler; and, verily, whosoever
knows this, thus comes to be that whole (Agni) who
is the space-filler.

6. Now, these (amount to) twenty-one Brihatîs[1];
and—the heavenly world being the twenty-one-fold
one[2] and the Brihati (the great one)—this (altar)
thus comes to be equal to the heavenly world, and
to the twenty-one-fold Stoma (hymn-form) and the
Brihati metre.

7. But, indeed, that Fire-altar also is the Metres;
for there are seven of these metres, increasing by
four syllables[3]; and the triplets of these make seven
hundred and twenty syllables, and thirty-six in
addition thereto. Now what seven hundred and
twenty bricks there are of these, they are the
three hundred and sixty enclosing-stones and the
three hundred and sixty Yagushmatîs; and what
thirty-six there are in addition, they are the
thirteenth month, and the body (of this altar),—
the trunk (consisting of) thirty, the feet of two,

---

[1] The Brihati verse consisting of 36 syllables, this makes a total
of 756 syllables, or the same amount as that of the days and nights
of the year, plus the days (36) of the intercalary month.

[2] Viz. inasmuch as the sun is 'the twenty-first,' cf. I, 3, 5, 11;
VI, 2, 2, 3: svargas tv âditya iti surake(tu)rûpo vâ lokah svargah
ekavimsatisamkhyâpûrakah. Sây.

[3] The seven metres, increasing by four syllables from 24 up to
48, consist together of 252 syllables, and hence the triplets of them
amount to 756 = 720 + 36 syllables.

the vital airs of two, and the head itself being the
(thirty-fifth and) thirty-sixth; and as to there being
two of these, it is because 'siras' consists of two
syllables.

8. Now the first ten syllables of this Brihati,
consisting of thirty-six syllables, make an Ekapadâ [1]
of ten syllables; and the (first) twenty make
a Dvipadâ of twenty syllables; and the (first)
thirty a Virâg [2] of thirty syllables; and the (first)
thirty-three a (Virâg) of thirty-three syllables; and
the (first) thirty-four a Svarâg [3] of thirty-four
syllables; and in that this fire-altar is built with
all metres thereby it is an Atikhandas [4], and (so)
indeed are all these bricks [5]. And the three
syllables 'ishtakâ (brick)' are a Gâyatri tripadâ,
whence this Agni is Gâyatra; and the three
syllables 'mrid' (clay) and 'âpah' (water) [6] also
are a Gâyatri tripadâ: thereby also he is Gâyatra.
And what is between (each two) metres is the

---

[1] The Ekapadâ is a verse consisting of a single pâda, and the
Dvipadâ one of two pâdas, whilst verses in the ordinary metres
consist of three or four pâdas.

[2] The Virâg is a metre consisting of 1 to 4 (usually 3) decasyllabic
pâdas; the one consisting of four such pâdas being, however,
commonly called Pankti. Besides this, the principal, Virâg, there
is, however, another consisting of 3 pâdas of 11 syllables each.

[3] This name, which is here applied to a verse of 34 syllables,
was in VII, 4, 1, 9 used of a verse of 10 + 10 + 11 + 11 = 42
syllables (Vâg. S. XI, 29); cf. Weber, Ind. Stud. VIII, p. 63.

[4] That is, an over-metre, excessive metre, consisting of more
than 48 syllables. The fire-altar, being built up with all the metres
(viz. with the Khandasyâ bricks, representing the metres, cf. VIII,
3, 3, 1 seqq.), would thus far exceed the latter number.

[5] ? Thus Sâyana: kityâgnir atikhandâ iti yat tena sarvâ ishtakâ
atikhandomayya ity uktam.

[6] That is, the materials used for making bricks.

Sûdadohas; and the food which is in the metres is the earth-fillings, the oblations, and the fire-logs; and what is called 'metres,' that is the space-filling (brick):—thus this comes to make up the whole Agni; and the whole Agni comes to be the space-filler; and, verily, whosoever knows this, comes to be that whole (Agni) who is the space-filler.

9. Now, these (amount to) twenty-one Brihatis; and—the heavenly world being the twenty-one-fold and the Brihatî—this (altar) thus comes to be equal to the heavenly world, and to the twenty-one-fold Stoma and the Brihati metre.

10. But, indeed, that Fire-altar also is the Year,—the nights are its enclosing-stones, and there are three hundred and sixty of these, because there are three hundred and sixty nights in the year; and the days are its Yagushmatî bricks, for there are three hundred and sixty of these, and three hundred and sixty days in the year; and those thirty-six bricks which are over[1] are the thirteenth month, the body (of the year and the altar), the half-months and months,—(there being) twenty-four half-months, and twelve months. And what there is between day and night that is the Sûdadohas; and what food there is in the days and nights is the earth-fillings, the oblations, and the fire-logs; and what is called 'days and nights' that constitutes the space-filling (brick):—thus this comes to make up the whole Agni, and the whole Agni comes to be the space-filler; and, verily, whosoever knows this, thus comes to be that whole (Agni) who is the space-filler.

---

[1] Viz. those required to make up the 756 Yagushmatîs.

11. Now, these (amount to) twenty-one Brihatis; and—the heavenly world being the twenty-one-fold and the Brihati—this (altar) thus comes to be equal to the heavenly world, and to the twenty-one-fold Stoma and the Brihati metre.

12. But, indeed, that Fire-altar also is the body,—the bones are its enclosing-stones, and there are three hundred and sixty of these, because there are three hundred and sixty bones in man; the marrow parts are the Yagushmati bricks, for there are three hundred and sixty of these, and three hundred and sixty parts of marrow in man; and those thirty-six bricks which are over, are the thirteenth month, the trunk, the vital air (of the altar),—in his body there are thirty parts [1], in his feet two, in his vital airs two, and in his head two,—as to there being two of these, it is because the head consists of two skull-bones. And that whereby these joints are held together is the Sûdadohas; and those three whereby this body is covered—to wit, hair, skin, and flesh—are the earth-fillings; what he drinks is the oblations, and what he eats the fire-logs; and what is called the 'body,' that is the space-filling (brick):—thus this comes to make up the whole Agni, and the whole Agni comes to be the space-filler; and, verily, whosoever knows this, thus comes to be that whole (Agni) who is the space-filler.

13. Now, these (amount to) twenty-one Brihatis; and—the heavenly world being the twenty-one-fold and the Brihati—this (altar) thus comes to be equal to the heavenly world, and to the twenty-one-fold Stoma and the Brihati metre.

---

[1] See p. 383, note 3.

14. But, indeed, that built Agni (the fire-altar) is all beings, all the gods; for all the gods, all beings are the waters [1], and that built fire-altar is the same as those waters [2];—the navigable streams (round the sun) are its enclosing-stones, and there are three hundred and sixty of these, because three hundred and sixty navigable streams encircle the sun on all sides; and the navigable streams, indeed, are also the Yagushmati bricks, and there are three hundred and sixty of these, because three hundred and sixty navigable streams flow towards [3] the sun. And what is between (each) two navigable rivers is the Sûdadohas; and those thirty-six bricks which remain over are the same as that thirteenth month, and the body (of this altar, the waters [4],) is the same as this gold man.

15. His feet are that gold plate and lotus-leaf—(that is) the waters and the sun's orb [5]—are his feet; his arms are the two spoons, and they are Indra and Agni; the two naturally-perforated (bricks) are this earth and the air; and the three Visvagyotis (all-light) bricks are these deities—Agni, Vâyu, and

---

[1] Viz. inasmuch as they are the foundation and ultimate source of the universe; cf. VI, 8, 2, 2. 3; and everything is contained therein, X, 5, 4, 3.

[2] Viz. inasmuch as the built Agni is the same as the sun, and the sun is surrounded by water; cf. p. 368, note 1.

[3] It is not clear whether these rivers are meant to be different ones from those flowing round the sun, or whether they are the same as 'washing against' the sun.

[4] Adhokteshu paryâyeshv agnyavayava - trayodasamâsâtmika âtmâ agnyâtmanâ dhyeyân.im apâm âtmety arthah. Sây.

[5] That is, in regard to the sacrifice, the gold plate and lotus-leaf are his feet, and in regard to the deity, the waters and the sun's disk. Sây. They are, nevertheless, counted as four.

Âditya, for these deities, indeed, are all the light: and the twelve seasonal (bricks) are the year, the body (of the altar, and the gold man); and the five Nâkasads and five Pañkakûdâs are the sacrifice, the gods; and the Vikarnî the (third) Svayamâtriṇṇâ and the variegated stone [1]; and the fire which is deposited (on the altar [1]) is the thirty-fifth; and the formula of the Lokamprinâ (brick) [2] is the thirty-sixth;—that (gold man), indeed, the body (of the altar) is the end of everything here [3]: he is in the midst of all the waters, endowed with all objects of desire—for all objects of desire are the waters [4]; whilst possessed of all (objects of) desires he is without desire, for no desire of anything (troubles) him [5].

16. Regarding this there is this verse—'By knowledge [6] they ascend that (state) where desires have vanished [7]: sacrificial gifts go not thither [8], nor the fervid practisers of rites without knowledge;'—for, indeed, he who does not know this does not attain to that world either by sacrificial gifts or by devout

---

[1] For this stone, which was deposited near the Âgnîdhrîya shed, and afterwards placed in the Âgnîdhra hearth, see p. 243, note 2.

[2] See VIII, 7, 2, 6.   [3] See X, 5, 2, 6–8.

[4] Sa eva . . . shattrimsadishtakâmayo hiranmayah purusha âtmâ sarvabhûtadevâtmanâm apâm agnyâtmanâ dhyeyânâm madhye vartate. Sây.

[5] Sâyana does not explain this last sentence.

[6] 'Only by knowledge is such a body (self) to be obtained by all, not by hundreds of religious performances.' Sây.

[7] Yatra svarûpe kâmâh sarve parâgatâ vivrittâh (? nivrittâh) svayam akâmam ity arthah, tad âtmasvarûpam vidyayâ svarûpena ârohanti âpnuvanti. Sây.

[8] Sâyana takes 'dakshinâ' as instrumental, in accordance with the comment offered by the Brâhmana, which, however, is probably not meant as a close grammatical explanation.

practices, but only to those who know does that world belong.

17. The welkin is the earth-fillings (between the layers of brick); the moon the oblations; the Nakshatras (lunar mansions) the fire-logs,—because the moon resides in (or with) the Nakshatra, therefore the oblation resides in the fire-wood: that [1], indeed, is the food of the oblation, and its support; whence the oblation does not fail (na kshiyate), for that is its food and its support. And what are called 'the gods' they are the space-filling (brick); for by (naming) the gods everything here is named.

18. It is regarding this that it is said by the *Rik* (X, 12, 3), 'The All-gods have gone after this thy Yagus,'—for all beings, all the gods, indeed, become the Yagus here. Thus this whole Agni comes to be the space-filler; and, verily, whosoever knows this, thus comes to be that whole (Agni) who is the space-filler.

19. Now, these (amount to) twenty-one B*ri*hatis; and—the heavenly world being the twenty-one-fold and the B*ri*hati—this (altar) thus comes to be equal to the heavenly world, and to the twenty-one-fold Stoma and the B*ri*hatî metre.

FIFTH BRÂHMANA.

1. Ku*s*ri Vâga*s*ravasa [2] once built a fire-altar. Su*s*ravas Kaushya then said to him, 'Gautama, when thou wert just now building up Agni, didst thou build him with his face forward, or backward, or downward, or upward?

---

[1] Viz. the staying (of the moon) in, or with, the Nakshatras, whose name is then made use of for a fanciful etymology.

[2] That is, Ku*s*ri Gautama, (son and) disciple of Vâga*s*ravas.

2. 'If perchance thou hast built him looking forward, it would be just as if one were to offer food from behind to one sitting with averted face [1]: he thereby will not receive thy offering.

3. 'And if thou hast built him looking backward, wherefore, then, hast thou made him a tail behind?

4. 'And if thou hast built him with his face downward, it would be just as if one were to put food on the back of one lying with his face downward: he surely will not receive thy offering.

5. 'And if thou hast built him with his face upward—surely, a bird does not fly towards heaven with its face turned upward [2]: he will not carry thee to heaven, he will not become conducive to heaven for thee.'

6. He said, 'I have built him with his face forward; I have built him with his face backward; I have built him with his face downward; I have built him with his face upward: I have built him in all directions.'

7. When he lays down the (gold) man with his head forward (eastward), and the two spoons (with their bowls) forward [3], thereby he (Agni) is built looking forward; and when he lays down the tor-

---

[1] The oblations are offered by the Adhvaryu whilst standing south, or south-west, of the fire, with his face turned towards north-east,—hence Agni, looking eastwards, would not see the food offered him.

[2] Yady agnir uttânas kitas tarhi yathâ uttânam vayah pakshî svayam âkâsam utpatitum na saknoti kim utânyam purusham dvâbhyâm pakshâbhyâm grihitvotpatitum na sakta iti . . . tvâm kitavantam svargam lokam prâpayitum na saknoty uttâna kayanâd ity arthah; abhivakshyatîti vahah prâpane lriti syapratyaye rûpam. Sây.

[3] See VII, 4, 1, 15. 16.

toise[1] with its head backward (westward), and the victims' heads turned backward, thereby he is built looking backward; and when he lays down the tortoise with its face downward, and the victims' heads with their faces downward, and the bricks with their faces downward[2], thereby he is built looking downward; and when he lays down the (gold) man with his face upward, and the two spoons (with their open bowls) turned upward, and the mortar turned upward, and the fire-pan turned upward, thereby he is built looking upward; and when he lays down the bricks whilst moving round (the altar) in every direction, thereby he is built (looking) in all directions.

8. Now, the Koshas, whilst driving about, once drove up[3] to an Agni with his head pulled out[4]. One of them said, 'The head (siras) means excellence (sri): he has pulled out his excellence, he will be deprived of his all!' and so indeed it happened to him.

9. And another said, 'The head means the vital airs: he has pulled out his vital airs, he will quickly go to yonder world!' and so, indeed, it happened to him.

---

[1] See VII, 5, 1, 1.

[2] Ish/akânâm ni/itvenopadhânam nâma ri/ulekhâdakshinâpasa-vyatryâlikhitâdilekhânâm uparibhâge darsanam. Sây. The broad side of the bricks not marked with lines is thus looked upon as their face.

[3] That is to say, according to Sâyana, whilst going about officiating at sacrifices, they built the altar in that way at some one's house.

[4] That is, with a head built on to the altar on the front side of the body; see the diagram of the syena/iti in Burnell's Cat. of Vedic MSS. (1870), p. 29.

10. Upwards, indeed, he (Agni) is built up, to wit, (in the shape of) the grass-bunch, the clod-bricks, the lotus-leaf, the gold plate and man, the two spoons, the naturally-perforated one, the grass-brick, the Dviyagus, the two Retahsik, the Visvagyotis, the two seasonal bricks, the Ashâdhâ, and the tortoise; and that fire which is placed on the altar-pile, assuredly, is then most manifestly his (Agni's) head: let him therefore not pull out (the head).

SIXTH ADHYÂYA. FIRST BRÂHMANA.

1. Now at the house of Aruna Aupavesi[1] these came once together,—Satyayagña Paulushi, Mahâsâla Gâbâla, Budila Âsvatarâsvi, Indradyumna Bhâllaveya, and Ganasârkarâkshya. They took counsel together regarding (Agni) Vaisvânara, but did not agree as to Vaisvânara[2].

2. They said, 'There is that Asvapati Kaikeya who knows Vaisvânara thoroughly[3]: let us go to him!' They went to Asvapati Kaikeya. He ordered for them separate dwellings, separate honours, separate Soma-sacrifices each with a thousand gifts. In the morning, still at variance with one another, they

---

[1] Khândogyop. V, 11, where another version of this story occurs, has here the name of Aruna's son, Uddâlaka Âruni; and, instead of Mahâsâla Gâbâla, it has Prâkinasâla Aupamanya.

[2] Sâyana takes this to mean, 'he (Aruna) was unable to instruct them in regard to Vaisvânara,'—so *runas teshâm satyayagñâdînâm pañkânâm vaisvânaravidyâm bodhayitum na samiyâya samgatah sakto nâbhavat,*—probably, however, 'samiyâya' is better taken impersonally ('there was no agreement between them'), as is done by the St. Petersb. Dict.; though Khând. XI, 3 favours Sâyana's view.

[3] Sâyana takes 'samprati' in its ordinary sense of 'now.' The knowledge of Vaisvânara implied here, according to Sâyana, means the knowledge of the supreme deity (paramesvara).

came again to him, with fuel in their hands[1], saying, 'We want to become thy pupils.'

3. He said, 'How is this, venerable sirs, when ye are learned in the scriptures, and sons of men learned in the scriptures?' They replied, 'Venerable sir, thou knowest Vaiśvânara thoroughly: teach us him!' He said, 'I do indeed know Vaiśvânara thoroughly: put your fuel on (the fire), ye are become my pupils[2].'

4. He then said to Aruṇa Aupavesi, 'O Gautama, as whom knowest thou Vaiśvânara[3]?'—'As Earth only, O king;' he replied.—'Yea,' he said, 'that indeed is Vaiśvânara, the foundation; and because thou knowest the Vaiśvânara Foundation (pratishṭhâ) therefore thou art firmly established (pratishṭhita) with offspring and cattle; and, verily, he who knows that Vaiśvânara Foundation, repels Death and attains all life. But, in truth, these are only the feet[4] of Vaiśvânara, and thy feet would have withered away, hadst thou not come hither; or the feet would be unknown to thee, hadst thou not come hither[5].'

5. He then said to Satyayagña Paulushi, 'O Prâkînayogya, as whom knowest thou Vaiśvânara?'

---

[1] That is, in the way in which pupils approach their teacher.

[2] Literally, 'Ye have entered (my tuition);' upetâ stha upâsinâ bhavatha. Sây.

[3] Or, perhaps, 'what Vaiśvânara knowest thou?'

[4] 'Pratishṭhâ' (rest, foundation) also commonly means 'the feet.'

[5] It is not quite clear whether the words 'or the feet, &c.' really (as Sâyaṇa takes them) form part of the king's speech, or whether they are merely meant as explanatory of the latter part of the king's remarks. If Sâyaṇa be right, the words 'the feet would be unknown by thee,' seem to admit of a double meaning, viz. 'thou wouldst

—'As Water only, O king;' he replied.—'Yea,' he said, 'that indeed is the Vaisvânara Wealth; and because thou knowest that Vaisvânara Wealth, therefore thou art wealthy and prosperous; and, verily, he who knows that Vaisvânara Wealth, repels death and attains all life. But, in truth, this is only the bladder of Vaisvânara, and thy bladder would have failed thee, hadst thou not come hither; or the bladder would be unknown to thee, hadst thou not come hither.'

6. He then said to Mahâsâla Gâbâla, 'O Aupamanyava, as whom knowest thou Vaisvânara?'— 'As Ether only, O king.' he replied.—'Yea,' he said, 'that, indeed, is the Vaisvânara Plenteous; and because thou knowest Vaisvânara Plenteous, therefore thou art plentiful in offspring and cattle; and, verily, he who knows that Vaisvânara Plenteous, repels death and attains all life. But, in truth, this is only the trunk of Vaisvânara, and thy trunk would have failed thee, hadst thou not come hither; or the body would be unknown to thee, hadst thou not come hither.'

7. He then said to Budila Âsvatarâsvi, 'O Vaiyâghrapadya, as whom knowest thou Vaisvânara?'— 'As Air (wind) only, O king;' he replied.—'Yea,' he

have become footless,' or 'not even Vaisvânara's feet would have been known by thee;' though in the latter sense some particle such as 'eva' might have been expected. Sâyana, however, seems to take these words in yet another sense (if, indeed, he had not another reading before him),—vaisvânara-yâgñinât pâdau te tava viparîtagrâhino amlâsyatâm amlânau gamanâsamarthâv abhavishyatâm yadi mâm nâgamishyah; ittham doshaparyavasânayuktam ekadesagñânam eva nâvasesha ity âha, pâdau te viditâv iti vaisvânarasya pâdamâtram tvayâ viditam na tu kritsno vaisvânarah; atah sâdhv akârshîr yat tvam âgato · sity abhiprâyah.

said, 'that indeed is the Vaisvânara of divers courses; and because thou knowest that Vaisvânara of divers courses, therefore divers rows of cars follow thee; and, verily, he who knows that Vaisvânara of divers courses, repels death, and attains all life. But, in truth, this is only the breath of Vaisvânara, and thy breath would have failed thee, hadst thou not come hither; or the breath would be unknown to thee, hadst thou not come hither.'

8. He then said to Indradyumna Bhâllaveya, 'O Vaiyâghrapadya, as whom knowest thou Vaisvânara?'—'As Sun only, O king,' he replied.— 'Yea,' he said, 'that indeed is the Vaisvânara of Soma's splendour [1]; and because thou knowest the Vaisvânara of Soma's splendour, therefore that Soma-juice never fails to be consumed and cooked [2] in thy house; and, verily, he who knows that Vaisvânara of Soma's splendour, repels death, and attains all life. But, indeed, this is only the eye of Vaisvânara, and thine eye would have failed thee, hadst thou not come hither; or the eye would be unknown to thee, hadst thou not come hither.'

9. He then said to Gana Sarkarâkshya, 'O Sâyavasa, as whom knowest thou Vaisvânara?'— 'As Heaven only, O king,' he replied.—'Yea,' he said, 'that indeed is Vaisvânara Pre-eminence; and because thou knowest the Vaisvânara Pre-eminence, therefore thou art pre-eminent among thine equals; and, verily, he who knows that Vaisvânara Pre-

---

[1] Or, perhaps better, 'of Soma's fire.' The Khândogya-upanishad has 'Sutegas (of beautiful splendour, or light),' instead of 'suta-tegas.'

[2] According to Sâyana, this refers to the cooking, or baking, of the cakes (purodâsa) connected with the Soma-sacrifice.

eminence repels death, and attains all life. But,
indeed, this is only the head of Vaisvânara, and
thy head would have failed thee, hadst thou not
come hither; or the head would have been unknown
to thee, hadst thou not come hither.'

10. He said to them, 'Ye then, knowing different
Vaisvânaras, have been feeding on different kinds
of food; but verily, the well-beknown gods have
attained, as it were, the measure of a span[1]; but
I will so tell them unto you that I shall make
them attain no more nor less than the measure of
a span.'

11. Pointing at the head he said, 'This, indeed, is
the Vaisvânara Pre-eminence;'—pointing at the eyes
he said. 'This, indeed, is the Vaisvânara of Soma's
splendour;'—pointing at the nostrils he said, 'This,
indeed, is the Vaisvânara of divers courses;'—
pointing at the space in the mouth he said, 'This,
indeed, is the Vaisvânara Plenteous;'—pointing at
the water in the mouth he said, 'This, indeed, is
the Vaisvânara Wealth;'—pointing at the chin he
said. 'This, indeed, is the Vaisvânara Foundation.'

---

[1] Sâyana apparently takes this thus: but the gods, knowing well
that (essential element) which is merely of the space of a span, have
become successful;—yat tv evam yathoktâvayavaih prithivîpâdâdibhir
dyumûrdhântair avayavair visishtam ekam vastu tat prâdesamâtram
prâdesapramimam iva devâh suviditah samyag gñâtavanto 'bhisam-
pannâh prâptaphalâ babhûvur ity arthah. Though this interpretation looks very plausible, the accent of 'suvidita' would scarcely
admit of the word being taken as a bahuvrîhi compound. In the
words which follow, Sâyana takes 'them (enân)' to refer to the
bodily parts of Vaisvânara, identified with the imperfect doctrines of
the king's disciples. It is, indeed, quite possible that 'the gods'
are here identified with the special Vaisvânaras, the unity of whom,
in the one Purusha, or Âtman (self), the Brâhmana endeavours to
inculcate.

This Agni Vaisvânara is no other than the Purusha;
and, verily, whosoever thus knows that Agni Vaisvânara as Purusha-like, as established within the
Purusha, repels death, and attains all life; and,
verily, Vaisvânara does no harm to him that speaks
of him.

SECOND BRÂHMANA.

1. Now, indeed, there is this twofold thing, to wit,
the eater and that which is eaten [1]; and when this
pair meets it is called the eater, and not the eaten.

2. Now that eater is the same as this Agni (the
fire and fire-altar); and whatever they assign to him
is his assignments; and these assignments (âhiti) are
mystically called oblations (âhuti), for the gods love
the mystic.

3. And the eater, doubtless, is the sun, and his
assignments (offerings) are the moon, for the moon
is assigned to the sun [2]. Thus much as to the deity.

4. Now as to the body. The eater, doubtless, is
the breath, and its assignments are food, for the food
is consigned to (the channel of) the breath. Thus
much as to Agni.

5. Now as to the Arka (flame). The Arka, doubtless, is Agni; and his joy are the oblations, for the
oblations are a joy [3] to Agni.

---

[1] Or, as Sâyana takes it,—this (world) is twofold, the eater and
the eaten.

[2] The moon here would seem to be considered as serving for
food to the sun, as it does to the gods. The commentary is not
very explicit on this point,—tasyâhutayas (?) kandramâh kandra-
masam hy âditya âdadhatity anena kandramasa âditye âdhânâd
âdhititvam pratipâditam.

[3] 'Kam' is used adverbially 'well,'—they do him good, they
please him.

6. And the Arka, doubtless, is the sun; and his joy is the moon, for the moon is a joy to the sun. Thus much as to the deity.

7. Now as to the body. The Arka, doubtless, is the breath, and his joy is food, for food is a joy to (the channel of) the breath. Thus much as to the Arka.

8. Now as to the Uktha (song of praise). The 'uk,' doubtless, is Agni, and his 'tham' is oblations, for by oblations Agni rises (ut-thâ, i. e. blazes up).

9. And the 'uk,' doubtless, is the sun, and his 'tham' is the moon, for by the moon the sun rises. Thus much as to the deity.

10. Now as to the body. The 'uk,' doubtless, is the breath, and the 'tham' is food, for by food the breath rises (increases). Thus much as to the Uktha. That Agni-like, Arka-like, Uktha-like one is the same as the Purusha; and, verily, the enemy withers away of whosoever, knowing this, thus serves that Agni-like, Arka-like, Uktha-like Purusha.

11. The fire, indeed, is kindled by the breath, the wind by the fire, the sun by the wind, the moon by the sun, the stars by the moon, and the lightning by the stars [1]:—so great, indeed, is the kindling both in this and in yonder world; and, verily, whosoever knows this is enkindled to that full extent both in this and in yonder world.

---

[1] Agnir prânena dîpyate, prânavâyor abhâve alpatve agner dîpanam nâsti; agninâ vâyur dîpyate vâyunâdityo vashtambham itrena tad dîpanam; âdityena kandramâh prabhâvaso gyotihsâstra-siddhah; râtrau nakshatrâni kandramasâ prakâsante divâ hi mahattarena sûryaprakâsena tirobhûtatvân na tadâ prakâsah; nakshatrair vidyut prakâsyate. Sây.

THIRD BRÂHMAŅA.

1. Let him meditate upon the 'true Brahman.' Now, man here, indeed, is possessed of understanding [1], and according to how great his understanding is when he departs this world, so does he, on passing away, enter yonder world.

2. Let him meditate on the Self, which is made up of intelligence, and endowed with a body of spirit, with a form of light, and with an etherial nature, which changes its shape at will, is swift as thought, of true resolve, and true purpose, which consists of all sweet odours and tastes, which holds sway over all the regions and pervades this whole universe, which is speechless and indifferent [2];— even as a grain of rice, or a grain of barley, or a grain of millet, or the smallest granule of millet, so is this golden [3] Purusha in the heart; even as a smokeless light, it is greater than the sky, greater than the ether, greater than the earth, greater than all existing things;—that self of the spirit (breath) is my self: on passing away from hence I shall obtain that self. Verily, whosoever has this trust [4], for him there is no uncertainty. Thus spake Sândilya, and so it is [5].

---

[1] Or, will, purpose,—kratumayaḥ, kratur niśḳayo ⹂dhyavasâya evam eva nânyathety avivakshitapratyayaḥ, tadâtmako ⹂yam purusho gîvaḥ. For this chapter (the Sândilyavidyâ) see Khândogyop. III, 14 ('man is a creature of will,' Prof. Max Müller).

[2] Anâdaram asambhramam (without mental affects). Sây.

[3] That is, of the brilliance of gold (suvarṇasamânategâḥ). Sây.

[4] Or, thought, knowledge (buddhiḥ), as Sâyaṇa supplies.

[5] Sâyaṇa takes this along with 'so spake Sândilya,'—ity evam etad âha sma uktavân sândilyo nâmarshir iti. The final 'iti' seems to be intended to indicate that Sândilya's opinion is adopted by the Brâhmaṇa.

FOURTH BRÂHMANA.

1. Verily, the dawn is the head of the sacrificial horse [1], the sun its eye, the wind its breath, Agni Vaisvânara (the fire belonging to all men) its open mouth. The year is the body of the sacrificial horse, the sky its back, the air its belly, the earth the under part of its belly, the quarters its flanks, the intermediate quarters its ribs, the seasons its limbs, the months and half-months its joints, the days and nights its feet, the stars its bones, the welkin its flesh, the sand its intestinal food, the rivers its bowels, the mountains its liver and lungs, the herbs and trees its hair, the rising sun the forepart, and the setting sun the hindpart of its body, the lightning its yawning, the thundering its whinnying, the raining its voiding urine, and speech its voice. The day, indeed, was produced as the Mahiman [2] (cup) before the horse, and its birth-place is in the eastern sea. The night was produced as the Mahiman (cup) behind (or after) it, and its birth-place was in the western sea: these two Mahiman (cups), indeed, came to be on both sides of the horse. As Haya (steed) it carried the gods, as Vâgin (racer) the Gandharvas, as Arvan (courser) the Asuras, as Asva (horse) men. The sea, indeed, is its kindred, the sea its birth-place.

---

[1] That is, of Pragâpati, in the form of a horse. For this and the next chapters see the beginning of the Kânva recension of the Brihad-âranyakopanishad.

[2] This is the name of two gold cups used at the Asvamedha; cf. XIII. 2, 11, 1 seq.; 5, 2, 23.

FIFTH BRÂHMANA.

1. Verily, there was nothing here in the beginning: by Death this (universe) was covered, by hunger, for Death is hunger. He created for himself this mind, thinking, 'May I have a soul.' He went on worshipping. Whilst he was worshipping the waters were produced. 'Verily, to me worshipping (ark) water (kam) has been produced,' thus (he thought): this, indeed, is the Arka-nature of the Arkya[1]; and, verily, there is joy (kam) for him who thus knows the Arka-nature of the Arkya.

2. The Arka, doubtless, is the waters; and the cream (froth) which was on the waters was compacted, and became this earth. Thereon he wearied himself, and the glow and essence (sweat) of him thus wearied and heated developed into Fire.

3. He made himself threefold—(Agni being one-third), Âditya one-third, and Vâyu one-third: that is this threefold breath. The eastern quarter was his head, this and that (intermediate quarters) are his fore-feet, the western quarter his tail, this and that (intermediate quarters) his thighs, the southern and northern quarters his flanks; the sky his back, the air his belly, and this (earth) his chest:—on the waters he was established any and everywhere, and so indeed is he established who knows this.

4. He desired, 'May a second self be produced for me.' By his mind he entered into union with speech,—(to wit) Death with hunger: the seed which was produced became the year, for theretofore there was no year. For as long as the year he (Death) carried him (within him), and at the end of

---

[1] See X, 3. 4. 3 seq.; 4. 1. 4. 15. 21 seq.

that time he produced him [1]. He opened his mouth
(to devour) the new-born one, and he (the child)
cried 'bhâ*n*'; thus speech was produced.

5. He bethought him, 'Surely, if I kill him,
I shall gain but little food [2].' By that speech and
that soul of his he created all this (universe) whatsoever there is,—*Rik* (hymn-verses), Yagus (formulas),
Sâman (hymn-tunes), metres, sacrifices, men, and
beasts. And whatsoever he created he set about
devouring; and because he eats (ad) everything,
hence the name 'Aditi'; and, verily, he who thus
knows the nature of Aditi becomes an eater of
everything, and all food becomes his.

6. He desired, 'May I again sacrifice by yet
another sacrifice.' He wearied himself and practised
austerity. From him, thus wearied and heated,
glory and vigour departed; and glory and vigour,
indeed, are the vital airs. The vital airs having
departed, that body of his began to swell. The
mind was yet in the body;—

7. He desired, 'May this (body) of mine be
sacrificially pure: may I thereby be possessed of
a self!' Thereupon the horse (asva) was produced;
and because that which was swelling [3] (asvat) became
pure (medhya) therefore the name Asvamedha (belongs to that sacrifice). He, indeed, knows the
Asvamedha who thus knows him [4].

---

[1] Viz. Pragâpati, the year: Agni. the Purusha, the Self.

[2] Or, I shall lessen my food (which would have become more
abundant if the child had been allowed to live and grow).

[3] The commentaries on the B*ri*had-âra*ny*akop. take this together
with the preceding clause,—and because that (body) was swelling
(asvat), therefore the horse (asva) was produced.

[4] Viz. Agni-Pragâpati, or Death, in the form of the horse.

8. He bethought him of leaving it unrestrained [1]. At the end of a year he slaughtered it for his own self, and made over the (sacrificial) animals to the deities : therefore they slaughter the consecrated (victim) as one that, in its nature as Pragâpati, represents all the deities. But the Asvamedha, in truth, is he that shines yonder (the sun), and the year is his body. The Arka is this Fire, and these worlds are his bodies. These two are the Arka and Asvamedha ; but these, indeed, become again one deity, to wit, Death. And, verily, whosoever knows this, conquers recurrent Death, and Death has no hold on him : Death is his own self ; he attains all life, and becomes one of those deities.

9. Now the line of succession (of teachers). The same as far as Sâmgîvîputra. Sâmgîvîputra (received it) from Mândûkâyani, Mândûkâyani from Mândavya, Mândavya from Kautsa, Kautsa from Mâhitthi, Mâhitthi from Vâmakakshâyana, Vâmakakshâyana from Vâtsya, Vâtsya from Sândilya, Sândilya from Kusri, Kusri from Yagñavakas Râgastambâyana, Yagñavakas Râgastambâyana from Tura Kâvasheya, Tura Kâvasheya from Pragâpati, Pragâpati from Brahman (n.). Brahman is the self-existent : reverence be to Brahman !

---

[1] For the construction, see IX, 5, 1, 35 ; on the negative form of the gerund (tam anavarudhyaivâmanyata) with a direct object, see Delbrück, Altindische Syntax, § 264.

CORRECTIONS.

Page 66, l. 11, and note 1. The *K*atush*t*oma is such an arrangement of the Stotras of a Soma-sacrifice in which the Stomas, or hymn-forms, employed increase successively by four syllables. See notes on XI, 5, 2, 9; XIII, 3, 1, 4 (sic).

P. 279, line 7. Perhaps this passage had better be translated thus,—And he who, without having performed these (rites), should officiate even for another person in the performance of any other sacrifices . . .

P. 296, l. 3 from bottom. Read,—Upavasatha.

P. 394-98, paragraphs 4-9 ; 11. Read,—repels recurrent death.

,, l. 5 from bottom. Read,—tasyâhutayas (?).

PART III.

Introduction, page xii, line 27. Read,—pa*s*ubandha.

P. xvi, l. 11 of notes. After—*S*yaita-sâman, add—II, 161-2).

P. xviii, l. 23. In *S*at. Br. V, 5, 3, 4, the Sho*d*a*s*in is distinctly mentioned as forming part of the Ke*s*avapanîya Atirâtra.

P. xviii, l. 4 of notes. Read,—'form' instead of 'from.'

P. xxv, note. Add,—So also *S*at. Br. V, 3, 4, 12 ; 4, 3, 2.

P. 38, l. 1. Read,—Vâgaprasavîya.

P. 62, l. 22. Read,—as it undoubtedly does in V, 4, 3, 18; as well as savyash*t*hâ, in Atharva-v. VIII, 8, 23).

,, end of note. Add,—In *S*at. Br. V, 4, 3, 23, sa*m*grahit*ri* certainly means 'charioteer.'

P. 113, l. 8. The chant here alluded to is the first or Hot*ri*'s Prish*t*ha-stotra, for which see part ii, p. 339. The Abhishe*k*anîya being, however, performed on the Ukthya, not on the Agnish*t*oma, model, this stotra, on the present occasion, consists of the B*ri*hat-sâman (see Introduction, pp. xvi, note 2 ; xxxvi).

P. 136, l. 4. Read,—Barhi-shada*h*.

P. 140, last line of text. For 'Âra*n*i' read 'Âru*n*i.'

P. 169, l. 18. Read,—'Those kindling-sticks . . . .

P. 171, l. 2. Read, Âshâ*dh*i.

P. 203, l. 10. Read,—'vâk' (voice).

P. 265, note 2. In the passage of the Ait. Br. referred to, the Vishuvat day is the central day of an Ekavi*m**s*arâtra, or twenty-one days' performance.

P. 252, l. 10. Read,—'sand' for 'seed.'

P. 360, note 1. Add,—See also VIII, 7, 3, 10, where that thread is identified with the wind.

P. 363, note 1. The reference is wrong ; for the real Satya-sâman, see part iv, p. 145, note 1.

,, 67, l. 24. In the opposite direction, i.e. in the direction away from us.

P. 369, note 1. The reference is wrong; for the real *Âitra-sâman*, see part iv, p. 145, note 1.

P. 379, l. 10. Read,—the breath serves everything here.

,, l. 20. For this Sâman, based on the word 'bhûs,' see part iv, p. 145, note 1.

P. 404, l. 15. Read,—having pre-eminently endowed the man with power, he sets him up. Cf. VIII, 7, 2, 3.

P. 415, l. 4. Read,—XIII, 53.

Transliteration of Oriental Alphabets adopted for the Translations of the Sacred Books of the East.

CONSONANTS.	MISSIONARY ALPHABET.			Sanskrit.	Zend.	Pehlevi.	Persian.	Arabic.	Hebrew.	Chinese.
	I Class.	II Class.	III Class.							
Gutturales.										
1 Tenuis	k	. .	. .	क	ग	ﻥ	ﻙ	ﻙ	ﬨ ﬣ ﬤ ﬥ	k
2 ,, aspirata . . .	kh	. .	. .	ख	व	ﺯ	ﯓ	ﻕ		kh
3 Media	g	. .	. .	ग	৩	ﺯ				
4 ,, aspirata . .	gh	. .	. .	घ	৩	২	ﻍ	ﻍ	ﬡ ﬥ ﬢ ﬣ	
5 Gutturo-labialis .	q	. .	. .	. .	. .	. .				
6 Nasalis	n̄ (ng)	. .	. .	ड़	৩ (ng)	. .	. .	. .		h. hs
7 Spiritus asper	h	'h	. .	ह	৩ (×)	. .	,	,	ﬢ ﬤ ﬡ ﬣ	
8 ,, lenis . . .	'	. .	. .	ळ	৩ (çh)	. .	—	—		
9 ,, asper faucalis	'h	. .	. .	. .	. .	. .	ﻥ	ﻥ		
10 ,, lenis faucalis . .	'h	. .	. .	. .	. .	. .	ﻉ	ﻉ		
11 ,, asper fricatus . .	. .	'h	. .	. .	. .	. .	ﻥ	ﻥ		
12 ,, lenis fricatus . .	. .	'h	. .	. .	. .	. .	. .	. .		
Gutturales modificatae (palatales, &c.)										
13 Tenuis	. .	k	. .	च	. .	৬	ﻉ	ﻉ	. .	k
14 ,, aspirata . .	. .	kh	. .	छ	. .	৫	. .	. .	. .	kh
15 Media	. .	. .	. .	ज	৬	. .	ﻉ ﻍ	ﻉ ﻍ	. .	. .
16 ,, aspirata . .	. .	. .	. .	झ	. .	. .	. .	. .	. .	. .
17 ,, Nasalis . .	. .	. .	. .	ञ	. .	. .	. .	. .	. .	. .

CONSONANTS (continued)	MISSIONARY ALPHABET			Sanskrit	Zend	Pehlevi	Persian	Arabic	Hebrew	Chinese
	I Class	II Class	III Class							
18 Semivocalis	y			ऱ	init.	)	ی	ی	'	y
19 Spiritus asper										
20 „ lenis		(s)								
21 „ asper assibilatus . .		(s)		ऱ			ن	٤		
22 „ lenis assibilatus . .		s	z							
Dentales.										
23 Tenuis	t			त		ے	ب	ٮ	ב ב	t
24 „ aspirata . . .	th		TH	थ						th
25 „ assibilata . .										
26 Media	d			द			ٯ	ٯ	ר ר	
27 „ aspirata . . .	dh		DH	ध						
28 „ assibilata . .										
29 Nasalis	n			न		ى	ں	ں	ר ר	n
30 Semivocalis	l		l	ल						l
31 „ mollis 1 . .				ळ						
32 „ mollis 2 . .										
33 Spiritus asper 1 . .	s		s (')	स	ॐ		)	ز	ם ם ם	s
34 „ asper 2 . .	z		z (ṣ)			ى	ز (ذ)			z
35 „ lenis			z (ẓ)				ز (ز)	ظ		z; jh
36 „ asperrimus 1 . .										
37 „ asperrimus 2 . .										

Dentales modificatae (linguales, &c.)

No.			Latin	
38	Tenuis	. . . .	t	
39	„ aspirata	. . . .	th	
40	Media	. . . .	d	
41	„ aspirata	. . . .	dh	
42	Nasalis	. . . .	n	
43	Semivocalis	. . . .	r	
44	„ fricata	. . . .	r	
45	„ diacritica	. . . .		
46	Spiritus asper	. . . .	sh	
47	„ lenis	. . . .	zh	

Labiales.

No.			Latin	
48	Tenuis	. . . .	p	
49	„ aspirata	. . . .	ph	
50	Media	. . . .	b	
51	„ aspirata	. . . .	bh	
52	Tenuissima	. . . .		
53	Nasalis	. . . .	m	
54	Semivocalis	. . . .	w	
55	„ aspirata	. . . .	hw	
56	Spiritus asper	. . . .	f	
57	„ lenis	. . . .	v	
58	Anusvâra	. . . .	m	
59	Visarga	. . . .	h	

VOWELS.	Missionary Alphabet I Class	II Class	III Class	Sanskrit	Zend	Pehlevi	Persian	Arabic	Hebrew	Chinese
1 Neutralis	o									ā
2 Laryngo-palatalis	è									
3 ,, labialis	ŏ									
4 Gutturalis brevis	a	(a)		अ						a
5 ,, longa	â			आ		fin. init.				â
6 Palatalis brevis	i	(i)								ĭ
7 ,, longa	î									î
8 Dentalis brevis	li									
9 ,, longa	lî									
10 Lingualis brevis	ri									
11 ,, longa	rî									
12 Labialis brevis	u									
13 ,, longa	û	(u)								ŭ
14 Gutturo-palatalis brevis	e	(e)			ε(e) ξ(e)					e
15 ,, longa	ê (ai)	(ai)								ê
16 Diphthongus gutturo-palatalis	âi	(ai)								âi ; ei, ēi
17 ,,	ei (ēi)									
18 ,,	oi (ōu)									
19 Gutturo-labialis brevis	o	(o)		ओ						o
20 ,, longa	ô (au)	(au)		औ	(au)					âu
21 Diphthongus gutturo-labialis	âu									
22 ,,	eu (ēu)									
23 ,,	ou (ōu)									
24 Gutturalis fracta	ä									ü
25 Palatalis fracta	ï									
26 Labialis fracta	ü									
27 Gutturo-labialis fracta	ö									

OXFORD
PRINTED AT THE CLARENDON PRESS
BY HORACE HART, M. A.
PRINTER TO THE UNIVERSITY

SACRED BOOKS OF THE EAST

TRANSLATED BY

VARIOUS ORIENTAL SCHOLARS

AND EDITED BY

F. MAX MÜLLER.

∗∗ This Series is published with the sanction and co-operation of the Secretary of State for India in Council.

REPORT presented to the **ACADÉMIE DES INSCRIPTIONS**, May 11, 1883, by **M. ERNEST RENAN.**

'M. Renan présente trois nouveaux volumes de la grande collection des "Livres sacrés de l'Orient" (Sacred Books of the East), que dirige à Oxford, avec une si vaste érudition et une critique si sûre, le savant associé de l'Académie des Inscriptions, M. Max Müller. . . . La première série de ce beau recueil, composée de 24 volumes, est presque achevée. M. Max Müller se propose d'en publier une seconde, dont l'intérêt historique et religieux ne sera pas moindre. M. Max Müller a su se procurer la collaboration des savans les plus éminens d'Europe et d'Asie. L'Université d'Oxford, que cette grande publication honore au plus haut degré, doit tenir à continuer dans les plus larges proportions une œuvre aussi philosophiquement conçue que savamment exécutée.'

EXTRACT from the QUARTERLY REVIEW.

'We rejoice to notice that a second series of these translations has been announced and has actually begun to appear. The stones, at least, out of which a stately edifice may hereafter arise, are here being brought together. Prof. Max Müller has deserved well of scientific history. Not a few minds owe to his enticing words their first attraction to this branch of study. But no work of his, not even the great edition of the Rig-Veda, can compare in importance or in usefulness with this English translation of the Sacred Books of the East, which has been devised by his foresight, successfully brought so far by his persuasive and organising power, and will, we trust by the assistance of the distinguished scholars he has gathered round him, be carried in due time to a happy completion.'

Professor **E. HARDY**, Inaugural Lecture in the University of Freiburg, 1887.

'Die allgemeine vergleichende Religionswissenschaft datirt von jenem grossartigen, in seiner Art einzig dastehenden Unternehmen, zu welchem auf Anregung Max Müllers im Jahre 1874 auf dem internationalen Orientalistencongress in London der Grundstein gelegt worden war, die Übersetzung der heiligen Bücher des Ostens' *The Sacred Books of the East.*

The Hon. **ALBERT S. G. CANNING**, 'Words on Existing Religions.'

'The recent publication of the "Sacred Books of the East" in English is surely a great event in the annals of theological literature.'

Oxford

AT THE CLARENDON PRESS

LONDON: HENRY FROWDE

OXFORD UNIVERSITY PRESS WAREHOUSE, AMEN CORNER, E.C.

FIRST SERIES.

VOL. I. The Upanishads.

> Translated by F. MAX MÜLLER. Part I. The *Kh*ândogya-upanishad, The Talavakâra-upanishad, The Aitareya-âra*n*yaka, The Kaushîtaki-brâhma*n*a-upanishad, and The Vâgasaneyi-sa*m*hitâ-upanishad. 8vo, cloth, 10s. 6d.

> *The Upanishads contain the philosophy of the Veda. They have become the foundation of the later Vedânta doctrines, and indirectly of Buddhism. Schopenhauer, speaking of the Upanishads, says: ' In the whole world there is no study so beneficial and so elevating as that of the Upanishads. It has been the solace of my life, it will be the solace of my death.'*

> [See also Vol. XV.]

VOL. II. The Sacred Laws of the Âryas,

> As taught in the Schools of Âpastamba, Gautama, Vâsish*th*a, and Baudhâyana. Translated by GEORG BÜHLER. Part I. Âpastamba and Gautama. *Second Edition.* 8vo, cloth, 10s. 6d.

> *The Sacred Laws of the Âryas contain the original treatises on which the Laws of Manu and other lawgivers were founded.*

> [See also Vol. XIV.]

VOL. III. The Sacred Books of China.

> The Texts of Confucianism. Translated by JAMES LEGGE. Part I. The Shû King, The Religious Portions of the Shih King, and The Hsiâo King. 8vo, cloth, 12s. 6d.

> *Confucius was a collector of ancient traditions, not the founder of a new religion. As he lived in the sixth and fifth centuries B. C. his works are of unique interest for the study of Ethology.*

> [See also Vols. XVI, XXVII, XXVIII, XXXIX, and XL.]

VOL IV. The Zend-Avesta.

> Translated by JAMES DARMESTETER. Part I. The Vendîdâd. *Second Edition.* 8vo, cloth, 14s.

> *The Zend-Avesta contains the relics of what was the religion of Cyrus, Darius, and Xerxes, and, but for the battle of Marathon,*

might have become the religion of Europe. It forms to the present day the sacred book of the Parsis, the so-called fire-worshippers. Two more volumes will complete the translation of all that is left us of Zoroaster's religion.

[See also Vols. XXIII and XXXI.]

VOL. V. Pahlavi Texts.

Translated by E. W. WEST. Part I. The Bundahis, Bahman Yast, and Shâyast lâ-shâyast. 8vo, cloth, 12s. 6d.

The Pahlavi Texts comprise the theological literature of the revival of Zoroaster's religion, beginning with the Sassanian dynasty. They are important for a study of Gnosticism.

VOLS. VI AND IX. The Qur'ân.

Parts I and II. Translated by E. H. PALMER. 8vo, cloth, 21s.

This translation, carried out according to his own peculiar views of the origin of the Qur'ân, was the last great work of E. H. Palmer, before he was murdered in Egypt.

VOL. VII. The Institutes of Vishnu.

Translated by JULIUS JOLLY. 8vo, cloth, 10s. 6d.

A collection of legal aphorisms, closely connected with one of the oldest Vedic schools, the Kathas, but considerably added to in later time. Of importance for a critical study of the Laws of Manu.

VOL. VIII. The Bhagavadgîtâ, with The Sanatsugâtiya, and The Anugîtâ.

Translated by KÂSHINÂTH TRIMBAK TELANG. 8vo, cloth, 10s. 6d.

The earliest philosophical and religious poem of India. It has been paraphrased in Arnold's 'Song Celestial.'

VOL. X. The Dhammapada,

Translated from Pâli by F. MAX MÜLLER; and

The Sutta-Nipâta,

Translated from Pâli by V. FAUSBÖLL: being Canonical Books of the Buddhists. 8vo, cloth, 10s. 6d.

The Dhammapada contains the quintessence of Buddhist morality. The Sutta-Nipâta gives the authentic teaching of Buddha on some of the fundamental principles of religion.

VOL. XI. Buddhist Suttas.

Translated from Pâli by T. W. Rhys Davids. 1. The Mahâ-
parinibbâna Suttanta; 2. The Dhamma-kakka-ppavattana
Sutta. 3. The Tevigga Suttanta; 4. The Âkankheyya Sutta;
5. The Ketokhila Sutta; 6. The Mahâ-sudassana Suttanta;
7. The Sabbâsava Sutta. 8vo, cloth, 10s. 6d.

*A collection of the most important religious, moral, and philosophical
discourses taken from the sacred canon of the Buddhists.*

VOL. XII. The Satapatha-Brâhmana, according to the
Text of the Mâdhyandina School.

Translated by Julius Eggeling. Part I. Books I and II.
8vo, cloth, 12s. 6d.

*A minute account of the sacrificial ceremonies of the Vedic age.
It contains the earliest account of the Deluge in India.*
[See also Vols. XXVI, XLI.]

VOL. XIII. Vinaya Texts.

Translated from the Pâli by T. W. Rhys Davids and Hermann
Oldenberg. Part I. The Pâtimokkha. The Mahâvagga, I–IV.
8vo, cloth. 10s. 6d.

*The Vinaya Texts give for the first time a translation of the moral
code of the Buddhist religion as settled in the third century B.C.*
[See also Vols. XVII and XX.]

VOL. XIV. The Sacred Laws of the Âryas,

As taught in the Schools of Âpastamba, Gautama, Vâsishtha,
and Baudhâyana. Translated by Georg Bühler. Part II.
Vâsishtha and Baudhâyana. 8vo, cloth, 10s. 6d.

VOL. XV. The Upanishads.

Translated by F. Max Müller. Part II. The Katha-upanishad,
The Mundaka-upanishad, The Taittiriyaka-upanishad, The
Brihadâranyaka-upanishad, The Svetâsvatara-upanishad, The
Prasna-upanishad, and The Maitrâyana-brâhmana-upanishad.
8vo, cloth, 10s. 6d.

VOL. XVI. The Sacred Books of China.

The Texts of Confucianism. Translated by James Legge.
Part II. The Yî King. 8vo, cloth, 10s. 6d.
[See also Vols. XXVII, XXVIII.]

VOL. XVII. Vinaya Texts.

Translated from the Pâli by T. W. Rhys Davids and Hermann
Oldenberg. Part II. The Mahâvagga, V–X. The Kullavagga,
I–III. 8vo, cloth. 10s. 6d.

VOL. **XVIII.** Pahlavi Texts.

Translated by E. W. West. Part II. The Dâdistân-î Dînîk
and The Epistles of Mânûskîhar. 8vo, cloth, 12s. 6d.

VOL. **XIX.** The Fo-sho-hing-tsan-king.

A Life of Buddha by Asvaghosha Bodhisattva, translated from
Sanskrit into Chinese by Dharmaraksha, A.D. 420, and from
Chinese into English by SAMUEL BEAL. 8vo, cloth, 10s. 6d.

*This life of Buddha was translated from Sanskrit into Chinese,
A.D. 420. It contains many legends, some of which show a certain
similarity to the Evangelium infantiae, &c.*

VOL. **XX.** Vinaya Texts.

Translated from the Pâli by T. W. RHYS DAVIDS and HERMANN
OLDENBERG. Part III. The Kullavagga, IV–XII. 8vo, cloth,
10s. 6d.

VOL. **XXI.** The Saddharma-pundarîka; or, The Lotus
of the True Law.

Translated by H. KERN. 8vo, cloth, 12s. 6d.

*'The Lotus of the true Law,' a canonical book of the Northern
Buddhists, translated from Sanskrit. There is a Chinese translation of this book which was finished as early as the year 286 A.D.*

VOL. **XXII.** Gaina-Sûtras.

Translated from Prâkrit by HERMANN JACOBI. Part I. The
Âkârânga-Sûtra and The Kalpa-Sûtra. 8vo, cloth, 10s. 6d.

*The religion of the Gainas was founded by a contemporary of Buddha.
It still counts numerous adherents in India, while there are no
Buddhists left in India proper.*

[See Vol. XLV.]

VOL. **XXIII.** The Zend-Avesta.

Translated by JAMES DARMESTETER. Part II. The Sîrôzahs,
Yasts, and Nyâyis. 8vo, cloth, 10s. 6d.

VOL. **XXIV.** Pahlavi Texts.

Translated by E. W. West. Part III. Dînâ-î Maînôg-
Khirad, Sikand-gûmânîk Vigâr, and Sad Dar. 8vo, cloth,
10s. 6d.

SECOND SERIES.

VOL. XXV. Manu.

Translated by GEORG BÜHLER. 8vo, cloth, 21s.

This translation is founded on that of Sir William Jones, which has been carefully revised and corrected with the help of seven native Commentaries. An Appendix contains all the quotations from Manu which are found in the Hindu Law-books, translated for the use of the Law Courts in India. Another Appendix gives a synopsis of parallel passages from the six Dharma-sûtras, the other Smritis, the Upanishads, the Mahâbhârata, &c.

VOL. XXVI. The Satapatha-Brâhmaṇa.

Translated by JULIUS EGGELING. Part II. Books III and IV. 8vo, cloth, 12s. 6d.

VOLS. XXVII AND XXVIII. The Sacred Books of China.

The Texts of Confucianism. Translated by JAMES LEGGE. Parts III and IV. The Li Kî, or Collection of Treatises on the Rules of Propriety, or Ceremonial Usages. 8vo, cloth, 25s.

VOL. XXIX. The Grihya-Sûtras, Rules of Vedic Domestic Ceremonies.

Part I. Sânkhâyana, Âsvalâyana, Pâraskara, Khâdira. Translated by HERMANN OLDENBERG. 8vo, cloth, 12s. 6d.

These rules of Domestic Ceremonies describe the home life of the ancient Âryas with a completeness and accuracy unmatched in any other literature. Some of these rules have been incorporated in the ancient Law-books.

VOL. XXX. The Grihya-Sûtras, Rules of Vedic Domestic Ceremonies.

Part II. Gobhila, Hiraṇyakesin, Âpastamba. Translated by HERMANN OLDENBERG. Âpastamba, Yagña-paribhâshâ-sûtras. Translated by F. MAX MÜLLER. 8vo, cloth, 12s. 6d.

VOL. XXXI. The Zend-Avesta.

Part III. The Yasna, Visparad, Âfrînagân, Gâhs, and Miscellaneous Fragments. Translated by L. H. MILLS. 8vo, cloth, 12s. 6d.

VOL. XXXII. Vedic Hymns.

Translated by F. MAX MÜLLER. Part I. 8vo, cloth, 18s. 6d.

VOL. XXXIII. The Minor Law-books.

Translated by JULIUS JOLLY. Part I. Nârada, Brihaspati. 8vo, cloth, 10s. 6d.

VOL. **XXXIV**. The Vedânta-Sûtras, with the Commentary by Sankarâkârya. Part I.
Translated by G. Thibaut. 8vo, cloth, 12s. 6d.

VOLS. **XXXV AND XXXVI**. The Questions of King Milinda.
Translated from the Pâli by T. W. Rhys Davids.
Part I. 8vo, cloth, 10s. 6d. Part II. 8vo, cloth, 12s. 6d.

VOL. **XXXVII**. Pahlavi Texts.
Translated by E. W. West. Part IV. The Contents of the Nasks, as stated in the Eighth and Ninth Books of the Dînkard.
8vo, cloth, 15s.

VOL. **XXXVIII**. The Vedânta-Sûtras. Part II. 8vo, cloth, with full Index to both Parts, 12s. 6d.

VOLS. **XXXIX AND XL**. The Sacred Books of China.
The Texts of Tâoism. Translated by James Legge. 8vo, cloth, 21s.

VOL. **XLI**. The Satapatha-Brâhmana. Part III.
Translated by Julius Eggeling. 8vo, cloth, 12s. 6d.

VOL. **XLII**. Hymns of the Atharva-veda.
Translated by M. Bloomfield. 8vo, cloth, 21s.

VOLS. **XLIII AND XLIV**. The Satapatha-Brâhmana.
Parts IV and V. [*In the Press.*]

VOL. **XLV**. The Gaina-Sûtras.
Translated from Prakrit, by Hermann Jacobi. Part II. The Uttarâdhyayana Sûtra, The Sûtrakritânga Sûtra. 8vo, cloth, 12s. 6d.

VOL. **XLVI**. Vedic Hymns. Part II. 8vo, cloth, 14s.

VOL. **XLVII**. Pahlavi Texts.
Translated by E. W. West. Part V. Marvels of Zoroastrianism. 8vo, cloth, 8s. 6d.

VOL. **XLVIII**. Râmânuga's Sribhâshya.
Translated by G. Thibaut. [*In preparation.*]

VOL. **XLIX**. Buddhist Mahâyâna Texts. Buddha-karita, translated by E. B. Cowell. Sukhâvatî-vyûha, Vagrakhedikâ, &c., translated by F. Max Müller. Amitâyur-Dhyâna Sûtra, translated by J. Takakusu. 8vo, cloth, 12s. 6d.

Anecdota Oxoniensia.

ARYAN SERIES.

Buddhist Texts from Japan. I. Vagrakkhedikâ; *The Diamond-Cutter.*

Edited by F. Max Müller, M.A. Small 4to, 3s. 6d.

One of the most famous metaphysical treatises of the Mahâyâna Buddhists.

Buddhist Texts from Japan. II. Sukhâvatî-Vyûha: *Description of Sukhâvatî, the Land of Bliss.*

Edited by F. Max Müller, M.A., and Bunyiu Nanjio. With two Appendices: (1) Text and Translation of Sanghavarman's Chinese Version of the Poetical Portions of the Sukhâvatî-Vyûha; (2) Sanskrit Text of the Smaller Sukhâvatî-Vyûha. Small 4to, 7s. 6d.

The *editio princeps* of the Sacred Book of one of the largest and most influential sects of Buddhism, numbering more than ten millions of followers in Japan alone.

Buddhist Texts from Japan. III. *The Ancient Palm-Leaves containing the* Pragñâ-Pâramitâ-Hridaya-Sûtra *and the* Ushnisha-Vigaya-Dhârani.

Edited by F. Max Müller, M.A., and Bunyiu Nanjio, M.A. With an Appendix by G. Bühler, C.I.E. With many Plates. Small 4to, 10s.

Contains facsimiles of the oldest Sanskrit MS. at present known.

Dharma-Samgraha, *an Ancient Collection of Buddhist Technical Terms.*

Prepared for publication by Kenjiu Kasawara, a Buddhist Priest from Japan, and, after his death, edited by F. Max Müller and H. Wenzel. Small 4to, 7s. 6d.

Kâtyâyana's Sarvânukramani of the Rigveda.

With Extracts from Shadgurusishya's Commentary entitled Vedârthadîpikâ. Edited by A. A. Macdonell, M.A., Ph.D. 16s.

The Mantrapâtha, or the Prayer Book of the Âpastambins.

Edited, together with the Commentary of Haradatta, and translated by M. Winternitz, Ph.D. *First Part.* Introduction, Sanskrit Text, Varietas Lectionis, and Appendices. Small quarto, 10s. 6d.

Oxford

AT THE CLARENDON PRESS

LONDON: HENRY FROWDE

OXFORD UNIVERSITY PRESS WAREHOUSE, AMEN CORNER, E.C.

Milton Keynes UK
Ingram Content Group UK Ltd.
UKHW040827120124
435829UK00019B/39